Praise for

C.E. MURPHY

and The Walker Papers series

Urban Shaman

"A swift pace, a good mystery, a likeable protagonist, magic, danger—*Urban Shaman* has them in spades."
—Jim Butcher, bestselling author of The Dresden Files series

Thunderbird Falls

"Fans of Jim Butcher's Dresden Files novels and the works of urban fantasists Charles de Lint and Tanya Huff should enjoy this fantasy/mystery's cosmic elements. A good choice."
—*Library Journal*

Coyote Dreams

"Tightly written and paced, [*Coyote Dreams*] has a compelling, interesting protagonist, whose struggles and successes will captivate new and old readers alike."
—*RT Book Reviews*

Walking Dead

"Murphy's fourth Walker Papers offering is another gripping, well-written tale of what must be the world's most reluctant—and stubborn—shaman."
—*RT Book Reviews*

Demon Hunts

"Murphy carefully crafts her scenes and I felt every gust of wind through the crispy frosted trees.... I am heartily looking forward to further volumes."
—*The Discriminating Fangirl*

Sp...

"An original and...
—*Roma...*

"The twists and turns w...   ...eads while devouring the next page."
—*USA TODAY*

Also available from

C.E. MURPHY

and Harlequin LUNA

The Walker Papers

URBAN SHAMAN
WINTER MOON
"Banshee Cries"
THUNDERBIRD FALLS
COYOTE DREAMS
WALKING DEAD
DEMON HUNTS
SPIRIT DANCES
RAVEN CALLS

The Negotiator

HEART OF STONE
HOUSE OF CARDS
HANDS OF FLAME

C.E. MURPHY

MOUNTAIN ECHOES

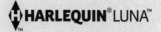

Recycling programs
for this product may
not exist in your area.

MOUNTAIN ECHOES

ISBN-13: 978-0-373-80351-4

Copyright © 2013 by C.E. Murphy

This edition published by arrangement with Harlequin Books S.A.

For questions and comments about the quality of this book, please contact us at CustomerService@Harlequin.com.

Printed in U.S.A.

for my father-in-law, Gary Lee
(why, yes, Joanne's Gary is named after him, in fact)

CHAPTER ONE

Friday, March 24, 4:15 p.m.

I came home to North Carolina just shy of a decade after promising I'd never go back.

Home was a funny word. I'd lived in Qualla Boundary during high school. That was longer than I'd lived anywhere else up until then, but in the intervening decade I'd lived exclusively in Seattle. But North Carolina still twigged as *home*, maybe because it was where my father had been born.

It was where he'd gone missing from, too, and that was why I was back.

Driving up from Atlanta was a slow immersion into memories. I had the windows of my rented Impala rolled down, and the rich rotting scent of winter collapsing into spring made a hungry place at the hollow of my throat. Of course, everything made me hungry right now—I hadn't yet recovered from a week's worth of exhaustive shape-shifting fueled by my body's resources instead of food. But that slightly sweet smell of death begetting life had always made me hungry, and I'd forgotten that until now.

The low hills with a haze of new leaves lining the roads; the roads themselves narrowing as I pulled away from interstates; the way strangers stopped along the roadside would nod a greeting as I passed by: those things I remembered more clearly. Then again, I'd spent an awful lot of my formative years in cars, crisscrossing the country with my father. Things I could see from a vehicle were most likely to stay with me, maybe.

Like the sign welcoming the world to the Qualla. It was smaller than I remembered it. I was taller than I'd been fourteen years ago when Dad had driven us past that sign for the first time, but mostly its size was relative to its importance in my life. Back then those carved white words on a brown road sign had been the most important thing in my life. *Welcome: Cherokee Indian Reservation.* At thirteen, going on fourteen, I'd never belonged anywhere for more than a few months, and that welcome sign was supposed to be the start of a whole new life for me.

It had been, too. Just not the way I'd expected it to be.

I slowed the car as I drove into the town of Cherokee. It was equal parts bigger and better than I remembered it, and exactly the same. The main street was four lanes rolling through town, no sidewalks to mention, just road, then parking spaces, then tourist shops flush up against them. A lot of low brown buildings with statues of headdressed Indian chiefs or protective gleaming black bears in front of them, and—new to me—signs making sure everybody knew which way to drive to the casino. It had opened the year before I left the Qualla, and the bigger-better aspects of Cherokee probably had it to thank. There'd been tourism money half the year before that, and unemployment the other half. That was the Cherokee I remembered, but I was just as glad it had moved on.

I got out of my car in front of the sheriff's station. Wind came down off the blue mountains and caught the skirt of my white leather coat with cinematic flair. For half a second I wished I was as cool as the woman reflected in the car window looked. Somebody that cool, though, probably wouldn't have a stomach full of butterflies, and her hands wouldn't shake as she took off her sunglasses. I'd burned bridges, mentally if not actually, when I'd left the Qualla. Coming back scared the crap out of me.

A man about my own age stepped through the station's open front door, leaned in the frame and said, "I'll be damned. Joanne Walkingstick's come home."

All the butterflies got squished as my stomach clenched. I'd Anglicized my last name the minute I left Cherokee, calling myself Walker. Excepting a handful of magic users, nobody had called me Joanne Walkingstick in ten years. I'd somehow forgotten that's who I would be, back here.

"You haven't changed," the guy said, which was wildly untrue, although in physical terms he was right. I was still six feet tall with short-cropped black hair, and ten years wasn't enough for most people to lose the youth they'd had graduating high school. I looked like me, albeit better-dressed.

The fellow in the door looked like himself, too, though it took me a good twenty seconds before I said, "Lester," and even that I said slowly. It took another moment to finish with "You cut your hair. And you're a *cop?*"

"Who better than the local troublemaker? Figure I at least have a clue what the kids are on about. I hear you're a brother in blue, too." Lester Lee pushed out of the door and stepped forward to offer his hand. I shook it automatically, still trying to get past the silver badge on his chest and the tidy police haircut. Last time I'd seen Les, he'd had hair to his ass and had been smoking pot during our graduation ceremony. Other than that, he did look like himself: pleasant dark eyes, wide cheekbones, reasonably fit and about four inches shorter than I.

"I was," I said a bit absently. "I just quit. I've had othe— Who told you that?"

"Sara."

"She's here." Of course she was here. Sara Buchanan, now Sara Isaac, was the one who'd called to tell me my father was missing. We'd been best friends about half a lifetime ago, right up until I blew it by sleeping with the boy she liked. In my defense, she'd said she didn't like him, and my social skills hadn't been well enough developed to recognize the lie. Either way, the friendship had ended. But we'd reconnected, if that was the right word for an encounter over half-eaten dead men, about four months earlier. When that case was over, I'd never expected to hear from her again.

"Lucas came with her," Les said, watching me.

My stomach went to knots again, though I wasn't surprised. Lucas Isaac had been the boy, back then. He'd gone home to Vancouver before my pregnancy became obvious, but he and Sara had kept in touch and eventually got married. I'd always refused to answer questions about who the father of my twins was, and had thought nobody knew. Judging from Les's expression, if everybody hadn't known then, they did now. That was awkward, so I ignored it.

"I'm more worried about my dad. Les, what's going on? Sara called and said he was missing, but she wouldn't say anything else." That wasn't exactly true. She'd said it was "my kind of thing," which I took to mean it appeared to be something paranormal in nature.

"She wouldn't—" Les broke off with a cough, then jerked

his chin toward the station. "Come in and sit down a minute, Joanie. We—"

"Joanne. Or Jo, please. I don't use Joanie much anymore." Actually it had only just struck me in the past few days that I'd left the little-girl nickname behind, but Les didn't have to know that.

He lifted an eyebrow. "You hated being called Jo." With that observation he went inside, leaving me to look at the dark square of doorway with a blush mounting my cheeks.

We hadn't been particular friends, Lester Lee and me. I hadn't been particular friends with much of anybody, truth be told, because I'd had a chip the size of Idaho on my shoulder. I had my Irish mother's pale skin, which made me unnecessarily self-conscious about coming to the Qualla, and the only long-term companion I'd ever had was my father. Coming into a high school of kids who'd known each other since birth made me horribly uncomfortable, and I'd mostly been a complete jerk through my adolescent years. I could not for the life of me imagine why Les knew I didn't like being called Jo, when I couldn't even remember talking to him more than five times in the years I'd been here. But he knew it, and I was once more smacked in the face with the realization that if I'd been less of a jackass, I'd probably have had a lot more fun in school. I sighed and followed Les inside the cop shop.

Last time I'd been in there it had been to hack my personal files in their computers, changing my last name from Walkingstick to Walker on my driver's license. By the time it propagated to the state system I'd left North Carolina and Joanne Walkingstick behind.

The station hadn't changed a lot since then. The computers were better and so was the system they were linked into. I probably wouldn't be able to hack it anymore. Of course, I wouldn't need to. I could just access any files I needed to change from the Seattle Police Department's computers. Or I could have before I'd quit not quite a week ago. I sighed, pushed my hand through my hair and went to sit in one of the surprisingly comfortable chairs by Les's desk. Sunlight hung on motes of dust between us, making the whole world seem like it was standing still. "All right. Hit me. What'd Sara leave out?"

"Luke's missing, too."

Static rushed my ears and for a minute I couldn't say anything. Then I laughed, short and harsh. "Before or after Dad?"

"Before. Sara and him came into town last Friday. Luke went missing Saturday night and there's been a manhunt on for him. Your dad was helping, but Monday night he didn't come back."

A house of cards collapsed in my mind, each card with a nugget of information on it. Monday had been the solstice. Dad was some kind of mystic. Those two things probably went together. Sara had called me Wednesday. Midafternoon, Irish time—I'd been in Ireland hunting banshees—which was morning here in Cherokee. Dad had been missing about thirty-six hours then, and Lucas for seventy-two. Aloud, I said, "You're sure Sara didn't tie Dad up somewhere so she'd have an excuse to call me?"

Humor creased Les's face, showing what he would look like in another forty years. Like his grandfather, the tribal elder for whom he'd been named. "The thought crossed my mind," he said, "but she was never an outdoorsy type. She'd never get the drop on your Dad."

"She's an FBI agent now, Les. She could get the drop on most people."

"Not," Les said firmly, "your Dad," which was probably true. I'd never thought of my father as particularly impressive, but he was the kind of guy who could sit down and disappear into the landscape even if you were looking at him when he sat. Wild animals tended to treat him as if he was one of their own. Sara had learned the ropes well enough to kick my puny ass, but I couldn't see her taking Dad out. "Not if her life depended on it," Les finished, as if following my thoughts.

"What if Luke's did," I said under my breath, but I didn't really mean it. Not mostly, though I was willing to bet Sara'd been almost relieved when my father went missing, if it meant she had an excuse to call me in. "Why'd she say it was my kind of thing?"

Les's humor fell away. "I know the elders gave you a drum, Joan— *Joanne*." He emphasized the name, reminding himself not to use the high school nickname.

A little shock ran through me. There'd been a bit of ceremony involved with the gifting of the drum and logically I supposed half the town knew I'd received it, but logic had never been my strong suit. I sat forward, elbows on my knees, and rubbed my eyes. "Yeah, they did. When I was fifteen."

"So what happened?" Les's voice dropped, his curiosity softened by what sounded like genuine respect.

I rubbed my face again, then sat on my hands so I'd stop doing that. "The really short version is I got pregnant and it screwed me up. Everything the drum suggested..." I shrugged. "Went off the rails. I only found the tracks again about fifteen months ago."

"So you're a..."

For the first time, I didn't want to answer the question, not because I thought he would laugh, but because of where I was. Sitting in the heart of Qualla Boundary, in all that was left of the once-vast Cherokee nation, in the midst of that, saying "A shaman," somehow sounded very arrogant indeed. There were too many charlatans and quacks out there buying, selling and bartering so-called shamanic gifts, and I'd spent way more of my life off the rez than on. For a minute I felt as false as any of those con artists. I'd never had any use for the mystical. Claiming I was now part of that heritage just seemed wrong.

Les, though, looked neither offended nor surprised when I said the word. He just nodded and let me work my way around to continuing. "Not quite like the traditional medicine men, as far as I can tell. When this all…woke up…I was told I was on a warrior's path. Healing's only part of it, for me."

Les's mouth twitched. "You always did like a fight."

That much, certainly, was true. It was utterly bizarre to talk to someone who had enough knowledge of a younger me to say a thing like that, but it was true. I shrugged one shoulder and tried again. "So why'd Sara think it was my kind of thing?"

"The mountain's been hollering, Jo. So loud even I can hear it, and I'm no shaman."

The mountain was hollering. That was an utterly preposterous thing to say, except I had just gotten off a plane from Ireland, where a screaming stone laid out peoples' destinies. Mountains hollering seemed right in line with that. I nodded. "What's it shouting about?"

"It started the night Lucas went missing." Les shrugged. "Your dad said it was trying to tell us how something was wrong. That's why he went up there, why he went alone. He was looking for Luke like all of us were, but—"

"But he was looking to heal the crying land," I finished.

Surprise and respect brightened Les's eyes. I could see a question coming, and lifted a hand to ward it off. I'd only just, in the past couple days, discovered my father belonged to a magical bloodline just as much as my mother had. My nomadic childhood had crystallized into a never-before-appreciated kind of sense: Dad had been taking us from one damaged site to another, trying, I now suspected, to give something back to barren earth. I hadn't yet wrapped my mind around the whole idea and wasn't prepared to discuss it. "What happened when he didn't come back?"

"It got worse. It's echoing all over the mountains now, so bad you can't tell where it starts. My grandpa looks like he's sucking lemons all the time, that's how much it's affecting him. It's worse for some of the other families."

"Is there anybody it's not affecting?"

Les's mouth quirked again. I'd had no idea that under the hair and the weed he'd had a pervasive, low-key sense of humor. "Tourists," he said. "White men. Whatever's happening here, Jo, it's not their story. It belongs to the People."

"I'm half-white, Les."

"Nah. You grew up in the Qualla."

I stared at him a long moment, a smile tugging at the corner of my mouth. "Just like that, huh? All the time I spent being a dick, chip on my shoulder, obstreperously ignoring my Cherokee heritage, it all gets hand-waved away because I spent a handful of teenage years here? Shit, Les, if I'd known it was that easy—"

"*Hadlv hehi,* Joanne?"

I answered in the same language without thinking. "Home is where the heart is, Les. Which means—" I broke off, my brain catching up to my tongue and immediately forgetting the words I needed. I hadn't spoken Cherokee regularly since I'd been a kid, less than ten years old. But Les was grinning at me, and shaking his head.

"Maybe you didn't learn that here, Joanne. Maybe you learned it out there on the road with Joe, but as far as I'm concerned, it means you grew up in the Qualla. So you're part of the People, even if your ma was white. Besides, most of us have white blood anyway. I mean, look at Sara."

I actually looked over my shoulder, half expecting her to be there. She wasn't, but I knew what he meant. Sara was honey-blonde with brown eyes and perpetually tanned skin, making her look like more of a California golden girl than somebody who laid claim to a quarter Cherokee blood. But kind of like me, her heritage came out in black and white: the high school yearbook snapshots emphasized the Indian aspects of her features, making the light hair seem less relevant. I turned back around and crooked a smile at Les. "Right. Christ, Les, were you this—"

His eyebrows rose as my face reddened again. "I was going to say this easy-going in high school, but my dim recollection is you were about as easy-going as anybody could be. This nice. Were you this nice in high school?"

"Yeah, pretty much. Bounced off you a few times, though, and figured you weren't interested."

I wasn't especially good at reading between the lines, but I was reasonably certain that Cherokee County Sheriff Lester Lee had just confessed to having had a crush on me in high school. I sat there speechless long enough for him to get uncomfortable and to go back to the topic at hand. "Anyway, so white blood or not, it doesn't mean the mountain hollers aren't our story. I'll call somebody to cover the station and I'll take you up there now, if you want."

Light changed behind me, somebody coming through the still-open front door, and a woman's voice, cool enough to shave ice, said, "Don't worry about it, Les. I'll take her up myself."

Oh, God. Caught between unrequited high school love and unforgiven high school rivalry. I slumped in my seat, trying to disappear myself. It didn't work, and after a minute, Sara Isaac, Archnemesis, said, "Come on, Joanne. It already took you long enough to get here. We haven't got all damned day."

CHAPTER TWO

"It—!" My voice rose and broke on the one-syllable word. My splendid white leather coat flared over the chair as I surged to my feet and faced her.

Sara, who was about six inches shorter than I was, took in the coat with a scathing, raking glance and managed to look down her nose at me. "Oh, *please*. Are you serious? What do you think this is, Joanne, a movie? The good guys wear white hats? My God, I thought you'd grown up a little."

A better person than I would have remembered that this was a woman whose husband had been missing for almost a week. That this was a woman who'd been obliged to call in her rival to try to find her husband. That this was a woman who looked like she hadn't slept much in the past several days, and who was gaunter than she'd been last I'd seen her.

I was by definition not that person. I snarled, "Yeah, actually, I am serious. Maybe the good guys *should* wear white hats, Sara. Maybe it makes them better target practice, but maybe it's more reassuring than a bunch of grim-faced mooks in black jackets muttering, 'We're the FB freaking I.' Jesus Christ, Lucas and my dad are missing and you're worried about my fashion choices? I got here as fast as I damned well could. I don't have an unlimited budget for international travel." In fact, having maxed out my credit card buying a last-minute ticket to Ireland and then the leather coat, I'd had to borrow the ticket-change fee from my friend Gary, who I'd then left in Ireland to keep an eye on my cousin, the new Irish Mage.

"What the hell were you doing in Ireland anyway?"

"I was *burying my mother,* okay?"

Sara's jaw snapped shut so definitively I heard the click. She had the grace to flush an attractive dusky red, and after a moment said in a much less antagonistic tone, "I'm sorry. I didn't know. I didn't even, um…" and decided she should stop there.

I finished for her, out of something I'd like to call the goodness of my heart and which I suspected was more like a gleeful willingness to twist the knife. "I didn't know her. Not well, anyway, and not at all until the very end. So I got here as fast as I could, Sara, and if you'd told me Lucas had gone missing almost a week ago I might have tried getting here that much sooner."

She stiffened all the way from her heels to the top of her head. I swear if it could have, all that honey-blond hair would have stood straight out like an angry cat's. "I didn't know it was—"

"'My kind of thing'?" I asked when she broke off, then couldn't help relenting a bit, palms turned up in something like apology. "Yeah, okay, that's fair. Look, do we have to do this, Sara? Didn't we get it out of the way in December?"

From her expression, no, we hadn't. Or rather, we had, but only when Lucas wasn't actually part of the physical scenario.

Reintroducing him and me added a whole new level to the emotional mess we'd created in high school, or at least it apparently did in Sara's mind. "I don't," I said to the ceiling, since I figured it was more inclined to listen than Sara was, "have designs on your man."

"How do you know? You haven't seen him in thirteen years."

I reversed my gaze to peer at Sara. "You really think he and I are going to, what, Sara? Fall into each other's arms in a fit of storybook love? He never even *liked* me, you idiot."

"He got you pregnant!"

"And then he turned tail and ran. Sara, I don't think liking somebody has much to do with sex for your average teenage boy. Opportunity, yes, fondness, not so much."

Les, whom I'd more or less forgotten about, cleared his throat. Sara and I both looked at him accusingly and he said, "Don't paint all of us with the same brush."

I wrinkled my face. "I don't need you being the voice of reason in the middle of my rant, Les."

He shrugged expressively. "I'm just saying some things are more worth doing if you like the person."

"So he *did* like you," Sara said, which was such a wild extrapolation from Les's statement that I flung my hands up in exasperation.

"Did or didn't, it was half a lifetime ago, Sara. Get over it. Or would you rather I tried really hard *not* to find Lucas while I'm looking for my dad?"

She turned ever-more scarlet, spun on her heel and stalked out of the sheriff's office. I stood there a moment, watching sunlight eat her silhouette, then turned to Les. "Is this what it's like for people who never leave their hometowns? Does everybody get permanently stuck in high school?"

"Sara left," he pointed out, but gave another shrug, this time one of agreement. "I think coming back makes us revert to form, maybe. Everybody knew who we were then. It's pretty easy to fall right back into those expectations. Try being the stoner who comes home a cop. That'll mess you right up."

"You ever tempted to slide?"

Les looked thoughtful, but shook his head. "Not really. Feels better to be part of the community, to be useful and make a difference in people's lives. It took some getting used to, but I wouldn't want to go back."

I glanced after Sara and sighed. "Yeah, I hear you. Guess I should try to remember that. Look, if I find anything useful, I'll…"

"You'll bring it to the elders," Les said, which made a lot more sense than anything I'd have suggested. "Don't forget you're not alone on the path here, Joanne."

I had, in fact, forgotten that, and for a moment it was far more interesting than chasing after Sara Isaac. I came back to the desk, half-curious and half-worried. "So why haven't they already solved it?"

"You'll see when you get up on the mountain." Les shook his head. "I'm not screwing with you. I think it's just better for you to see for yourself. I don't have the eyes for it."

Self-conscious, I touched my cheekbone just under the eye. They weren't gold right now because I wasn't drawing down power, but I felt a little like a marked man anyway. Then my fingertips brushed the scar on my right cheekbone, the one I'd gotten the day my shamanic powers had awakened, and I guessed maybe I *was* a marked man. "All right. Anything else I should know before I go up there?"

"Yeah." Les's grin flashed. "Sara drives like an old woman on those mountain roads."

I laughed and dug my keys from my pocket on the way out the door.

Sara was in her own rental, a Toyota Avalon. I laughed again, shook my head, and dangled my keys. She shook her head. I sat on the Impala's hood and waited. It only took about forty seconds for her to throw her door open, stand up in it and snap, "I'm not letting you drive me up there, Joanne. I remember how you drive. And what were you laughing at?"

"My, um. My, uh…" I crinkled my face. Captain Michael Morrison of the Seattle Police Department, less than a week ago my boss, and now featuring as the romantic lead in the movie of my life, was thirty-eight years old. That seemed a little long in the tooth for the word *boyfriend*. And since I'd jetted off to Ireland within minutes of us finally mentioning the elephant in the room that were our feelings toward one another, we hadn't really discussed different terminology. *Significant other* was a mouthful. *Partner* connoted long-term commitments, which I was kind of hoping for myself, but didn't think seemed appropriate under the current circumstances. I cleared my throat and finally said, "Morrison. Captain Morrison, the guy who gave you my number in Ireland? He drives an Avalon. Highest safety rating in its class. That's very FBI of you, or something. Get in the Impala."

"I am not driving anywhere with you in that thing."

She sounded like Morrison. I rolled my eyes. "Come on, Sara. It's a brand-new car, not a classic roadster. It has seat belts. I promise not to drive over the speed limit."

She closed her car door and took two wary steps toward me. "Promise?"

"Cross my heart." I actually did, and Sara, still suspicious, came and got in the Impala. I got in, buckled up, waved at Les as I started the engine, and gunned it.

Dust kicked up, Sara screamed like a little girl and I laughed until the tears came as we zoomed toward the mountains. I slowed down, too, because driving while blinded by tears wasn't a good idea, but I thought I was funny as hell. Sara waited until we reached a stop sign, then hit the meaty part of my shoulder so hard the *thwock* echoed against the dashboard. Still grinning, I rubbed my shoulder and didn't even say "ow," because I deserved it. "Yeah," I said instead, "but you shoulda seen your face."

Sara, through her teeth, said, "This is not a time to be joking, Joanne," and two days of worry that I'd been holding off through force of will alone came to boil acid in my belly.

I was not close to my father. I hadn't actually talked to him in years, not even a happy birthday or merry Christmas. I blamed him—unfairly, as it turned out, but then, it turned out most of the blame I laid was unfair—for raising me on the road, for always looking at me like he'd been saddled with a kid he didn't know what to do with, for more or less everything wrong with my life that I couldn't lay at my mother's feet for abandoning me. I had issues. Hell, I had subscriptions. And I was only just discovering how badly I'd misread, oh, every situation that had shaped my life since infancy. I'd only resolved things with my mother after she was dead, which was not a statement most people got to make.

I was desperately afraid of the same thing happening with Dad. I had regrets with Mother, but I hadn't known her very well. Dad had raised me. If I lost him and the chance to settle things between us, I didn't think I'd ever forgive myself. Classic scenario, thinking I had time, in so far as I'd ever thought about it at all. Which I hadn't, because I'd been busy being The Wronged Party, but a little forced perspective over the past week had changed that, and now—

Now my hands were cold and shaking and bile scored the back of my throat. I swallowed. "This is exactly the time to be joking, Sara, because otherwise I'm going to freak the hell out, okay? I know you're stressed and I'm sorry, but so am I an—"

"Funny way of showing it."

"Yeah," I said softly, "yeah, that's exactly what I'm trying for. Funny-ha-ha ways of showing it. You probably told Lucas you loved him the last time you saw him. I can't even remember the last time I talked to Dad, much less what I said, so in fact, yes, I'm trying hard to act like none of this matters very much so I don't burst into tears. Okay?" She didn't say anything, so after a minute I said, "Okay," and went back to the business of driving. Slowly, or at least less fast than I'd started out.

The road leading up to the mountains was better than I remembered. Either it had been resurfaced recently—sometime in the past ten years—or the late-model rented Impala had better suspension than my 1969 Mustang. Actually, it probably did, or at least better suspension than Petite had had when I drove her out of the Qualla. I'd done the restoration work myself over the course of a decade, but I hadn't gotten nearly that far on her before I'd left. The smoother ride made driving faster easy, and I had to keep a steely eye on the speedometer to keep myself from panicking Sara. Truth was I hadn't driven Appalachian roads in so long even I didn't think I should be speed-demoning over them, but I could hardly say that aloud and lose face in front of my high school rival.

"I didn't think you ever cried." Sara spoke to the window, not me, and it took a moment to realize she was probably addressing me anyway. Then I snorted.

"Used to be my motto, I guess. Never let 'em see you bleed."

"Yeah. I used to think you were so tough. So cool."

"Sorry to spoil the illusion."

It was her turn to snort. "I got over it a while ago." She shifted in her seat, then muttered, "Or not. You were still a jerk when we met in December but you were fearless. I guess maybe I thought you were still all that. Pull over here."

"There's nowhere to pull over." I pulled over anyway. Mountain rose on one side of us and dropped off on the other, with a road slightly wider than a horse track between. It reminded me of Ireland, except their horse-track roads had stone walls on both sides, not mountains.

Sara gestured for me to get out, then climbed across the seats and got out on my side. Had to; pulling over, such as it was, put her door up against the mountainside. Ten years earlier I wouldn't even have objected to the lack of room. "Up or down?"

"Up. I'm pretty sure there's a better way in but nobody would show it to me." Sara walked along the road a few yards, searching for a trail I couldn't see, then stepped off the road and disappeared into foliage. I tried to remember when poison ivy started to bloom, then shrugged and followed her. At least I was wearing a long-sleeved coat.

Sara, whom Les had accused of not being the outdoorsy type, was already a couple dozen feet up the mountain by the time I fought through the roadside brush. She bounced from one foot to another, lithe steps that took her higher while I scrambled along behind, wondering how it was I was climbing my second mountain inside a week when I didn't make a habit of climbing them at all. This one was easier than Croagh Padraig: that had been slippery shoal and switchback rock face, while this one was wooded, mossy and offered things to hold on to. I kept an eye out for poisons ivy and oak, and called, "Who wouldn't show you the better way?" after Sara.

"Everybody. The elders, the locals, nobody. I guess growing up here doesn't count for much if you come back wearing an FBI jacket. A hundred and fifty years after the Trail of Tears and half of 'em still don't trust Feds, even if it's one of their own."

"They kind of have a point."

"That's why I didn't make an issue of it. Besides, I grew up here. This used to be my path up to the hollers and the backwoods."

"Dad's house backs up to the mountains. I used to just go out the back door. We could've gone that way."

"Except this is the path I showed Luke." She glared at me over her shoulder.

I sighed. "I'm sure he didn't go through Dad's house to go hiking on Saturday night, Sara."

Her mouth pinched. Clearly that was not the answer she'd been looking for. She'd wanted me to say I never took him up in the mountains myself. I supposed I could have, but that would have been a lie, and no doubt would only make things worse at some point. She said "Anyway" a little too loudly, and went back to climbing. "Anyway, this is the long way around to where the mountain is crying—" She broke off again and shot me another glare.

This time I stopped, scowling the short distance up at her. "Sara, there's almost nothing you can say that's so weird I'm going to flip out. Les already told me about the hollers, er, hollering—"

"Can you hear them?"

"I'm not listening."

"What's that mean?"

I tipped my chin back and looked at the pale blue sky as if it could give me patience. "It means I'm not listening. I'm not using any power right now. I like to get the lay of the land through normal means first if I can, but more important, if the earth is screaming loudly enough that half the Qualla can hear it, then it's probably going to knock me on my ass when I turn the Sight on, and I'd rather be sitting down, not climbing a mountain, when that happens. Okay?"

"Oh. Okay." Sara waited another moment, still frowning at me, then shrugged and kept climbing. After a minute she crested a small ridge and waited for me there. I popped up beside her a few seconds later and exhaled sharply.

A scar across the mountainside drew my eye first, earth that hadn't yet healed from the centuries-old tobacco farm that had been there. The broad-leafed plants were no longer part of the landscape, done out of business by bigger farms or given up on by families who'd lost too many members to the variety of diseases smoking offered. Mostly big business, though: even my grandfather, who had died of lung cancer, hadn't given up his tobacco farm until it cost him more to run than it profited.

Surrounding that scarred earth, though, bluegrass and new leaves shimmered over hills so old they'd forgotten what it was like to have rough edges. A stream cut through the holler's floor, feeding more life than the eye could see. Insects and birdsong hummed through air soft enough to touch, soft enough to wrap myself in and settle down where I belonged. I put my hands over my mouth, tears pricking my eyes. Sara, in mystified horror, said, "God, you really can cry."

"It's been a long time since I've been home." I pressed my lips together behind the tent of my fingers and tried to find somewhere safe to look. There wasn't really anywhere, not with Sara to one side and the silent valley before me, but the tightness in my throat faded and after a while I cleared it. "The whole never-let-'em-see-you-bleed thing sort of went to hell when this all started up."

"'This'?"

"The shaman thing." As soon as I said it, I remembered Sara had a starkly different recollection of our childhood interests than I did, and she verified that with a peculiar look and a comment. "You were into that when we were teens, Joanne."

"Not after Lucas. I shut it all down. It came back about fifteen, sixteen months ago, and I swear to God every little thing makes me sniffly now. You'd think I was making up for lost time."

"Maybe you are." Sara, as uncomfortable with my sudden emotional confessions as I was, waved at the valley. "Come on. We cut through here and the next holler is where the elders are waiting."

I slipped down the hill behind her, trying not to catch my coat on branches. "Is that were Lucas and Dad went missing from? I mean, last place they were seen?"

"You could say that."

I squinted at her shoulders. "You're being cryptic. So was Les."

"Joanne, just shut up and come on. You'll see why in a few minutes."

I mumbled dire imprecations, but followed along, eating three of the chocolate bars I'd stored in my coat pockets. An apple, too, a local breed so I didn't feel guilty about ditching the core in the woods as we clambered along. Sara glanced back at me once and I offered another chocolate bar, which made her eyebrows rise. "The backseat of your car is full of candy-bar wrappers, too. How many of those things have you eaten?"

"About twelve."

"And you're still skinny," she said in disgusted disbelief, and surged ahead before I could explain. Ten minutes later we crawled over the top of another ridge, and the chocolate turned to oil in my stomach as I finally understood why neither Les nor Sara had wanted to explain what was going on in the mountains.

The world had disappeared.

CHAPTER THREE

The valley's heart looked like something out of *The NeverEnding Story*. Gray misty nothingness hissed and swam at its center, held in place by wards so strong they were visible without the Sight. Wards of white magic, white as only power offered up by many could be, and the many were men and women I hadn't seen for ten years or even longer.

They were impossible to recognize, magic sheeting over them so strongly that their features were lost to it. I could tell that a steel-haired man stood at the northern end of the holler. He was the focal point, probably the oldest of those gathered. If you'd told me he'd been standing there since the beginning of time and would be there until the end, I'd have believed it. His presence was rooted in the valley floor, determined against the nothing. Others stood not just at the cardinal points but at the half points, too, seven more of them in all. Another two dozen or more hung back, not part of the power circle but not far from it, either. I took them in at a glance, but mostly I couldn't look away from the nothing. The Nothing. It deserved a capital letter.

It strained at the wards, doing its best to break free. Malevolence boiled at its heart, an age-old anger with intent and desire shaping it. My muscles locked up, fight-or-flight dissolving into simple fright. No one should have to look into that stuff, much less stand guard against it. I wanted to run, and couldn't make myself move.

"Joanne?" Sara touched my arm, making me flinch. I nearly seized her hand, grateful for human interaction, but I suspected she wouldn't appreciate it. Or maybe she would, if the Nothing unnerved her as badly as it did me. "What do you see?"

"I see—" Oh. She meant what did I See, not what did I see. I shuddered. If it was bleak and scary without the Sight, I really didn't want to see it with otherworldly vision. "Look, if I fall over, don't let me roll into it or anything, okay?"

"...okay."

I nodded, shivered and, despite Sara's assurance, knelt rather than dare trigger the Sight while still on my feet. It would be harder to fall over if I was kneeling, but more relevantly, it would be harder to run away, which my feet were already trying to do. I even leaned forward and put my hands in the moss, bracing myself before letting myself See the world through a shaman's eyes.

I'd told Sara the truth. I liked to get the lay of the land through ordinary vision before using magic, for two reasons. One, once I used the Sight, it was easy to overlook nonmagical things I might have otherwise noticed. Two, I was always a little afraid the astonishing light-filled beauty of the shamanic world would be so compelling I would never go back to normality.

Not today. The brilliant blue light of sap coursing through

tree branches, the resolute deep earthy red–brown of the mountains, the very brightness of the sky, were all distorted, as if the Nothing at the valley's center sucked them down. The shamanic wards helped, but as I watched it became clear they were merely mitigating the situation, not solving it. Their white power bent inward, as well, dragged into the Nothing's gravity well, and under that strain, the southwestern point of the compass faltered.

Without hesitation one of the extras stepped forward, put his hand on the shoulder of the woman standing at that point and strengthened her segment of the ward with his own magic. Over the course of a minute, maybe two, his aura blended and joined with the circle as hers became more distinct and separate. She finally stepped back, dropping to her knees with weariness, and two of the others came to help her away and offer food and drink.

I croaked, "How long have they been there?" and felt, rather than saw, Sara shake her head.

"Since your dad went missing. It'll be three full days in a few hours."

"Jesus." The three dozen people in the valley couldn't possibly have held that stuff off by themselves, not for that long. Every elder in the Qualla had to be stepping in, and probably every youth with any hope or hint of power in their bloodline. Maybe even many who didn't, but who could focus their energy in a positive way, as my friends had once done for me back in Seattle. Half the rez had to be in on this, to make it work. Most of them wouldn't even be believers, because really, although there was a pretty good sense of community amongst the People, and a lot of people turned out for the festivals and things, we were all modern-day people in a modern-day world. Magic wasn't part of most people's lives. But they still had to be showing up in the holler to stand their ground, or the whole place would have collapsed in on itself already.

And yet they wouldn't let Sara help. Sara who I knew had a spirit animal, a badger, because I'd helped her find it almost fifteen years ago. Sara who had some vestige of power because of that. Sara who certainly knew how to place her trust and faith in the hands of others, a necessary gift in a fight against something like this.

Sara who was a federal agent, and who could not be trusted. I wanted to cry.

The black heart of Nothing seized on that impulse, enriched it, pulled it up, emphasized despair over possibility, and for the first time I heard the mountain sobbing.

It came from deeper than the power circle reached, came all the way from a different level of reality where a low red sun hung bright and hard in a yellow sky. It came from the place the Native peoples of America were born of, the Lower World, and it cried at having lost its children not just now, but in the always. The dark magic devoured them, had devoured them through the centuries, had taken them with smallpox and measles and alcohol, and came again now to take them in whatever new way it could.

Anger roared within me, an infantile response to an unfair world. I wanted to throw everything I had against the Nothing, throw all my power in its teeth and prove to it that it couldn't take everything away. I wanted to soothe the torn earth and promise its future was brighter than its past, and to offer healing magic from inside me to calm its pain. That impulse, like the first, was seized upon by the Nothing. It tried to dig claws into me but instead skittered across the mental shields that had finally become second nature.

I jerked my hands from the soil and cut off the Sight so violently I shivered with it. Sara crouched beside me, a hand on my shoulder. "Joanne? What happened? You went all...blue."

"It tried to kill me." I shuddered again and shoved my hands through my hair, trying to scrub away the feeling that it was all standing on end. "It hooked right into my despair, but it couldn't grab hold of the magic. Thank God for that goddamned werewolf."

"The *what?*"

"Werewolf. Never mind, I'll explain later. I gotta do better with the emotional shielding, but we'd be really fucked if it had gotten the magic. Sara, that stuff is...really bad." I'd gotten to my feet while I gabbled, but I couldn't quite get myself moving toward the power circle.

Sara's voice went deadly neutral. "How bad?"

I'd heard that voice before, when she'd asked about her agents after we fought the wendigo. It was her preparing-for-the-worst voice, and when it had been her agents, she'd appreciated me not pussyfooting around the truth.

But that was work, and this was her family. I said, "It's hooked into the whole history of the People," carefully. "Not just the Cherokee, but across the continent. It's gained strength from every genocide wrought against Natives, and it's trying to reach forward to wipe more of them out. It's, um..." I pulled a hand over my face. "Shit. Look, I just dealt with this in Ireland. I mean, like three days ago. It's corruption in the Lower World and I thought it wasn't as bad here as it was in Europe, but maybe it's just...different."

"Joanne," Sara said in the same neutral voice, "what about Lucas?"

"I don't know. I really don't know yet."

"But..." she said, even though I didn't think I'd left an unsaid *but* dangling at the end of that. Maybe I didn't have to. Maybe having known me when I was a kid meant she heard them even when I didn't put them there, or maybe—more likely—being an FBI agent made her understand there was almost always a *but* when it came to bad things.

I closed my eyes, wishing I had another answer, then opened them again so I wouldn't feel like a coward when I looked her in the eye and said, "But if your husband and my father went into that stuff, we should both start getting used to the idea they're not coming out."

Sara regarded me steadily for a long moment, then said something that made me like her again, really genuinely like her, for the first time since we'd been teenagers: "No."

She walked down into the valley toward the horrible Nothingness, and to my surprise, I followed her with a smile.

From up close, the eight men and women in the power circle were barely more discernible than they'd been from a distance. Hair color under the pouring white magic told me they weren't all elders. In fact, from the apparent height and breadth, the person at the southern end of the circle was still a kid. The woman who'd been replaced was in her forties, and looked up as Sara and I came down the hill. Her face was drawn, but she pushed away the bottle of water someone else offered and got up as we joined them.

Rather, as *I* joined them. Sara might not have been there for all the woman cared, which seemed a bit unfair. I started to introduce myself, but she interrupted with "Joanne."

Not a friendly sort of "Joanne," but more a how-dare-you-appear-in-my-presence kind of "Joanne." I blinked at her, utterly bewildered. "Yes?"

"I'm Ada Monroe."

A small thermonuclear explosion went off in my belly. Heat rushed up, burning my face and setting my ears on fire. "Oh."

I probably should have recognized her. She had silver

threads in black hair now, crow's feet around brown eyes and twenty or so extra pounds, but she was the same woman she'd been thirteen years earlier. She'd been happier then, but then, she'd also just adopted the infant she'd been unable to have herself, and possibly more relevantly, hadn't just staggered out of a power circle that had been heavily borrowing from her life force. I said, "Oh," again, as the nuke in my stomach settled. "Hi. Are you okay?"

"What are you *doing* here?"

"I'm...*oh*. It's my dad, Ada, not Aidan. Um. Aidan?"

She nodded stiffly and a thrill of pleasure shot through me, then muted under wondering if she'd kept Aidan's name because it was similar to her own. "Aidan," I said again. "God, no, Ada, I'm not here for him. He's your son. Sara called and said Dad was missing. Of course I came."

"Of course you did." She packed a truly amazing amount of sarcasm into four words, which was probably fair, given I wasn't certain when I'd last talked to him. I exhaled and studied my feet a moment. First Sara's paranoia, now Ada's, and I hadn't hardly gotten past the Qualla's front door. There were probably another half-dozen bombs I didn't even know about just waiting to go off.

My feet seemed unconcerned by the possibility. I nodded, accepting their complacency, and looked up again. "Of course I did," I said again, more gently. "And from what I can tell, what you're doing here is helping make sure nobody else goes missing. I had no idea you were—" I hesitated, fumbling over the word. I'd learned a lot of them recently, words that meant magically talented: *adept, connected, talented.* I didn't know which she would respond to best.

What she didn't respond to well was the hesitation. "I'm not like you Walkingsticks, but my grandmother was a shaman's daughter. I have some of the blood."

"I didn't mean—" I wasn't going to get out of this alive, and stopped trying. "I'm here because I hope I can help."

"Then what'd you come with *her* for?" Sara suddenly became a presence again, one that Ada could look down on. I half turned toward Sara, who held her jaw so tight I could see muscle twitch. Anger, less profound than what the Nothing had called up, did a little stompy dance inside me. Sara and I might not be the best of buddies, but she deserved better than a total shut-out just because she'd become a Fed. But from how she stared resolutely away from Ada and the Nothing, it was pretty clear she wouldn't take a stand. Maybe she felt like she'd betrayed her own by going into the line of work she had. Maybe she was afraid they'd stop looking for Lucas entirely if she rocked the boat at all. Maybe she just wasn't confrontational by nature, though she'd been happy enough to get in my face.

Why didn't matter. She could take it if she wanted to, but I didn't have to enable it. I turned back to Ada with my best butter-wouldn't-melt expression. "Sara called to tell me that my dad was missing, Ada, and her husband's missing, too. Why wouldn't she be here? Besides, I've worked with Sara in the past. I know what a professional asset she is, and I'd think everyone would be grateful for a trained agent on a search-and-rescue operation."

Ada snapped, "This is Qualla business," and I, very softly, said, "And Sara is a Qualla agent. The government's done a lot of harm, I'm not arguing, but if everybody in the Qualla turns their back on people who pursue federal careers, then there's not much chance those people are ever going to be able to help, or in the end even want to. Don't cut off your nose to spite your face, Ada. Now, can you tell me anything about what's going on here, or bring me to someone who can?"

Mouth set in a thin line, Ada pointed toward the northern

end of the holler, then folded her arms under her breasts and turned away from us. I went where she directed, Sara catching up to say, semigrudgingly, "Thank you. That was a dumb thing to do, but thank you."

I nodded acceptance of the thanks, but asked, "Dumb?"

"She's your kid's mom, Joanne. You really want her angry at you?"

"Sara, if she wants him to loathe me then I'm sure it's already far too late for that. Three minutes defending you is not going to change anything, and she pissed me off. You deserve more respect. I mean, you're what, twenty-nine now? And you're leading investigative teams with the FBI. That takes a lot of ambition and dedication. It doesn't—it shouldn't—matter if you're a federal agent. You're not the enemy."

My little rant had taken us around the Nothing to the holler's northern end. Sara, bemused, murmured, "I don't know what you've done with the Joanne Walkingstick I drove up here with, but I like this version better," as we were approached by an old woman I recognized. Carrie Little Turtle, whose steel-gray hair was still twisted in the same relentless braids she'd worn almost fifteen years earlier when she and Les's grandfather, also Lester, and three other elders had given me the shaman's drum that currently rested on my dresser back in Seattle.

Carrie looked equally at home in jeans or deerskin, the latter of which she was wearing now, with feathers woven into the under-skirt. She also wore so many rings and bangles that I wasn't quite sure how she could lift her arms. Like Ada, she gave Sara a faintly scathing look, but since I was half certain Carrie actually remembered the Trail of Tears, I was less inclined to put my neck out in Sara's defense.

Sadly, she gave me a far more scathing look than she graced Sara with. "Where's your drum?"

"…Seattle…"

Carrie clicked her tongue so loudly I suspected they immediately started discussing my shame in the next county over. "Well, I didn't," I started, then tried, "I mean, I wasn't," before finishing up in a burst of desperation: "I was in *Ireland,* see."

"And they don't use drums in Ireland? Never mind." For a woman eighty years older than God, she had some fine talk-to-the-hand action going on. I subsided without even trying to speak, feeling like a scolded puppy. "This is a bad time to come home, Joanne Walkingstick. You should have come home a long time ago."

My guilt did a quick reverse into belligerence. "Really. A long time ago or not at all? Because tell you what, Carrie, *that,*" I said with a jab of my finger toward the power-bound Nothing, "scares the shit out of me, and if you've got some way to deal with it that I don't have to play along with, I might actually be okay with that. I can just hightail my ass back to Seattle and all y'all can quiet the mountain down yourself."

"Ah," Sara said almost inaudibly, "there you are."

"You think you can help the mountain? Stop *that?*" Carrie made much the same gesture I had, only somehow she filled it with derision, which actually stopped me cold.

There were two possible options. One was she genuinely wasn't afraid of a boiling mass of Nothing that creeped me out so badly I was unconsciously doing everything I could not to look at it. If that was the case, Carrie Little Turtle was not only more of a badass than I was, but she was more of a badass than I could ever imagine hoping to be.

The other, far more likely option, was that she was every bit as terrified as I was, had no idea how to protect her land, her people, or their history, and had no intention of letting anyone see it. I bit back a response just as short-tempered as Carrie's and eased the Sight on so I could take a look at her aura.

It spun with turmoil, earthy dark green and brown nearly overwhelmed by sharp bursts of red panic and bright orange throbs of pain. Her whole left torso was afire with orange, in fact, squeezing and straining her body, and her aura's stuttering pulses reminded me of a faltering heartbeat. A whole metaphor rolled out of that in an instant, how the mountains were Carrie's heart and this nothingness at their center was breaking it, that the stress reflected in her body was representative of what happened in the Carolina hills—

Then I got my English degree under control and realized no, actually, the woman was having a heart attack right in front of me. I yelped and shoved my hand over her heart.

Healing magic shot from me like it was desperate for something to do. Like the chance to heal Carrie was a chance to heal the mountain, though realistically I knew the metaphor wasn't going to stretch that far. But the problems of age and stress, those I could deal with. Carrie's heart muscle was old and worn out, arteries stiff with build-up. With a touch, I had the instant sense of how long she'd been breathing poorly, of how long she'd been growing weaker without fully realizing it.

For months I'd used detailed visualizations to heal, mapping my mechanic's skills at fixing cars to healing the human body. I didn't need to do that anymore—in the end, with my full belief behind it, healing was essentially instantaneous—but the images came anyway. Blocked arteries were clogged fuel lines that needed to be scraped clean; loosened bits of plaque were the floating debris that needed to be flushed from the system. It was easier with a car, of course, since cars usually had valves that could be unfastened and drained, whereas yanking a coronary artery out so gunk could wash free would probably be bad for the patient. Still, the basic idea was solid, and the image held in my mind for less than a breath as my silver-blue power coursed through Carrie's body.

Her next breath came more easily. Red still dominated her aura, but the orange flares of tension were gone, the tightness and weight in her chest no longer wearing her down. She clutched her left breast, classic heart attack motion, but there was neither pain nor fear in her expression, only astonishment.

Astonishment, then joy. "You *have* come home. You've come back to the path. I thought you were lost to it, all those years ago. I thought you didn't carry the drum because it meant nothing to you."

My throat tightened up again. I said, "The drum," then had to swallow and try a second time. "The drum never stopped meaning something to me. It was the only thing that did for a long time. Well. That and my car."

Amusement crinkled Carrie's eyes, which I hadn't even known was possible. "I remember the car. We thought perhaps when its restoration was finished, your soul would be healed. Have you completed it?"

I blinked, taken aback. "Um, actually, yeah. I even put in a manual transmission like I'd always promised her. That was just a couple months ago, at Christmas. And I sort of…" Had really pulled my shit together around then, too. That was when my mentor Coyote had returned, and when I'd finally really began to understand what being both a healer and a warrior meant.

But the alarming bit was I'd always envisioned my car—Petite, her name was Petite, and she was a 1969 Mustang Boss 302 I'd rescued out of somebody's barn the summer I turned sixteen. The first thing I'd replaced was her spiderwebbed windshield, and for the past fifteen months I'd envisioned my soul as exactly that mess of a windshield. It made Carrie's theory equal parts viable and too damned weird to contemplate. I shivered all over, trying to put it out of my mind. "Anyway, I came back because Sara told me Dad was missing, but there's obviously a hell of a lot more going on. I Saw what that stuff is doing, how deep it's reaching—you Saw that, too?"

Carrie shook her head, which I didn't expect. "I only see how it eats at the mountain. What more do you See?"

"Oh, God. It's—"

The power circle fluctuated again, but differently this time. Not a weakening in one place, but responding to a sudden vast surge of power from within the Nothing. A concussive force blew out, like it was testing for vulnerable spots through sheer strength of magic. The skirt of my coat blasted backward. Sara went head over heels. Carrie stayed upright only because I grabbed her arm and grounded myself, shamanic magic telling the earth I was there and requesting its support.

The wards almost held. They flickered and faltered, white magic shimmering to more individual colors, but at seven points of the compass, they held, keeping the Nothingness from gobbling up more of the mountain.

At the eighth point, at the most northerly edge of the circle, hungry gray mist rushed out, taking advantage of an old man's weakness.

For one frozen moment, Carrie and I stood together, numb and unable to move, as Les's grandfather collapsed at our feet.

CHAPTER FOUR

Two things needed doing and I couldn't make a choice: step up and hold the line against the Nothing, or drop to my knees and heal Les's grandpa. Carrie, thank God, snapped into action, pointing an imperious finger at Grandpa Lee as she flung every bit of her age, rage and will against the surging wall of Nothing. There was nothing elegant about the transference of power, not the way the other one I'd just seen had gone. She just stepped in, forcing her strength to merge with the other seven. Raw edges flared and burned white as they struggled to hold the shields together and accommodate Carrie's rough entrance. The mountain shrieked pain and fear, and triumph rolled through the gray, but too soon. Carrie would die before she let the Nothing win, and she had just gotten topped up full of glowing blue healing magic. Les's grandpa had been the weak link for a heartbeat there, but Carrie was the strong one now. It wasn't going to last, but it didn't need to, not with me there.

Not as long as I got my act together and got Lester Lee Senior on his feet again. I shaved off part of my concentration and built a shield around him and me, one that ran deeper and stronger than usual. I didn't want the Nothing leaking out the edges of the power circle shielding to get even one tendril inside Les Senior while I patched him up. The world went pleasantly blue around us, a bubble of active magic so solid I hoped warheads couldn't budge it. Then I put a hand on Les Senior's chest and had a quick look around inside him.

I got more than an eyeful of what I expected, too. Most times I got a sense of someone's physical well-being. This time he was so worn and raw I Saw straight into his garden, the metaphorical center of self that reflected a person's well-being. Les Senior's was parched and dry, red earth cracked and once-lush plant life brown and drooping. It didn't feel like age—God knew my pal Gary, who was at least as old as Les Senior, wasn't suffering from any kind of drying–out of his garden. This was more like Les Senior was being sucked dry. More like he'd given everything he had, and was now too exhausted to replenish himself. There was nothing else wrong with him, no clotted arteries or other common maladies of age. Gratitude surged through me. It wasn't often I got to save two people back to back, but between Les Senior and Carrie, I was batting a thousand.

Bizarrely, fixing exhaustion was more delicate work than stopping a heart attack. Cardiac arrest was all about violence and instantaneous reaction, and shutting it down had taken the same response. Exhaustion was something that built up, and Les's garden was so parched that throwing a metaphorical river in would just drown him. I tamped the power down to a trickle, easing the gas on, as it were, and let it drain in slowly enough that his garden's earth had time to absorb the replenishing magic instead of being flooded by it. I couldn't let myself pay attention to what was going on outside my shields, trusting that Carrie and the others had it under control. Or at least trusting they could triage until I was done getting Les Senior's feet back under him.

He opened his eyes sooner than I expected, blinked a couple times, and somehow didn't seem surprised to focus on me. "I'll be fine. Go on."

I swear, the old man was like Carrie, made of sprung steel and baling wire. Nothing was gonna keep them down, not until they marched out of this world and into the next, where they would probably start setting things to right all over again. I still said, "You sure?"

Les Senior nodded, and I pointed out a direction away from the boiling Nothing. "You get the hell away from that stuff, you hear me? Don't be stupid just because you're conscious."

Amusement darted through his brown eyes and he nodded again. I let the shields down slowly, keeping them thickest to my left, where I'd last left the Nothing, until I was certain the world around us hadn't disappeared entirely. It hadn't. I pointed to my right. "You go that-a-way."

Les Senior went as directed, and only when he was well away and into the arms of others did I get to my feet and put my hands on Carrie's shoulders. "My turn."

"We need you out there. Fighting."

"I need to know what I'm fighting. I've got to See what's at the heart of this thing. And you just came a hair's breadth from a coronary. You don't need to be shouldering this burden right now. So move it."

I got the dirtiest look in Creation, but bit by bit Carrie transferred the weight of shielding she'd taken on to me. The power fluctuating between the eight compass points strengthened considerably as I took more of it on. Partly because I was a heavyweight in the mojo department, but partly because this transition was deliberate, rather than somebody shoving themselves in to plug a bursting dyke. After about two minutes, Carrie stepped out, and I...

...stepped up.

Because I wasn't kidding anybody, least of all myself. I had a pretty goddamned good idea who, or at least what, was behind the pit of Nothing trying to eat out the heart of my homeland. Barely three days ago I'd effectively nailed a cross to my enemy's door, made it clear we were about to reach a header. I'd *seen* him for the first time, the Master whose power was death and corruption, and I'd come damned close to losing my life.

I *had* lost my mother, forever and for always, to the fight against him. She'd come to protect me one last time, and had burned out everything she'd ever been, in that battle. There were old souls and new ones in this world, and my mother's had been old, but it would never be reborn. That was the price she'd chosen to pay to keep me alive. It had given me the last bits of breathing room I needed, because it had turned out I wasn't quite ready to face him after all. She'd left him wounded and embarrassed, and there was no chance the mess in Carolina was coincidence, not after that.

So I wasn't screwing around when I joined the power circle. I didn't let them have it all at once, because I'd noticed an alarming tendency for blown-out electrical grids and other exciting ramifications of announcing my psychic presence in a grand slam. But I came to the party to play, and by the time Carrie's power faded out and mine replaced it, I was feeling pretty white-hot with magic. If there was *any* chance I could snuff out the Nothing, I was going to take it right now.

I expected resistance. I expected it to seep inside me and find my fear again. I expected it to ratchet that up to eleven, and for grim determination and a whole lot of stubbornness to get me through. I was prepared for that, leaning forward a little, saying, "C'mon, I can take it," with my body language. I thought I *could* take it, now that I was ready for it. The fear hadn't been as bad as the Master hitting me in the teeth with pain, and I'd survived that. Only just, but this wasn't the time to quibble over details. So I was braced, ready for whatever the Nothing threw at me.

I was not prepared for sympathetic magic to skyrocket across the power circle, south to north, and catch me in the breast-bone. Catch me right where my magic had lodged itself for all the long months before I'd really accepted it, in fact. Not my heart: my center. I wasn't prepared for its vainglorious brilliance, four shades of brightness that whipped and blended together so fast they became white. And I was *really* not prepared for the boom of power that erupted when that magic and my own fused.

A visible ring bounced through the power circle like a shock wave, vibrating the mountain under our feet. Vibrating the air, vibrating sound, vibrating everything: I could've been standing under the bells at Notre Dame and gotten less resonance.

The gasp couldn't have been audible, not beneath all the power noise, but it felt audible. Everyone took a step forward, a step closer together, like we were drawn in by that power burst. Part of my brain screamed an objection, not wanting to get any closer to the Nothing than it had to, but it wasn't the part in control. I moved just like everyone else.

The Nothing shrank. Rolled in on itself, no farther than we'd stepped forward, but it got just a little bit smaller. Emotion spiked through the power circle, hope and confusion and flaring confidence. We stepped forward again, magic ricocheting between me and the southern point like some kind of earthbound display of Northern Lights. My power sluiced along the outsides of the other adept's magic, encompassing it with silver and blue. The four bands of bright colors spun inside mine, and everybody else's swam alongside ours, drawn back and forth at light speeds. From inside I could See the different auras, though only faintly: mostly they remained blended to brilliance, subsuming themselves to the massive working of white magic. We all took one more step forward, coming much closer to the Nothing, and a sense of nervous anticipation swept through the working. Six of them were waiting: waiting to see what the southern and northern compass points to their circle did next.

I wasn't sure voices would carry through the Nothing between us. I clenched my stomach, preparing myself for a fight, and sent that feeling of determination through the magic.

It bounced back at me so fast it felt like laughter. A grin stretched across my face, wild and a little crazy. I spread my arms, knowing I was much too far away to catch the hands of the elders nearest me, but feeling like it was a statement: *Come and get me. Catch me if you can.* The same feeling crashed back at me from the other side of the circle, all kinds of reckless and foolhardy and ready for a fight. I knew the feeling intimately. I'd been like that as a kid. Who was I kidding: most of the time I was still like that. I hadn't been set on the warrior's path just because there was a big bad monster who needed taking out. I was sort of an aggressive little punk most of the time. Mouthy and full of 'tude, even—or especially— when it wasn't warranted.

God knew I had plenty to introspect over, but even I thought this was sort of a weird time for it to crop up. I told myself it was the familiarity of emotion in my partner's magic, and let it go. There were far more important things to worry about right now.

Like how to crush the Nothing into a tiny ball of, er, nothing. We had some kind of major power blend going on here, far stronger than I'd anticipated. Stronger than the Master had anticipated, too, I was willing to bet. But I didn't know if the Nothing could be undone, or only captured. Wondering made my head hurt, so I took action instead of thinking anymore, and squeezed my shields down.

The first couple advances we'd made had been instinctive. This was deliberate, and there was a world of difference. The Nothing made a sound, a shriek of anger that reverberated in my ear bones. It collapsed in, shrinking visibly as the southern adept squeezed, too, and as the others followed our lead.

Glee rose up from my counterpart. Glee and triumph and all sorts of other premature but obvious emotions that I was inclined to share. I'd had a hell of a couple of weeks. I thought I deserved one easy win, especially if it made my homecoming a little easier. But I wasn't quite foolish enough to do a touch-down dance yet. Shriveling evil magic was not the same as eliminating evil magic, and I wanted it good and eliminated. My shields were rock-solid, and I wrapped them in the idea of a net, just to help squish everything down a little more. Step by step we closed in around the Nothing, and with every step the others became more confident. It made a positive feed-back loop, creating stronger magic because our belief in it was stronger. I had no idea how much time passed before I touched hands with my right neighbor, and then moments later with my left, but suddenly we were a physical construct as well as a magical one, and the Nothing roiled and shrieked and spat fury in the circle created by our linked hands.

Someone finally spoke aloud. Not either of my closest co-horts, and not the next people over, either. I could see them, but the Nothing still rose tall enough to block the other three from my line of vision. I figured it was the southern compass point, the other one who was flinging as much magic potential around as I was. She had a light voice, still a teenager's voice, which fit with the glimpse I'd had of a slight figure, on my way into the holler.

"It's a time traveler," she said. "It's trying to slide through. Forward, backward, I don't think it cares very much as long as it pulls bad shit through. We've gotta cut it out. We've gotta remove it from the timeline entirely. That's the only way it's gonna be vulnerable enough for us to smash it."

I had the impression she was lecturing me specifically. That kind of made sense, since everybody else had been here for days, and she had no way of knowing I'd recognized the Nothing's time-slip capability, too. She sounded pretty sure she knew how to deal with it, and for a half second I wondered if I could've been her, self-assured and rife with magic, if I hadn't blown it so badly half a lifetime ago.

Not that it mattered, because I *had* blown it, and I'd largely come to terms with that. I let regret go, said, "Sounds like a plan," to my unseen counterpart, and let her take the lead.

For the first time, an edge of alarm slipped through the power circle. Her alarm, not mine, which made me think maybe giving her the lead hadn't been so bright, but it also seemed not only rude but potentially dangerous to yank it back now. Besides, I wasn't at all sure how a person went about yanking things out of time to castrate them. I knew how to yank things around *in* time, albeit clumsily, but that didn't seem like the skill set necessary here. The kid across the circle had sounded sufficiently confident that I'd assumed she did know.

Eventually I was going to learn that assumptions were dangerous, but today was clearly not that day. I breathed, "Calmly, calmly," and sent a ripple of healing power through the circle. I didn't usually use it as a soporific, but it seemed to help. I felt the multistranded adept's aura and power strengthen again.

An image popped into my head. I didn't know if it was my own or my counterpart's, though if it was hers I really wanted that nifty telepathic aspect to my magic. Either way, the idea of a sensory deprivation tank came to mind. That, in essence, was what we needed to do to the Nothing. Except where I was supposed to find a tank so secluded that *time* didn't affect it, I didn't know. Well, except maybe on the event horizon of a black hole, but that led to all sorts of other really bad possibilities that I wasn't eager to explore.

It did, though, give me an idea. Space was affected by time: anything that light passed through kind of had to be. But the idea of the dark side of the moon introduced itself to me, and I seized on it. It wasn't *really* dark, I knew that, it was just that we never saw its other face, so maybe that was close enough. I was willing to take it.

I filled my shields with that idea: cold black timelessness, lingering in the silence, no pressure or need for change. It wasn't perfect, but it was pretty good, and the cold started crackling the edges of the Nothing. That was shamanism: change instigated by belief. I could turn the air within that crushing shield to a space vacuum without harming any of the nonspacesuit-clad elders in the power circle. And that little inkling of time that was still part of the equation, that was no big deal, that was—

—slipping.

Slipping, cracking, sliding out of control, bringing the Nothing back into the world because it still had something to latch on to. I clamped down, trying to ignore it, trying to hold on to the possibility of taking something entirely out of time, trying to remember just how much depended on me doing that, and felt a jillion little bug feet run up my spine and send shivers all over me. They all leapt off, my spine abandoned by an infinitesimal number of bugs, and I lost control of the magic.

Panic and dismay shot up from the other side of the circle. The dismay cut deep, much deeper than the fear. The Nothing erupted again, knocking us all over the holler. I crashed against soft dirt and immediately staggered to my feet, weaving physical shields together again, determined to catch the stuff before it got out-of-control large again. It was much smaller than before, but not *gone,* dammit. All around me, power stuttered back into wakefulness, everyone who'd been thrown around trying, as I was, to hold the Nothing to a smaller size. My counterpart's magic rushed through us all, connecting us like railroad ties, until it slapped into me and we once more had a functional power circle around the Nothing. The younger woman's magic was flushed with anger, fitting against my own anger tidily. I was able to hang on to its edges easily, improving our connection with the sense of long familiarity.

It all came home to me a little slowly. I'd worked with sympathetic magic before. Recently, even, up on a mountaintop in Ireland. Maybe it had something to do with mountains. Anyway, I knew the strength of blending familiar, familial magics, but I hadn't expected it in the Qualla.

Which, in retrospect, was really, really stupid, because the Qualla had the two people on Earth who were closest to me by blood.

It wasn't a teenage girl at all, the counterpart who stalked up to me with frustration and anger in brown eyes. It was a prepubescent boy, a twelve-year-old nearing his thirteenth birthday but not his voice change, and he said, "You're twice as old as I am, *Joanne.* I thought you would be *good* at this stuff," with all the disdain in the world.

It was not, all things considered, how I'd envisioned re-meeting my son.

CHAPTER FIVE

Aidan Monroe had inherited his father's golden-brown skin tones and hair so black its natural highlights were blue. He'd also gotten some of the same shape to his nose as Lucas had, mitigating my own beak somewhat. But I could see bits of me in him, too: the shape of his eyes and jaw, particularly with said jaw thrust into a too-familiar scowl. He was rangy like I'd been—like I still was—and there wasn't any hint yet of whether he would grow into shoulders like Lucas's or not. He was barefoot, red clay under his toenails, and his ragged-ankle jeans and sleeveless T-shirt could've belonged on any kid from the mid-20th century on.

I thought he was beautiful.

I mean, I guessed mothers were supposed to, but I hadn't been a prime candidate for mother of the year when I'd gotten pregnant and given him up at age fifteen. If anything gave me potential mother-of-the-year status, in fact, it was *having* given him up. I had a lot of emotional investment in that decision, but not a lot of sentimental investment, even if that seemed like a fine hair to shave. The point was, I hadn't been overwhelmed with his infantile beauty, so I was a little surprised to find myself wanting to smile and pat him on the head like he—or I—had done well, just by him being cute.

Given that he was already glaring at me, I manfully restrained myself and instead shrugged. "I probably should be, but I'm a lot further behind on my studies than you'd expect. Sorry." The word, while flippant, was also sincere: I'd have preferred to unveil myself to Aidan in all my shining glory, instead of fumbling the ball just before the end zone. I was pretty certain that was the right sports metaphor.

He squinted and rolled back on his heels, a sign of surprise so like my own body language I had to fight not to laugh. I supposed lots of people did that, but seeing it on him was a little like looking in a reverse-gender mirror. Offhand, I suspected he hadn't expected an apology from me, or anything less than a like-for-like chip on my shoulder.

To be fair, everybody who'd known me, anybody who might have told him about me—and he *clearly* knew who I was—would have told him to expect that chip. To expect whole icebergs, probably, not just chips.

For half a second I lost my battle with the smile, because I was obviously surprising him, and surprise allowed for a possibility of change, and that, at its heart, was what my magic was supposed to latch on to and work with. Shamanistic magic right there in action, even if no actual magic was being worked.

Aidan didn't like the smile. It gave him something to be pissed off about, which was why I'd been trying to suppress it in the first place. "Are you *laughing* at m—"

"No."

The poor kid looked so surprised again I had to bite the inside of my cheeks to keep from laughing for real that time. "Aidan—it's Aidan, right?" I'd asked his mother that once already, but somehow it seemed important to clear it with him, too. He nodded, somewhere between sullenly and suspiciously, and I said, "Right. Aidan. No, I'm really not laughing at you. I'm laughing at me a little, maybe, because somehow I didn't expect to see you so soon, and because it's sort of embarrassing to admit a kid pushing thirteen almost certainly has it all over me in terms of mystical training. I mean, holy crap, kid, did you see you out there?"

I waved toward the Nothing, which was a much smaller seething ball now, and being held in place by the six elders who'd been working with us, and two others who'd joined them when Aidan and I broke out to have some awkward family time. I'd hardly even noticed them taking over for me, I'd been so busy gawking at Aidan. "You were awesome. What was I *supposed* to do there at the end? Maybe if we can do it now…?"

Aidan's eyes went deep gold. Molten gold, a crazy color I was pretty sure mine didn't reach, not even in the depths of magic use. He turned that heated gaze on me, slamming it right between my eyes, like he was looking into my head—

—and my garden ripped to life around us. The mountain holler faded, short-shorn grass and neat stone pathways appearing under our feet. A waterfall began burbling, and crumbling stone walls rose up out of the earth, farther away than I'd ever seen them. Ivy wrapped around the trunks of strong young hickory trees, which made me mutter and flick a finger, clearing the ivy away. It scattered from the trees and returned to the walls where it used to grow, thin climbing branches working to break them down further. A breeze swept through, carrying the scent of flowers from somewhere, and I could almost pretend that my staggering was actually me setting off in search of where those blooms were growing.

Almost. Mostly, though, I was just staggering and gaping. "How the hell—! What the hell! What are you—"

The garden turned to mist, blue sky turning yellow and the sun turning red. The ground was red, too, redder than the deep earth of the Appalachians, and the grass growing up around us was purple in some places and yellow in others. Familiar enough territory, except I had no idea how Aidan had slammed us not just into, but *through,* my garden and into the Lower World. "What are you d—"

Raven, my cheerful, chattering spirit guide, exploded into being with a clatter of wings and noise. He dove around Aidan's head fast enough to make me dizzy, pulling at Aidan's long hair and tangling his beak in it. My long-suffering Rattler spirit also appeared, though less exuberantly. He wound around Aidan's feet, tongue flickering in and out, then returned to wrap around my ankles. Rattler had had a much more difficult couple of weeks than Raven, and I really needed some not-forthcoming downtime to get him back on his feet. Belly. Whatever.

Aidan, evidently waiting on something, stoically ignored Raven. Me, I crouched to stroke Rattler's head and watched Raven's antics with bemusement. Not even my mother had been able to pull my spirit guides into focus, but then, Mother had been a mage, not a shaman. I had plenty of questions, but for once I kept my mouth shut, more curious about what Aidan's expectations were than about how he'd hauled us into the Lower World.

Finally it became clear that whatever he was waiting on wasn't going to put in an appearance. Full-on teenage horror filled his face. "Oh, my God. You don't even have all your *spirit animals.* You're *useless.*"

He disappeared from the Lower World, leaving nothing but a set of footprints behind in the red earth, and I flung my hands up with a shout of exasperated laughter.

Raven *klok-klok-klok*ed at me and came to settle on my shoulder, where he could peer at me from a third of an inch away. "What," I said to the bird, "does he think I can't get back if he leaves me here? Is this some kind of test?" I sat down. Rattler slithered into my lap and coiled up comfortably small. I stroked his head again, smiling as he leaned into the touch like a cold-blooded scaly cat. I'd spent enough time as a child tromping around snake-littered woods that I'd never imagined having an affinity, much less fondness, for a rattle-snake, but Rattler was something special. And I was sure that I'd think so even if he hadn't saved my life more than once.

"Perhapsss," he said once he was cozy and lazy in my lap, "perhaps you should take this opportunity to seek out your third, as he thinks you ssshould."

"Third what, spirit animal? I don't know, that seems like it would be giving the little punk the upper hand. 'Hop to it, birth vessel! Heed my wisdom!' Like that." It probably wasn't fair to call Aidan a punk. He probably had every reason to be upset with the woman who had skipped out on her magical heritage and failed to come back home firing the big guns in a moment of need.

And besides, it wasn't like I had any room to go around throwing stones. I *had* been a pain-in-the-ass punk teen, with what was turning out to be less justification than Aidan probably had. I said, "Sorry, kid," aloud and mentally retracted the *punk* nomenclature with the intention of retiring it permanently.

Rattler, who apparently didn't care what I called Aidan, said, "It isss foolish to not ssstrike when the opportunity arissses," with an acerbic tang. I could tell, because his sibilants got stretchier when he was annoyed.

I rubbed the top of his head. "So I should ignore the fact that someone I barely know and maybe shouldn't trust because of that brought me here, and just head gung-ho into a spirit quest?"

"Do you missstrust him?"

"Nah." That was a much softer and far less flippant answer. "Nah, I don't know him at all, but I guess I'd trust him way past where I could throw him. He's got power and he's got a lot more training than I do. Maybe I should listen." A chortle bubbled around my chest. "Because, you know. That's always been my strong suit up until now."

"Sssometimes," Rattler said, and it was amazing how dryly a snake could speak, "sometimesss it isss all right to learn from past missstakes." He slithered out of my lap and coiled around me in a tight circle, closing it up by taking his rattle in his mouth. Raven gave an excited caw and bounced into flight, wheeling around my head like he was drawing circles in the sky to match the one Rattler made on the ground.

"Right," I said to both of them. "This is me, getting the message. When your spirit animals start drawing your power circles *for* you…." I traced a hand along Rattler's sinuous spine, stopping at the cardinal points to murmur a little breath of nonsense that mostly meant I was paying attention to where they were. If I wasn't careful, soon I'd be doing rituals and all the other silly stuff that went along with being a magic practitioner. It was bad enough that I adopted this weird semiformal language structure when I started talking about magic. I really didn't want to get any more New Agey than I was, though I was much less biased against the whole scene than I'd been when I'd started out.

A soft wash of magic splashed up while I was trying to convince myself I was still normal and not hippy-dippy. Blue and silver swirled around each other, reaching for the sky-circle Raven had drawn, and thoroughly putting paid to any dreams of normalcy. I snorted at myself and closed my eyes, listening for something that would do as a drum and drop me into the quiet dark space where spirit animals roamed.

My heartbeat did the job, thumping in my ears more loudly than usual. I counted the beats until I started to drowse, my shoulders going slack and my hands loosening from the curls I'd held them in. I'd done the spirit quests for both Rattler and Raven while in the Lower World, though I hadn't meant to either time. It seemed appropriate to be doing a third one here, too, though I had no sense of whether it would be like Raven's appearance or like Rattler's. Raven's had been fairly traditional—well, except for the part where it had been conducted by an evil sorceress—with several creatures coming to say hello before Raven picked me. Rattler had simply shown up in the nick of time and saved my bacon.

My bacon was, for once, not in need of saving, so when a white butterfly drifted through the darkness, I figured it was just checking me out, and probably indicative of a more traditional quest. That was good. I was down with tradition, for once. The butterfly faded, and only after the fact did I remember my last encounter with butterflies had made a serious stab at ending the world. My stomach clenched up and I tried to remember what other totem animals I'd dealt with. I did not want a parade of bad associations contaminating my quest for a third spirit animal.

Raven, who in the Lower World was much more real than in the Middle World, smacked me alongside the head so hard I got dizzy even with my eyes closed. I took that as an indication that I was probably making things worse, told my brain to shut up, and held my breath, like that would make my brain shut up.

It didn't. Nothing ever made my brain shut up. It went right back to worrying about the various spirits I'd seen before Raven in the quest run by an evil sorceress. Rattler, with a sense of exasperation as great as Raven's, let go of his tail to bite me. I yelped, but it did at least remind me that I'd seen a snake, too, during that particular ritual, and that it had turned out I did indeed have a snake spirit who was no more wicked than Raven. Possibly less so, in fact, since Raven had a teasing sense of humor and Rattler didn't have much of one. So maybe if the horse from that first session showed up, it wouldn't mean I was in trouble after all.

No horses showed up. No badgers or tortoises or rams had shown up during some of the quests I'd done for other people. No nothing, in fact: apparently the butterfly was just an errant wanderer, lost in the ether. Grumpy, I said, "This is getting us nowhere," and opened my eyes.

The entire landscape was covered in walking sticks.

CHAPTER SIX

I squeaked and shoved my hands against my mouth to keep it from turning into a full-on shriek. It wasn't that I was afraid of bugs. Even if I was, walking sticks were such peculiar bugs that they moved out of the realm of Potentially Scary all the way into That Is So Weird It's Cool, which wasn't usually frightening. Even more, this was at least the third time I'd suddenly been faced with an onslaught of walking sticks, but there were zillions of them now, far, far more than I'd encountered on other spirit journeys. Purple foliage bent under their collective weight, and the ground shifted subtly as they moved around. It bordered on creepy.

They had not crossed the tiny power circle Rattler made. Rattler was eyeing the nearest ones like he thought someone had just provided the largest smorgasbord in history, and also like he suspected he really shouldn't start chowing down on other denizens of the Lower World.

One of them was eyeing me as blatantly as Rattler eyed it. It was nearly as long as my arm—not my forearm, but my whole arm—and striped green and yellow, which made it stand out against the multicolored earth. Its legs were long enough to wrap around me, and I was reasonably certain that although walking sticks were nominally herbivores, its mandibles could take a sizable chunk out of tender body parts.

It lifted one spindly leg and tapped its foot on Rattler's scales, just like it was knocking to be let in.

Way at the back of my head, a penny dropped. This was at least the third time I'd been faced with an onslaught of walking sticks. The other times had also been in spirit realms, and both times the bugs had gone away again with a sense of resignation. Of waiting.

And now they were knocking to get in.

I gently disengaged Rattler's grip on his tail and put my arm out. The walking stick bumped its nose against my fingers, kind of like a big dog sniffing before deciding I was okay, then stepped onto my hand and traipsed lightly up my arm.

Eye-to-eye and nose-to-nose with a giant bug was not somewhere I'd ever imagined I'd be. Its eyes were black and shining, and its mouth really was big enough to make divots in flesh. Despite its size, it had almost no weight, which reminded me of Raven. Raven was huge, but bird-boned even if he wasn't also a spirit animal, and his weight was always surprisingly negligible. Rattler seemed to have more oomph to him, but the walking stick was pure delicacy. It leaned in until its forehead touched mine, and a little spark of embarrassed recognition popped through me.

It wasn't like I hadn't thought of it when the bugs had come visiting previously. My last name *was,* after all, Walkingstick. I hadn't imagined it was pure coincidence that innumerable stick bugs had decided to parade over me as I scrambled through the Upper World. I just hadn't quite realized they were early-stage spirit animals waiting for me to be ready for them.

I dearly wanted that mind-meld pose to make everything cascade into clarity, sense and reason. I wanted to suddenly understand the stick's purpose, to understand what it offered and why, and wrap that all together with my magic so I finally had a full grip on it. Raven had always been my guide between life and death. Rattler's gifts were multifaceted, as variegated as his scales: healing, fighting, shapeshifting; he encompassed all of those aspects.

There was really only one thing left that I could do, one major power component that had been dogging me since before I was born. Something so big I figured it *had* to warrant a spirit animal of its own, even if I had no clue why a walking stick was the manifestation of that power set. It was so big and so absurd I didn't even like putting it into words, but having just jumped back and forth around the entire history of Ireland, I was pretty damned certain that for some unbelievably stupid reason, the last of my phenomenal cosmic power set was freaking *time travel*.

I could not for the life of me imagine why anyone would be given the power to travel through time, even if it had become manifestly clear to me that doing so was more of a perspective-offering scheme than a "Woo hoo! I can change history!" kind of thing. I could not, in fact, change history. The timeline was pretty fixed, with only minor variations permitted. So far the best I'd been able to do was get an understanding of time loops that had been opened a long time ago, so that I could close them on this end of time.

"We are unchanging," the stick bug said in a surprisingly feminine voice, and I sat bolt upright, blinking at her. She did not blink back, what with having no eyelids, but somehow conveyed a sense of sedate blinking anyway. I waited, but she didn't say anything else, which made me have to think about what she'd said.

I wasn't certain, but I thought stick bugs were a bit like crocodiles: an evolutionary path that got it right early on, and didn't mess with anything afterward. I thought they'd been pretty much the same animals for tens of millions of years. From that perspective, unchanging and being associated with time travel made a certain amount of sense. I'd been able to haul myself through time by fixating on something as comparatively new as a Neolithic cairn. If stick bugs had twenty million years of unchanging evolution to draw on, they were probably damned fine focal points for time travel.

It made me wonder if some of the other animals whose fossil records were relatively unchanged were also time-traveling spirit animals. I was just as glad my last name was Walkingstick and not Sharkbait. "Right," I said out loud, to stop myself going down that line of thought. "You're…I mean, welcome. Welcome to our funny little magic family. It's, um…it's nice to meet you."

A smooth talker I was not. But then, despite all my hopes, nobody had ever shown up with that Shaman's Handbook I'd been asking for. Spirit animals, like everybody else, had to make do with my clumsy, if usually well-meant, expressions of greeting and methods of coping. "This is Raven," I said to the stick bug, as politely as I could, "and this is Rattler. Guys, this is…"

Stick was a lousy name, and I couldn't exactly call her *Walker,* because that's what Captain Michael Morrison of the Seattle Police Department, formerly my boss and with any kind of luck shortly to be my partner, called *me.* Besides, I had Rattler and Raven. "Walker" didn't fit with that, alliteratively speaking. "Renee," I decided. "This is Renee the stick bug. She's the last of our merry band, and…" My shoulders slumped. "Does this mean we're going to do more time traveling?" I perked right up again, though, suddenly eager. "Oh, but maybe with you along it'll be easier. It might be kind of cool if I'm not fighting against the tide so much. Can we go see the Library at Alexandria? There must be stick bugs of some sort in Egypt to cross-reference..."

Renee still didn't blink, but she kind of looked like she wished she could. I wondered if spirit animals knew what they were getting themselves into when they signed on, or if like most people, only realized after the fact that something had gone horribly wrong. I took a deep breath, straightened my shoulders, and tried hard to look like a shaman she'd want to stick with.

No pun intended. I dissolved into giggles at myself. Raven flapped around my head in delight while Rattler and Renee exchanged expressions of despair. It was no use. I was never going to be the proper dignified medicine woman of legend. They would have to take me as I was. I got up, Renee still balanced on my arm, and bowed to the legions of stick bugs still flooding the Lower World. "Thank you," I said to all of them, but especially Renee. "Thank you for putting up with me, for coming when I needed you, and for facing whatever hell you're likely to go through with me until we've got this thing beat. I'm a terrible ingrate, but I do know how much I owe you. All of you," I added to Rattler. He slithered around my ankles, effectively pinning me in place, but accepting me, too. Raven plonked down on my shoulder and stuck his beak in my hair, so I was spirit-animaled from head to toe.

It felt pretty good, actually. I felt pretty full of life and confident, which was a damned sight better than I'd felt facing the Nothing in the Middle World.

A Nothing that was still up there, but maybe now I had the weapons to fight it. I stroked Renee's long heart-shaped head with a fingertip and she tipped her chin up to do something that registered as smiling at me. "So what do you think?" I asked her. "Can you help me snip that stuff out of time? If you're unchanging, then maybe time doesn't mean anything to you, so you're not constrained by it…. Raven, can you take us home?"

He *klok*ed with surprise, since I usually asked him to take me in and out of the Dead Zone, not the Lower World. But I figured anything that could transition between life and death probably shouldn't be too stymied by mere world-walking. Nor was he, springing off my shoulder to lay down a path of yellow bricks with each wing beat. I followed along behind, Renee and Rattler fading with each stride, until I stepped back out of the Lower World and into the Carolina holler with no visible signs of having been on a spirit quest. I felt the three of them at the back of my mind, though, murmuring and examining one another, and, I suspected, giving me a good hard once-over as they decided whether I was redeemable.

The whole trip to the Lower World had taken about as long as it took for Aidan to back off from me by a couple of steps. I was never going to really get used to that: traveling within the space of my head while my body stood there in the real world like an empty puppet. It usually only lasted a few seconds—longer spirit journeys did, or at least should, involve safe territory and someone to watch over me—but it was always disconcerting to realize I'd gone through a transition while other people were scratching their noses.

Usually, though, nobody else noticed. Aidan, however, froze midstep, toes planted in the dirt and heel still elevated as he stared at me. Then he surged forward again, eyes full of golden fire.

This time, however, he slammed into shields that were strong enough to keep young gods at bay, and bounced off hard enough that he actually lost his balance. I snagged a hand out to catch his biceps, and kept my voice low. "Not twice, kid. You caught me off guard once and bullied your way into my garden, but not twice. First off, that's *rude*. Second, it's rude. And third—"

"Yeah, yeah, I get it, it's rude."

"Dangerous. You don't know me, and you don't know what's inside my head or what I've faced. For all you know, I'm set up with a guard dog at the gate, and the only thing that kept it from attacking you was me knowing who you were."

"*Attack?* What kind of shaman would *attack* somebody?"

"One who's on the warrior's path." I let him go at the same time he yanked his arm out of my grip, and he couldn't decide if that meant he'd escaped or if I'd relented. Either way, he pushed his lower lip out in a pout that was all too familiar, and muttered, "I've never heard of somebody being on the warrior's path. Shamans are healers."

"Lucky for you I am. Ever met a sorcerer, Aidan? They use shamanic magic. It's just corrupted. If you go blowing into somebody's soul space like that—"

A disdainful sneer appeared. "Now you're trying to scare me. It won't work."

"—then you might open yourself up to let that corrupted magic in. Or do you think *that*—" and I jabbed a finger at the Nothing "—is just something the earth spat out after eating too much spicy food? Don't go making yourself vulnerable if you can avoid it. Having said that—"

"Why do you think you get to tell me something like that? You're not my mother!"

Of all the conversations I didn't want to have with half of Cherokee looking on, this one was close to the top of the list. But I'd already had it with Ada once and it wasn't like the answer had changed in the half hour since then. "I know

I'm not your mother. I am a shaman, though, and I probably have more experience with black magic than most. I'm *sure* I've got more experience rushing in where angels fear to tread, and in paying the consequences for that. Forget being careful because I'm asking you to. Be careful so your mother doesn't have to worry about you."

Aidan scowled like he thought I was trying to pull a fast one, hiding my own concern for him under the mask of the word *mother,* which could technically mean either me or Ada. I wasn't, actually, because I wasn't that clever, or at least not that manipulative. I was concerned about him, but my concern landed in the grand scheme of "Hi, kiddo, I accidentally let the Major Bad Guy know you existed, so along with trying to find both of our missing fathers, I'd also like to make sure you don't get creamed by monsters" rather than what I imagined were Ada's more standard maternal worries.

I looked at the Nothing, and at Aidan, and for once in my life realized I should probably tell him about all of the Master garbage that was likely to come raining down on him, rather than keeping it bottled up inside myself and trying to fix it all myself. I did not, however, think that the middle of a holler with half the town listening in was the time or place to do it, so I said, "And I was trying to say thanks, before you derailed me," instead.

His scowl deepened suspiciously. "What for?"

"Rude and dangerous as it was, shoving me into the Lower World gave me a chance to find that last spirit animal. Which you knew as soon as I stepped out of there, didn't you? That's why you came at me again. Man, you really—"

He really reminded me of me, was what I wanted to say. I had certainly been as impulsive and angry as a kid, and probably wasn't much different now. But wisdom reared its ugly head and I managed to stop talking before I said something unforgivable. "You really know what you're doing. I wouldn't know how to recognize somebody lacking a spirit animal if it bit me."

Aidan gave me a sideways look, which was pretty talented, given that we were still facing each other straight on, and said, quite slyly, "If the spirit animal bit you, or if the person who didn't have it did?"

"If it bit me I'd be sure it was there." The conversation had turned completely nonsensical in three sentences, but we were both grinning, which was a great improvement. Maybe the kid was just edgy because of my unheralded arrival. Maybe he wasn't quite as much of a punk as I'd been. Either way, I suddenly thought that maybe I could like this young man, and better yet, maybe he could like me. "Look, this is as rude as you just were, but...walking sticks?"

His grin turned into a much more solemn expression, though it didn't quite lose the smile. "Yeah. Yeah, it makes Mom kind of crazy, because she doesn't really want me to be anything other than boring and normal, but at the same time she's kind of proud, you know? I mean, if she wasn't she never would've let me start training with Grandpa, and I started like half my life ago, so..."

"Gra— You mean my *dad?*" If it was possible for a brain to wobble and wiggle like a bowl of dropped Jell-O, mine did it right then. "You've been studying with *Dad?*"

Aidan shrugged with the insouciance only available to children on the cusp of teen-hood. "Well, yeah, didn't you? I mean, he said you guys drove all over the country your whole life, and he's been telling me about all the cool stuff he did, I mean, not that he called it cool, but it was, healing the land and—"

He kept talking, but I heard nothing more than Charlie Brown *wah-wah-wah-waaah!* sounds for a few seconds. For about that length of time, I couldn't even see Aidan: my vision went kind of red and staticky, though I wasn't exactly enraged. More gut-punched, more shocked and cold-handed and betrayed. Dad had taught me the Cherokee language when I was a kid. That was the only studying I'd ever done with him. It had been less than a week since I'd discovered he had magic of his own, or begun to suspect the reasons—now confirmed by Aidan—why we'd spent my childhood driving around America.

It went beyond *"not fair"* that Aidan was now studying magic with him. *"Not fair"* didn't even begin to touch it. It was *"why,"* and *"what did I do wrong,"* and *"did he just not want a daughter"* and a thousand other black-streak thoughts dashing around the static Jell-O in my head. The ball of Nothing was roiling and pitching nearby, reacting to the depth of my emotion. Reacting to it more than I was, really, because I could hardly let myself touch on any of those bleak thoughts before bouncing off in pain. But I didn't want the Nothing to latch on, so I stuffed the shock down deep, buttoning it up until I could take it out and admire it later. Aidan's voice faded back into comprehensibility. "...knew you had magic too, so I thought you'd studied with him...."

I heard myself speaking rather faintly and hollowly, as if I was on the far end of a bad telephone connection. "He knew I had magic, or you did?"

"He did." The poor kid knew he'd stepped in something and had no clue how to extricate himself. "Are you, um... Are you okay?"

"Yes. No. Sort of. Not really." My nostrils flared as I dragged in a deep breath, stood with my eyes pressed shut a moment or two, then exhaled as deeply and opened my eyes to force a smile. "I'm fine. Or a reasonable facsimile thereof. I didn't actually study magic with Dad, no, so you're definitely ahead of me in that game. Anyway, walking sticks. What do you know about them?"

Aidan hesitated, clearly not sure if he should respond to my obvious emotional distress or the facade I was putting on. In the end, though, he was twelve, and went with the surface story. "I know your walking stick shoulda helped with *that*." He pointed a thumb at the Nothing and scowled at me, visibly returning to the slightly sullen wariness of before. That seemed fair enough. I hadn't exactly imagined we'd get on like a house on fire from the moment we met. I was a little wary of him, too, despite our moment of camaraderie. A faint edge came back into his voice. "I mean, look, dude, no pressure, but you're the grown-up here. You're supposed to be more awesome than I am. I thought you were gonna show me what to do."

"How about we give it another shot?"

Aidan looked somewhere between dubious and envious. "You only just got back from your spirit quest. You think you've got a handle on shi— things?"

"Probably not, but that's never stopped me before." That wasn't quite true. My magic had come in over the past ten days, far more cohesively than before. I believed I could handle whatever new aspects Renee's gifts uncovered, because I'd handled everything up until now, and I was finally firing on all cylinders. "Let's go see."

Ada Monroe's voice stopped us cold: "No."

CHAPTER SEVEN

Aidan sounded like every kid in the world mortified by a parent at an inopportune time: *"Mom!"*

"I said no, Aidan. You've just come out of that power circle after being in there for fifteen hours. Do you even know what day it is? You need sleep and food." Ada shot me a daggered look, which was only partially unfair. It wasn't like I'd known Aidan had been on his feet and fighting the good fight for more than half a day. On the other hand, given how wiped out Ada and Carrie had been when they staggered from the circle, I probably should not have automatically assumed Aidan would be raring to go.

Except he was, which I could See in his superbright aura as much as in his impatient squirm. "I'm fine, Mom, really, and if Joanne and I do this thing now maybe everybody can get some rest. It's bugging the whole Qualla, not just us up here in the mountains, so c'mon, Mom, please? *Pleeaaaaaaaaase?*"

She gave me another hard look and I raised my hands. Even if I could See he was in dandy shape, I was not about to get caught in the middle of this particular stomping match. Among other things, I had no other way to prove that, no, really, I thought of him as her kid. I was not the one who got to make decisions for him.

Unfortunately for me, she snapped, "Is he right? Is he fine? Can you two fix this?"

"We can try. As far as I can tell, he's just fine, yeah. He's got a lot of raw power." As much as I did. Maybe more, which was alarming, given that I'd called down a Navajo Maker god with the strength of my magic. "But that doesn't mean you're wrong, because I have no idea how long he'll keep burning this bright. He might just fall over from exhaustion halfway through. I've been known to do it," I said defensively as Aidan's expression indicated I was betraying his trust. Two minutes ago we'd been antagonists, but for the moment I'd been moved to his side of the fight, and could thus betray him. How quickly the lines shifted.

"I'm *fine!* Really, Mom, come on, please? I just want to help."

Ada glanced at Carrie, which took the weight of responsibility off my shoulders. The old woman looked between all three of us and sniffed. "With Joanne here I imagine we can keep the Nothing under control until you've gotten some rest, Aidan. Don't worry," she said dryly. "I don't expect we'll do anything exciting without you."

Aidan gave me a perfectly filthy glare and stomped away without saying another word. Ada shrugged at the world in general and followed him. Sara was right: they went up the holler instead of heading toward the hedges we'd scraped our way through. There had to be another, easier pathway in, probably via a different mountain. Well, I was going to show it to Sara once I found it, whether the rest of them liked it or not.

"Or will we?" Carrie asked the moment Aidan was out of earshot.

I pursed my lips and turned back to the Nothing. It didn't scare me as badly as before, but I thought that was bravado and suspected if I scratched it, panic would knock me over again. "The big advantage to waiting for Aidan is he's too young to be scared senseless of that stuff. It's hard to believe the world might actually get eaten when you're twelve. Not much sense of personal mortality yet, and that entrenched self-confidence might help wipe it out."

"But...?"

"But he's twelve and if something goes wrong I'd rather he wasn't here to be part of it or feel like it was his fault."

"Could work the other way," the old lady said philosophically. "Could be that if he's not part of it and something goes wrong, he'll blame himself."

I examined that from the attitude *I* would have had at his age, and said, "More likely he'll blame me."

"True." She snapped her fingers, making me jump to her beat, and I scurried into place at the northern edge of the power circle, where I'd been before. Carrie marched down to the southern edge, taking Aidan's place, and we tapped the shoulders of the people in those positions, asking to be let in.

Frankly, I wasn't sure I should be letting Carrie participate any more than I wanted Aidan to. Five minutes ago she'd been having a heart attack. I had every confidence in her new-found well-being, but that didn't mean it was an especially good idea for her to go throwing herself right back into battle. On the other hand, Carrie Little Turtle was every bit as intimidating to the adult me as she'd been to the teen me. I was just slightly too scared to suggest she sit this one out.

Besides, she was one of the elders, along with Les Senior, who had presented me with my drum. It meant we shared an affinity, and while that wouldn't be anything like as strong as my magic pairing with Aidan's, it was still a bonus. My walking-stick spirit animal was settled in now, a sense of eagerness building within her, like her whole purpose was invested in doing something about the Nothing that was a slash in time. I'd seen walking sticks neatly slice and fold up leaves for consumption, and had the vivid idea that was *exactly* what Renee was going to do with the Nothing. Suddenly buoyed, I flexed my magic through the circle, checking to see if everyone was willing to follow my lead.

Their power responded, falling in line behind the ripples I sent through. No one seemed to have a need to put themselves forward, no one presenting a history of shamanic practice that I should heed. There were shamans in the Qualla, but if this had been going on for three days, they had to be spelling one another as the focal point for the circle. I suspected Aidan had been playing that role for this particular circle until my arrival. Later I might feel guilty about being the interloper, but right now I was just glad everybody was willing to let me and Renee hone the magic to a fine point and obliterate the bad stuff.

The imagery was easy, with the spirit stick's input. She was utterly serene in her self-confidence, in her certainty of what she represented. Odd little details floated up from her as the magic began to parcel up the Nothing, cutting it away and reducing it to uselessness. She, and other stick bugs like her, had had wings once, but that in no way reduced the eternal sameness of their structure. They had needed wings in the past, and might need them again in the future, but it didn't change what they were. It was a mere flick of a...and I couldn't imagine a spirit animal, much less a stick bug, was actually using the words or images, but the sense I had was *a mere flick of DNA,* whether wings came or went. The wings were inherent, and therefore unchanging. She was as her mother had been, and her mother's mother, all the way back to the beginning. That, too, spawned a bizarre language choice for an insect: *parthenogenesis,* females breeding without males, begetting more females, all the way back to the beginning. Renee was eternal, imperturbable, and unflappable. The Nothing, built on pain and rage and death, had nothing on that calm confidence in always.

It fought, though. Holy crap, did it fight. Everything that had hit me in the moment I saw it redoubled: the lonely ghosts, last of their people, who simply stopped eating when everyone around them had died. Worse, sometimes: the ones who could not quite bear to die themselves, and lived empty and hollow, a single red man among the whites. Good Indians, the dead kind, or the ones who gave up on tradition and lived as the white men did, in soulless houses and crammed into clothes that kept the world off the skin. They were pinpoints of agony against a backdrop so bleak it could barely be comprehended, thus making individual pain all the more exquisite.

The memory of empty villages rose up within me, of empty plains discovered by European settlers who never understood just how many people had died long before their arrival. Disease traveled faster than hordes of men, leaving nothing—*Nothing, Nothing, Nothing,* like the Nothing trying to eat its way through the holler—leaving nothing in its place, nothing to discover except a sense of superiority, that the poor pathetic natives of this new world had never even explored and peopled these amazing broad lands. I kept unwinding my hands from fists, trying not to feed the Nothing with my own rage and frustration: that was half my heritage disappearing into the wind, and even today most people didn't grasp just how many Natives had died when the West discovered the Americas.

My heartache had nothing on Carrie's. Carrie was old, old enough that it had been her grandparents, people she *remembered,* telling her stories of loss. Her memories extended to people who had been born in the middle of the nineteenth century, people who had watched family walk away on the Trail of Tears. So many of them had died, and the Nothing wanted to finish the job.

In the space of a heartbeat, I realized that was *exactly* what the Nothing wanted, and made a desperate attempt to throw a shield between it and the people trying to contain it.

The Nothing, all parceled out into the sharp thin blades and deadly edges of Renee's imagery, sliced through my shields and drove deep into the hearts of the Cherokee elders.

Not into me. *My* shields, my personal shields, were sacrosanct. I had gone through too much hell and breakfast lately to let them falter, but I was not prepared to shield seven others with such vigor, not with so little notice. Knives bounced off me, shattered, turned to splinters of black and disappeared, but so many more of them drove through the elders and burst out of their spines, sucking the Nothing out the other side.

The Nothing pulled their life forces with it as it fled. All the magic we'd been working, all the effort and passion we were pouring in to wiping the Nothing away: it had been waiting for us. Why it had taken so long to respond, why it hadn't attacked when Aidan and I were working together and raising the power usage to a whole different level, that I didn't know, but I knew we'd been set up, and that we were now taking the fall.

No. I did know. *We* hadn't been set up.

I had been set up.

I'd said it to myself already: there was no chance the problems in Carolina were cropping up a few days after the mess in Ireland just by coincidence. Between my mother, Gary and myself, we'd taken out some major talent on the Master's side over the past couple weeks, and in the midst of all that I'd let it slip that I had a son.

The Nothing hadn't struck at Aidan because it was waiting for me, and the mind behind it had lulled me into a goddamned sense of self-security. It had *given* me the chance to almost defeat it, taken me off the defensive, and then hit like a pile driver when I thought I had it in the bag.

That all fell into my mind at once, like crystal drops from heaven, so utterly clear I could've killed myself for not seeing it coming. But I had bigger problems right then, and at the same time I was recognizing I'd been had, I was also rushing into action.

I threw a second shield up, pouring all the power I had available into it. It splashed into full live-action color behind the elders, a desperate attempt on my part to hold their life force inside a sphere where I might have a chance at putting it back where it belonged. The shield was as strong as I could make it with my attention split: I was also running hell-bent for leather toward Carrie with the conviction that if I could save her, I'd be off to a strong start for saving the others. She was the one I'd just healed, after all. She was the one I should have the deepest connection to.

She was barely fifteen feet away, and by the time I got to her, her body was cold. *Cold.* Not just breathless, not just without a heartbeat, but *cold,* like she'd been dead for hours. Part of me knew it was already too late and the rest of me went two directions at once. I slammed a fistful of healing power into her chest, trying to jump-start her heart, and at the same time I plunged recklessly into the Dead Zone, shrieking for Raven's assistance as I went.

He appeared, his beaky face as grim as I'd ever seen it. The Dead Zone resolved around us. There was an unusual emptiness to it, a distance that went deeper than its near-infinite size and its endless, featureless blackness. Raven hung in the air before me, banging his wings to hover there, and said, *"Quark,"* so intensely I half thought it was an actual word.

It wasn't, and the next wing-flap keeping him hovering also smashed my ears, boxing them while he shouted, *"Quark!"* again. Every wing-beat from there drove me back a step, until I realized he was sending me home and blurted, "But her soul...!"

Raven gave me as flat and angry a look as he could, and what faint hope I had slithered away. I'd watched the Nothing rip the life essence out of everybody, but when people died their souls passed into the Dead Zone, there to be found by whatever gods or spirits they believed would carry them through to the next world. That was how it worked.

Except Carrie's soul hadn't passed through the Dead Zone. I'd almost managed to bring somebody back once, when her life essence had been ripped away but her soul had passed into the Dead Zone. That time, the woman had been so startled by her death that she hadn't even registered it as violent, and had simply moved along. This time I didn't have even that much chance. Carrie's soul had been flayed right out of her body along with her life essence.

If I was really lucky, there were enough pieces of her soul sticking to the insides of my shields that I could put it back together. I stepped back out of the Dead Zone as fast as I'd gone in. Carrie's body was arching under my hand, exactly like my healing power was a burst of electricity trying to restart her heart. That was how little time had passed. I looked up, the Sight raging full-on, and my stomach fell.

My shields hadn't held the stolen life forces in. My brain scrabbled around that, trying to understand why, and landed on a six-year-old's answer, the kind of thing that fixes itself in a kid's mind and the adult never quite lets go: of *course* the shields hadn't held. Their essence had been gobbled up by Nothing, and everybody knows you can't hold nothing.

This was not the kind of deeply held childhood belief that would get anybody on the entire planet except me in trouble. I vowed that I would later stab an ice pick through the part of my brain that was still six, and got up, shaking with anger, to face down the Nothing.

It had taken everything it was built on, all the wounds and pain born of genocidal history, all the raw power of life it had just obliterated, and it sharpened itself on the whetstone of the fresh terror spiking from everyone else in the holler. It whipped around, no longer a Nothing, but instead becoming something honed, a personification of not just death, but murder. An executioner, an executioner's ax. It wasn't that anthropomorphized, but that was the sense of it, its weight ready to fall.

And there were so many people in the holler for it to fall onto. Dozens of them, everyone who had come up from town and from across the county to try to help heal the crying mountain. There was so much power here, and so much good will, and it was ripe for the plucking. My shields, strong as they were, would be spread too thin across this much space. I could not protect them. Not by fighting. So I did the only thing I could think of.

I dropped my shields.

CHAPTER EIGHT

The Executioner went still, like a giant gray smear of evil suddenly catching its breath. I wasn't sure how sentient it was, though I had considerable faith in the sentience behind it. It was its Master's dog, just like the Morrígan had been, just like all the others had been. And the Master really ought to be smart enough not to fall for me making myself vulnerable this way, but the fact of the matter was, if he'd done it to me, I'd have gone for his throat, too, never mind what the smart thing was. So I wasn't entirely surprised when the Executioner swung toward me, slow and ponderous like a thing trying to fool me with its slow ponderousness.

It was not a Nothing anymore. My brain wasn't going to pull that trick again. I could catch an Executioner. I wasn't sure what I was going to do with it once I caught it, but that was a problem for later. Hopefully not much later, but later. I flexed my hand, waiting for just the right moment, and when it moved, I drew a rapier out of thin air.

An elf king had made it for a god, and I'd taken it away from the god. Like any decent magic sword, it had useful qualities, like being summonable from the ether, rather than having to carry it around a modern world. But like any decent magic sword, it also had flaws—or I did. For the past year I'd been alternating between learning how to use it and paying the price for not having my healing magic and my warrior's path in balance. For most of the time I'd owned it, I could either fight with it, or I could fill it with magic. I couldn't do both without suffering significant backlash.

But that was yesterday's news.

Today the sword blazed blue, my power searing through it. Healing power invested in an edged weapon made for powerful mojo. For a moment I thought what to do with the Executioner after I'd caught it was going to be moot. An adrenaline rush of battle thrill erupted within me, and I met the creature halfway, more than ready to spike it.

To my complete shock, the Executioner chickened out.

It split in half, gray cloudy body ripping down the middle and both sides passing so close by that I felt the cold misty rush against my cheeks and arms. I spun around, howling in childish offense as it reamalgamated and fled up the mountainside.

Fled toward Ada and Aidan, just now cresting the path leading from the holler.

For the second time in as many minutes I dropped every personal shield, but this time I threw everything I had up the path, willing it to get there before the Executioner did. Aidan's name echoed around the mountain, cried out not just by me but by half the valley's population.

Sound and shields and evil all hit him in nearly the same instant. He and Ada both turned as voices screamed warnings, and I couldn't tell if they fell because the Executioner hit them or because my shields slammed into place so hard as to knock them to the ground. I *knew* the Executioner hit my shields: I felt the impact reverberate in my bones, and caught a taste of whiplash as it struck back at me, too, forgetting or not caring about the distance. I sucked back just enough magic to instigate rudimentary shields and it gave up. Not, I thought, because it couldn't have taken me, but because Aidan was potentially more poorly shielded, and it was hungry for as much power-bearing life force as it could suck down.

I was halfway up the mountain when Ada Monroe slammed a four-foot-long hickory log against the Executioner's spine.

It misted to pieces again, and the log crashed against the shields I was holding around Aidan. A roar of approval chased me up the mountain, my own voice fronting it as the leading shout. The Executioner came together again, its ax-like aspects increasing as it prepared to strike Ada down. She swung her hickory bat again, and to my astonishment, I Saw power streak the air. Green, the determined, resolute color that most buildings and protective structures were imbued with. It hit the Executioner with more force than I'd have expected, and by that time I was only ten steps away. I launched myself at it in a superhero jump, fully intending to slam my sword into its shady skull from above.

It howled in fury and for the third time, fled. I cast the sword aside as I came down, seized Ada's shoulders when I landed, and bellowed, "You! Are! AWESOME!" into her face. Then we both dropped to our knees on either side of Aidan, whose brilliant, multivariegated aura was spinning wildly with fear, surprise, confusion, pride, anger and a dozen other emotions I couldn't focus on long enough to name.

Pride won out, at least temporarily, because he, too, was bellowing, "MOM! DID YOU SEE THAT! YOU'RE AWE-

SOME!" at Ada, and smacking at both of us as we tried to make sure he was all in one piece.

I couldn't See any indication that the Executioner had ripped any life force away from him, but his aura was so overwhelming I wasn't sure how I'd be able to tell. I just didn't know him well enough. I looked up at Ada, meeting her eyes, and we both blurted, "Is he okay?" at the same time.

"I'm *fine*." Aidan sat up, suddenly remembering his dignity. In remembering, he looked so much like my friend Billy's thirteen-year-old son I giggled. Aidan glowered at me and I wiped laughter away.

Once it was gone I remembered the chaos left in the valley below, and all hope of humor faded. I got up and stared down the path I'd taken, realizing it was not humanly possible for me to have climbed the distance I had in the time I had. *Rattler?*

Ssspeed is an easier gift in the otherworlds, he answered wearily, *but when necesssssary…*

"Thank you," I whispered aloud. *"Thank you."*

I felt his pleasure in the acknowledgment, and let the poor snake drift back into resting. I badly needed to spend some quiet time in a drum circle, letting it fill me up and replenish my spirit snake. I'd done a little of that work in Ireland before Sara called, but not nearly enough. It wasn't looking especially promising to get any done in North Carolina, either. I let out a long, slow breath, and murmured, "I'm sorry," to everyone in the valley.

Then I pulled up my big-girl pants and headed back down the mountain, because I certainly had some explaining to do, and we had seven bodies to carry out of the hills.

Sara was kneeling by Carrie Little Turtle's body when I got back down. Aidan and Ada had followed me, but their footsteps had stopped when they'd gotten close enough to get a sense of what had happened. Others were gathered around the other dead women and men, most faces still too shocked to begin moving on to grief. I went to Sara and Carrie, though I pitched my voice to carry around the fallen circle. "We were sucker punched. This whole thing was a bait and switch. It was trying to get at me. That's probably why Dad went missing."

"Who the hell are you, that an evil wants you this badly?" A big-boned man spoke from across the circle, accusation raw in his question.

Despite everything that was happening, I doubted he wanted to know my long, drawn-out history with the Master and his minions. After a long minute I settled on a response that might or might not mean anything to him, but did, in its way, answer the question: "I'm Joanne Walkingstick."

Apparently it answered the question a lot better than I'd thought it would. A ripple of recognition and a strange mix of relief and hostility swept the gathered mourners. The hostility wasn't much of a surprise. I hadn't exactly left the Qualla on good terms, and I'd come back to preside over the mass murder of seven elders.

The relief was unexpected, given that I *had* just presided over a mass murder. Not deliberately, maybe, but still. It gave me the sneaking suspicion that my family name carried a lot more weight and a lot more respect than I'd ever imagined. I was going to punch my father in the nose when I found him again. Sara, quietly, said, "That thing ran away. Is it over?"

"No. I'm going to have to go hunting." Hunting magic wasn't easy, at least not for me. It didn't leave discernible tracks, and unless I knew exactly what I was looking for, I often couldn't see the scars it left on the landscape where it gathered. "We need to get everyone back down into town, though. We—"

"Can you magic them down there?"

I blinked. "Er. No. That would be cool. But no."

"Then you need to go hunt and the rest of us will deal with the bodies."

I opened my mouth and shut it again. Sara had a point. A very good one, actually, thwarted only by one minor detail. "I need Les. Or somebody else who actually grew up in the mountains, Sara. I spent some time tromping around when I was a teenager, but I'd be kidding myself if I didn't think I'd get my ass lost up here by the time I was five minutes out of this holler. Can you…?"

"If I was good enough in the mountains to guide you I'd have found Lucas by now."

"I'll take her." Aidan had come up behind us. I twitched around to see him and bit my lower lip. The warmth was gone from his face, leaving blue shadows under his eyes and his skin sallow. He focused on a spot just beyond Carrie, close enough he could pretend he was looking at her without actually doing so. Being brave, in other words, and it broke my heart.

As gently as I could, I said, "That would be really great, if it's okay with your mom. But honestly, you look like you need some rest, Aidan. I know you want to be doing something. It helps a little, having something to do. But if you're going to guide me through the mountains, I need you to be totally sharp so we don't both end up lost."

He thrust his jaw out and dared a glance at me, trying to determine if I was serious or just wheedling him into getting some rest. His eyes flashed gold, probably checking my aura for truthfulness, and his shoulders relaxed a millimeter. "I guess that maybe makes sense."

"Yeah. Ada? Is it okay if he takes me up into the mountains in the morning?"

Ada's mouth thinned. "We'll talk about it when we get home."

In my vocabulary that constituted a yes. I smiled with relief at Ada, then looked hopefully at Aidan, whose shoulders relaxed just that little bit more. I guessed he thought it meant yes, too. Then we both turned to Sara, waiting to see if that was an acceptable solution.

Her eyebrows were drawn down. "Won't the trail go cold? Isn't every minute you're sitting here losing us time in the manhun—"

She stopped before I had to say it, her scowl growing darker as I picked up in the silence she'd left off. "It's not like setting dogs on a scent or following a predisposition toward certain brands of cigarettes or patterns of cash withdrawals that might let you find a suspect. Magic doesn't leave a trail like that. It's not going to get any colder by morning."

"If we let it go tonight, can things get worse?"

"Oh, yeah. It could always get worse." I looked skyward. "It could be raining."

Sara smacked my shoulder, just like we were teens again, and muttered, "I can't believe you said that. No, I meant is it likely to attack? Is it going to tear the mountain up? What was it, anyway? Not a demon."

"No, not like the wendigo. This is a spirit creature. An evil ghost, kind of. It's made up of all the hate and indifference and deliberation that slaughtered the First Nations, and of their pain and loss and fear and anger, as well. It's like a ghost on steroids, and it's been deliberately awakened and is being directed. At all of us in general and at me in particular."

"What does it want?"

I shrugged. "To obliterate us. But it retreated for a reason. Either we were more than it expected, or more likely, it's resting and getting used to its new strength. I think it's not going to try anything again just yet."

"And if you're wrong?"

"Then it'll probably come looking for me, so with any luck everybody else will stay safe."

"How often does 'any luck' come in to the equation?"

"Not often enough." I got up as a familiar *thup-thup-thup* began echoing against the mountains. "Are those helicopters?"

A few seconds later, two Medivac choppers crested the mountains and maneuvered around each other to find landing space at the foot of the holler. Wind and dust and leaves kicked up, spraying everyone and sending arms over faces to block the updrafts. A fair number of paramedics jumped out and came running up the hill, bent double until they were well away from the choppers. Their expressions went unusually blank when they saw the bodies. I was sure they'd been briefed, but a briefing wasn't the same as laying eyes on seven uninjured dead people sprawled in an otherwise idyllic setting. Sara got to her feet and met them, taking charge naturally. None of the people who had refused to talk to her earlier objected, either. I took an uncharitable moment to regard them all as hypocrites, then got over my judgmental self and went to see if I could help.

I couldn't. I got turned away faster than a bad smell, and was left cold-shouldered by the men and women who carefully helped lift bodies onto the Medivac sledges, too. That, as far as I was concerned, *wasn't* hypocritical: I was far more an outsider than Sara, and I'd been responsible in some fashion for these deaths. They fully deserved to handle and respect their dead without my interference, even if some of the dead had been important to me, too. I backed up the holler a ways, wondering if I could find my way to the trail Aidan and Ada had planned to take out of here. Given that I'd just sworn I'd get lost the moment I left the holler, I figured I should wait until the valley cleared and I could fight my way back down through the trees, the way Sara and I had come. I expected her to ride away in the helicopters, and she did.

Only after the choppers were gone and the sounds of their blades had faded did people begin to move out. Slowly, in small groups that supported each other and chose not to look at me. I could have followed them, but watched them go instead, even Ada and Aidan, the former of whom had the grace to glance toward me in invitation. I shook my head and she went along with the others, until I was alone in a mountain holler with the sun fading fast on the western horizon.

In a world with a proper sense of drama or mystical nonsense, the ghost of my father would no doubt have come slowly down the hills as the sun disappeared. I was just as glad the world wasn't inclined toward that kind of theatrics, since I really didn't want Dad to be dead. I did, though, sort of want...*something*. Some kind of connection to the land, I guessed. Something that said, "It's okay, Jo. You belong here, too. The ghosts of your ancestors welcome you home," or something to that effect.

What I got was a slight chill as a breeze picked up, and a greater awareness that late March was maybe the perfect time of year in the Qualla. Summer's mugginess hadn't come on full yet, nor were the bugs out in full force. Though I'd been serious about the likelihood of getting lost if sent out here alone, I'd also spent quite a bit of time in the mountains, especially after the twins had been born and I'd thoroughly branded myself an outsider and a loser. Then I went to college in Seattle, and while the Pacific Northwest was covered in forests, I'd stayed out of them. Only in the past year had I gotten back to the outdoors at all, and it had reminded me how much I'd liked being part of the world in that way. But the Northwest's trees were nothing like down here in the Appalachians, and these were the ones that made my heart sing with familiarity. I wanted to curl up beneath them and pull a blanket of leaves over myself so I could sleep in the land and belong again.

Except I couldn't, because there were seven dead people on their way home, and I had to first pay my respects, then go find what had killed them and stop it. I swayed a little, preparing myself for motion, but as the stars began to appear, crickets started singing, and some of the night wildlife began rustling through the underbrush. I closed my eyes, feeling raccoons and possums and shrews scrambling through the woods, and got a far-off sense of a puma who wasn't supposed to be there any more than I was. Deer were settling down for the night, and there were individual human settlements still awake and pulsing with energy here and there amongst the hollers and hills. The road wasn't so far away I couldn't hear it over night's quiet, and there was a steady stream of traffic. I imagined most of it was heading down the mountains into Cherokee as more and more people learned of the deaths.

I thought maybe Les Senior would be presiding over the vigil tonight, no doubt feeling his own near miss keenly. I wondered, had my own father not gone missing, if he might have been the shaman most qualified to perform death rites. There was so much about my own family that I didn't know, and standing out here on a mountain was not going to teach me any of it.

I stayed there anyway, until it was fully dark and the likelihood of me snagging a handful of poison oak on the way back to the road was extremely high. I laughed at myself, because of course I hadn't thought of that possibility while I was indulging in the dramatic lonesome-warrior-on-a-hill pose, and then I went home to Cherokee to see what help I could be.

CHAPTER NINE

Old Cherokee tradition laid the dead to rest by sunset the day they died, or the day after, and had someone remain with the bodies to make sure sorcerers didn't steal the soul in the meantime. My recollection was that as a teen I had thought it was a supremely bullshit, embarrassing, hokey-dokey ritual that no one with any grip on the modern era would admit to participating, never mind actually believing, in. And to be fair, most people didn't. That was why it was tradition, not modern practice. On the other hand, there were people who kept to the old traditions, and I was pretty certain at least some of the dead would be among them.

Besides, the forced perspective of the past year made me reconsider my stance to a significant degree. Now I not only didn't think it was bullshit, but since the elders' bodies wouldn't have gotten back to town until just before sunset, far too late to bury them, I was also incredibly grateful that there would be someone watching over them. Even if it was just an undertaker, that would be good, but I had hopes that there might be a genuine vigil. I was pretty certain the bodies didn't have any souls left to steal—recovering those souls by taking out the Executioner was going to be my job—but it was good to know they'd be observed and shielded from further desecration.

I supposed one very powerful medicine man might keep all seven of them safe, but it seemed more likely to me that if anybody was taking the old rituals seriously, that there would be at least seven: one for each body. I wasn't surprised, when I got back to town myself, that there were far more than seven gathering for a vigil. Cherokee was a small community, and seven deaths was a lot to take in at once. A slow stream of vehicles drove down toward the high school. There was a natural amphitheater up in Cherokee County itself, where this kind of tragedy would be dealt with on a deeper, community-wide level later. But for tonight, the high school became the default location for large gatherings, just like it would be in many other small towns. I followed the taillights and parked my rented Impala on the outskirts of the lot, where it wouldn't be boxed in, should I need to make a quick exit.

I stopped cold at the school doors, not because of horrific teenage memories, but because the last time I'd been in a high school, it, too, had been the source and gathering place of a tragedy. That had been the same day my shamanic powers had reawakened, and a bunch of teens had been murdered by a lunatic demigod. The terrible silence in the school had struck me: the murmur of shocked voices, the barely echoing footsteps in the halls, the arms around one another, and the blank helplessness sketched on the faces of children were all echoed in the devastated community now entering Cherokee High. It wasn't something I particularly wanted to immerse myself in again, especially since I'd had more connection to some of the victims here. Not much more, maybe, but a little.

"Come on, Joanne." Sheriff Lester Lee passed by, putting just enough hitch in his step to let me fall in beside him.

I did so, shoving my hands in my pockets and not quite seeing the hopelessly familiar, totally changed halls around me. "I thought you'd be in there already. I'm late."

"I was filling out incident reports. The medical examiner has the bodies right now. She'll be bringing them in later, after the autopsies. She won't find anything, will she?"

"I don't think so. Is there someone, a medicine man, someone, with them?"

"Of course. Is it going to be important?"

"I hope not."

Les nodded, accepting that, and I had a surreal moment of wondering whether this was what life would be like if everyone took the mystical and magical as matter-of-fact. It wasn't that I thought everybody in the Qualla *would* take it seriously, but I'd met more people here in the past twelve hours who were accepting of magic than I'd met in the past year. Most of the time I found myself stuttering around explanations that didn't matter anyway, because people made up their own stories as soon as the magic faded. Les, however, was calm, cool, collected, and obviously not going to put this out of his mind. "Grandpa says you saved his bacon up there on the mountain today. Twice."

"Only once. He was out of the power circle when this happened, either way. If I hadn't been there, he certainly wouldn't ha…" It finally struck me that Les was obliquely saying "Thank you," and that arguing over the details was not gracious. I cleared my throat. "You're welcome. He's welcome. I'm glad I was there. I just wish…" I made a useless little gesture as we entered the gym, where hundreds of people were gathered.

I stopped and smiled in spite of myself. There was a cohesive look to the people gathered, a certain similarity of facial shapes, of skin tones, that I hadn't seen for a while. Seattle's Native American population was a lot smaller than the area's historical settlements could account for. I'd unconsciously missed seeing a solid representation of the Native element, and seeing it again made me happy.

It also made me aware that while I'd resented being paler-skinned than so many of my classmates when I was a teen, as an adult it was clear to me that the thing that had really made me stand out was my bad attitude. There were people in the gym who looked like they'd walked straight out of three hundred years ago, but there were as many whose lighter skin had a sun-warmed ruddiness to it, or who had African influence in their genetics. Every single one of us still laid legitimate claim to Cherokee heritage. Too bad I'd been such a punk when I was a kid, and too bad I already knew time travel wouldn't fix it if it could.

"You all right, Joanne?" Les, who'd gone on ahead, noticed I wasn't at his side and turned back. "It's all right, you know. You can come on in. Nobody's going to blame you."

"That wasn't it." Though it was a perfectly reasonable fear, now that he'd reminded me of it. I caught up again and we made our way through the throng to find Les Senior on his way into the music room that lay across the hall from the gym.

"This is where we will watch over them until morning. There are too many eyes in the gym now. Too much anger and hurt that a sorcerer could steal and use. The elders and the medicine men will take turns shepherding the dead and counseling the living. It would be good to have a Walkingstick sit with us," he said to me as we went into the music room.

I blinked around at the room, mumbling about how it had hardly changed as a method of trying not to show my surprise at the invitation. Both Lesters waited with a degree of patience that told me I wasn't fooling anyone, so I cleared my throat, then nodded. "Sure, yeah. I mean, I'd be honored. It should be Dad, not me, but…yeah. If you're sure. Not everybody's going to like it."

The wrinkled corners of Les Senior's mouth quirked upward. "They don't have to. There are some advantages to a people who still at least pretend to respect their elders. Can you make this room a safe place?"

That, I was much more confident about. I nodded. "In fact, if we've got the time and some chalk dust, maybe, we could build a protective circle around the whole school. It wouldn't hurt any of us to have that sense of security, not after today. Grandpa Les, I'm—"

"It was not your fault." He didn't do the same talk-to-the-hand gesture Carrie had used earlier, but the tone of voice was very similar. My throat tightened and tears burned in my eyes at the reminder. It barely seemed possible Carrie was dead, even if I'd seen her fall.

"I'm not sure it wasn't," I said hoarsely. "I've turned into a walking bull's-eye lately."

"Did you ask for this? Did you call down evil and welcome it into yourself? Did you cast it on your family here and gain strength from their sorrow? No. A target is not responsible for the weapon pointed at it, Joanne."

"Maybe not, but that doesn't mean I don't feel responsible as hell for the…"

"Collateral damage," Les Junior said, which I would not have done even though they were the obvious words. I wasn't about to refer to seven dead elders as *collateral damage,* like I was a heartless military machine and they were faceless enemies, or even faceless allies.

"Fallout," I said instead, but the other phrase hung there too. Both of them were war terms, and for the first time it actually hit me that I was in fact at war. That I had been all along, not just from my rebirth as a shaman fifteen months ago, but since my mother had given me up to Dad so I'd be safe from the Master for a little while longer. For more time than that, even, because I finally understood that I was the latest in a long tradition of warriors on both sides of my family, men and women who had been holding the line against darkness for thousands of years. I wet my lips and exhaled. "I'm sorry anyway. Whether it was my fault or not, whether I could have stopped it or not, this is horrible and I'm sorry. And I'm glad you're okay."

"So am I," he said in a measured tone that told me just exactly how much of my guilt he was sharing. Survivor's guilt rather than instigator's guilt, maybe, but we were both up to our teeth in coulda-woulda-shouldas.

Sheriff Les took us out of it with the deft touch of a professional: "Grandpa, if you want to get a couple others to help you get the room ready, Joanne and I will go find some chalk dust and lay that circle. Jo, are you going to need anybody to help you raise it?"

"No, I'll be fine by myself. It might even be smarter to keep other people out of it right now. That attack up in the mountains—" We left Les Senior and headed for the custodian's offices, though I couldn't really imagine them having chalk dust in this day and age. There would be something, though.

Les picked up my story thread, nodding an already established comprehension of what had happened. "Sara said it was a setup, trying to draw you in. Probably trying to suck you dry, too. That everybody else got caught up in it."

I gave a terse nod, trying to figure out how that possibly made me not responsible for seven deaths, but set the thought aside. Wallowing was not going to help. "So it's probably better for me to be the only target."

"Why didn't it take you down?" Les either had school keys or a skeleton key, because we went straight to the custodial rooms and he opened them without stopping to ask anyone for help. I raised my eyebrows and he looked slightly sheepish. "They haven't changed the locks since before we graduated. I stole school keys when I was about fifteen and made all my own copies. There's salt in massive buckets in the back corners. For the two or three times a decade when it snows."

Despite everything that had happened, I laughed. "You were a criminal mastermind. I had no idea." We lifted buckets, mops, long rolls of heavy colored paper, moved floor waxers and vacuums, and dumped a box of glitter onto ourselves before we managed to get to the salt. I brushed as much glitter off as I could, but I still looked like I lived in a snow globe as Les wrestled a dolly into place and we hauled two giant buckets of salt onto it. "We're going to need a bigger boat."

"There's a trolley over there, but we just piled about three hundred pounds of school supplies on it."

"That was not well-planned." We were both sweating glitter by the time we got four buckets of salt onto the trolley. Les banged something else onto the front of the trolley, the buckets hiding it from my line of sight, and by unspoken consent we hunched over the handles and took the most indirect route out of the school, trying to avoid being seen by mourners. I felt like I was fifteen again, in fear of the law catching me, and again, despite the circumstances, giggles kept cropping up. We finally got ourselves outside and straightened up like we'd successfully escaped, and Les flashed me a bright grin.

"If I'd known you were that good at sneaking in high school...."

I grinned back. "Who knows what trouble we could've gotten into. Okay, look, this is a lot of salt but it's a lot of ground to cover, too. We're going to have to be scarce with it, but it also needs to be a solid line."

He scooped up the thing he'd thrown onto the trolley: a thin-nosed funnel about eighteen inches deep, pretty much perfect for laying down a salt circle. I stared at it. "That can't possibly be meant for salt. I mean, in the snow you need salt to scatter, not make tidy lines."

"It's for repainting the parking-lot lines. There's another piece that it fits onto for power-pressured paint, but I didn't think we'd need it."

"You're a freaking genius."

Les, modestly, said, "I am. How perfect a circle does this need to be?"

"The rounder the better, but it's more about intent than perfection. The important thing is to make sure nobody breaks it when they're coming or going. I don't know how we'll manage that."

"I'll get some of the deputies to direct traffic and assign someone to keeping the salt fresh where the cars are coming in. How's that sound?"

My eyebrows rose. "Great. Won't they think you're insane?"

"Probably, but they'll do it. Look, I can go set that up, but I can't do it and help you lay the circle at the same time."

"That's fine. I can handle this. Thanks, Les."

"You sure you're going to be all right? You never did say why that thing up there in the mountains didn't take you out."

"Because I have psychic shields to shame the Rock of Ages. I'll be fine, Les. Go get the traffic situation sorted out."

He went with only one last backward glance, which made

me smile. He was pretty cute. I wondered if I'd thought so in high school, and concluded I'd been a moron if I hadn't. And I'd definitely been a moron, so probably I hadn't. Amused at myself, I filled the paint-dripper with salt and started building a circle around the school.

It was pushing midnight by the time I was done. People were beginning to sing inside, songs that blended from gospel to traditional Cherokee music and occasionally slid into something modern, poppy, and still somehow appropriate. I walked back around the circle, checking the consistency with the Sight—the salt glowed the same purposeful green that the school and other protective constructs did—and was satisfied. I took up a place closest to the mountains where the Executioner had fled. Nothing like literally placing myself between the people and the evil. I bowed in all four directions, then sank power into the land, asking it to respond and protect.

Magic zinged through me like fireworks. I'd only joined the power circle on the mountain; I hadn't opened it. The difference between opening a circle with two spirit animals and three was astounding. It added a depth of awareness that made the air itself come to life, dust and seeds shining in the dark. I felt the age of the land, the solemn incontrovertible strength of the mountains, and felt how even as we ravaged the planet, mankind's touch was still a light thing on it: *it* would endure, whether we did or not. *It* had survived cataclysms before, and would again. *It* would bring life forth again, carried in those seeds and motes of dust, and in time the scars left by humanity would fade and heal. It could easily cast me away, deny my hopes and leave my people open and vulnerable to the dark magic gathering in the hills.

But it didn't. It answered, living magic rising from the earth to answer my call. Its green was so dark as to be nearly black, rich with age and confidence. It met my silver-blue and amalgamated it, comforting and strong, until I was the unknown spark that had started the fire. It would continue burning now, keeping those things within it safe from the world outside, until I asked it to come down. I would feel the people coming and going, and if corruption tried to slip through, I had no doubt I would sense it. I'd never had such a strong sense of the earth itself, or of such a connection to it. I whispered, "Thanks, Renee," aloud, and felt the walking stick give a little nod of pleasure in the depths of my mind. Raven and Rattler felt smug, like this was much better, this was the way things really *ought* to go, and I grinned as I left my place in the power circle to go back into the school.

Les met me at the doors, his eyes shining. "You did it, didn't you? The circle is up."

"Yeah. Why?"

He tipped his head toward the gym, then took a sort of skipping step in that direction. "You should have seen it. It was like someone wrapped the whole place in a blanket. The mountain echoes cut off and everybody relaxed a little. I'd never seen anything like it. They're calmer now, all of them. It's like the air gave us a hug."

I chuckled quietly. "That's good. I'll leave it up until they're ready to be buried. Maybe it'll help."

"Won't that wipe you out?"

"Nah. It's like turning the key to spark an engine. Once the engine is going you don't have to keep turning the key. As long as the earth is willing to help, the magic is self-sustaining." I followed Les into the gym, where I, too, could feel the decrease of tension. There was still a lot of sorrow and anger, but the fear had faded. That was a relief, since this many unhappy people powered by fear could turn into a mob very fast, and Les didn't have anything like the resources to contain an angry mob. Well, unless you counted me among his resources, but that made me start wanting a holocaust cloak and a wheelbarrow.

This time as I came in, a ripple went through the crowd. Everybody knew by now that Joanne Walkingstick was back in town, and that I'd had something to do with what had happened on the mountain. Calming power circle or not, there were a lot of suspicious faces and hurt gazes as I stuck close to Les. "This was maybe not a good idea."

"Too late now." He led me through the gathering, his badge giving him just enough authority that nobody got in my face. Not, at least, until we'd crossed the gym and were about to go into the music room. Then a big block of a man put himself between us and the door, and folded his arms.

"I don't think you deserve to sit with the dead, Walking-stick. You ran out of here a long time ago. You should go back where you came from."

Les murmured, "Grandpa Les asked for her, Dan," while I tried to figure out who the guy was. The name rang a bell, and I took half a step back to get a better look at the guy.

"Dan. Danny Little Turtle?" Danny had been big in high school, too, but he'd filled out enough to be mistaken for a wall by casual observers. He'd been a football player, a big man on campus, and I was the tall skinny walking chip-on-the-shoulder who showed up and wasn't impressed. To the best of my memory, "Oh, God. I'm so sorry, Dan. I'm so sorry about your grandmother. I liked her," were nearly the first words I'd ever said to him.

"So much you got her killed. Get out of here, Joanne. Go back to Seattle. We don't want you here." His animosity picked up followers, men and women who were less aggressive by nature but glad to follow a lead.

Les started to look grim, and I touched his elbow to ask him to let me handle it. His expression didn't change, but he didn't break into the discussion yet, so I took that as my chance. "First off, you're right. I left a long time ago and I have a lot of nerve coming back right now. A lot more nerve, coming here, into your memorial services. I'm sorry for intruding, and if you don't want me helping keep vigil, I won't. It's not my place."

There was nothing like agreeing with somebody to take the wind out of their sails. Dan's scowl got darker, but he couldn't argue when I was offering to do what he wanted. I kept my voice pitched exactly the same way, just loud enough to carry around a group of people who had suddenly gotten very quiet. "Grandpa Les thinks this horrible mess isn't my fault, and I wish I believed him, but I'm not trying to kid anyone. Even if it's not something I did, it's something that's happening to bring me back here. I wouldn't have come back if Dad hadn't gone missing."

"I'm surprised you did anyway."

That was way too shallow to hurt: I cut myself deeper than that every day. All I said was, "Yeah, I know," because while I wasn't exactly surprised at myself, I couldn't imagine anyone else being anything *but*. "I'll do what I can to help here, Danny. I can't undo these deaths. I hope like hell I can prevent more. And if I go away again when this is over, I hope at least this time I won't be running away, and that maybe someday I'll be invited back. It's the best I can do. It's not enough. We all know that. But it's the best I can do."

All that shamanic training was doing some good. I'd set Dan and everybody else on their ears, at least, shaking the foundations of what they expected from me. It was a good place to start, and for once smart enough not to push it, I gave Danny a respectful nod and said, "Thanks for letting me say my piece. I'll get out of the way now. I don't want to disrupt things more than I have."

I went ahead and left through the doors we'd been heading for. Les and Dan both followed, the latter to make sure I wasn't going into the music room. When I headed past it to the end of the hall, he went back into the gym. Les, though, caught up with me and said, "'If'?"

There was only one *if* in what I'd said that he'd be asking about. "I couldn't say 'when I go away again' without losing any possible street cred I'd just earned."

"Ah. Yeah. I guess. I guess it was too much thinking you'd come back and realize everything you were missing, all inside a day."

I crooked a smile. "Give it time. I haven't even been here twelve hours yet. Look, I'm gonna do just what I said. I'm going to stay out of the way. Tell your grandpa I'm sorry, okay? But I don't think it's a good idea to push it with Danny, and there are probably others in there who think the same thing. They'll be all right without a Walker in there."

"A Walker?"

I sighed. "Walkingstick. I changed my last name when I left. Abandoning my roots, all of that. Don't tell me you never noticed in the computer files."

"I never looked." Les had a funny expression. "Not on our files, anyway. I looked you up a few times online, but I was looking for Joanne Walkingstick. Guess that's why I never found you."

A crop of nervous butterflies awakened in my stomach. This didn't seem like a good time to admit I'd never even thought of looking him up online. "I guess I didn't think in terms of how changing my name might make me kind of disappear. But here I am now." I spread my hands in demonstration, then nodded toward the gym. "You'd probably better get back in there. I'll keep an eye on the power circle and if anybody needs me my mobile is, er, I mean, my cell phone number is—" I rattled off the number feeling silly, and mumbled, "I was in Ireland, everybody calls them mobiles there."

"I'll call if we need anything." Les headed back into the gym and I watched him go, uncomfortably aware that his high school interest in me didn't seem to have passed. Otherwise *if* I left versus *when* I left wouldn't have mattered, never mind things like whether he could find me online. It all made me miss Morrison horribly, which was probably not in the least what Sheriff Lester would like to hear. I took my cell phone out of my jeans pocket and checked the time. One in the morning in North Carolina was only 10:00 p.m. in Seattle. I slid down against a wall and called Morrison, fingers tangled in my hair while I waited for him to pick up.

He didn't. After five brisk rings, his voice mail invited me to leave a message. I sighed and said, "Hey, it's me. I just, um. I miss you. Gimme a call if you get a chance, okay? I'm back in the States, I'm in North Carolina, I'm… It's too much to put in a voice mail. Call me when you can." I hung up, then went and did as I'd promised Les I would—checked the power circle.

It was in fine condition, as I'd predicted. I stayed within it, but wandered the school grounds, breathing in the warm night air and listening to bugs sing. Probably it would've been smartest to try snatching a few hours' sleep, but despite what I'd told Les, I wasn't positive the circle would remain active if I paid so little attention as to take a nap.

Eventually I wound up in the mechanic's shop, which was as close to home as anywhere in the world might be. I'd spent a lot of hours banging around in there when I was a teen, and the smell of grease and oil put me right back where I belonged. There was still a wreck of a stereo against one wall—it might have even been the same one—and I dug through a box of dust-covered CDs until I found a classical one. I put the CD on repeat and settled into a corner, letting myself drift into a semisomnolent state where the swoops and falls of Beethoven filled me with a slow-building exuberance. It wasn't as good as a drum circle, but it did the job. I felt Rattler finally beginning to regain his strength, after two weeks of being put through the wringer. I retained just enough awareness to know nothing wicked struck from beyond the power circle. Hours later, the circle's connection with the earth let me know that the sun was rising, and I slowly shook off the music's power and got to my feet.

Everybody in the gym who was still awake had to be exhausted. I thought maybe I could run to the supermarket and come back with all the doughnuts in town. It was a cheap way to buy myself into the community's good graces, if it worked. I left the shop and went back into the main part of the school, passing the music room on my way to check and see how many people had made it through the night awake.

A couple steps past the music room's open door I stumbled, my brain catching up to what I'd seen there. I backed up, one hand already on the door frame for support, and the other one knotted over my stomach like I could keep sickness at bay until I was certain of what I'd seen.

The floor was littered with the vigil-keepers, whose mouths and eyes gaped in rigid horror. Above their unseeing eyes, fingertip-size burns were seared into each forehead. A few of them had fallen in ways that suggested they'd been running and had simply been felled where they moved, bodies instantly going into rigor mortis. It was so macabre and senseless that for long moments I just stood there, swaying, unable to see what else was wrong in the room. Finally, though, it struck me.

The elders' bodies were missing.

CHAPTER TEN

Saturday, March 25, 5:38 a.m.

From the outside. I had set the circle to warn against threats from the outside. I hadn't thought to check for evil already within the school, and I wasn't certain it would have triggered any wards even if it had. Not the way I'd set it up, anyway. The thoughts ran through my mind, splashes of cold and hot, while I stared at the wreckage in the music room.

I didn't notice when I started moving. I just saw it happening from above, watched myself turn around and walk out of the music room like my body had decided to go on walkabout while my spirit stayed with the dead, struggling to understand how I could have prevented another massacre.

By not letting Danny Little Turtle push me around, obviously, but I'd thought we were safe and I'd thought he had a point. I would never, ever refuse a request from an elder again.

My stomach dropped and I looked more carefully at the bodies. Somehow, inexplicably, Les Senior was not among them. I didn't know if he'd stepped out for a bathroom break or what, but he'd been spared a second time inside of twenty-four hours. For one heartbeat I was grateful, and for the next I wondered if he'd cut a deal with somebody to make sure he survived.

I shuddered. The motion snapped me back into my body, which was getting into the rented Impala and offering a genial wave at the guys maintaining the traffic patterns and salt circle. By the time I really felt like I was behind my eyeballs again, I was halfway out of town. When I figured I had a good ten minutes' head start on any pursuit, I broke the law and made a cell-phone call while driving.

Les picked up on the second ring, his voice hoarse like he'd been talking all night. "Sheriff Lee."

"This is Joanne. Something's gone wrong."

The rough quality left his voice. "What? Where are you? I'm on my way."

"I'm not at the school anymore. The elders are missing and their vigil-keepers are dead." I couldn't think of a way to soften the blow, so didn't try.

His breath hitched, then turned gruff with professionalism. He reminded me of Morrison right then, and I wished desperately that the captain had picked up last night. "They're dead and you've left the premises? Joanne, that doesn't look good."

"Heh. I know. I know, and I'm sorry, but I made a huge mistake and I'm going to try fixing it before it gets any worse. The trouble wasn't coming in from outside, Les. It was already in the school, waiting for us. *Dammit!*" That was twice I'd been sucker punched, and I was starting to get pissed.

"You've made a mistake by leaving, Jo. Please come back

before I have to explain to anyone why you left the scene of a crime."

"It's not a crime." It was, of course. Just not the kind Les was going to be able to do anything about.

"Joanne." The professional edge was getting harder. "If you don't come back I'm going to have to consider you a suspect. You kn— *Jesus.*"

That, I judged, was the sound of him getting to the music room. "*Jesus,* Joanne, what happened here? Where are the bodies? The—the first bodies, I mean? You don't have them, do you?"

"No. Either somebody in the school attacked the vigil-keepers and stole the bodies, or…" I didn't much want to think about, much less say, the *or,* because I was considerably more convinced of its probability than of someone making off with seven dead people and not being noticed.

Les, grimly, said, "Or what?"

I sighed. "Or they got up, killed their watchers, and left on their own." I was in the mountains now, and wishing the phone's reception would start cutting out so I'd have an excuse to hang up. I didn't want to convince Les that there were seven undead running around the North Carolina hills. I wished I didn't feel so confident of it myself. It said something about my life that undead seemed more likely than body snatchers.

"Joanne.…" Les's exhalation came over the line, and his words were measured. "Just come on back so we can talk about this, all right?"

"Sorry, Les. I'm losing reception. I'll talk to you later." I hung up, then swore creatively for about a quarter mile, and called Sara. "Go to the music room. Les is going to need your help."

"Joanne?" Sara sounded fuzzy with lack of sleep, but like

Les, she sharpened right up. "What've you gotten us into now?"

"A fine mess, and I'm sorry. Look, please don't tell Les, but I'm heading back to the holler where the Nothing came up from. It's the only place I've got to start."

I heard her say, "Got to start with what?" but I was already hanging up. I tossed the phone into the passenger seat and put both hands on the wheel, breathing, "C'mon, little buddy, let's see what your punk-ass V-6 can do."

The Impala, which had as much heart as could be expected from a late-model automatic transmission, jumped from forty to ninety in a respectably short distance, and for a few glorious minutes I didn't think about anything except getting there *fast*. The car's tires weren't quite wide enough to stick to the mountain curves as well as I'd like, but he and I knew each other well enough by the time we got through the lower turns to take the higher ones at satisfying speed. I'd cut my teeth on these roads, learning to drive both safely and dangerously well, and some things you didn't forget. Driving was the one skill at the police academy I'd come up aces in, and sometime soon after I got back to Seattle I was going to have to make a little drag-racing confession to Morrison, who would never, ever understand the impulse. Neither for the speed or for the thrill of the illegality of it, though at least I wasn't a cop anymore, so I would at least save the department that embarrassment if I ever got caught.

Not that I ever got caught.

I overshot Sara's holler-entering-site by a good distance, heading farther up the mountain to see if a pull-out gulley I remembered still existed. It did, as a big chunk of raw earth and dust where somebody had once cleared the land for tobacco. I killed the engine, got out, and slammed the car door closed. The noise echoed off the mountains and down into the gulley on the other side of the narrow road. For just a second it struck me as the only sound of civilization in all of creation, and the old soft beauty of the landscape impressed itself on me.

The sky was misty gold and pink, with just enough clouds hanging on the horizon to hold the color. The trees were still black with night, not yet giving up to daytime colors, and down in the gulley, steam rose off water that was warmer than the early-morning air. It couldn't be more than half an hour past sunrise.

Which meant that realistically, I had to be way ahead of a bunch of animated dead bodies. There was no way they might have gotten up here faster than I had. Zombies were not known for their speed.

I fact-checked that against every zombie movie in history and decided to ignore movies. My personal experience indicated that zombies were, as tradition had them, slow. They also stank to high heaven, an experience that couldn't be replicated in film, but which ought to give me some warning. Except these would be very fresh zombies, which might not stink so much.

I was not helping myself any, and neither was the awareness that I was not armed the way I'd been at Halloween. I had my sword and my magic, but I longed for Petite and the small arsenal I'd built into her trunk recently. It wasn't much, just a sawed-off shotgun, some rock salt, three pairs of handcuffs and two wooden stakes, which I filed under "just in case" and assumed I would never actually have to use. Vampires did not exist. Dammit.

I'd taken a look around the pull-out while muttering all that to myself. There were fresh footprints, but not much in the way of tire tracks, which meant one of two things. Either this was not the other way into the holler, as I had hoped it would be, or the locals had been going to a tremendous amount of trouble to keep Sara from finding it. Unless there was also a major moonshine distillery up along the trail, I couldn't imagine why they would go to so much bother, so I figured it wasn't the way in. I sighed and decided to leave the Impala there, and walk back down to Sara's roadside entrance to the holler. It would keep the car from getting banged up by traffic driving up the mountain the way I'd just done. I locked the doors and headed for the roadside.

Carrie Little Turtle, moving at lightning speed, came out of nowhere and tried to rip my face off.

The only thing that saved me was the sheerly instinctive flight reaction of falling over backward because something was in my face. I screamed loudly enough to be heard the next county over and kicked a booted foot into Carrie's belly as she leapt at me. She weighed nothing, all that baling wire and sprung steel turning out to be personality more than physical strength. She went flying over my head and crashed to the earth somewhere beyond me. I dug my fingers in the clay, reminded myself that zombies were slow and came to my feet with a fistful of dirt in one hand and a blazing blue sword in the other.

The other six dead elders spread around me in a half circle, their hair bleached stone-white and their skin only a half shade darker. Their eyes were eaten with darkness, blood red where the color once had been. Their fingers were grotesquely long, nails discolored and sharp, and each of their forefingers looked as if it had been burned. Just like the marks on the vigil-keepers' foreheads.

"Not zombies." I actually said it aloud, surprising them at least as much as I surprised myself. "Definitely not zombies. Wights. I think I'll call you wights. Is that all wight with you?"

Three of them snarled, possibly in response to the pun, and

showed teeth that had decayed into yellow masses of dripping bile. I took that as a no, but before I could think of anything else stupidly witty to say, they came at me.

I envisioned the handful of clay as carrying the weight of the earth itself, and flung that weight at the nearest wight. It fell, pinned down and screaming under a shimmer of gunmetal-blue magic. I was starting to like that shade. It appeared to be the color my magic took on when it was really working in harmony, warrior and healer together again for the first time at last. The wight struggled, but healing power trumped death magic this time around, and I felt like having the bright morning sun on my side was a win.

The second wight avoided my rapier with a deftness I wouldn't have attributed to the undead. I mean, I'd been sword fighting for almost a year now, and I'd skewered a thing or two in my time. Even with pinning one wight down magically, I could manage a lunge and thrust. But the second wight sucked its belly in and twitched to the side like it was invested with a rattlesnake spirit, too, lending it speed it had no native right to.

And that left the third one to jump on my head.

I went down under its weight, shouting and swearing. Its nails scrabbled at my shields, unable to break through, and for the umpteenth time in a week I cast a rueful thanks toward the werewolf whose attack had finally forced me to permanently activate those shields. I wasn't exactly invulnerable, but I was a whole lot harder to hurt now, which made this kind of fight a little less scary.

Still, there were seven of them and one of me. Shields were great, but if they decided to work together, I could be drawn and quartered before I blinked. I forgot about pinning the one monster down and shoved my left hand upward, willing magic to take a physical, concussive form.

The wight on top of me blew upward like it had been caught in Old Faithful and went spinning off to crash against the mountain somewhere. The remaining four closed in all at once. I threw magic in quick blasts, catching them repeatedly and knocking them back, but they kept getting up and coming at me again. They sauntered around my swordplay like I was a kid with a stick. After a minute or three, Carrie and the other one I'd blown off joined the others, so I was surrounded and starting to feel like the hapless kung fu student in the movie, right before everything comes together and she suddenly kicks everybody's ass.

Except instead of kicking ass, I was slowly wearing down. That was almost entirely new territory for me. I was accustomed to drawing ridiculously deeply on my own strength, without the need for a power circle. Moreover, I'd leveled up in the past couple weeks, gaining more access to greater power. There was no way a bunch of undead monsters should be able to wear me down so fast. But not only was I starting to stumble, it seemed like they were getting faster and stronger with every hit they took.

A little belatedly, I realized that these things had been created by somebody sucking all the essential force out of seven people, and that throwing bolt after bolt of life magic into them was probably not the best way to defeat them.

For just an instant I wished the snarky little voice in the back of my head was still there. The one that told me when I was being an utter ass, and when I was making really stupid mistakes. Unfortunately, that voice had been the lingering ghost of a much younger me, and she and I had fully integrated now. All I had left was my own voice muttering, "Moron," and somehow it just didn't have the same ring to it. I reined in the magic and even drew it out of the sword, so it was just me and a silver rapier against seven wights on a mountainside.

It was the moment they'd been waiting for. They moved as one, so fast I could barely see them. One actually sacrificed itself, leaping belly-first onto my sword. It slid all the way to the hilt, wrapped its long-fingered hands around my wrist, and held on.

Like Carrie, it didn't weigh very much, but it didn't have to weigh a lot in order to completely inconvenience me. Apparently being skewered by a relatively ordinary sword wasn't enough to hurt an undead, never mind kill it, because its grip on my wrist didn't loosen at all. I couldn't shake the thing off, and while I was trying, five others did their best to tear me apart. One jumped on my back and wrapped its arm around my throat, going for a rear naked choke hold. I thrust the idea of a fender between its arm and my throat, creating a little more barrier, strengthening my shields there a little, but then another one started gnawing on my ankle and I started to discover inherent shields were one thing, but fighting half a dozen enemies at once were another. I ran backward as best I could, planning to smash the one on my back against the mountain. Instead I tripped on the one chewing my ankle and fell over.

On the positive side, while I didn't think it was possible to knock a dead man breathless, the impact did at least cause the wight to loosen its grip around my neck. I kicked frantically and rolled away, feeling the earth rumble beneath me. There was a vehicle on the mountain somewhere, a huge roaring V-8 engine like Petite's eating up the road. I thought it was a kind of nice sound to die by, and surged to my knees against the weight of two more wights pulling me back toward the ground. None of my spirit animals were about strength. Rattler was fast, Raven was clever, Renee was…timey-wimey-wibbly-wobbly, as best I could tell. I needed a freaking bull to draw on.

Or a burst of healing magic used entirely on myself, rather than shoved out into the world. I'd never done that before. It was worth a shot. I concentrated on the idea of a turbo thruster, where the stoked-up, over-oxygenated engine was the muscles in my arms. Blue fire lit up in my biceps, triceps and deltoids. I bellowed from the bottom of my diaphragm, using all that focused energy to fling the wight on my sword upward. Straight up, with the intent to not just dislodge it, but toss it halfway across the mountains.

It would have worked better if the damned thing hadn't still been clinging to my wrist like a leech, but its unnaturally long fingers lost their grip and I shook the sword free. The wight flopped over instead of flying off, and dragged my arm right back down with its weight. But I was now firing blue power on all muscular cylinders, and bashed my left hand into its face. It drove straight into the earth. I surged to my feet, twitching with the need to act and trying without much success to fight down an unholy glee. This had to be what Olympic athletes felt like at the top of their game: purely unstoppable, fully in their bodies, utterly certain of the physical response they would achieve.

I bet Olympic athletes hardly ever had wights shove a fingertip against their foreheads and begin to siphon off their physical prowess. The wight's blank face curdled into a hideous smile, and beyond it I saw the others, including Carrie, coming toward me for a final time. My shields slipped and scrambled even as I fundamentally understood what was happening: I was pouring so much power into my own body that there was bleed-off, enough that the monsters could suck some of it up as it spilled out of the shields. And I'd overloaded myself just like a nitroed-up engine: it wasn't going to come down until the fuel ran out. I had a lot of fuel for them to burn through.

I hated to think what they would do with it, once I was depleted and they were all topped up.

My vision got woozy, way faster than I'd have thought possible, and I had the utterly childish thought *"this is not fair!"*
before I dropped to my knees, wondering faintly how I was
going to get out of this one.

Petite, my big, beloved 1969 Boss 302 Mustang, custom
purple paint job and Washington State vanity plates declaring her name, hit the brakes behind me, spun a flawless 180
in a spray of red dust, and came to a shuddering stop not ten
inches from my nose.

Morrison flung her door open, stood up with his duty
weapon in hand, and shot Carrie Little Turtle between the
eyes.

CHAPTER ELEVEN

Carrie dropped. The wight siphoning off my magic screamed and leapt backward, soaring over Petite and landing on her opposite side, closer to Morrison than me. He sighted and fired again, smooth and cool and calm. The wight dodged, taking the bullet in a shoulder instead of the throat, but it wouldn't go any closer to Morrison. Or to me, for that matter, which was good, because I was too busy being astounded to do anything but gape.

Morrison was in jeans, which was utterly unheard of. Jeans and a snug white T-shirt, equally unheard of. He was also wearing his shoulder holster, which pinned the shirt against his chest even more snugly, and emphasized the line of his shoulders and waist. His silvering hair was bright in the morning sunlight, and he looked absolutely unconcerned that five of the six remaining wights were edging closer to him.

Not much closer, though. They got within fifteen feet, then

hissed like they were burning and backed away again. Morrison shot the second one a second time, this time catching it in the forehead as he'd done with Carrie. It collapsed, too. The others howled, rushed forward, came within a few feet of Petite, and screamed their rage and fury as they fell away again.

"Steel." I whispered the word, and it gave me the strength to stand. Petite was a classic, her sweet body made up of steel, not fiberglass or aluminum or carbon fiber like modern cars. And there wasn't a monster in the books that didn't have a revulsion to cold iron. Still whispering, I said, "Keys."

Morrison, who shouldn't have been able to hear me, reached into Petite's interior, turned the engine off and tossed me the keys without ever dropping his weapon's training on the wights.

I snatched the keys out of midair, took three long steps to Petite's trunk, opened it, and popped the sawed-off shotgun out of its custom holder. I loaded it and another few steps brought me to Morrison's side. He, still very steady and calm, said, "Shoot or run?"

I cocked the shotgun, and by the time we started pulling triggers, the wights were running for the hills. The dust from Petite's arrival wasn't yet settled when they disappeared from sight entirely. Morrison lowered his weapon and cast me the very slightest hint of a smile in his sideways glance. "Do we go after them?"

"Sure, if you've got boots of seven leagues so we can catch up to them WHAT THE HELL ARE YOU DOING HERE?!?!" I threw the shotgun aside and flung myself into Morrison's arms, which would have been a lot cuter if I was eight inches shorter and seventy pounds lighter than he. Instead we were of a similar height and he probably only had thirty, maybe forty, pounds on me. Instead of a romantic-lovers-reunited embrace it was more of a crashing, staggering thud against Petite's frame, while I howled and shrieked and beat my fists against his back in utter, stupefied joy. "Oh, my *God,* Morrison, did you *see* yourself, holy shit, you were freaking *fantastic* what are you DOING here how did you FIND me what the HELL!!!"

To my pure, unadulterated delight, he was every bit as silly as I was, roaring laughter into my shoulder as he hugged his arms around my waist. He smelled so good, Old Spice and dust and sweat and wind, and beneath my shouting he said, "Muldoon called me when you left Ireland. I've been driving for two days. Walker, are you *sparkling?*"

I'd forgotten about the glitter bath Les and I had taken, and said, "What? Yes," before returning to a bellow of semicoherent delight. "PETITE, you've been DRIVING PETITE?! I didn't know you drove so well! You said my relationship with my car was pathological! YOU DROVE MY CAR ACROSS THE COUNTRY, YOU CRAZY MAN! IN TWO DAYS!"

Morrison, who was nothing if not good at taking my outbursts in stride, went on like I wasn't a maniac shouting into his shoulder. "—called that woman, Sara, when I got to the outskirts of town—"

"WHY DIDN'T YOU CALL ME!"

"I wanted to surprise you. She said you'd headed up into the mountains and something was wrong, so I floored it."

"YOU FLOORED IT! I DIDN'T THINK YOU KNEW HOW TO FLOOR IT!"

Morrison said, "Of course I do," and then he kissed me.

It was an extremely effective way to get me to stop shouting. After a minute we sort of collapsed into Petite's driver's seat, which was not a comfortable place for two people to be. I had not known from previous experience how awkward it was to get two people from the driver's seat into the passenger seat, either, but we managed. It might have been easier if I hadn't been trying to remove Morrison's shoulder holster and shirt at the same time, but that was not a detail that occurred to me in the moment. We were both giggling and swearing by the time we got into the passenger seat. Morrison fumbled for the seat latch and I grabbed it, sending the seat ratcheting back at top speed. I fell on top of him, laughing, and tried to mumble an apology that he stopped with a kiss, and then some more kisses.

I wanted to sit up so I could see him better, but I couldn't make myself untangle my fingers from his hair long enough to do it, not even when he skimmed my shirt off and slid his hands over my skin. Petite's windows were steaming up, despite the door being open and the rising sun heating the air around us. And then for quite a while I stopped noticing much of anything about the world beyond us, or anything that wasn't Morrison's scent and touch and warmth.

Saturday, March 25, 8:25 a.m.

I was not *asleep*. I just wasn't very conscious, although the only thing keeping me from being unconscious was the fact that my left ankle had been pressed against the gearshift long enough to develop a permanent bruise that was starting to make my whole calf hurt. Aside from that, though, I was…

…well, actually I was hideously uncomfortable, because my jeans had never made it much past my calves, either, and were cutting off circulation, and my right knee, where it was wedged between Morrison's thigh and the door, was also stuck to Petite's leather seat. I hated to think just how much of *Morrison* was stuck to the leather.

Not the important bits, anyway. I smiled, then woke up enough to grin, and within a moment was laughing quietly. I hadn't been so overwhelmed by sheer adolescent horniness since I'd *been* an adolescent, and overall, the aftermath of bubbly giggly joy was a lot better than my teen experiences. Maybe there were big bad things out there in the world, but if I was with Morrison I could handle anything. I felt effervescent. Stuck to a muggy, hot black leather interior, but effervescent. My laughter faded back into smiles and I mooshed a kiss against Morrison's shoulder, just happy to be there.

Morrison turned his head and kissed my hair, murmuring, "I haven't done that since I was a teenager," with a smile of his own.

"Really?" I lifted my head to look at him from so close we both went cross-eyed. His eyes were still a lovely blue, even crossed. "You're very good at it for someone who hasn't done it in twenty years."

I got an up close and personal glimpse of his best exasperated look, though for once it seemed tempered by fondness. "In a *car,* Walker, I meant in a *car.*"

I propped my elbows on the seat above his shoulders so I could see him a little more clearly. "I can't believe the staid and steady Morrison has ever had sex in a car. What kind of car was it?"

He stared at me. "Does it *matter?*"

I laughed out loud and kissed him again. "Probably to everybody but you. Hey," I said, suddenly a lot more softly. "Hi. You rescued me. Thanks."

"Probably a once-in-a-lifetime opportunity. I had to take it." Morrison curled his arms around me and pulled me back down against his chest. "You're welcome."

I smiled, thought of all the things that were going wrong just beyond Petite's front end, and sighed. I'd had a very long couple of weeks, and no sleep the night before. I figured we deserved five more minutes of slightly glittery snuggling before we got on with the dirty business of hunting wights. I nestled against Morrison, listening to his heartbeat, and the next thing I knew, the sun had jumped a hand-span in the sky and Sheriff Lester Lee was leaning in Petite's open driver's-side door with a look of betrayal and disgust on his youthful features.

Morrison took a deep waking-up breath, the kind that signaled having gone from totally asleep to totally prepared to shoot something inside a blink. His pistol was in the driver's seat, which I hadn't consciously noticed until I discovered my hand on his forearm, stopping him from picking it up. Les, expression flat with displeasure, picked it up instead, and removed it from sight. Morrison tensed very slightly beneath me, though I could see him processing Lester's uniform and accepting that if anyone had the right to move his weapon it was the local law enforcement. I still murmured, "It's okay. Les is one of the good guys."

Les growled, "Get dressed, Joanne," stood up, and turned his back on us.

I looked back at Morrison, aware that this situation was not at all funny. His blue eyes crinkled up at the edges, and we both buried our faces in each other's shoulders, trying to muffle high-pitched, teenage giggles. It didn't work at all, because getting caught having sex in a car was even less dignified as adults than as teens. For a few seconds Petite rocked with our mirth, and we were still giggling and smirking as we found our clothes—mine had littered glitter into the backseat, the foot-wells and on Morrison—and obediently got dressed. Morrison slid his hand into my hair and stole one more kiss before we opened the passenger door and sort of half climbed, half fell out in an undignified tangle of limbs. I zipped my jeans, laced my fingers through Morrison's, and tried to look apologetic through my grin as Les turned to face us.

"You think this is funny, Joanne?"

"No. Well, yes. I mean, this part? Yes. The rest…" Guilt started getting the better of me and my smile fell away.

The truth was, I had desperately needed—well, Morrison riding to my rescue had been a huge win, but the aftermath had been pretty high up on things Joanne needed, too. Up to and including the nap. I knew people were dying, I knew I'd lost the trail of not just the wights but the Executioner that had created them and I knew taking time out to get laid looked incredibly, mindlessly selfish. And it probably was.

But on the other hand, my mother had just sacrificed her immortal soul to save my life, my father was missing, and my son had come a hair's breadth from getting eaten by a soul-devouring monster. I'd had very little sleep and insufficient emotional support. I was perfectly willing to admit my timing was terrible, but given the all-or-nothing crisis my life tended to be, it wasn't like there was going to be a *good* time to throw my hat in and say, "Go away, the next few hours belongs to me."

So I shoved guilt into a box and booted it to the curb. "Les, this is Captain Michael Morrison of the North Precinct Seattle Police Department. Morrison, this is Sheriff Lester Lee. We're all on the same side here."

Les gave me a look that said obviously Morrison was a lot more on my side than he himself was, and that he, rationally or not, resented that. Morrison read the look as clearly as I did, and I could all but feel him file that one away to ask about later. Les didn't exactly put it aside, muttering, "Give me one good reason I shouldn't arrest you for fleeing the scene of a crime," with half-credible threat in his voice.

"Because you know perfectly well I didn't kill those people, and because I'm guessing if there are any prints scorched into their foreheads, they match up with the bodies who were already in the room."

He muttered incomprehensibly, then with slightly more volume said, "For public displays of indecency, then."

He had me dead to rights on that one, even if we were up on a mountaintop and he was the only public around. I was still smart enough to change the subject. "What's going on down there that you're up here?"

His expression went black. "The news media picked up last night's deaths. When you called I was already arguing about whether this had to become a federal case, but with the second wave the FBI has taken over. Murder on the Qualla. Six months from now it'll be a movie of the week. Sara's taking point—"

"Really? This isn't her jurisdiction."

"It's her or let somebody who's got no business here at all come in. At least she knows what's really going on."

I winced. Sara had already taken a mystical case in the teeth because of me, when the serial killer she was hunting turned out to be a man-eating monster called a wendigo. I doubted she was even done clawing her way out of that trail having gone cold, and now she was going to be leading another investigation that would have no satisfactory answers. Personally I was grateful it would be her leading it, and not some stick-up-the-ass white man who had no use or respect for the Cherokee culture. Professionally, I wished it was the stick-up-the-ass white guy, because two cases like this in a row could destroy Sara's career. "So, what, she sent you up here to…?"

"Find out where the hell you'd gone, and why." Les glared at Morrison again. "She's going to love the answer."

"There are two bodies over there," Morrison said in his mildest ever voice. Then I *did* feel guilty, because I'd totally forgotten the magnificent arrival had meant Morrison had needed to shoot some people. On the other hand, they hadn't been very people-like anymore, and I was reasonably certain that if he'd been all torn up about it, we'd have ended up discussing the case and what exactly he'd just had to do, rather than falling into my car like a couple of hormone-addled teenagers. Guilt went away again. I was beginning to like this new, stable, grown-up me.

Les said, "There are?" through his teeth, and whatever mild-manneredness or calm Morrison and I had been sharing evaporated. We exchanged glances, then peered over Petite, beyond Les, to where Carrie Little Turtle and the other wight had fallen.

There were no bodies. There were empty clothes and white dust smears on the red earth, but there were no bodies. After a brief, loud silence, Morrison said to me, "The zombies didn't do that."

I pinched the bridge of my nose. "No. No, they didn't. Les, they were…the…they…" Even talking to a believer didn't mean it was easy to say, "Apparently they disintegrated after Morrison shot them," though after another try or two I got that out.

Les's voice dropped an octave. "He *shot* them?"

"Les, they were undead. Wights. Revenants. Something, I don't know. I'm calling them wights. Their hair was white and their eyes were red and they sucked the life out of the people keeping vigil and they were trying to do it to me. I tried fighting them with magic and it was like fighting fire with gasoline. They slurped it right up. So although I'm very, very sorry I'll have to tell Danny there is no body for him to bury, I am frankly very glad Morrison showed up and shot a couple of them. So you go tell Sara it's all gone horribly wrong, and I'll go into the mountains and stop these things."

"Not without me, you won't. You said yourself you'd get lost."

I had. And I'd also said I'd let Aidan be my guide, which

seemed like an even worse idea now than it had at the time. "Sara needs to know—"

"You have her phone number."

That, while true, was a detail that had slipped my mind. I stared thoughtfully at the Impala. "Ever read a mystery novel set in the '80s and thought, 'Man, if they'd had cell phones this book would only be twenty pages long?' No? It's just me? Okay then." The point I was really trying to make was it had also probably been easier to send people on important but time-consuming errands when the whole world hadn't been carrying space-age communicators in their pockets. I got the phone and called Sara, who told us all in no uncertain terms to get our asses back down to town. "You," I said to Les when I'd reported this, "may be obliged to take that as a direct order. Me, I'm not even law enforcement anymore—"

"Thank God," murmured Morrison, which made me grin even as I kept talking.

"—and Morrison is, um. On vacation?"

"Emergency family leave," he said, and my heart flip-flopped.

"And if you go up in the mountains by yourselves we're going to have four people missing instead of just two."

That kept being a valid argument. I took a breath, but Morrison said, "I know you can't track with the magic, Walker, but I've Seen what you See. Can't you just use the Sight to get yourself pointed back at civilization? Towns look different than wilderness, don't they?"

I shut my mouth. Les shut his. After a minute I said, "So we'll go wight-hunting now, then, okay?"

"Aidan will never forgive you."

"That," I said firmly, "is a risk I'm willing to take. He's twelve. He really doesn't need to be putting himself in the line of fire. So if you'll go report in to Sara, Morrison and I will go hunt these bastards down the old-fashioned way." With shotguns and salt, but Les didn't need to know that.

He scowled, but he was stuck between a rock and a hard place. I was certain Sara wouldn't inform her superiors that the local LEOs were being uncooperative, because she wouldn't want any more publicity than necessary, either. On the other hand, the local populace was likely to be uncooperative, and Les's presence would smooth things over. He couldn't really stay, even if it was his personal preference. He finally jabbed a finger at me. "You keep me informed."

"I will." I meant it, though he didn't look like he believed me. After another minute of glaring, he got in his car and went away, leaving me and Morrison to exhale loudly. I said, "This is a mess," as I put my phone in my pocket and collected the shotgun from where I'd tossed it.

Morrison didn't say anything, and after a few seconds the not saying anything got very noticeable. I stopped digging supplies out of Petite's trunk and looked at him curiously.

He had the cautious expression of a man who wanted badly to speak and was certain it would explode on him. I put the gun and the ammo back in Petite's trunk and closed it, both to assure him I was listening and that I wouldn't shoot him. "What?"

"Was that, ah. Was that…?"

Really, I shouldn't have had the foggiest idea what he was asking. Five words, two of them repeated and one a filler rather than a real word, did not an actual question make. But I understood perfectly, and a soft breath rushed out of me in something like a laugh. "No. No, that's Les. I guess he had kind of a crush on me in high school. I had no idea until yesterday afternoon. No, it's… That's Lucas. Lucas Isaac."

I folded my arms over my chest and looked down, lower lip caught in my teeth. Then I sidled around Petite's big back end so I was closer to Morrison, because I knew the body language I was using was all *"go away, I don't wanna talk about it,"* which wasn't exactly true and wasn't the impression I wanted him to get. I just wasn't *good* at talking about it, having kept the secret bottled up for well over a decade.

Morrison was the first one outside of the Qualla who'd sussed it out, anyway. I'd told him my real name, the full Irish-Cherokee hybrid tongue tangling disaster of it, last summer. He'd gone and looked up one Siobhán Grainne MacNamarra Walkingstick, aka Joanne Walker, and had discovered I'd had children while still in high school. After asking very carefully if I'd been raped—there were no police reports indicating I had been, but God alone knew what a fifteen-year-old might choose to report—and hearing the answer was no, he had let the whole thing go with a great deal more grace than I would have shown.

But that was then, and everything was different now. I was different, we were different, and our whole potential future was different. Maybe that was so huge it should all be put off for later consideration, but I was still of the mind that with my life, there was no telling whether there would be a later to consider. So I cleared my throat and tried to answer all the questions he'd been too gentle to ask over the past year. "We hadn't really been in the Qualla all that long. A year, I guess. And I had a chip on my shoulder like you wouldn't believe."

Morrison tried to hide a snort of laughter and completely failed. I laughed, too, and looked up, my cheeks hot. "Yeah, okay, you'd probably believe it." I looked down again, because I still didn't like telling this story, even if I'd come increasingly to terms with having to. "Anyway, Lucas came in that fall from Vancouver, and he was really cute. Really cute. And I had a terrible crush on him, and Sara was my best friend and she said she didn't like him, which wasn't true but I didn't get it. Anyway, I was desperate to make him like me so I did the obvious. The really, really dumb obvious. It didn't work, of course, and to make it worse I got pregnant. And being fifteen...I don't know. Maybe I thought being pregnant would suddenly make him like me and it'd all be fairy-tale princesses from there on out, but what happened was he hightailed it back to Vancouver at Christmas break, and I had twins about a month early. The little girl died."

I rolled my jaw, stopping Morrison from saying anything. It had been thirteen years ago and I'd never meant to keep the babies anyway, but it still made a sick sad place inside me to think or say those words. "Aidan was adopted by a local woman. It was an open adoption, of course, I knew she would be taking him, she knew I was having him, none of it was secret, It was all just what we both wanted. I don't know if he's ever even met Lucas. I haven't seen him—Lucas—since he left. I met Aidan yesterday. Seems like a good kid. He knows who I am, which I didn't know if he would, and Ada, his mom, she's a little touchy about me being here even if everything was open and okay, but anyway, so Sara grew up and married Lucas after all, which I learned last December. And on Wednesday she called to tell me my father was missing but she somehow forgot to mention that Luke was, too. So she's furious at having to call me and I think she's equally terrified I won't find him, and that I will and suddenly some long-buried passion will spark and we'll, I don't know, steal Aidan and run away together."

"Should I be worried?"

That was so unexpected I lifted my gaze again. Morrison did not look like a worried man. The corner of his mouth was lifted, and his blue eyes were concerned, but not in a way that suggested he felt threatened. He was concerned about me, that was all, and when I inadvertently smiled at the question, his own smile broadened a bit. He came over, put his arm around my shoulders, and tugged me into an embrace. "Thanks for telling me. I knew some of it, but not the details."

I put my forehead against his shoulder. "I knew you did. You're a gentleman, by the way. For not pushing it last summer."

"You said nobody'd hurt you. I had to trust you on that. I figured you knew where I was if you wanted to talk."

"Is there a universe in which you thought I might actually come talk to you?"

"You just did."

"Yeah, but you couldn't have seen that coming a year ago. Could you?" I leaned back, trying to gauge his expression.

"A year ago you were my employee, Walker. Anything you wanted to say to me then would have been in a different confidence than what you tell me now, even if it's the same information." He brushed my chin with his thumb and smiled.

"Did you know I love you?" The question popped out, followed by a blush so hard it made my eyes water. I'd said it on the phone, but that wasn't the same as saying it right to his face, and besides, it seemed awkward on the tail of the conversation we were having.

His grin only got wider, though. "Then or now? Now, yes, I've been starting to suspect. Then? Then it didn't matter, because I was your boss." He hesitated. "And you took the promotion, so I wasn't sure."

The Promotion. Morrison had made that job offer very carefully, after we'd shared a kiss that hadn't exactly happened in the real world. I'd had the impression then that he was testing the waters, seeing which I wanted more: him, or to become a police detective. "I wasn't ready. I was still way too much of a mess, and…and besides, you'd kind of thrown down a gauntlet. You said, I don't know if you remember, but the day I came back from Ireland you said you thought I could be a good cop. Of course, that was right after you said you'd always liked me, so I probably should've taken it with a grain of salt, but—"

"I did like you. I *can* tell the difference between a Corvette and a Mustang, Walker. It was the woman sitting on the hood that got me flustered. Then you realized I was your new boss, and it seemed like we were better off off to a bad start than making up." Morrison's eyebrows darted up and he amended that, turning into something of a confession: "It seemed like *I* was better off if we stayed on bad terms."

A smile tugged the corner of my mouth in turn. I leaned against Petite, sliding my feet wide so Morrison could lean against me. "You have no idea how glad I am to hear you can tell Corvettes from Mustangs. Any doubts I might have had are now put to rest."

"Were you having doubts?"

"No." I sighed and put my forehead against his shoulder again, easier now that I was scooted a bit lower than he. "Pretty much not since I threw that temper tantrum in the restaurant over Barbara Bragg." I'd come a breath from going all *Fatal Attraction* on Morrison's paramour, and then read Morrison the riot act for putting himself in danger while I was trying to save him. It had not been my proudest moment. "Sorry about that."

"It's all right. Though that was some of why I wasn't sure about what you felt. It seemed fairly clear there in the parking lot, but you took the promotion after that. And you did turn out to be a good cop, Walker. You proved that to me."

"I guess I had to. Maybe not just to you, but to myself, too. But the whole shamanism thing, it's pulling me another direction."

Morrison's voice dropped. "Is it what's pulling us back into Petite's front seat?"

He was right. We were in serious danger of scootching our way right back in there. I groaned and shook my head. "No. It's pulling us, or at least me, up into the mountains, and if you want to know the truth, Boss—"

"Not 'Boss.'"

I smiled briefly. "Morrison. Whatever I call you, the truth is I don't know how to find what's up there, much less how to handle it."

"I'm sure it'll find us, Walker. The rest we can figure out."

There was nothing better than having a handsome man completely confident in your abilities, except maybe having one who also intended to go into battle with you. I kissed him, then squeezed away before we did fall into Petite's front seat and went searching for the shotgun I had carelessly tossed away. I was surprised Les hadn't read me the riot act on that, too, when I found it half-under the Impala. I bent to scoop it up and my phone rang, making me clap my hip as I stood. Morrison straightened, his gaze watchful as I answered with a "Yeah?"

"You answered too fast to be driving back down here, and I don't want to know why you're not," Sara said. "But belay those orders anyway, because Ada Monroe just came to the school. She says Aidan has gone missing."

CHAPTER TWELVE

I didn't know what my expression was, but Morrison came closer and put his hand at the small of my back. My heart's tempo had picked up to an improbable degree, drowning out Sara's voice. My face felt flushed and my fingers were freezing, but then those reversed while my stomach churned. Sara, distantly, was saying, "She says his bed hasn't been slept in and the back door was open. Their property backs up onto the mountains, Joanne."

"He's twelve," I protested faintly. "How far could he have gotten in eight hours?" It was a stupid question. Even assuming he'd gone into the mountains at the very slow pace of a mile an hour, that made for a lot of square mileage to cover. Realistically he would know at least a few miles of the land well enough to move much, much faster than that, even at night. I stopped being able to extrapolate how much distance he could have covered. It was busywork anyway, my brain trying desperately to distract itself with numbers while adrenaline pumped through, urging me to move.

"The town is putting a search party together already, and he's been reported missing in the NCIC and CUE, but—"

"But I'm already up here. CUE?" I knew the National Crime Information Center, but CUE was new to me and would give Sara something to talk about while I folded my hand around the phone and triggered the Sight. Petite herself flared reassuring, solid green, and Morrison had faint red tinges of concern dancing through his purple and blue aura. The mountains were brilliant with color, new leaves on trees burning electric blue, the sap running strong and bright. Bugs and larger animals made different-colored shadows against the blue pulsing life in the trees, but I was looking beyond that. Way beyond.

The Sight wasn't exactly X-ray vision, but for my purposes it was close enough. I couldn't track magic, but I could *See* it, and Aidan's aura was brilliant and distinctive. Phone still folded in my hand, I turned my attention up into the hills, searching for the blaze of near-white blend that was Aidan Monroe's presence.

Nothing. I gritted, "We'll find him," over Sara's explanation about the Community United Effort, and hung up. "Horrible energy-sucking monsters have been moved into second place on the priority list. Aidan's missing."

"Your son."

"Yeah. Ada's son," I said after a moment, because it was bizarre hearing someone else say those words aloud. I thought of Aidan as my son in the privacy of my head, but to the world outside my head, he was Ada's. "Not that I'm trying to write him off. It's just that she's put all the time and effort in. All I did was give birth. A long time ago." I wet my lips, then swallowed. I meant it, but that didn't mean I wasn't worried.

Terrified, even. "I don't want anything to happen to him, Morrison. He's just a kid, and my screwed-up life is coming in to haunt him."

"Your life…" Morrison paused long enough to make me give a hard little laugh.

"Isn't screwed up, is that what you were going to say? Thanks, but it is. More than most."

"Differently from most." He thought about that, then exhaled and admitted, "More than most. Speaking of which, Walker, it's a bad time, but how are you doing with the Patricia Raleigh incident?"

"Did she die?"

"No."

"Then I'm fine." I wasn't certain it was true. Two weeks ago I'd shot a woman to keep her from killing my detective partner. I hadn't shot to kill, and she'd survived, but shooting someone was a big deal all by itself. For me, though, it had also been the spark setting off two weeks of explosive, nonstop action. That kind of thing looked cool in movies, but was exhausting when it really happened. I was going to have a hell of a lot to work through when things slowed down.

At the rate I was going, that would happen when I was about eighty. "I'll be fine, anyway," I amended. "Don't worry about it right now. We have other problems. Aidan apparently knows these hills like the back of his hand, and he really wanted to go with me yesterday when it looked like I was going monster-hunting. If he's gone hunting by himself…."

"He'll be fine," Morrison promised, and since, like George Washington, Morrison never told a lie, I accepted the reassurance gratefully. He edged me aside to pick up where I'd left off: packing the shotgun and other bits of the arsenal I'd put in Petite's trunk over the past several months. "I'm glad no one stopped me for speeding. I had no idea what you had in the trunk. Is anything in here illegal?"

"I have permits for all of it. Were you really speeding? Of course you were." I took a back holster for the sawed-off shotgun out of the trunk and slung it on, but I was trying to stare at Morrison over my shoulder while he slid the shotgun home. It had a comfortable weight to it, though I bet after a day's hike it wouldn't be so comfy. "You really just drove across the country in two days, Morrison? Did you *sleep?*"

"Not much. I made good time through the Midwest and stopped at a motel for about six hours."

I turned around to stare at him with my heart and my libido both speeding up. I'd driven that route when I was seventeen, all the way through South Dakota and into the speed-limit-free zone of Montana. I had a fair sense of what *good time* meant, in those regards, and I knew for damned sure what Petite's upper speed range was. *I* had made it across the country, North Carolina to Seattle, and avoiding Ohio, which was lousy with cops, in about forty hours, including sleep, stopping for food, and climbing a mountain to look at the wild horse monument built there. My average speed had been around 75 miles an hour, and that took traffic jams into account. My *top* speed had been close to Petite's nominal upper limit of 130, but I'd never quite pegged it. One of my goals in life was to bring her to Utah and let her rip on the salt flats.

The idea of Morrison tearing across the country at an average speed in excess of sixty miles an hour was one of the sexier images I'd been presented with lately. My cheeks flushed. Morrison looked amused. "You all right, Walker?"

I'd said it before, but it was worth repeating, except this time I said it in a lower, more throaty voice. "I didn't know you drove that well."

"Driving fast isn't the same as driving well." He gave Petite a sideways glance, then admitted, "She can move."

My grin was big enough to split my head. I patted Petite proprietorially and beamed some more as Morrison put on his best official-cop face and went back to ransacking Petite's trunk. He didn't ask about the flask of holy water or the wooden stakes. Then he went around to the driver's side, flipped the seat forward, and took out two more completely unexpected items from behind the seat.

The first was a black leather coat, which he shrugged on and magically transformed from Michael Morrison, Seattle police captain, to Mike Morrison, In Need of a Motorcycle and Possibly Not The Boy You Bring Home To Mother, After All. There was suddenly not enough air in the whole world. I got dizzy. Morrison glanced at me and smirked. I blushed. He laughed, and I said, *"Well!"*

"Glad you approve." Then he took the other item out and offered it to me.

My blush turned into something much more profound. The heat rising in me made my heart ache with surprise and joy, and I took what he offered carefully.

My drum. The skin drum given to me by the elders, Carrie Little Turtle included, when I turned fifteen. Aside from Petite, it was easily my most prized possession. Almost two feet across, its thin leather was stretched across a wooden frame. Crossbars were set into the frame's insides, providing a handhold. Feathers and beads trailed from leather strings around the frame's edge, and the images painted onto the drum skin were as bright and vibrant as they'd been nearly thirteen years ago when it had been given to me.

But the peculiar thing was, they had changed. Or one of them had, at least. A raven still arched over two other animals, their orientation giving the drum's circle a top and bottom.

On the left was a rattlesnake, poised to strike. But on the right, for more than a decade, a wolf or a coyote—I'd never been sure which—had faced the rattlesnake. Six months ago the painting had begun to fade and warp like it had been soaked, but the drum itself never lost any of its tension. I hadn't been able to tell what was coming up in the coyote's place, though even I had understood the change indicated a waning of my mentor's influence on me.

Now, though, the image was there, fresh and clear as if it had always been the one painted onto the drum. A praying mantis, long legs folded and heart-shaped face examining the rattlesnake across from it. I touched it cautiously, a little afraid it would smear, though I knew perfectly well it was magic, not paint, staining the leather. I said *Subtle,* inside the confines of my head, and all three of my spirit animals radiated amusement. Most people didn't go around announcing to the world what form their spirit guides took. I guessed I couldn't do anything like most people did, and lifted my smile to Morrison. "Thank you."

He looked incredibly pleased with himself. "I thought you might want it."

"You…" I shook my head, still smiling. I was alternating between having the best and worst moments of my life the past couple weeks, crashing from one to the other with no real warning. Despite the low moments, Morrison's presence and thoughtfulness were pulling everything heavily toward it being the best of times. "You have no idea how badly I've been wanting this. Thank you. You're going to roast in that coat, up in the mountains."

"I'd rather have it in case we're out there all night. Unless you can keep us warm."

My eyebrows did a lascivious waggle, all of their own accord. Morrison laughed, but he had a good point. I went to get my own coat and a backpack while he tucked his gun—Les had left it on Petite's roof—back into its holster.

Ankle-length white leather was even less practical for mountain climbing than Morrison's black bomber jacket. I stared at my new coat, still in love with it but having a moment of vicious practicality regarding the upcoming cost of maintenance on the thing. On the other hand, the only other coat I had with me was the winter-weight parka I'd been wearing when I went to SeaTac two weeks ago, and there was no way I was wearing *that* hiking. Feeling a little silly, I pulled the shotgun holster off and the coat on, wondering if the former would fit over the latter.

To my surprise, it did. I belted the holster and turned around to find Morrison looking at me with much the same stunned gaze I'd delivered unto him a few minutes ago. I ducked my head, self-conscious as he had not been, and studied the toes of my stompy boots as I listened to him cross toward me. He tipped my chin up until I met his eyes, and then with great solemnity, said, "Nice coat."

My discomfort vanished and I laughed aloud. "Did Gary put you up to that?"

"No, why?"

"That's what he said, too, that's all. Thanks. I kind of liked it."

"You look like one of the good guys." Morrison kissed me and went back to Petite, leaving me all but dancing in his wake. The whole point of the coat was to look like a good guy. I felt like I could take on anything if I was projecting the right image.

We were packed up in less than five minutes. My backpack didn't fit all that comfortably over the coat and shotgun holster, but it was better than stuffing my pockets with ammo. I locked Petite, informed the gods that if anything happened to her they would have me to reckon with, and Morrison and I walked into the Appalachian Mountains like a modern-day Lewis and Clark.

We were barely forty feet in before Morrison made a sound of satisfaction and called me over with a crooked finger. Bent grass, broken branches and hints of heel prints were visible, the wights' high-speed escape left its mark. Either that or this *was* the path most people had been taking up to the Nothing Holler, which I suggested to Morrison in apologetic tones. He said, "I think you'd better fill me in," and I did as we hiked up the mountainside.

He didn't interrupt often, once with a "They'd really make it that difficult for Sara because she's a Fed?" that wasn't so much disbelieving as a sigh at the human condition, and later with a quiet "It wasn't your fault, Walker."

"People keep saying that. Doesn't make it any easier to believe." We crested the mountain as I finished catching Morrison up, and there we paused, taking in the view. I loved Seattle and the sharp, ragged Rockies in its distance, but North Carolina's soft old mountains and hazy landscape were welcoming in a way the Pacific Northwest would never seem, to me. I inhaled deeply, and Morrison cast me a cautious look.

"Miss it?"

"More than I realized." After a beat, I recognized the real intent behind the question, and shook my head. "Not enough to come back, except maybe to visit. Too much water under this bridge. I'm pretty dedicated to Seattle at this point."

A flash of regret sang through me as I remembered the expression on my friend and mentor Coyote's face when he'd realized that I really wasn't ever going to give up my cool Seattle street stomping grounds for the heat and wilderness of Arizona. It wasn't a lot of regret, especially with the reasons for my decision standing right here beside me on a low-rolling mountaintop, but the echo of Coyote's fear in Morrison's question brought it to mind. His eyebrows quirked, suggesting he was reading something of my emotions in my face, but I didn't think this was a great time to explain I was thinking about another man. "Trust me, Morrison. I'm coming home with you when this is over."

"Good. The trail goes two directions here. Which one do we take?"

Even I could see there was a reasonably well-beaten path heading off to the east, in which direction lay the Nothing Holler. Sara had not, I thought, tried very hard to find the easier path into the holler.

The other trail was considerably less obvious, only visible if I crouched and squinted at things. "This way. The path less traveled by."

"No one can accuse you of taking anything else." Morrison forged ahead until I caught up, said, "Snakes," and lifted my booted foot in comparison to his shod one. It wasn't so much that I'd come prepared for tromping through viper-infested forests as I'd been wearing my favorite stompy boots when I'd left Seattle. They just happened to go up to the bulge of my calf muscle, which was high enough that most startled snakes would get a fang full of leather instead of flesh.

Morrison blanched and fell behind me. For a while we worked our way up, down, through, around, over, under, and occasionally between valleys, hollers, trees, dells, streams and shrubberies. The wights' path was mostly clear enough to follow, though I called Morrison forward a few times when I wasn't certain. The second or third time I breathed, "What, Boy Scouts?" and he said, "Eagle Scout," without missing a beat.

I laughed. "Of course you were. I'm surprised you're not a troop leader now."

He said, "No kids," in a tone light enough that it was weighty. I narrowly avoided tripping over my own feet as we got started again. It wasn't so much that somebody had to have children themselves to lead Scout troops as clearly that was how Morrison envisioned himself doing it, and that was a thought I hadn't gone anywhere near. And I wasn't going to go any closer to it, either, not now and not for any time in the immediate future.

The sun was overhead before we broke over another crest that lay a whole rich valley out beneath us. A creek not quite big enough to be a river dribbled down the center, visible here and there between breaks in a full-on old-growth forest. The water's song bounced around the valley just enough to be heard when the wind caught it, and the scent of early wildflowers rose up with the buzz of captivated insects. It was as idyllic a setting as I'd ever seen.

Morrison, softly, said, "But if you *insist* on moving back South..." which reminded me of the glimpses I'd had of his inner garden: wilderness, as lush and varied as this place, though much more informed by the Pacific Northwest's landscape. I had miles to go before I caught up with his spiritual development, and I doubted it was something Morrison spent much, if any, conscious time on.

"We'd need a helicopter to get in and out. I don't think I'm man enough to hike three hours each way every time I wanted to go see a movie. Seriously, though, yeah. I can't believe it's not settled. The water must be coming in and out of a cave system, or somebody would have followed it upstream and built a homestead here." I slid the Sight on, wondering if I could get a glimpse of the water system.

Instead a roar of pain and anger rose from the earth, black wiping out the color and life I saw with normal vision. I fell back a step, shocked, and felt Morrison's hand at the small of my back again. Not really supporting me so much as letting me know he was there. I could get used to that.

It took a minute or two for the roar to die down, and even then it didn't disappear, just faded out. I could nearly See that a settlement *had* been made in this valley, once upon a time. Small buildings, cleared spaces, campfires, and children's laughter filled my mind, though I knew they were imaginary. I didn't see ghosts, not the way some people did. But I *could* See the centuries-buried fire circles, the fallen structures of homes and meeting places. The Cherokee had built wattle and daub homes with thatched roofs, previous to Western encroachment. This valley had been home to buildings like those, and to dozens, maybe hundreds, of people. Their bones faded into view the same way the buildings had, buried deep and forgotten by time. Bit by bit I realized the trees weren't actually old-growth, not the way I was thinking. Their roots ran deep, blue strength making concentric rings in the trunks, but they were a couple hundred years old, not centuries on end. One of the fires had burned through the valley, left untended by the dying. Nothing deliberate had happened here, no massacre, no driving the natives out. It had been destroyed through illness, smallpox and influenza carried on blankets and racing ahead of the conquering people.

"No," I said very quietly, "we wouldn't want to live here after all." I shut the Sight down. As I did, something flared at the corner of my vision. I steeled my stomach for a second hit from the death valley and triggered the Sight again, turning north toward the brightness.

Aidan's aura, unmistakable with its broad tangle of colors, and from the frantic pulse to his magic, he was fighting for his life.

CHAPTER THIRTEEN

Three things hit me at once: I could not get there fast enough. No matter what was happening, I simply could not get there fast enough.

I could not throw magic that far, not without at least being able to see my target.

I could not do less than try.

I whispered, "Renee," aloud, and for the first time tried to trigger time-shift magic on purpose.

I had done it before, inadvertently. Done it at Morrison's home, in fact, and therefore his presence at my side boosted my confidence. I had thrown my spirit forward, gone out of body to see what was happening in a room I couldn't get into. I still had no recollection of how my body had caught up to that passage of distance. It had just snapped into focus, catching up somehow, and in retrospect I thought I'd done something a little like folding a square of time. A tesseract.

If Mrs Who could do it, so could I.

I cut free from my body. Distance was irrelevant in the spirit world. It was all about expectations, there. One moment I was beside Morrison and the next I was beside Aidan, whose body language was pure last stand: *they* were going down, or he was.

They were the wights. All five of the remaining ones, whose presence made a sick lurch in the space that was nominally my stomach. There were seven more people back in town who had died in more or less the same way the wights had, by having their lives sucked away through black magic. I should have told Sara to burn those bodies, because I couldn't think of anything else that would guarantee they wouldn't rise like these ones had. I guessed they'd be buried by sundown, but I wasn't at all sure that would be enough. I hoped like hell that once this was over, I would remember to call and tell her that. And that there would be cell phone reception that would let me. And that was the last time I worried about anything but me, Aidan and survival for a little while.

Renee was a firebrand inside my skull, stitching things together with her long sticklike legs. I reached for my sword and remembered two things at once: first, it hadn't been a good weapon against the wights, and second, I was immaterial. I had nothing to hold a sword with.

The attempt to draw magic, though, got the wights' attention. Two, then three of them, moved away from Aidan, drawn by the source of raw energy that was me. My shields were in place, rock-solid, but without a body to house my power in, I blazed all over the landscape, a delicious temptation. I still didn't know how to fight them, and had probably made it worse by de-bodying, but if it was me or Aidan, I much preferred them siphoning off me. Not so much because I was confident of my survival, but because if somebody was going to die here it was not, by God, going to be the twelve-year-old. As the wights closed in on me, I forced myself to think. They were undead. Monsters created by sucking the life force out of others, as they had none left of their own.

The question, then, was what happened if I sucked the power out of *them*.

The wiser part of my brain suggested it would be nothing good, but I didn't see a lot of choice in the matter. I extended my hands and waggled my fingers like they were tasty energy sausages, and the wights pounced.

This time I let them land. I kept my shields in place, kept them ratcheted up to full power, and I scrambled for mental imagery that would let me try turning the whammy on the wights. Draining things wasn't so hard. Oil tanks, gas lines, even air from tires. The thing they all had in common was a valve of some kind.

I didn't much want to use the most common human drainage valve for this particular experiment. I settled for sticking my fingers into the mouth of the nearest wight, and imagining an oil tank releasing its black gooey contents onto the ground.

The good news was they had no shields at all. Nothing prevented me from doing as I imagined.

The bad news was its corrupted life force came out *exactly* as I imagined, as horrible stench-ridden sticky black goo. I shouted in disgust. It would have been more effective with a voice, but it made shock waves anyway, magic reverberating against the air. The wight pulled backward, screaming. Black oil stretched from it to my fingers, thickening instead of thinning. Its life drained away, corruption skimming down my ethereal arms and searching for ways in.

It weighed a tremendous amount. I'd mostly had experience with things trying to kill me. Attempts at corruption had been relatively subtle, but there was nothing subtle about this. It coated me, growing stickier and more alarming as it rushed over my torso and toward my face. The wight I was draining kept screaming even as it faded, but there was a vicious tri-

umph in its cold eyes as it screamed. I started to get the idea
that I had once more made a terrible mistake. I wasn't turboed
up like I'd been before, but possibly leaving my body behind
and attacking a bunch of soul-sucking monsters while one of
my spirit animals was going great guns working magic inside
my head had not been all that well thought out.

I wished for the umpteenth time that someone had given me
a goddamned handbook, and then I put that thought to bed
forever, because I'd gotten this far without one and I wasn't
dead yet. I could hold on through this. I could take on every
inch, every ounce, every spot of nastiness these things had,
and when they'd poured it all onto me I could wrap it up in
a big shining blue-and-silver bow, and obliterate it. All I had
to do was hang on while they gnawed and pierced and did
their best to get inside me. I shut my eyes, sealed my mouth,
did my best to pinch my nostrils together. No access. I was a
seal, with crazy ear flaps that kept water out.

Rattler stirred at the base of my skull. I hastily assured him
I did not want to actually turn into a seal right then. He settled again, and I stuck with the imagery. Nothing was going
to get inside me, and I was going to suck these bastards dry.
The first one's howl began to lose confidence, like it had believed it would break through and then have all of my potential for its pickings. My own confidence picked up. I could do
it. I was *going to* do it, one at a time or all of the rest of them
at once, I didn't care, and then Aidan wouldn't have to fight
a battle nobody his age should be seeing. A kind of *give-me-
your-best-shot* triumph crashed through me.

So did a freight train's worth of white magic.

Every ounce of my attention had been wrapped up in the
wights. I had nothing left to keep my metaphorical feet on
the ground. Aidan's power slammed me backward into the
forest. Bark and bugs and leaves and twigs smeared through

my spirit and my impression of the world, and only gradually slowed me down. Six months ago they'd have stopped me cold, because my consciousness would have accepted them as totally solid, the kind of thing a body would crash into and slither down. Now not only could I register them as ephemeral, but also myself.

Under other circumstances I might have been proud of myself for that change of belief. Under these ones, I wished I hadn't come quite so far in accepting the new way my world worked, because it left me thirty trees back from Aidan and the wights as they went into a throw-down.

I'd lost the one into whose mouth I'd shoved my fingers. The muck connecting us had been vaporized, sparks of it still lingering in the air. I got myself heading the right direction again and shot back to the fight.

All five wights had risen into the air, bodies arched with exultation. Near-white magic danced between them, sucked out of Aidan at an impossible speed. I was close enough now to shield him, and threw a wall of magic between him and the undead.

Or I tried, anyway. I didn't know if he felt it coming or if my timing was just excruciatingly bad, but in the half an instant between throwing the magic and it manifesting, his power changed. He wrenched it back from the wights with brute strength that even I admired, rechanneled it and threw it like a massive missile, intent on destroying the wights. I squeaked, but it was too late.

Aidan's magic backfired. I knew exactly what it felt like, because I'd had it happen myself. He was a healer, and healing magic had strong opinions about being weaponized. I was astonished it hadn't happened when he bowled me over, but my guess was that had been solely intended to save me, not damage the wights. Magic, the living stuff of the soul, had a sense of the intent behind its use. Violently saving somebody was borderline okay. Taking the fight to the bad guys was something else. That was why my own path had been such a tricky one to get right. I hoped Aidan would never have to walk it. But right now he was dangerously close to trying, and I watched his magic roll up and shut down.

For what I bet was the first time in his life, his spiritual presence became quite ordinary, if spiked with fear. I Saw him struggling to call the magic again, and watched it retreat deeper into him, until there was nothing left but a scared kid.

A scared kid with a black mark on his soul.

Renee finished her work, and my body surged through time and space, slamming my spirit back into place. It rattled my teeth, but not my vision.

With all his magic tamped down, I could See the streak of darkness that had lodged in Aidan's center. It was a small scar, but it sizzled and stung like cold iron melting magic away. It was growing fast, like his magic had been holding it in place and it now suddenly had room to expand. I took a half dozen running steps, my hands alight with power, though I already knew it wasn't an infection I could simply wipe away. I would have to go into his garden—be *invited* into his garden, after the fuss I'd made yesterday—and we would have to tackle that growing corruption together.

Two steps away from him, the wights threw down a thunderous wall of magic that cut me off from Aidan entirely. I bounced off, shocked, and shot a look upward. They were gathered together, cannibalizing the magic that sustained them in order to build a funnel between themselves and Aidan. The black mark inside him expanded exponentially, seizing his retreating magic and bending it to its own will.

I slammed my sword into existence and bashed it against the cascading magic, but its strength called on exactly the same things that had made me vulnerable to my mother's power: in

Ireland, Mom's magic had known mine well enough to break in. Here, Aidan's magic knew mine well enough to keep it out. And I was unaccustomed to forcing myself in where I wasn't wanted, magically. I doubted it had been high on Mom's list of honed talents, either, but she had, after all, been one of the bad guys when she did it to me.

I was not one of the bad guys, but the power draw was reaching a crescendo. If I didn't act now, something bad was going to happen, and I didn't even have enough imagination to wonder what. I whispered, "Sorry, kid," and let my spirit go a second time.

This time I dove deep, as deep into the mountain as I could go, then turned tail and began scrambling back toward the surface, but on the other side of the magic pouring from the sky. I was a mouse, a badger, a wombat, any digging thing. The images were familiar to me from my first journeys into my garden, but this time I was digging my way toward Aidan's. He could be righteously furious and I could be properly apologetic later. Right now we had bigger problems, and the only way to defeat them was from the inside out.

I focused on the black streak consuming Aidan, aiming for it. Within seconds, I burst through the surface on the inside of the wights' casting of magic.

Aidan's eyes were black and soulless, his mouth contorted with wicked glee. He raised one hand, calling on power. I redoubled my shields, even though he shouldn't be able to throw any more magic around, and was glad I did. The blow that hit me had the Master's strength behind it, cold and enraged and viciously satisfied all at once. It was diluted, compared to what he'd thrown at me in Ireland, but there was no mistaking the source of power. I skidded backward but kept my feet, cementing the belief that the Master was weaker than he'd been. In Ireland he'd sliced and diced me for the fun of it, and I hadn't been able to raise a finger against him, much less shield myself.

Unasked for, a bunch of pieces fell into place. We'd pretty well knocked the Master around the block, in Ireland. We'd slain his dragon, wiped out his banshees, killed the banshee queen, destroyed the Morrígan, and then punched a bunch of holes in him and sent him scurrying back to his realm to lick his wounds. And when I said "we" I mostly meant my mother, Gary and Méabh, the warrior queen of Connacht, because during a lot of that activity I'd been busy taking it in the teeth. Perhaps I could consider myself the sacrificial lamb, hanging out to get everybody's attention while my allies did the heavy lifting, but really I just thought they'd saved my bacon a lot.

But put it all together, and we *had* dealt the Master some serious blows. He'd used the banshees for blood rituals and power collection, and we'd cut that source off. He'd barely been fed in the past thirty years, and had to be going mad with hunger. The wights were power siphons, not such a far cry from the banshees, only without hundreds of years of practice behind them. I still didn't think it was coincidence it had come home to North Carolina, but it seemed likely he was scrambling to rebuild his power base. Anything we did to draw the line here meant he would be weaker yet, and for me, planning to face him down, that was a good thing.

So I did not fight back. Not for a lot of reasons, the primary one being I had no wish to risk Aidan any further. But also because any active magic I used could be sucked down and used to power up the wights, whereas if I could keep them pouring out the strength they'd taken from Aidan, they might just burn themselves out. It was a dangerous gamble with Aidan's life, but I was confident of being able to keep that, at least, together. I did, quietly, say, "C'mon, kid. Let me in." I was three steps away. If he would invite me into his garden, we could stamp out the stain building in him.

The stain, though, was very dark and strong by now, though it had only been growing a few seconds. I could See glimpses of his spirit animals, torn with agitation as they fought with, and gradually for, the darkness overtaking him. Two of them were familiar: a raven and a walking stick. I said, "Screw this," considerably more loudly, and then, "Raven?" in a normal tone.

He erupted from my shoulders like flights of angels. In the magic-rich environment, he was less a concept and more of a bird, weight to his wings instead of just the beautiful tendrils of light that he often manifested as. "Go talk to him," I said, and he chortled and darted toward Aidan.

The wall of magic leapt over me, compressing around Aidan. I snapped back into my body. Raven dove, quick and desperate, and I saw a flash of Aidan's walking stick leaping like it was trying to connect with my spirit bird.

Instead, it hit the shrinking wall of magic, and time flexed.

Everything turned rubbery, including my legs. The air rippled, starting with Aidan and rushing out at great speed. It felt nothing like my train wreck through time in Ireland, but I was convinced something similar was happening. Maybe the difference was I had Renee along to smooth out the bumps.

Or maybe the difference was that the twelve-year-old epicenter of the quake had *his* spirit walking stick along, and it had a much clearer idea of how to surf time than I did. Aidan's eyes were entirely black and his expression was one of unholy delight. I shrieked for Renee and dug my heels in, throwing everything I had at the idea of staying put in time.

The world ripped apart, shock waves redoubling around us, then expanding out in a pulse faster than the eye could see. Almost faster than I could See, for that matter: a leading edge of discoloration showed me where it was headed, and gave the impression that it was picking up speed and intent as it rolled. Whatever the time wave wanted, *I* did *not* want it leaving the valley. There was enough sorrow and pain for the wights to feed on in this protected haven. The idea of what they, hooked into Aidan's magic, might be able to do with the world outside the valley didn't bear thinking about.

I forgot about rescuing Aidan and threw everything I had at the mountainous borders of the valley. It was too far, just like Aidan had been too far, but I was desperate. Shields flickered in the distance, gunmetal faint against the blue sky. They were weak. Feeble, because raw cosmic power or no, a valley was a lot of territory to cover, and I lacked confidence in being able to do it. I saw the power surge roll toward them like a tsunami, and braced myself.

It hit, wobbled, and passed through. A huge amount of magic rolled back at me, caught by the shields, but some of it kept going. I had no idea what that meant in terms of the world outside this valley. Within it, the trees bent until they snapped, splinters erupting into the air. Birds and animals shrieked. So did I, for that matter, ducking and flinging my arms over my head. Branches and falling trees bounced off my shields, pummeling me. When the destruction finally stopped, I lifted my head, eyes wide.

Aidan was gone. The wights were gone. A village stood around me instead, men and women frozen in their activities and staring at me. Cherokee men and women, wearing traditional leather clothing: pants, tunics. A few women wore woven shirts from some fiber I didn't recognize. They were all barefoot in the spring weather. I felt overdressed.

And for some reason, that thought reminded me of Morrison.

CHAPTER FOURTEEN

My first impulse was to run like hell back to the other end of the valley, where I'd left the love of my life just before hauling a chunk of real estate somewhere else in time. My second and third impulses were pretty much the same, but by that time the locals had worked through their first, second and third impulses, too.

Some of them threw down what they were carrying and ran shrieking. Others fell down and pressed their faces to the earth. One decided the only smart thing to do was shoot me.

Despite being on the wrong end of the arrow, I kinda liked him for it. The arrow *spanged* off my shields, which made several more people fall down. I decided discretion was the better part of valor and started backing away. There was a creek around here somewhere. No doubt if I fell in it I could get myself far enough downstream to not threaten these people, which made me wonder if my vaccinations were recent enough for it to be safe for me to even be breathing near them. I wondered if Aidan's were, since he probably had at least one more set of them due before adulthood arrived. I would *not,* God damn it, permit myself, Aidan or Morrison, whose vaccinations I was confident were up-to-date, be the carriers for every disease that smeared across the Americas post-European-contact. Even if I had to single-handedly heal every living soul on the continent, I would not let that happen.

For one crazy heart-lurching moment I wondered if that was even possible. Probably not without killing myself, but it was one of those closed time loops anyway: the Native American population had largely not survived European contact, therefore I had not gone through healing millions of people. I still had another heart-fluttery moment where I held on to the idea, imagining how the world might look on my end of time if I'd managed to somehow effectively vaccinate a continent's worth of people against the diseases that were coming to wipe them out.

The timeline was not that flexible, and I knew it. If I managed something like that I would end up returning to a future that was nothing like the one I'd come from. Alternate worlds. I knew the potential for them existed: I'd seen too many of the paths I hadn't taken roll out before me to doubt it. And much as I'd like to see a world where American natives rose up as a major power, I didn't want to lose the life I had, either. The timeline would have to remain as it was.

I fell into the creek about then, and despaired for my white leather coat.

The creek turned out to be more of a river, in this day and age. It snatched me up and tossed me downstream. Another arrow or two came flying my way, but they had a sense of *"Yeah! And stay away!"* about them, rather than real threat. I got knocked and buffeted around, shields keeping me from any dangerous injuries, and after a while hit a shallow enough stretch that I was able to fling myself out of the water. Dripping and battered, I scrambled out of my coat and held it up to see how badly damaged it was.

It wasn't torn, scraped, stretched, bruised or marked up. In fact, although I was soaked to the skin and had water pouring from my hair into my eyes, it wasn't even wet. The only water on it was where my hands clutched its shoulders, and there, it beaded and rolled away. I boggled at it, then turned the Sight on, searching for an explanation.

Apparently the coat was taking on the properties of superhero outfits, which never seemed to get shredded when heroes ran off at supersonic speeds or got shot up by the moron of the week. It had some shielding of its own, a faint shimmer of gunmetal. My subconscious evidently did not intend to let another Morrígan shred the coat's sleeves again, or indeed to allow my clumsiness to soak and ruin the leather. I was deeply, deeply grateful for my subconscious, and also very slightly resentful that it didn't think the rest of me was worth keeping dry. Especially since I couldn't think of a way to use the magic to dry myself after the fact. At least I wasn't coated in glitter anymore. Muttering, I put the coat back on and looked around, trying to get my bearings.

Morrison and I had come into the valley close to its southern end. The village site had been closer to the northern end. I was somewhere in the middle now, and Aidan was nowhere to be seen. Neither were the wights, which was something, at least. Not a good something, but something. I wished I knew what year it was, then straightened up. *Renee?*

It is before the time of tears.

Before the time of tears. The Trail of Tears. The Cherokee had been forcibly relocated in 1838, but they were the last of the Five Civilized Nations to be moved. The first had gone in 1831. But the people I'd seen didn't look like they'd had any European contact. They were isolated, so it was possible they'd just been overlooked, but I asked *how* long *before the time of tears?*

She sighed. I supposed eternal bugs were not deeply concerned with the piddling details of human history. After some consideration, she said, *The sickness has only begun to come,* which I thought might narrow it down to somewhere in the late 1600s, but could be as early as 1493, for all I knew. I still said, "Thanks," out loud, then sighed as deeply as Renee had. "I don't suppose you know where Aidan went."

My sister is distant. The path between us is dark. She is ill. Perhaps dying.

My heart went into triple time. "Does that mean Aidan's dying? Raven?" He was the expert on life and death, after all. He *klok-klok'd* a couple of times and gave a shiver of wings, leaving the impression that no, it didn't necessarily mean Aidan was dying, but it meant Aidan was certainly not well. I restrained myself from saying I could've figured that out without help. I tried to calm my heartbeat, and put the question of Aidan aside for a moment.

"What about Morrison? Renee, did he… Did we… Did everything in this valley slide come loose from time?" It had sure felt like it. I wasn't at all certain things beyond the valley hadn't also come loose, but that was more than I could deal with right now. Renee nodded complacently and I let go a shuddering breath. Morrison was here somewhere. He was not dead, lost, eaten or any of the other potential bad things that could have happened in a time slip. I just had no way to contact him.

I couldn't help taking my phone from my pocket and checking for a signal, just in case. There wasn't one, of course, nor was there any other sign of life from the damned thing, because it, like me, had gotten soaked in the river. I wished for a cup of rice, then realized I had salt in my backpack. Wet salt, which would do me no good.

My stomach clenched with sudden hope. I also had the shotgun and a small pack of live ammo. I slithered the holster off, checked the gun over, then unloaded the packed salt ammo and replaced it with shotgun cartridges. I didn't want to go hunting. I just wanted to make a really big, very modern noise in a quiet preindustrial valley. If Morrison was out there, he could respond in kind. And then if he had any sense he'd stay put. Actually, if I had any sense, I'd stay put, because Morrison clearly had a lot more woods know-how than I did, but it was pretty much a given that I had no sense. I raised the shotgun, sighted, and blew a hole the size of my fist in a hickory tree about twenty feet away.

The report sounded roughly like the fall of Jericho. It would have been loud even in the modern day, with the distant but discernible drone of airplanes and car engines as part of the background noise. Here, now, with nothing but the wind and birds, it was terrifying, and that was speaking as the person who'd caused it. I staggered a bit with the gun's kick, lowered it, and rubbed my shoulder.

An answering pistol shot cracked the air. I howled triumph, thrusting the shotgun at the sky like a rebel leader, and did a dance of relief. Then I packed everything up, slung the coat and pack on, and headed south along the riverbank. Maybe Morrison would think to come down to the water. It was the easiest meeting point for two people who had no way to communicate.

I'd gotten almost no distance at all when another sound ricocheted through the valley. It wasn't nearly as loud as the gunshots, but much steadier and quite sharp, like rocks being knocked together. I stopped, ears perked, and listened.

Dat dat dat dat. Brief pause. *Dat.* Longer pause. *Dat.* Another longer pause. *Dat.* Another longer pause. *Dat,* brief pause, *dat,* long pause. *Dat,* long pause, *dat dat.* Considerably longer pause. *Dat,* long pause, *dat dat.* It went on like that while I stared helplessly up the mountains.

Of course Morrison knew Morse code. *Of course* he did. *Of course* he would try to communicate with me that way. Except I knew the same two letters in Morse code that everybody else in the world did, S and O, dot dot dot and dash dash dash, and that was the sum total of my knowledge. He banged out an O, but one letter out of several was not enough to illuminate his meaning. Feeling helpless, frustrated and remarkably uninformed, I started down the river again. Morrison kept banging away for a while, including a pause long enough to suggest he was wiping the slate clean and starting over, and then did the whole thing a second, then a third, time. Then he went silent, either waiting for my response or assuming I'd understood and was doing as he'd instructed.

Or possibly murdered horribly by natives led to his location by his activities, but I was fairly certain murdered horribly would be accompanied by at least some gunshots, so I stuck with my previous assumptions and made my way south as fast as I could. At least I might be able to get some sense of where we'd been, and head up the mountain from there, hopefully to locate him. I'd pick up some rocks of my own when I thought I was far enough south, and start playing Marco Polo.

As far as I could tell, no one from the settlement had chosen to follow me. That was a relief. We had enough to worry about without adding potentially, and understandably, hostile natives to the mix. *Renee, can you get us back home?*

I can guide you. The power is yours alone.

I'd gotten used to Raven's playfulness and Rattler's snarky tongue. I was not prepared for a pedantic spirit animal. I shifted my eyebrows upward in a sort of snooty *ooh-la-la* response, and had the distinct impression a bug glared at me from the inside of my own head. Well, as long as between the two of us we could get home, I wasn't going to worry about that aspect too much. Finding Morrison and Aidan could take top priority. I stopped a few times to drink from the river, wondering vaguely what kinds of interesting bugs were in it, and whether healing magic would flush them out or if I should be boiling this stuff. I guessed I'd find out.

I heard it before I saw it, a soft crashing through the woods. There were still deer and the occasional report of mountain lions in the Appalachians in my time, so I slipped behind a tree and stood as quietly as I could, waiting to see what would burst out of the trees. I was hoping for a puma, since I'd never seen one, when Morrison stepped out of the branches. He had a wary hand near his gun, and an intent expression on his face. I squeaked and whispered, "Morrison!"

His shoulders visibly relaxed and he moved his hand away from his gun. I scooted around the tree and hugged him as he said, "Walker. Thank God you understood me. I didn't know if you knew Morse," into my shoulder.

"I don't. What did you tell me to do?"

"Head downriver." He set me back, hands on my shoulders and his eyes as disturbed as I'd ever seen them. "Where the hell did you *go?*"

"Oh. I was doing that anyway. I hoped you might think of it, too." I frowned. "Where did I go? Downriver, just like you sa—"

"You disappeared, Walker. You turned north, your face went blank, and a few seconds later you…I don't know what happened." The strain in his face came out in his voice. "The air rippled. Not as badly as it did later, but it rippled and the sun jumped in the sky. I don't know how much time I lost. But from the moment the air changed, you were gone. I saw your magic for a few seconds. I don't know what it was doing, but it looked wrong. Dangerous. Like you stretched and snapped away. What the hell happened?"

Watching him try to maintain composure put stepping out of time on my short list of things to never do again, certainly not in front of a witness. I hadn't thought about what it would look like, or what might happen to people moving through normal time while I took a shortcut. I suspected losing a few minutes was the least awful potential side effect, and that much, much worse ones could be in store. I'd cut maybe a couple of hours of travel time by doing the leapfrog. If I'd skipped a century, the ripple might have turned Morrison to dust.

It is likely, Renee said, and I pressed my fists to my mouth, feeling sick.

"I was in a hurry," I whispered behind my hands. "Aidan was fighting the wights. I had to get to him. I'm sorry." I was not about to explain how badly I could have screwed him up, but I would never, ever do it again. "I'm sorry."

Morrison, bless him, accepted the apology with a nod and cut to the important business: "Did you save him?"

My shoulders slumped. "No. He tried saving me, instead, and the wights got hold of his magic. And I think I didn't get him shielded well enough yesterday. I think the Executioner left a mark on him, and once the wights plugged into that…"

"That's what happened with the valley? With the shock wave? I saw your power again—why can I see it now?"

"I don't think you can, mostly. But it takes on a visible element sometimes. When I'm using a lot at once."

Morrison looked relieved, which seemed fair enough. He wasn't magically adept himself, and for all that he'd taken my gifts in very good stride, I doubted a lifetime of being able to see my magic at work was really what he'd had planned. "You were trying to stop that ripple. What was it?"

"A time-quake." It was a terrible, stupid word, but I didn't have a better one. "The Nothing, I told you it was born from the genocides on this continent, right? Right. It wanted to open that up, spread it around the modern day. And it turns out Walkingsticks—my family—have an affinity for sliding through time. So getting their claws into Aidan may have let them rip a hole open right back to the source."

Morrison closed his eyes a moment. I all but heard him going through his paces, working his way around to being able to say, "Are you telling me we've traveled through time?"

"Um. Yeah."

He opened his eyes again, expression very steady and eyes very blue. "To when?"

"I don't know exactly. Somewhen between 1492 and 1831."

"That's a lot of time, Walker."

"I know. Probably more on the 1492 end, but...your vaccinations are up-to-date, right?" He gave me a look and I mumbled, "I thought so, but I had to ask. My spirit animal says it's before the sickness came, but I'm not sure how much sense of human time scale she really has."

The corner of his mouth twitched. He pulled his hand over it, wiping the smile away, but it crept back into place. "You realize you sound insane."

"Me? You're the one who told me when I called and woke you up at 3:00 a.m. that I shouldn't worry about my cell phone not working when I tried calling Gary, since he had been lost in time. I might sound crazy, but you've adapted to it. You adapted faster than I did."

"Walker, after working with Holliday for four years, when you turned up with magic it was either accept it or leave the job. If you and I are here, why isn't Aidan?"

"I don't know. Every time I've gone hopping through time I've stayed in the same place physically." Except that wasn't true, as manifestly demonstrated just a few short hours ago, when I'd skipped through both time and space in my attempt to rescue Aidan. "Shit." I stepped away, looking up the river like there would be answers somewhere in the soft haze. "Aidan's magic opened the time loop, but if the wights or the Executioner were in control, then they may have focused on another location. Somewhere they could suck up a lot of power, pain and death. Then all they would have to do is go home again and release it."

"What would that do?"

"Bad things. Humans are like rats in cages anyway. It doesn't take much to set us off. If you dumped a continent's worth of pain and anger on top of our high-tension lives already, I'd think we'd be looking at riots and murder in the streets."

"Is that how it happens?" Morrison sounded genuinely curious, enough so that I looked back and wrinkled my nose.

"I don't know. Maybe sometimes. Mostly it's probably just natural reaction, something getting pushed a little too far and society breaking down. But it doesn't take all that much to break it down, so if thousands of people were pushed just a little bit further than usual thanks to black magic with cruel intent behind it, then yeah, I think it could happen that way. We're susceptible, and there are people and things out there who want to take advantage of that."

"To what end?" Morrison shrugged when I frowned at him. "Criminals want something, Walker. To lash out, to have something they don't, to protect someone, to prove themselves. They're like anyone else, right? They want something. What do spirits or monsters *want?*"

"Freedom." The word popped out before I thought about it, but that gave me some confidence in it. "The freedom to inflict pain or increase their power. That's what Herne wanted, to take Cernunnos's place at the head of the Wild Hunt. Immortality, freedom from mortal shackles, whatever you want to call it. Power. Virissong wanted the same thing. When he couldn't get power in his earthly guise he…" I waved my hand, indicating I used the next words loosely. "He sold his soul to the Devil and became a sorcerer. He got trapped in the Lower World and wanted out to pursue the gain of power in the Middle World. All of them, everybody who's walking to the Master's beat, that's what they want. Dominance over a subjected world. A lot of them don't seem to realize they're just stepping stones, doing things that nourish the Master. Or maybe they don't care."

"The Master."

"My enemy." It sounded equally preposterous and resigned. "He's a death magic. Maybe *the* death magic. I don't know. He almost took Cernunnos out a while back, and Cernunnos is a god. I hadn't thought anything killed gods."

"Heroes do."

For some reason that made my heart hiccup. I wet my lips and shook my head. "He's not a hero. Death is necessary. I don't like it, but I understand it. Cruelty, power mongering, murder, hatred…I have to believe we could get by without those things. That they're what feeds something like the Master. If he was just about death, fine, I wouldn't like it, but I'd see why he was necessary. But Cernunnos is a death god, Morrison. He rides to collect the souls of his faithful. He has a purpose. He provides sanctuary and guidance to his followers. The Master might give his minions a task, but it's always to his own empowerment. He's reductive. Everything he takes is at a cost to another, like he's stomping out the light just because he can.

"I can't defeat him." I wasn't kidding myself about that. I

put my palm on a nearby tree, feeling the life in it. "I can't go around the world and clear out the pettiness and hatred and entrenched warfare from every single person. Even if I could, unless we all attained some kind of mystical enlightenment, I'd imagine the whole cycle would start over again. But I *can* kick him in the teeth. That's what my family does, apparently. We keep kicking him, and every time we do, I guess maybe it makes a little more space for light in the world. Seems to me like that's worth it."

"You're a romantic, Walker." Morrison folded his hand over mine on the tree trunk, then folded me into his arms.

I snorted. "Yeah, but don't tell anybody. Anyway, so if I want to stomp him down, I guess what he wants is to wipe me out, too. This is a generational thing. If he can wipe out my family, either side, both sides, of it, then he's got that much more room to spread misery and pain around the world."

"So it's personal."

I breathed laughter. "Yeah, I guess so. God." I straightened, horrified. "God, Morrison, is my family *causing* this? I mean, I know he's been trying to get at me since before I was born. What if having us to focus on is keeping him going?"

"What if having you to focus on is keeping him from wreaking havoc somewhere else? That's not something you can tackle, Walker. All we can do right now is find Aidan and fix this thing. So. How do we find Aidan?"

Any hope of answering that was wrested away as two dozen Cherokee warriors melted out of the forest and made it very clear that we, like kids playing cowboys, had been captured by Indians.

CHAPTER FIFTEEN

Morrison breathed, "Walker..." and I said, "Stay calm," just
as softly. Realistically, between my shields and our weapons,
even two dozen warriors couldn't hold us. They had no idea
how badly they were outnumbered, and I had a gut-deep re-
luctance to show them. "We're not in any danger. Be cool."

Morrison's chin tucked in and he shot me a disbelieving
sideways look. That was as far as it went, though. He even
very cautiously raised his hands, as did I, in what I hoped was
not only a universal, but also a time-honored way of saying,
"Look, Ma, no threat."

Our captors' dark eyes all immediately focused on the pistol exposed by the movement of Morrison's coat, and on the
heavier shift of my back holster and shotgun. One of the men
took a step forward. I snapped, *"Thla!"*—no in Cherokee.

I could not have shocked him more if I had turned green

and sprouted feathers. He froze, staring at me, and the entire group started jabbering at once.

My Cherokee was not good. I was badly out of practice to begin with, and in these circumstances, literally out of date. I got the gist of what they were saying, but hell, so did Morrison, who had no Cherokee language at all. The gist was "How the hell does this woman—is it a woman with that weird short hair? Yes, it's a woman, you idiot, how the hell does this woman with her ugly weird clothes and ugly short hair and ugly pale skin know the language of the People? Hell if I know! Ask her!"

I stammered through "I'm of the People, of a far-away tribe," to expressions of growing disbelief. One of them said something to the effect of, "You speak the language of the People poorly."

I nodded in embarrassment. I would no doubt speak it poorly by their standards anyway, given that the language had almost certainly changed over the past few hundred years, but my lack of fluency made it a lot worse. I wished to hell I could reach back in time and waken the depth of immersion speech I'd had when I was about eight. There'd been a year or so there when Dad and I spoke almost exclusively Cherokee, until I turned into a brat and started refusing. I wanted to kick my younger self, which was not an unusual sentiment for me. This time, however, I had Renee, and gave her a hopeful mental poke. Not so much for the kicking myself, but maybe for the awakening long-dormant language memories.

She gave me a priss-mouthed look, but then she slipped into what felt like a meditative state, as if she was centering herself to bring up what I needed. I whispered, *Thank you,* and in the meantime tried scraping together what I did remember on my own. "We're lost."

A snicker that was pure body language and no sound at all

ran around our group of captors. I muttered and tried again. "I'm a shaman—"

Suspicion and clarification settled on them in equal parts. It wasn't particularly couth, in my mental image of things, to go around announcing one was a healer, and I thought they might feel similarly. People who actually claimed to be shamans were possibly more likely to be sorcerers. On the other hand, the expected unexpectedness displayed by a shaman probably went a long way toward explaining my bizarre costuming.

The next round of rapid speech went completely over my head. It ended with the spokesman pointing interrogatively at Morrison as a headache began pounding behind my left eye. I had understood Méabh, who had stepped out of the other end of time speaking ancient Irish. I had understood Lugh and Nuada and I understood Cernunnos, none of whom spoke English as a matter of course. I had no idea why I couldn't understand these men.

Except I hadn't been able to understand my cousin Caitríona and Méabh when they'd *both* started speaking Irish. The magic translator had shorted out somehow then.

And I spoke Cherokee. Not a lot, but apparently enough for the magic to figure I was okay on my own. It took everything I had not to clutch my head and rattle it in frustration. Instead, I hissed, "Can you understand them?" to Morrison, who nodded in rightful bewilderment.

It would not help our case for me to stomp around in circles shouting imprecations at myself and my magic. Instead I took the deepest, most calming breath I could, and suggested, "You talk to them, then."

"*Me?*"

"Just try, Morrison. I think they'll be able to understand

you. It's this sort of field effect. It worked with Caitríona and Méabh in Ireland, anyway."

Morrison's expression suggested *I* had begun speaking a foreign language, but he turned to the Cherokee spokesman and said, "No. I'm her companion, a…" He shot me another look, obviously wondering if shamans typically had handlers who helped keep their feet on the ground.

They didn't, as far as I knew. The spokesman, however, didn't seem to think a handler was a particularly strange thing for me to have. He spoke again, rapidly. Morrison's shoulders went back and this time the look he cast at me was faintly alarmed. "No. Yes? I don't know. Walker, they want to know if we've been touched by the gods, if that's why we look so pale. If I say no are they going to kill us?"

"They're not able to kill us." That, at least, I was firm on. "And tell them no, pale-skinned people aren't gods, they just come from far away."

"Are you trying to change history, Walker?"

"Yes. I'll let you know if it works."

Morrison made a sound of actual amusement and said exactly what I'd said, in English, except the Cherokee spokesman understood him when he clearly hadn't understood me. I wanted to hop up and down with frustration. Magic was *stupid*. Cool and awesome and amazing, but also *stupid*. Morrison and the spokesman exchanged several sentences, including mine and Morrison's names, and—this much I caught—the spokesman's, as well. He was Gawonii, and I was beginning to think he was the guy smart and brave enough to have shot at me.

"They think they should take us back to talk to their shaman. What do you think?"

"I think it won't…" I stopped, then reconsidered. "I was gonna say I think it won't get us any closer to finding Aidan, but I could be wrong. Just because I can't track magic doesn't mean their shaman can't. Ask if they've seen any other new-comers. No, never mind, if they'd seen those wights they'd be trying to kill us, not talk to us. Yeah. Tell them we would be honored to meet their shaman."

That, at least, was a right thing to say. Two dozen satis-fied Cherokee warriors formed up around us, and marched us three hours upstream down the river I'd just followed down-stream. It was late afternoon by the time we got back to the village, and now that we were safely captive, every single per-son turned out to give us a once-over.

The children thought we were hysterical. They darted be-tween the warriors, snatching at my coat and Morrison's jeans, tugging at shoelaces and making quick grabs at our gun hol-sters. Morrison smacked one kid's enterprising hand as it got too close to his pistol. The boy yelped, then skittered back with the air of a child uncertain if he should be infuriated or thrilled. He, after all, had *actually touched* one of the strang-ers, which I figured had to be worth quite a lot of street cred.

The adults were equally curious, but far more wary. The men escorting us said what they knew about us—that much I could follow—and it was clear many of them weren't cer-tain if they believed we weren't gods or spirits of some kind. I wasn't sure if claiming we weren't helped or hurt us, but I did know for damned sure I was not going to reinforce the idea by agreeing to it.

The deeper we got into the village, the older the crowd be-came. There weren't nearly as many elders as I expected, and it was clear the younger men and women were fiercely pro-tective of them. Finally the gathering split, revealing a woman whose presence was so powerful that if she'd been carved of stone and unable to move, I wouldn't have been surprised.

She was strong-boned, her hair threaded with white, and if she had been beautiful in her youth it had faded into something more enduring than beauty. Rock seemed more bending than she, and oaks more swayable. She stood with an alacrity that belied the weight of stone within her, and made chattering sounds to shoo our warrior escort back. They scampered like children, losing none of their dignity as they did so, and the medicine woman stalked a slow circle around us. More than stalked: I didn't need to trigger the Sight to feel the power she laid down, creating a barrier with her will alone. It rang of keeping things in, and I did not want to test my mettle against it.

"You are strong with spirits," she said to me, and to my shock I understood. Renee clicked with satisfaction and I sent a wave of gratitude toward her, then nodded as respectfully as I could at the ancient shaman. She sniffed and stalked around us the other direction, but she certainly wasn't lifting the power circle. If anything she was strengthening it with a counterpart, walking widdershins to her first and redoubling the magic flexing through. I'd never seen anyone do that before, and didn't dare call up the Sight to take a good look at it. I honestly had no idea what would happen if I started pulling down power within the confines of her circle. I didn't think it would end well for me.

When she'd completed the second circle she stood in front of us, arms folded and scowl magnificent. Better than anything the Almighty Morrison had ever thrown at me, and he'd come up with some doozies over the years. "You do not belong here," she informed me, with exactly the right inflection to suggest I had better get explaining, Or Else.

I genuinely did not want to find out what her Or Else constituted, and equally genuinely didn't think I could convince her with anything less than the truth. "I'm a Walkingst—"

She cut me off with a motion so sharp I actually felt a slice of power touch my throat, numbing my vocal cords. "Use the language of the People."

Jesus. I glanced nervously at Morrison and muttered, "Can you understand me when I speak Cherokee?" in that language. His expression went carefully blank and I ground my teeth. In English, I said, "Sorry. She wants me to use Cherokee and I don't know how to make the magic translate so you understand."

"We have bigger fish to fry, Walker. Talk to her."

There were a thousand reasons I loved that man, but his determined practicality had to be in the top ten. I gave him a grateful and perhaps slightly soppy smile, then turned back to the elder.

Her black eyes were sparkling, and I had the distinct impression she'd understood us. If I ever got hold of whoever made shamanic translation magic work, I was going to eat their brains until I understood it all. Speaking slowly, because even if my memory of the language had resurfaced, the centuries had still changed it, I said, "I will speak the language of the People if you will forgive my clumsiness with it. My family spirit is the *Udalvnusti*."

"The unchanging," she said. "But you are greatly changed from our ways."

In English, under my breath, I said, "You have no idea," then gave an explanation my best shot. "My spirit guide has brought me here to find my son, who was stolen by sorcerers and brought to this time."

"He is not here. There is no one here corrupted by sorcerers, or dressed as you dress."

"I think they took him to this time but another location. Do you know of...of a place of great pain? Of great fighting or illness?"

Her eyes darkened. "Everywhere. Stories came with the

traders, stories of people with skin like his—" and she nodded at Morrison, who was as fair-skinned and Irish as his name "—and with the stories came sickness, though we never saw men with skin like yours." She included me this time, fairer-skinned by far than she was, though I had a slightly gold burnish compared to Morrison. "We are what is left of ten villages, we who were not sick or became well again. We came to this valley, where there is water and game, and where we thought the sickness could not follow. Did sorcerers bring it?"

"No." I sighed. "Sickness can be carried on blankets and clothes, on trade items. That's why your people got sick before they ever even saw white men. I..." I had to try. It was useless, it would make no difference in the long run, but I had to try. I switched to English, because I knew she understood me and I didn't have words in Cherokee to describe a vaccination process. "If the pox sickness comes, there's a way to protect your people against it. Take scabs from the wounds and grind them up, then sniff them. It'll make most people a little sick, and some will get very sick and die. Maybe one in ten. But if you don't, it might be as many as nine in ten."

"Walker?" Morrison sounded horrified.

"It's how the Chinese vaccinated against smallpox for hundreds of years."

"How do you *know* that?"

"Because I used to play the what-would-happen-if-I-got-thrown-back-in-time? game, back before I started getting thrown back in time. I used to look things up to prepare myself for not having running water or penicillin or whatever." I could tell from Morrison's expression that this was not a game he was familiar with. "Look, it doesn't matter, but it's a real vaccination process and...and I have to try."

The elder's attention was hard on me. "You know of our future. It pains you."

"Yeah. Yes," I said more politely, and the stone in her turned to granite.

"Then retreating deeply will not help. The darkness comes no matter what we do."

I remembered, vividly, how Méabh and Caitríona had both seen a darkness on the horizon, an oncoming storm, and for a heart-wrenching moment I was desperately grateful that visions of the future were not part and parcel of my usual skills. "Tell your grandchildren to adopt white men into their families, and to have those white men buy land. That land will be all that belongs to you, when the darkness comes."

She looked utterly blank. "Buy and belong?"

"Just remember the words," I said unhappily. "Teach them to your grandchildren, and to theirs, and someday it'll make sense."

Morrison said, "Walker?" again, and, tense with frustration, I muttered, "Most of the Eastern band of Cherokee, the people who managed to stay in the Carolinas and Georgia instead of being forced onto the Trail of Tears, were allowed to stay because a white man they'd adopted owned hundreds of acres of land and let his adopted people live there. That and the Qualla were all the Cherokee had left. It doesn't matter, all right? I can't help, and I know it, but I have to *try*."

"Maybe you are helping," he said quietly. "Maybe this moment is why they end up with the land they do, instead of everyone being relocated to Oklahoma."

"If it is," I said bitterly, "it isn't enough."

"No." All the compassion in the world was in that one word. "But it's all you can do."

For a moment I could do nothing but stand there with my eyes shut, hoping the tears wouldn't leak through. The old woman touched my chest, fingertips light against my breastbone. I opened my eyes, looking down at her as she spoke.

"There are always sorcerers and darkness in the world. We will never do enough. But we hear, and listen, and try, and for that the Great Spirits love us, and gather us to them when our battles end. I will teach my grandchildren your strange words, and we will breathe the sickness in hopes of remaining well, and remember you for the gift of trying."

Tears spilled down my cheeks, both for her gratitude and for my futility. She wiped them away and tasted one, which at least shook a startled laugh out of me, and she smacked her lips. "Your body is poisoned with bad air and sick food. I would be full of tears, too. You should stay and breathe our clean air and eat our good food until you are cleansed."

I made an instant resolution to eat only organic vegetables and moderate amounts of grass-fed meat for the rest of my life, but shook my head. "I would love to, but I can't. I have to find my son. Do you know of where sorcerers would go to gather death magic and pain and hatred?"

"That is not a way any of the People should live, even those who are not of the People. But when our scouts and hunters go far, they return from the north with tales of war. They tell stories of the Northern and Eastern tribes driving each other further to the West, into the plains lands where they fight again with new enemies. They say the land is as red as the Lower World, stained with blood of the People." She brought down the power circle around us, face strong and sorrowful. "Go that way, and you may find the heart of darkness."

CHAPTER SIXTEEN

They insisted on feeding us before we left, and since I wasn't sure when I'd eaten last, I was glad to accept. They fed us a veritable feast of deer and possum and a few things I couldn't identify, all of which was enough to make my constantly hungry belly round and content for a little while. The elder, whose name I never did get, thought we should wait until morning to leave, and it was hard to argue on a full belly and a couple of days of no sleep. Morrison and I were given blankets to share, blankets woven and patterned in styles I'd never seen.

"This is what it looked like," I said to him, under the cover of a crescent moon and the blankets. The Milky Way sprawled above us, clearer than I'd seen it since I was a kid in the wilderness with my dad. The only sounds were the wind carrying light voices and the avid songs of horny bugs, and the only scents of small fires and clean human beings. "This is what America looked like before Europeans got here. All of this life and all of these images we'll never see on our end of time, because it's all been destroyed."

"Then hold on to every minute of this," he suggested, "because we're the only ones who ever get to see it. Walker, do you have any idea…do you have any sense of how incredible this is? I'm not sure you do."

I turned my face against his shoulder and closed my eyes. "Which part, that we're chasing black magic across time, or that we've just finished having dinner with a people who nearly went extinct?"

"Either," he said, quiet and steady. "You do that, Walker. You phrase everything like that, making light of it. Some things deserve more respect than that. The power that pulled us into that deserves more respect. *You* deserve more respect, even from yourself. Especially from yourself."

"Heh." It was sort of a laugh, muffled against his shoulder. "You're probably right."

"I am right."

"I can't, Morrison. I can't take it seriously that way. I'd be overwhelmed. Making stupid jokes is the only way I can cope. I don't know how you and Gary take it in stride. I mean, Gary, God. Gary goes charging along just asking for more all the time. I wish I was like that. I wish I was like you, unflappable."

Morrison chuckled. "You think I'm unflappable? Even with the number of times I've blown my top at you?"

"It's not like I haven't given you cause. But when it counts, yeah. You're unflappable. Witness our current situation, for example. I told you we'd time traveled and all you said was, 'So what do we do next?'"

"I've spent a lot of years cultivating an unflappable exterior, Walker. Would it make you feel better to know I was as amazed as a kid on the inside?"

"Maybe."

We lay down, Morrison taking my hand and putting it over his heart, which beat a lot more quickly than a quiet evening stargazing might account for. "I am," he said quietly, "in awe. It's hard to doubt you, Walker, even if what you're selling is outrageous. I'd like you to be able to see that."

"I'm still not used to this. I know it's been more than a year and I should probably have adjusted by now, but I still feel like I'm running to catch up. There are so many fires burning, and apparently I'm the one with the skill set to put them out. If I could just get them doused so I could sit back and breathe for a while, maybe I could take the time to be impressed. I'm just afraid if I take the time now I'll lose whatever handle I've got on things. I have to be sarcastic and unimpressed so I don't scare myself into immobility."

"It might be easier from the outside," he conceded. "I can afford to be impressed, from out here. But you should be proud of yourself, Joanne. You've come a long way."

"'Joanne.' That's not fair. I can't get my head around the idea of calling you Michael."

"You'll adapt. I'll wait."

"Good, because I think you're going to have to. Maybe when we get back to Seattle we can practice. I'll say Michael and you'll turn around and respond naturally, just like it was your name or something."

"We don't even have to wait until we get home."

"No, I'm sure that's important. I'm sure there's some kind of rule about not making drastic changes to your lifestyle when you're not in your home environment, because otherwise it won't stick when you go home."

Morrison laughed. "All right. We'll work on it being all right for you to be impressed that we're time traveling first. Time traveling, for God's sake, Walker," he said, and suddenly sounded like a kid, bubbly and full of excitement. "We're stuck at the beginning of European contact with the Americas. That's *incredible*."

"Yeah." I grinned against his chest and wrapped my arm around him, pulling myself closer. "Yeah, actually, I guess it kind of is. We should…" I laughed. "We should go find a rock in this valley and carve our initials in it, or something, and check for it when we get home."

I could hear Morrison's grin. "In the morning." He curled his arm around my shoulders, nestling me close, and fell asleep with the efficiency of a soldier. I stayed awake a while, listening to him breathe, watching the moon edge across the sky and the bands of the Milky Way change colors, until movement caught my eye. I pushed up a few inches.

The elderly shaman was watching us with a smile. She nodded at my sleeping partner, tapped the side of her head like she was suggesting the man had wisdom worth listening to, then slipped away into the darkness. It wasn't until morning that I realized she'd built a power circle around us again, keeping us safe from nightmares and restless sleep.

It also wasn't until morning that I thought to ask how far north the scouts meant, when they said they'd seen war to the north. The answer came back *days,* and I was a little numb with worry as we accepted some water skins and deer jerky to see us on our way. We followed the river until it disappeared into the hills, me silent and Morrison surprisingly chipper. When the water went underground, he stopped and scraped dirt away until he'd exposed rock, then crouched by it thoughtfully. "What is this, anyway? Granite?"

It had been a long time since my high school geology classes. I peered at the rock. "I think so. Granite and, um. Quartz, maybe."

"Quartzite," Morrison suggested. "That's the sparkle in the stone. So I'd need a diamond cutter. Can you do it?"

"Do what?"

He looked over his shoulder at me, blue eyes mirthful. "Carve our initials in a heart, Walker. Leave a mark to know ourselves by."

"Oh. Oh! Really? I was joking." I leaned on the exposed rock beside him, palms against it, feeling the slow ancient wearing down of the mountain. Its patience ran deep. Much deeper than my own, and made me think that, "Initials in the rock seems kind of crude." The mountain's life echoed in my hands, undisturbed by the idea of being carved. It didn't mind what I did to it—it would endure far beyond my brief years, but that was why I didn't want JW+MM carved into it forever.

Morrison straightened up, looking faintly disappointed. "If you say so."

"Hey, Mr. Pouty Pants. Give me a minute before you get all sullen." The stone was surprisingly malleable under my magic's questing pressure. I'd done body work on dozens of cars, and the mental process wasn't so different. Heat bent metal, water pitted stone; I combined the images to build cold fire in my palms, and spread it out across the exposed rock face. Stone shifted and deepened, lines melting into existence instead of being chipped or ground. After a few minutes I released the magic and stepped away, letting Morrison examine my handiwork.

His smile was slow in coming, but as strong as the hills themselves. He pulled me into his arms, offering a kiss to go with the embrace, and we departed the valley hand in hand, the petroglyphs left behind.

"We're never going to get there." Morrison surveyed the mountains running north and east of us and shook his head.

"Even assuming we don't run into unfriendly natives, I don't see how we're going to cover the distance we need to. If Aidan's out there being used as a repository, we're on a schedule."

"I've been thinking about that. Not about the schedule. The schedule's not our problem. He got pulled where they wanted him, and I didn't have the presence of mind to lock on and go with him. Which is probably just as well, because it would have stranded you in that valley, out of time and with no idea what had happened. So I'm going to work under the assumption that if there's war, death, misery and mayhem going on, that they're going to stay there sucking it down until they've drained everybody dry."

Morrison eyed me. "All right. If the schedule isn't the problem, then how do we solve the problem of traveling through hundreds of miles of unfriendly territory?"

"You're not going to like it." In fact, he was going to not like it so much I couldn't help grinning with anticipation.

He took in the grin and became suitably wary. "What is it?"

"You made a *very* pretty wolf, Morrison."

It took a full five seconds for the implication to sink in. Then his eyes widened with genuine horror. "Oh, no. No way, Walker. No way are you turning me into an animal again."

"Wolves can travel thirty miles a day just hunting, and they're top-of-the-food-chain predators. Nothing except humans and maybe a desperate puma is likely to attack one, whereas as humans we'd be much more vulnerable to any predators and very, very slow by comparison. Thirty or forty miles a day in clear territory, which the pre-Columbian Eastern seaboard forests are not. Do you have a better idea?"

Dismay stretched Morrison's mouth downward. "Walker, do you have any idea *what happened* while I was a wo—" Color stained his cheeks and his mouth snapped shut. I suspected we both very much wished he hadn't started to ask the question.

I didn't, in fact, know what had happened. Not specifically, because about thirty seconds after I'd gotten him back into human form I'd jumped on a plane to Ireland, and we'd mostly been talking about me since we'd been reunited. I had an unpleasant idea of what might have happened, though. Tia Carley, the werewolf I'd ended up neutering, had been as attractive a wolf as Morrison, and I was pretty sure she'd taken a fancy to my boss. There was no delicate way to ask, and besides, I really didn't want to know. After a few seconds of mental fumbling, I answered with what I *did* know: "You saved five people's lives while you were a wolf, and got me out of that cave system in one piece."

Some of the color faded from his face and an acknowledgment pulled at one corner of his mouth. I didn't know if he needed a way out, but I was more than happy to give him one. If there had been wolfy hijinks with him and Tia, I did not want to know. Not one little bit at all. He said, "I also terrorized some security guards and half a dozen Seattle cops," though most of the discomfort had gone out of the confession.

"I'm just glad nobody shot you. I was scared to death someone would. I'm really sorry about that, Michael. I had no idea it would happen. The dance performances…"

"Were transformative." Morrison's eyes sparkled, noticing how I'd managed to use his first name, but neither of us said anything, like it was an elephant in the room. "It's all right, Walker. I got over being upset right around the same time you said I love you."

It was my turn to blush. I bet we could stand here for a week taking turns at it. "Does that mean you're going to let me turn you into a wolf again?"

He groaned, turned to the vista, and pushed his hand through his hair. "Do I have any choice?"

"Sure. I could try turning you into a puma or a horse or

something, except a horse couldn't get through the under-brush well and I bet anybody who saw us might take a shot at a puma with your coloring. Ghost puma. Anyway, I think the wolf was your choice, which suggests you've got an affinity, so it's a better idea to try it." A grin started working its way forward. "Is that your mental image of yourself, Morrison? A lone wolf, standing against the tide of evildoers? That's very teenage epic fantasy of you."

He gave me such a flat look I laughed again. "It could be worse."

"Really. How?"

"You could think of yourself that way and not be a hero." I kissed him while he looked flummoxed, then got my drum out and beamed at him. "Take your clothes off."

"What?"

"Take your clothes off. They don't transform with you. You can carry them once you're shifted."

For a while his expression remained steady and patient, like if he waited long enough there would be an explanation as to how he had ended up on the back end of American history about to strip naked and run through the woods as a wolf. When it became clear no explanation was forthcoming—because really, he already knew the answers—he took his clothes off while I fought between watching unabashedly and trying to find somewhere else to look.

Watching won. He folded his shirt into his coat, toed his shoes off and stripped to his skivvies. He had an awfully nice body. Not overdeveloped, but not soft, either. Just right, like Goldilocks's third bear. He said, "I'm not sure I've ever taken all my clothes off outside in broad daylight," at the same time I said, "You know, I used to think you were kind of soft around the middle, but *damn,* Morrison."

Apparently we were both trying to distract ourselves from

him taking his underwear off. It worked, anyway, and he sat down on the bundle of folded clothes, saying, "I knocked off ten or fifteen pounds last spring, after I realized the woman I was increasingly interested in was eleven years younger than me. I didn't want to have a heart attack while she was still hale and hearty, if things worked out there. Your turn."

"My turn what?"

"To take your clothes off." He smiled at me. "If I'm going to sit here naked while you bang that drum, so are you."

I really wanted to find a viable argument, and really couldn't. Morrison got a self-satisfied smirk as I pulled my shirt off, so I threw it at him. He caught it and folded it along with his own clothes. I muttered, "I don't think I've ever taken all my clothes off outside in broad daylight before, either. Is this one of those things that's supposed to bring couples closer together?"

Morrison's voice dropped somewhere below the belt. "That sounds like a better idea than shapeshifting." Then, in a much more ordinary and amused voice, he added, "I didn't know it was possible to blush that far down. You're too thin, Walker."

I looked down and blushed even farther down. My navel was in danger of turning pink. "I didn't, either. And I know. I keep eating, but all the shapeshifting really took it out of me."

"The shapeshifting?"

"In Ireland." There was a lot I hadn't told him yet, and naked on a mountainside didn't seem like quite the right time or place to do it. I started anyway, getting as far as "I," and then ran into "Oh, hell." I hadn't drawn a power circle, and now I was naked. By the time I was done building one, I had moved beyond embarrassment into a comfortable Zen attitude, and clung to it with all my slightly Puritan little heart. Morrison tied our clothes and weapons into bundles, but otherwise watched the whole process with a grin that made him look about fourteen.

The positive upshot of all that was there was a great deal of energy crashing around inside the power circle. Most of it was sexual and anticipatory, but it wasn't difficult to channel it into shapeshifting magic. I called for Rattler, who awakened with a sense of approval. I wasn't in the habit of doing things properly, like building power circles and working up energy to help ease a transition from one form to another, but this time I'd done it right and he liked it. That helped, too, and so did Morrison having gone through the transformation process once before. He knew right down to his bones that I could do it, and so his bones were surprisingly willing to adapt to the new shape I poured them into.

There was no drawn-out painful half-man, half-wolf aspect to the change. Shamanic shifting didn't work that way, and from what I'd glimpsed with Tia Carley, neither did werewolf transformations. It was one, then the other, with little more than a shimmer of magic between the two to mark the transition. My power washed over Morrison in a gunmetal bath and left a huge silver-white wolf in his place. He took a very manlike sharp breath, but otherwise held himself still, becoming accustomed to the new form.

That was *much* better than the first time, when he'd understandably panicked, given in to the animal brain, and run like hell. Delighted, I put my drum into the bundle of clothes and weapons, then turned my magic inward, slipping into—

Not a wolf shape. Wolves were not my thing. Coyotes were. That hit Morrison like a blow, even in wolf form, and I felt him withdraw emotionally.

Frustration bubbled up inside me. That was twice already Coyote had come between us, even though there was absolutely nothing *with* Coyote to come between us. And I couldn't address the problem now, because as far as I knew, even humans shapeshifted into animals couldn't speak like humans while in the animal form. To make it worse, Morrison gave a cranky snort, picked up his gear and trotted away with it in his mouth, clearly saying, *"Let's get on with it, Walker."*

I was going to bite him as soon as my own mouth was free. Thus resolved, I picked up my gear, too, and we ran into the forests.

My ill temper couldn't hold a candle to the joy of running headlong through wilderness. We were both enormously large canines, weighing the same as we did in our human forms. The clothes were mildly inconvenient, and my jaw got tired, so the first time we stopped for a brief rest I shifted back to human form. It took a while to repackage everything, but then I slung Morrison's gun holster on him with his clothes and weapons stuffed into it. He squirmed a bit, but looked more satisfied with the results, so I hung mine on a branch so I could walk into it once transformed. Morrison managed, after some trial and error, to latch the shotgun's holster around my ribs, and we were off again.

We didn't change back to human form for two days, instead hunting, drinking and sleeping as canines. Very little disturbed us, and our supremely sensitive senses of smell allowed us to avoid anything that might have chosen to. I had no idea how much distance we covered. My thoughts simplified: we were hunting. When we reached the quarry, the hunt would intensify. Until then, nothing mattered but reaching it.

On the third day, the scent of blood came into the air. Morrison and I both slowed, tasting it, judging it and naming it: *human.* It was still far off, but we were reaching our destination. Morrison cocked an ear and I shook my head. It was too soon to change back to humans. Too far to go, still. But we would have to be ever-more careful. Our size would make us seem dangerous, and Morrison's brilliant white pelt would be a prize by itself.

We knew what we were approaching: the tang in the air told us.

It was still a shock to burst into a mountain meadow and see a war being fought on the river plains below.

CHAPTER SEVENTEEN

With Rattler at attention in the back of my skull, I changed to human form, then swiftly built a power circle around Morrison before calling up the magic to transform him. His first words were "Was that necessary?"

"The power circle? Yeah, you need to see—"

"The coyote."

For about three seconds I genuinely didn't know what he meant. Then the top blew off my head and I flung my hands in the air. "For crying out loud, Morrison, are you *serious?* You're thirty-eight years old! Are you really this insecure over my ex? I've known Coyote my entire life. He's been my mentor since I was thirteen. He's taught me most of what I know about magic. I've got an affinity for the shape through long familiarity, so *what?* It doesn't mean I'm going to bail and go make little coyote puppies with him happily ever after. Seriously, you've been gnawing on this for *three days?*"

"You wouldn't turn me back into a man so we could discuss it."

I threw my hands up again. "Oh, my God! Really? You think I deliberately kept you in wolf form so we couldn't talk about it? I just thought we were moving, Morrison, no reason to keep shifting back and forth. Canines have nice warm fur coats to sleep in, they hunt well, they can drink from streams more easily than humans. Are you *serious?* Holy crap, Morrison, seriously, where is the insecurity coming from? You're the most secure person I've ever *met.* And I told you before, me, Cyrano, there's nothing there. There could have been, in a whole different world, but no. It's you, it's been you all along, and I can't believe you're so damned worried about it! What do I have to do?"

"Not shapeshifting into a coyote would help."

I put my face in my hands, dragged them down, and showed him the reds of my eyes. "You're insane, Morrison. You're bonkers. The coyote is as natural to me as a wolf is to you. What did you want me to do?"

"You could have tried."

"No! No, I could not have. God dammit, Morrison, I turned into a werewolf, all right? I tried to kill Gary. Cernunnos nearly crushed my head, putting me in my place. I'm *sorry,* but no. I am not going to go down that road just to make you more comfortable. Almost anything else, yes. I will bend over backward to make you happy. But you're just going to have to suck this one up, because the wolf might be your personal affinity, but in my pantheon it scares the crap out of me."

That was obviously the exact wrong thing to say. Morrison stiffened right up and I made gargling sounds of frustration in my throat. "Not you. You don't scare the crap out of me except in the sense of yes, for God's sake, I am in love with you and I have no idea how to deal with that because you may not have noticed but I've kind of got the emotional spectrum of a turnip but I've never been so happy to be this scared and—"

I ran out of steam, my shoulders dropping as I looked away. We were both still naked. Having a naked shouting match on a mountainside should have been funny, but it wasn't. Not at all. "You drove my car across the country, and I was happy," I said dully. "Don't you get that, Morrison? The only other time somebody drove that car I just about ripped her ears off. But I was happy Petite brought you to me. I was happy to see you behind the wheel. You don't get more inside me than that, Michael. You just don't."

After a very long silence, he said, "You hadn't told me about Muldoon."

I closed my eyes and sank down to fold my arms around my knees. "When have I had time?" It seemed like we'd been doing nothing but talking since we'd reunited, but we'd also been running hell for breakfast all over the countryside. I'd caught him up on what was going on in North Carolina. I hadn't even touched on what had gone down in Ireland.

Another very long silence passed before he said, "I'm sorry."

I laughed, a tired, broken little sound. "Me, too. Seriously, Morrison, what the hell."

"You've known him your entire life, you share a magic I can't even touch, you have an affinity for his chosen animal form, you love him, he's good-looking, and he's your age."

"Jesus." I pressed my fingertips against my eyes, then twisted my neck so I could see Morrison. "You're really hung up on the age thing, aren't you? I didn't even know how old you were until I got a look at your driver's license last year. It doesn't matter. And I'll share as much of the magic with you as I can, if that's what you want, but you're my rock, Morrison. You're what keeps me connected. You're what I want to come home to. Yeah, I love Cyrano, but I wouldn't give up everything for him. I wouldn't give up anything for him, when it came down to it, and it did. You, I'd..." *I'd die for you* was the way that sentence ended, but it wouldn't be something Morrison wanted me to say or do, so I let it fade away.

He heard it anyway, and said, "Don't," quietly, then came to sit beside me. He was warm, even not quite touching me, and I wanted to lean against him and shiver in his body heat. After a while he said, "I am hung up about my age. I always have been."

I laughed again, a tiny, high-pitched and not very happy sound that was intended as an invitation to explain that re-mark. He took it for what it was. "I wanted to be a cop ever since I was a kid. I took college courses so when I graduated high school I only had three years of classes to get through. I finished the academy six weeks before I turned twenty-one, so I was very aware of being the rookie who was just barely allowed to go into bars. I made detective three years later, as soon as it was possible. My hair started going silver when I was about twenty-six, and I was self-conscious about that, too. I got promoted to lieutenant after three years in Homicide, be-cause Captain Nichols liked me, knew I was dedicated, and thought it would be good for the department to have new blood in its ranks. Because of that, I was thirty-three when I was made captain, and I was chosen over a lot of older, more qualified men."

Morrison exhaled slowly. "And now I'm just about the right age for people to start muttering about a midlife crisis, and I've fallen in love with a woman eleven years my junior. So, yeah. You could say I'm hung up about my age."

"You're crazy," I said again, a lot more softly this time, and did lean against him, shivering against his warmth. He put his arm around my shoulder, cautiously, and I shifted a little closer. "And I'll be damned. The Almighty Morrison is human after all. You do have neuroses and flaws like the rest of us."

"The Almighty Morrison. Is that what you call me? I liked 'Boss' better. Or does that mean I'm forgiven?"

"You're forgiven as long as you quit getting your knickers in a bunch over Coyote."

"I'll do my best."

"Then you're forgiven. I had no idea you were so self-conscious about your age, Morrison. You're, um." I pressed my lips together, looking at the valley below us. "You're a very private man. There's a lot I don't know about you."

"That," he said, "may also be a source of my concern. You know Cyrano very well, and I'm aware I'm…" He chuckled very softly indeed. "Private. Is there a word that goes beyond that?"

"Guarded. Discreet. Reserved. Chary. Restra—"

Morrison held his hand up. "*Chary,* Walker? I know you have an English degree, but *chary?*"

"How often does a girl get an excuse to pull a word like that out?"

He breathed a laugh. "All right. I get the idea, anyway. *Chariness* ties into the age awareness. The privacy helps create a barrier that—"

"Elevates you," I said. Morrison made a sound like he didn't care for the choice of phrase, but he didn't argue. "You're the boss. It's your job to know your people. It's not their job to know you. It puts me at a disadvantage, Boss. You probably know me better than I know you, and to make it worse I've been wearing my heart not so much on my sleeve as smeared across Seattle for the past year. Not just about you, but with all of this. The magic. Everything. And you've been there for it all." My eyebrows rose. "And apparently you fell in love with me anyway, which makes me worry about your judgment."

He laughed aloud this time, which was what I wanted. My heart ached, partly at the realization that I didn't know him all that well, but more at having actually unearthed something about him, even if it was insecurity. Maybe especially because it was insecurity. I was a bundle of insecurity myself, so it was nice to know he didn't actually have every aspect of his shit utterly, totally and completely together. "I want to go home," I said against his shoulder. "I want to go home and learn more about you. Which means we need to get all this other crap dealt with, so if you don't mind us going back to the part of the conversation where I thought the power circle was necessary…?"

He grunted, suggesting he hadn't actually heard me saying that. It seemed very guy of him, which also made me feel a little better. Perhaps the Almighty Morrison didn't actually notice every single thing that went on in his jurisdiction, whatever he decided that might be. "You need to See what I See out there, Morrison. You need to See why I couldn't risk performing magic openly. Get dressed first," I advised, and did the same myself. It felt strange putting clothes on after three days in fur, but at least I warmed up. It wasn't really cold, but the view was chilling even without adding the Sight in.

Morrison asked, "What's going on, Walker?" as he finished pulling his T-shirt on.

I shook my head, preferring to show rather than tell, and beckoned him over before he put his shoes on. "Same routine as before. Stand on my feet." I swung around so my back was to the valley, and he stood on my feet. I put my hand on his head and said, "See as I See," which wasn't poetic or spell-like at all, but at this juncture, I didn't think I needed my poor rhymes to set the magic in place.

Morrison's eyes filtered gold, then darkened.

I didn't need to look again. The images were seared in

my mind. Arguing with Morrison had been a lightweight relief, compared to what the valley presented. The war was bad enough, groups of men pushing back and forth toward a broad expanse of river. I half envisioned misted blood rising in the air, and wasn't certain if it was my imagination or not. There were places where the earth ran with blood, rivulets large enough to be seen from the distance amassing and pooling in hollows.

At the heart of it, as if orchestrating, a lash of black lightning cracked down, down, and down again. Its silence was worse than any sound could be, and each time it shattered the sky, a single individual was illuminated by the power of darkness.

The lightning was fed by five points around the battlefield, places where the fighting was bloodier and more vicious than anywhere else. Malevolence rose from the Native warriors, a madness driving them beyond what warfare had once been to their people. The wights hung above those battles, drawing on the warriors' fury and rage, and every time another man died, what was left of his soul was gobbled by a wight and sent back through the black lightning.

"What is that?" Morrison's voice said he knew, but that he needed me to confirm it.

I did, and let him go as I spoke. "It's Aidan." I faced the slaughter with numbness rising in me. "This isn't even Europeans coming in and making a hash of things, not as such. This is just warfare between nations."

"You mean we can't stop it."

I shook my head. I felt very calm, very rational, and knew it was a front. I was willing to embrace it, though, because otherwise I would fall into the screaming heebie-jeebies over not just the battle, but Aidan's presence in it, and the dark power he was drawing in. "We couldn't stop it anyway. But it's… It really annoys me, you know? The presentation of Native

Americans as being pure, innocent, and one with the land until the Europeans arrived. But it's still really easy to think that all of the bloodshed and death was implemented by Westerners. It's harder to remember that some of these groups were nation states of their own, and conducted warfare on their own. I fell right into that trap. I figured all the pain the Executioner was drawing on came from the incomers, but no. A lot of it was self-inflicted. Europeans might have triggered it, but... anyway, I know when we are, now, more or less. Mid-to-late seventeenth century, I'd guess. They're Iroquois and Huron out there, I think. They've been pushed west by the Europeans, don't get me wrong. From what I've read, the war they waged before Westerners arrived was much smaller scale, and now they're fighting for their land and their lives."

As a kid I'd resolutely ignored all the Native American history that had been offered up, but in the past year I'd begun paying attention to the histories of those people whose shamanic heritage I was drawing on. I'd mostly read about the Cherokee, but the Iroquois had put together maybe the fiercest, largest armies against European settlers and, inevitably, against other Native tribes as they were all forced out of their original lands. They'd eventually turned on the members of their own league of nations. It had not been a good time.

"How can you tell?"

"I'm pretty sure we're in the Ohio River Valley. Probably in Kentucky." A wry smile pulled at my mouth as Morrison turned an astonished expression on me. "I spent most of my childhood driving around America, Morrison. I know where things are. We headed north, maybe a little northwest. You pretty much have to run into the Ohio River if you go far enough that direction, and there's a big damned river out there. The details have changed, but it's not like there's a volcano waiting to go off nearby and change the whole face of the countryside."

Morrison shrugged his eyebrows, faintly impressed. "What are the Iroquois doing down here, then? I thought they were from the Northeast."

"They were, but they moved south and west when the settlers came. There was a huge war that got smeared all over the countryside as resources got scarcer. Mostly beaver pelts, I think." I wished I'd studied it more, but nobody had warned me I'd be in need of real-life application of the knowledge. "Besides, even if I'm wrong about when, the what is pretty obvious. Wholesale slaughter, captivity and death. And it's all being dumped into Aidan, who's going to bring all that misery back to our time once everybody here is dead."

"What are we going to do?"

"We're going to go in and get him before that happens. There's a little tiny bit of good news out there. You see those flashes?" I pointed down, then glanced at Morrison again, making sure the Sight was still working in him.

It was. His blue eyes were gold, utterly unearthly with his silver hair. Oblivious to my shiver, he looked where I was pointing and nodded.

"That's white magic." I winced. "Life magic. Positive magic. Not magic performed by white guys. You know what I mean." Morrison nodded and I fumbled on. "Basically it means there's someone down there doing what they can to stop this. Iroquois or Huron shamans, maybe. Someone who hasn't been corrupted or captured yet, anyway. We're not going for Aidan right away. We're going to go see if we can team up with whoever's on our side, and maybe together we'll have a better chance at stopping this."

Morrison took his attention from the massacre below.

"Walker, I hate to ask, but how far are we going to go to stop this?"

"You mean am I going to do down there and shoot Aidan if I have to?"

Morrison nodded. I set my jaw. "Yeah. If I have to. In the leg or arm or something where it'll get his damned attention. It's about the worst idea I've ever had, but if I can shock him into breaking free for even an eye blink I can get inside and try to help him fight the wights and the mark the Executioner left."

"And if that doesn't work?"

"It will."

"But if it doesn't?"

"It will."

A smile cracked Morrison's face. "That may be why I love you. All right. How do we get in there without getting killed?"

"That," I said, "I can manage. I invented an invisibility cloak thing ages ago. The only danger is whether the wights or Aidan notice I'm working magic, but I think they're involved enough in what they're doing, or they'd have already wiped that guy out." I nodded again toward the intermittent flashes of power struggling to hold against the tide of blood. Morrison took my hand, and I called up just about the oldest trick I knew, bending light around us in a sphere of *"we're not here."*

"We're good. Let's go."

Morrison hesitated. "I can still see us."

"Look with the Sight."

He blinked a few times, then bobbled with surprise. The shields around us warped the world beyond just a little, light refracted ever so slightly wrong. "Too bad we can't use this on police raids."

"Just as well. Imagine how many drug runners would get off by declaring their rights violated by magic."

"If any of them dared admit it." We shut up after that, concentrating on barreling our way down the low mountains and into a battlefield. I wished the invisibility shield worked both ways, so I didn't have to see the myriad ways people could die by edged and blunt weapons. Our feet became caked with mud and gore, and the smell went from bad to worse to vomit-inducing. Morrison kept me going after I did throw up, and for a few minutes I wasn't certain if he would get through with his innards intact. But we weren't hampered by fighters attacking us, and I was happy using my shields to keep them farther away than they might naturally have come.

Grim with determination, we worked our way toward the irregular sparks of healing magic that burst through the gloom, until suddenly we were in the heart of a pitched battle, men dying and killing all around, and the frantic blip of light was immediately in front of us. I risked it all, dropped the invisibility shield and bellowed, "Hello?"

The blood turned to roses, and my father walked out of the chaos.

CHAPTER EIGHTEEN

My knees cut out. Morrison caught me, which took faster reflexes than most people possessed. I wrapped my fingers around his biceps, trying not to collapse further as emotion hammered through me. Mostly shock, but also relief and a vast surge of anger.

I swear to God, Dad hadn't aged a day in the years since I'd last seen him. His black hair was still worn long but not loose: it was braided now, falling over his shoulder in a thick chunk. He was barefoot—my father never wore shoes if he could avoid it—and clad in jeans and an unbuttoned plaid shirt.

He hadn't aged, but he had changed. His eyes, at least, had changed. They blazed yellow, as gold as mine ever got. Or they did for half a second, anyway. Then they snapped back to ordinary brown, though his pupils were so large they just about ate all the brown. The misting rose petals became blood again.

Morrison, who was the only one who could find his voice,

and apparently his sense of humor, as well, said, "Joseph Walk-ingstick, I presume," and stepped forward, me in tow, to offer a hand. "Michael Morrison. It's a relief to find you, sir."

Dad shook Morrison's hand absently, like it was more or less reasonable to be meeting modern-dressed white men in the middle of seventeenth century Indian wars, and finally managed to say, *"Joanne?"*

Somebody chucked a spear at us. I snapped my hand up, strengthening shields that didn't need it, and the weapon bounced away. A brief, startled silence rushed through the warriors around us, and a few more slings and arrows came our way. They all bounced off, too, and that was that. They went back to slaughtering each other, evidently satisfied that we were insufficiently easy targets.

Dad's eyes glimmered gold again, then widened. I sup-posed he was checking out my shields, my aura, my whole general shamanic showcase. A mix of regret and pride slid across his face, sharpening the line of his cheekbones. I'd got-ten his cheekbones and Mom's nose, making for some fairly prominent features. My eyes were between theirs, too, hazel to Mom's green and Dad's brown. They tended to pick up more of the green, but the power-indicating gold reminded me more of Dad. And I had Dad's shamanic magic and my mother's magery running in my veins, setting me on the rare warrior's path.

Oh, yeah. I was my parents' child, through and through.

"Aidan is here." Even I was surprised at the coldness of my voice. "Is Lucas?"

Dad's expression went flat. So did something inside of me. He said, "I'm sorry," and a wall of white noise rose up, drown-ing out the sounds of battle in a static rush. Morrison didn't, or couldn't, catch me this time: after a while I became aware I was on my knees, fingers dug into the red mucky earth, and that my breathing was harsh and shuddering. Scalding tears dripped from my eyes, still hot as they hit the backs of my hands while I stared wide-eyed and barely seeing at the ground beneath me.

I hadn't seen Lucas Isaac in more than thirteen years. I hadn't been much looking forward to it, either, because the best way I could imagine a reunion turning out was awkwardly. I'd wanted the chance, though. I'd wanted to see how he'd grown up.

That wasn't exactly true. I did want to know how he'd grown up, but what I meant by that, in my heart of hearts, was that I'd wanted to see if he'd apologize for having been a chickenshit and running back to Vancouver. I'd long since accepted we'd never been fated for a happily ever after, and while I understood why he'd done it, I still thought if he'd grown up well he might have apologized.

Dad started talking again, or maybe he was repeating something he'd already said. "...called me Sunday afternoon, after he hadn't come back from an overnight camping trip in the mountains. He had his compass, and plenty of food and water, but..."

"Why hadn't she gone with him?" That was Morrison, the consummate professional.

A smile flickered through Dad's voice. "Sara is the five-star-hotel camping type. She never liked getting out into the woods and getting dirty. She likes things tidy." The sound of the smile faded. "So I went up to where she'd dropped him off and followed his trail. It wasn't hard. He'd gone to—" He hitched, and I felt the weight of his gaze on me. I didn't look up. My breathing was still ragged. "He'd set up camp in a hollow Joanne used to visit, a couple miles back in the hills."

My stomach dropped again and I bent closer to the ground, making fists to put my forehead against. I knew where Dad was talking about. It had been my sanctuary, far enough from town I couldn't hear anything but the loudest engines or the occasional airplane. I'd pretended I was a remote survivor of the olden days, or a modern one thrown back in time. That was where the time-travel game had come from, the one Morrison had evidently never played. I'd brought Lucas there because it was special to me, and I was trying so hard to make him like me. I hadn't been back since I'd realized I was pregnant. I wondered how often Lucas had gone back.

Dad answered the question without meaning to. "You'll want to go, Jo...anne."

Jo. The nickname my father had used for me all my life, no matter how much I protested. He was Joe, I was Jo, like I was some not-quite-good-enough not-a-boy knockoff. I'd come around to rather liking it since Gary started using it, but it still left a mark when Dad said it. He could keep right on calling me Joanne forever, as far as I was concerned. I got hung up on that instead of thinking about why Dad thought I should go back to the holler I'd once shared with Lucas. It was better that way.

Dad went back to talking to Morrison, since I was clearly not going to participate in this conversation. "He camped overnight, and I think he must have decided to find another route home. It took him through the Nothing Holler." There was no doubt in his voice that we knew what he was talking about. We were here, after all, on the wrong end of time, and we'd gotten here somehow. "His trail led right into it. I followed, but I was too late. It came out here, and I think he must have died before he even knew what had happened. I'm sorry, Joanne. I know you liked him."

"I barely knew him. Sara is going to be destroyed." It was pure displacement and I knew it, but I had to do something that would let me get on my feet again. If shoving Lucas's death into a box was what it took, that's what I would do. Later I would let myself wonder if Aidan had known him at all, and what the news would do to him. I shut that thought down. *Later.*

It took everything I had to get up. Morrison put a hand under my elbow, supporting me, and it took everything I had not to shake him off, too, which wasn't at all fair to him. My jeans were filthy with blood and mud, and my hands were only clean in the spots where tears had fallen. The coat, the ridiculous gleaming white coat, still gleamed white, unaffected by the mess I'd pressed it against. That was what good guys did, wore white. Made themselves targets, so no one else would get shot at.

Lucas Isaac had not deserved to get shot down, and I was going to wreak some unholy vengeance in his name.

"How did you *get* here, Jo?"

I snarled, *"Joanne,"* and saw Morrison's surprise as much as Dad's recoil as I continued, still snarling. "The Nothing killed Carrie Little Turtle and six, no, thirteen others. At least half of them rose again as wights. They kidnapped Aidan—" which was playing fast and loose with accuracy but was close enough for government work "—and when Morrison and I went after him they used Aidan's power to open a window to this place. Morrison and I got sucked in, but we weren't tied into the death magic here, so we ended up in a different location. It took us three days to get here. And all that time Aidan has been sucking down death magic. When everybody here is dead, they're going back to the future—" and I had been trying so hard to avoid that phrase "—and they're going to release it. They're trying to finish the job Columbus and Ponce de León started. They want to wipe out the Native Americans, and anybody else they can take along with them."

"Why?"

"Because they thrive on chaos and pain, and the Native genocides are the biggest thing on this continent for them to feed off. If they restart them in our time, and draw more people into ethnic wars or psycho survivalist modes, they'll keep gaining power. This is Mom's enemy, Dad. This is the Master. This is his attempt at a checkmate. He's trying for an endgame, and there is no way he gets to have that on this territory. I'm going to clean this mess up and then I'm taking it home and I'm going to finish this shit."

Morrison made a noise that sounded suspiciously like a cheer, cut off deep in his throat. My father, less inspired, stared at me in consternation. "You know about your…about your mother?"

I'd forgotten. I'd forgotten that I hadn't spoken to Dad in years, much less in the past year when the magical world had come up and bitten me on the ass. I'd forgotten he had no way of knowing what had happened. That I hadn't even told Morrison about the postmortem reconciliation with my mother, never mind having told Dad, whose entire knowledge of my relationship with her was based on my childhood resentment of her having left me with him. That he couldn't possibly know that I'd finally, finally learned that he himself was an adept, a shaman of some considerable power, and that magic was, if not exactly old hat, certainly part of my everyday life now.

And I did not want to explain it to him while standing in the middle of a battlefield with death and hatred raging around me and feeding monsters that were in turn filling a little boy with all that darkness and evil. So I said, "Yes," and left it at that.

It took Dad a good long minute to get past that. He eventually said, "You said Aidan is here," in a voice that suggested we had a lot to talk about, but that he agreed Aidan was in fact much more important.

I pointed at the still-increasing flashes of black lightning. "He's right there. Getting nailed by that crap every few seconds. What have you been *doing* out here, Dad?"

"Trying to stay alive." A string of tension came into the words, and I had another moment of recollection: Dad was a shaman. A healer. He couldn't take the fight to the other guys even if he wanted to, and I didn't know if he wanted to. He was not like me.

Nobody was like me, and I knew I should have some sympathy for him because of that, but I was all out of sympathy. Lucas was dead. We were all out of time, not just in the sense of being displaced by centuries, but also in terms of the black lighting flashes coming closer and closer together. The war around us was reaching its peak. Very soon there wouldn't be enough people left to sustain the increase, and the power would break. And I was a moron, because they weren't going to wait until everybody was dead. They would move as soon as the frenzy hit its highest point, taking all the passion and pain and anger at its strongest, before it broke and began to fall away again.

If we didn't get to Aidan before the black lightning became a single sheet, we would be out of time for real.

The thought had a horribly familiar feeling. It was obvious, but it seemed like it, or one like it, had gone through my head about a thousand times in the past few days. Everything kept coming around to rescuing Aidan. Of course it did, but it seemed like the idea shouldn't need to reestablish itself every couple of hours. It seemed like it should be at the forefront of my mind all the time.

"It's a loop in itself." My father and Morrison both looked at me, but I was staring at the power pouring into Aidan. "You bastard. You fucking clever bastard. You've got me spinning my wheels, don't you. A tiny little time loop built right into my head. It spikes with *'we've got to rescue Aidan!'* So we start off in that direction, but then we hit something personal that's got just as much punch. Things I've been avoiding or haven't had the chance to think or talk about for months. Important things, but they keep cropping up when I should be making a mad dash for Aidan, and it takes a while to shake it off. And then we start all over. We've got to rescue Aidan! And off we go. It keeps happening."

I couldn't count how many times over the past few days Morrison and I had gone through that loop. It wasn't like we'd been spending hours or days moping around being romantic, but we'd hit that emotional circle half a dozen times, and collapsed into sleep afterward more than once. Every time we did it, it lost us a little time and gained the Master and his minions a little more. "You clever fucking bastard," I said again. "But I'm fucking wise to you now. It's not going to work again. Dad, is this one of the places we stopped when I was a kid? Did you work to heal the land here?"

My father's eyes bugged, just about going *poing!* like a cartoon character's. "You knew I... Yes."

"All right. This is what we're going to do. We're going to get as close to Aidan as we can, and you're going to do the magical equivalent of opening up a vein. Whatever it takes to awaken the link between the power you laid down then, and us being here now."

"Jo, we do—"

"Joanne." It was petty as hell and I wasn't going to let it go. Gary could call me Jo. Morrison could call me Jo. Pretty much everybody in the damned world could call me Jo, but my father was going to have to earn it.

There was a beat in which Dad swallowed before saying, "Joanne. We don't have a power circle in place, and I don't think we'll be able to build one under the weight of that magic. It'll kill us."

"No. It'll be rough, but we'll be all right." That, to my surprise, was Morrison, who sounded far more calm and confident than I would have if I'd had to say it. I didn't lack confidence. It was just that I'd be arguing with my daddy, whereas Morrison had no emotional baggage on this claim.

"Jo-Joanne, you don't understand the kind of power you're asking me to use—"

"Yeah, I do. It's the kind of power you would normally need a big, strong power circle and ideally at least three others of your bloodline to work. It's the kind of power you might ask the Great Makers to help you handle, because without a god's touch it might burn you out. And calling on gods isn't something you do without a power circle unless you're me, so I understand your concern, Dad."

Under different circumstances, my father's expression might have been funny. He hadn't gotten as far as rearranging his expectations of me. They were all just being smashed around like billiard balls in his mind, bouncing and rattling chaotically, no pattern yet establishing itself. Under different circumstances—like circumstances in which he had told me about and guided me in my mystical heritage—I might even have felt sorry for hitting him over the head with his suddenly take-no-prisoners shamanic daughter.

Under these circumstances, however, I repeated, "I do understand, Dad. I just don't give a damn. You're either going to do this or I'm going to have to do it myself. The magic you laid down in the future will probably respond to me because I'm your daughter, but it won't be as responsive as it would be to you. We need that link to help get us back to our own time. I'm already going to have to cut Aidan off from the lightning and provide any magical offense we need, so it would be *really helpful* if you just did what I'm asking."

"It's impossible."

"Then do the impossible."

"What am I going to do?" Morrison kept right on sounding calm and sensible, for which I loved him beyond reason.

"You're going to shoot every wight that comes near us between the eyes, and leave an archaeological record that will bewilder the hell out of anybody who goes digging around here five centuries from now." I handed him the shotgun and my other weaponry, and he gave me a shockingly fierce grin. Properly armed, we both turned to my father, who was still struggling to rearrange his expectations.

That was good. He was off balance. Shamanic change happened when people were off balance. I said, "Come on," and slammed the invisibility shields up around us again. Dad staggered into step behind us and we slipped across the battlefield.

We were within fifty feet of Aidan when he said, "I see you, Joanne."

CHAPTER NINETEEN

"Well, shit." I dropped the invisibility shield, because if he saw right through it there was no point in expending energy to keep it up.

Aidan was sprawled in a throne of bones. His skin was deadened, not quite bleached white, but nothing like his normal, healthy tones. His eyes were black and gold, much more disturbing than just one or the other, and his hair was turning white from the roots down. All he needed was a skull from which to drink blood and the image would be complete. My father whispered, "Aidan," and the boy's gaze switched from me to him.

"Grandpa." He sounded just like a surprised little boy, which gave me hope. Surely if he was entirely absorbed by evil he would have just given a hollow laugh or smote Dad where he stood. In the heartbeat while he was being surprised, I flung a psychic net out, seized him with it, and yanked.

To my pure astonishment, it worked. Aidan crashed against the net's ropes as I hauled it in, but he didn't fall through or throw it off. Triumph exploded in me and for a moment I thought maybe it really would be that easy.

Then the next sheet of lightning fell, and I discovered it didn't care if Aidan was sitting on his throne of bones or bumping on his skinny little-boy butt across the mud and muck. It was perfectly happy to follow him, like electricity to a rod. Aidan howled with offended dignity and thrashed around, but there was strength in the gunmetal threads of my magic. Right then I thought a bomb could go off inside it and I'd have a good chance of holding it in. I pulled Aidan closer, fist over fist, even though the magic probably could have reeled him in without the physical action on my part. But it was all about expectations, so I pulled him in like a fisherman working the nets, and inside of two breaths he was at the heart of our little gathering.

Black lightning fell on us. It electrified Aidan, arching his body and spilling another inch of whiteness into his hair. When he came out of the arch he had a ghoul's grin, all sharp white teeth in a skeletal face. I said, "Now would be good," to my father, and braced myself for the next rain of lightning.

It hit my shields, not Aidan. I'd never made a shield so small and tight that also had to encompass more than one person, but this one had to hold. We were in a tiny bubble of melting silver-blue, the black magic's weight so heavy it split the gunmetal into its base tones. I kept my feet through sheer willpower, using Aidan's terrible changes to strengthen myself. If I fell, so would he, and that was unacceptable.

"Walker?"

"It keeps things out."

"All right."

I had no idea when Morrison and I had moved into the

phase of a relationship where whole conversations were contained within single words and unrelated sentences, but I was glad we had. Having gotten the answer he needed, he methodically checked his weapons, then smoothly lifted his pistol, moving so easily it appeared he had all the time in the world, and began to shoot.

Not wildly. Not Morrison. He wouldn't do that. Every action he'd taken filled up just the right amount of time while the wights left off their harvesting and came for us. The lightning did them no good if Aidan wasn't taking the magic into himself. Morrison fired, the sound explosively loud within the confines of my shields, and the shields did what he'd been asking about: kept things out, but didn't keep them in. He could shoot, and they, in theory, couldn't break through. He moved around the shield bubble, firing steadily, taking down the bad guys with each shot. It wasn't like they were trying to avoid him. They just kept coming.

He shot five, and they still kept coming.

Seven, and they still kept coming.

Two more, and his duty weapon was empty, and they still kept coming. He tucked it into the holster and began with the shotgun, but they still kept coming.

I was a *moron*.

I'd assumed it was just the five wights that had come back with Aidan, but that was a stupid, stupid assumption. They'd had days to drain the dead and create more of themselves. The more of them there were, the more food was funneled to a hungry Master, and the faster a crisis point built. We didn't just have to get Aidan out of here. We had to wipe out dozens, maybe hundreds, of living dead, or the time we went home to would be a ghost world.

Our time wasn't a ghost world, so that meant we would succeed. I promised myself that and tried very hard to ignore the fact that I felt nothing, *nothing,* in this time and place that meant time couldn't be changed here. I'd run up against a wall of magic when I'd tried to save Lugh, in Ireland. Someone had already changed the timeline close to when he died, and it had refused to alter anymore. There was no such wall here. It implied that, despite my insistence that the timeline was pretty fixed and didn't care to be mucked with, that this was a time and place in which it might be muckable.

For one desperate moment I wondered if that meant I really could have changed the whole future if I'd tried hard enough. If I could have saved the aboriginal Americans, and taken the price from the future I knew. Then Morrison said, "Walker," again, this time with a note of warning, and coulda-woulda-shouldas faded. We needed to survive here and now, and the timeline needed to continue as unchanged as it could be, because this was what built the world we knew. Some other me in some other adventure could try the other road, and maybe my dreams would tell me how that turned out.

For now I ground my teeth, fixed the idea of the net around Aidan as hard as I could, and latched it in my mind instead of in my hands. Then I took Morrison's pistol and reloaded it with the spare clip from my own duty weapon, which I hadn't had time to give up after quitting the police force. It had been in Petite's trunk along with the shotgun, which I also took and reloaded when it emptied. Then for good measure I loaded my duty weapon and tucked it into Morrison's belt.

In the twenty seconds that took, my net frayed. When I turned back to Aidan, he lurched at me with his hands clawed, cold fingers latching around my throat. Black magic pulsed out, strangling me, and exultation gleamed in his discolored eyes.

I whispered, "Wrong approach, kiddo," and grabbed his pinkies, wrenching them back. His fingers loosened and his triumph turned to churlish outrage. Black magic roared and spat around me, struggling to find a chink in my armor. There were none, not this time. He could pour all his magic out trying to break through, and I would come out aces.

He realized it at the same time I did, and the outpouring ceased. He collapsed in my arms, his eyes and skin returning to normal, though his hair remained half-bleached. I caught his weight and he tipped his chin up, all exhausted little boy, and whispered, "Mommy?"

I burst out laughing. Honest-to-God belly laughs, the kind that brought tears of mirth to my eyes. I whooped and wheezed, patted his cheek, and spoke to who or whatever was trying to sucker punch me from inside him. "You might've gotten me with 'Mom,' but you pushed that one way too far, buddy. This kid's mommy is somebody else entirely." My laughter faded into cold fury. "Now let him go, you son of a bitch. He's not your vessel, and don't think he means so little to me that I would let that happen."

The words had a familiar ring. Cernunnos had said something very similar just a few days ago, when I was the one boiling over with dark magic. He would have crushed my windpipe to make sure I didn't become the Master's doxy. I wasn't certain I had the nerve to do the same to Aidan, but there were no other ends to which I was not willing to go. This particular battle could go on for the rest of my life, if necessary, and I was okay with that.

"Walker," Morrison said a third time, and we were out of bullets, out of choices and out of time.

Aidan's face split in an ugly grin. The black came back into his eyes, gold flecks warning that he was reaching for magic again. His skin paled, becoming even more wightlike than before, and I braced myself for the inevitable blow.

My father said, "Now," and clean healing power smashed my shields down from the inside.

I'd forgotten about him. I really had. Between Morrison and Aidan, I'd just forgotten about my father, and about what I'd told him to do.

He'd done it in spades. He'd done what the valley shaman had done: reinforced a power circle by going over it again in reverse, except he'd used the bubble of my shields as the base for his power circle. The entire bubble, every surface, top, bottom, sides, where it intersected with the ground, everything. He'd lined it with his own magic, with the pure, deep healing power that he'd developed and honed over a decade and more of traveling America's wounded places. I had no idea if he'd called on any gods. Not any I knew, anyway, and not any I could see, which made me think that he hadn't.

Which meant the magic that battered mine down was all my father's, and that I knew *nothing* of healing, if this was what a Walkingstick could do.

My father's briefly glimpsed aura was green and gray, protective, resolute colors. The magic that burst outward was white, blazing white, a color I'd only ever seen come from the amalgamation of many magic practitioners working together. As it slammed into my shields, it took their power, drained all the magic I was throwing out to keep us safe, to keep Aidan in my grip. It flashed even brighter with that addition, purifying to an even greater degree, but I wasn't kidding myself: Dad's unleashed magic was the most hugely positive power I had ever encountered. He didn't need me for this. My presence only added some shine to a knowledge that ran deep into the earth.

It rolled over the battlefield as quickly as the time bubble had overrun the Appalachian valley, and left roses in its wake.

Some of them were literal: the bodies of the dead changed, softening, becoming things of beauty instead of victims of violence. The wounded staggered to their feet fully healed. Rose petals stuck to their skin instead of blood, and they brushed them away in bewilderment. Wights fell, disintegrating into sweet-smelling dust. The rage in the air gentled. It didn't end: roses, after all, had thorns, but it was mitigated, and the worst of the battle broke apart.

It wouldn't last. There would still be wars fought between Native tribes, between Indians and Europeans, between settlers and the people who had lived on these lands for millennia. But for the moment, at least, the poison was broken apart, and the weight of darkness was lifted.

A handful of wights remained, still spread across the battlefield at the points that had most strongly fed the black lightning. I felt their panic erupt as their power fell away. Then they rallied, coming toward us in a flash, dark magic gathering in a whirlpool as they approached.

A heartbeat too late, I spun toward Aidan.

One slash of light illuminated the dark vortex as it enveloped him, and then he winked out, swallowed whole by time.

"We need to go." My father's voice was completely different, deeper and more determined than I'd ever heard it. I whipped back toward him and squinted, even with the Sight turned off. He blazed with power, spirit animals standing tall and strong on his shoulders. A walking stick on his left, above his heart, and the others were fainter, less easy for me to recognize. Renee appeared on my own shoulder, brought to life and visibility by the magic Dad was working.

That was as clear a statement as I needed, but I still hesitated. "Where did he go?"

"We have to go find out. Come on, Joanne. I can't hold this for long."

I could, but there was no point in saying so. I reached for Morrison's hand. He looked between me and my father, put the guns away, and laced his fingers through mine.

"We were here when you were eight," Joseph Walkingstick said in a strained voice. "That's when I laid down power here. That's when I'm connecting to. I'm twenty years off target, Joanne. You're going to have to get us the rest of the way home."

"Okay." If Dad could haul us through three or four centuries, there was no reason Renee and I couldn't do the fine-tuning. I expressed the thought to her and she hummed, an unexpectedly sweet sound that I took as agreement. I wrapped us all in another shield, feeling it tremble. Dad had taken a lot of power out of me when he'd cleansed the valley. I didn't begrudge what he'd done, but if I'd known it was coming I'd have protected myself better. And Aidan.

I put that thought aside. It wasn't going to do any good. Instead I thought about—well, not quite home. I thought about Petite, parked there on the mountain pull-out. Thought about her solid steel presence there, a new presence: she hadn't been in the Carolina mountains in thirteen years. She was an equally fixed and mobile point, which seemed appropriate for a time-travel focus. I breathed, "Okay," again, and time spun out around us.

At first we stayed where we were, the valley subtly changing shape around us. Then it began changing more rapidly, and then I had the rushing sensation of great speed, like we were tearing down long highways with Petite's windows rolled down and Jim Steinman's *"Nowhere Fast"* blasting on the radio. The idea of that road pulled us south, carrying us back through the mountains until we were in the right place, closing in on the right time. Petite was a ghost in my mind, not there yet, but strengthening.

Time stuttered, stopped, and spat us onto my grandmother's front lawn.

CHAPTER TWENTY

The lawn was scraggly with bluegrass, and the house it fronted needed some TLC. Ranch-style and too small to boast many rooms, it did have a big inviting front porch and a long porch swing with faded lemon-yellow cushions. Hills rose up about forty feet behind the place, the back door obviously opening up into the mountains. A hard-packed dirt driveway boasted a huge old powder-blue Pontiac.

A little girl toddled out of the house and climbed into the porch swing. Hairs rose on my arms and nape as the familiar squeak made the child smile and swing more enthusiastically. Then she tumbled out and jumped down the steps one at a time, counting and providing sound effects as she went, "One! Bang. Two! Bang. Three! Bang." At the bottom she said, "Bang!" one more time for good measure, then ran across the lawn, through my legs, and skidded to a stop a few feet beyond me. I wobbled, feeling like someone had walked on my grave. She turned around, eyed me, or certainly appeared to, then turned away again and picked up a bug from the grass. "Hello, ladybug. Hello. I'm Joanie. Hello, ladybug. I love you!"

Morrison said, "Walker?" incredulously. It was amazing how much meaning he could invest one word with. I swallowed and didn't answer.

A woman I didn't actively remember came onto the porch and leaned against a rail, smiling at the mini-me expressing fondness to a ladybug. The woman wore bell-bottom jeans over bare feet, and a homemade cotton tunic with an embroidered slash at the collar. She was tall and striking, if not exactly pretty, and she wore her black hair in twin braids. Dad whispered, "Ma," and with heart-sinking dread I knew when we were.

My father, twenty-five years younger and shockingly handsome, came out behind my grandmother and leaned against another porch rail, watching three-year-old Joanne with the same fondness my grandmother showed. He was eating cookies. I looked back at my small self. She had chocolate smears on her hands and mouth, and an ant working its way up her leg in search of the sugar.

"The Jones house has been empty a few years," my grandmother said. We all looked at her again. Dad-the-younger hitched himself onto the rail, one leg dangling, the other bare foot planted on the soft old wood. My mother had said he was beautiful when he was young. I, blinkered by a child's blinders, had had no idea how right she was. His long hair was loose and he was wearing jeans and a cut-up T-shirt that showed off smooth brown arms. If catalogs had featured Native models in that era, he would have been world-famous. No wonder Mom had fallen for him.

At the moment he looked mildly amused. "You don't want us underfoot here?"

My grandmother's eyebrows rose. "You left when you were seventeen, Joe. I didn't think you were in any hurry to be back under my roof."

That was the same age I'd left the Qualla. I hadn't known Dad had left early, too. I glanced at the now-him, but he was watching his mother with open pain on his still-handsome features.

"You're both welcome here as much as you like, of course," Grandmother said, and Dad flashed a bright grin.

"Nah, you're right, Ma. We'd be better off in the Jones's place. How much work does it need?"

"As much as anything that's been empty awhile. Won't cost much, though. There's not much good growing soil around them. Too much tobacco sucking up the nutrients. You're really thinking of staying, then?" She kept it under wraps, but there was a bright note of hope in her voice. "She has so much potential, Joe. We could teach her so much if you stayed here."

"No, Ma. I told you before. Shell left her with me to keep her out of sight. Teaching her is too risky, no matter how much potential she's got. I'm supposed to be keeping her safe, not putting her in the line of fire."

My grandmother clucked her tongue. "That's nonsense. I know that Irish girl turned your head, but there are no monsters in the dark, Joe. Sorcerers are stories to frighten children with. No one is hunting Joanie."

"Maybe you're right, but I promised Shell I'd keep her safe, and this is the best way I can see to do it. If she's right, then if Joanie hasn't been initiated as a shaman there's no reason for anything to come after her."

I closed my eyes, impotent anger throbbing in my temples. I was sure Dad had meant well, but surely anybody who'd seen *Star Wars* knew that hiding the truth never turned out well for anyone. My entire life might have been different if he'd listened to my grandmother.

She, with the patience of a woman who figured she was in the first skirmishes of a protracted war, let it go. "Well, tell you what. I've got to go see Carrie this morning, but you and Joanie can stay here and eat all the cookies, and I'll get the keys to the Jones place from the real-estate agent while I'm in town. I'll pick you up after lunch and we can go take a look at it, see what you think."

Dad, my Dad, the now-Dad standing next to me on the lawn, whispered, "No, Ma. Stay home," but the one on the porch smiled and nodded. "Sounds fine, Ma. Tell Carrie hello."

"She wants you and Joanie to come see her."

"She wants Joanie to come see her," Dad corrected cheerfully enough. "Nobody cares about me now."

My grandmother smiled. "That's what happens when you have kids."

"Tell her we'll come down in a couple days. I want to get the mountains back under my skin for a while."

Grandmother hesitated on the steps, looking back at Dad when he said that. "I'll never understand why you left, Joe, not if the mountains call you back so strongly."

Dad put his fist just beneath his breastbone. "Had to, Ma. It was pulling me."

My heart missed a beat at the familiarity of that gesture, and of that feeling. The same sensation had been dragging me through magical mishaps for the past fifteen months. I'd had no idea Dad had felt it, too. There was so damned much I didn't know.

Grandmother nodded and left, the Pontiac's massive engine roaring down the mountains. I guessed my father and I had come by our love of classic cars honestly. Dad turned, watching her go long after the car was out of sight, then gave me a hard look. "What are we doing here, Joanne?"

"Hell if I know. I was aiming for home. I don't know why we hiccuped. This is… I mean, this is…"

"Yeah, it is. About half an hour from now she'll be dead."

"What?" Morrison, who had been watching the younger me with fascination, came around at that. Little Joanie, undisturbed by any of our discussion, kept playing with bugs.

"She died in a car wreck," I said when Dad's silence drew out. "Right after Dad and I came to visit when I was about three. We left after the funeral and never came back until I was a teenager."

Dad said, "I didn't think you remembered that," in an accusing tone.

I sighed. "I didn't. I don't. Exactly. I just…I got reminded a couple of weeks ago. It's been a rough couple weeks." I said that a lot. I hoped someday it would stop being true.

"I'm going to go stop her." Dad walked away, his footsteps bending the patchy grass underfoot. I didn't know how that worked, except this was real to us, even if we were ghostlike to our other selves. They couldn't see us, but maybe we could affect them. Morrison and I both stared after Dad, not quite believing he really did intend to go stop my grandmother until he disappeared down the road. Only then did Morrison turn to me in concern. *"Can* he?"

"No. I don't think so. Probably not." I thought about the sensation I'd had on the battlefield, the idea that the timeline in that particular place was still malleable, and worried at my lower lip. "Maybe."

"What happens if he does?"

"I don't know."

"Are we going to stop him?"

"I don't know." My younger self was industriously digging

a hole in Grandmother's lawn. Her fingers were filthy, nails caked with dirt, and she looked as happy as a pig in mud. I had no memories of doing that kind of thing. I remembered playing cowboys and Indians at Little Bighorn, rolling down small steep hills and scrambling breathlessly up the other side, alternating between being a cowboy and being an Indian. "Bang bang bang!" as I finger-gun shot up one side, and *fwipping* imaginary arrows down the other. I remembered sticking my fingers into the scars bullets had left in those hilltops. I remembered kicking sand and dust up in Nevada, never knowing I was disturbing the remains of nuclear test sites. I remembered a lot of things, but none of them seemed to have the childish simplicity of digging a hole to China, which appeared to be my small self's goal in life.

I would be a completely different person if I'd grown up on the Qualla. I was sure if we'd stayed here, my grandmother would have eventually worn Dad down, and I'd have begun shamanic studies at a much younger age. I might never have crossed paths with Coyote, and I almost certainly would never have met Morrison.

But it was my grandmother, my father's mother, and it obviously still tore him apart that she'd died. Maybe he wouldn't have stayed, anyway. Maybe the promise to my mother—to *Shell,* I'd never imagined Sheila MacNamarra with a nickname—maybe that would have kept him moving, especially if he thought he would lose the argument about my training. Maybe nothing would have changed, except my grandmother would still be alive. I said, "I don't know," again, and sat down in the grass with my hands covering my face.

After a moment a light touch brushed my arm. I spread my fingers to see little Joanne peeking at me. "Are you my momma? You look like me. We both has fweckles."

"Have freckles," I corrected automatically, then closed my

eyes, because I couldn't stand looking into my own interested baby face. "No, sweetheart. I'm not your momma, even if we both have freckles."

"Are you sad? Is that why you hiding you face?"

I made a soft sound. "I'm a little bit sad, yes."

She patted my arm. "Don't be sad. I has a ladybug. Hewe." She offered me the bug on a dirty fingertip.

I unfolded my hand to stroke its ghostly back. I couldn't feel it, and wasn't sure why she could pat me when she'd run through me once already. I suspected it had something to do becoming aware of me after she'd dashed through me, and let it go at that. "Thank you for sharing your ladybug. It's very nice."

"Is you happy now?"

I couldn't help smiling. "Yeah. Yeah, I am. Thank you, Joanie."

"You welcome!" She scampered off again, revealing Morrison watching me—us, I supposed—with an expression of wonder.

"You think *I* take things in stride, Walker?"

"It's not the first time I've had a conversation with my younger self. This one was nicer than most. Usually I excoriate myself. Of course, I also usually learn something."

"What'd you learn this time?"

"That she's a nice little girl and probably deserves to grow up into somebody less messed up than I am. Maybe I should go help Dad try to save my grandmother."

Morrison's voice got very quiet. "Don't." I blinked up at him and he met my gaze, concern rising in his blue eyes. "You do that, Walker, and everything changes, right?"

"Maybe. Probably. I don't know. I've never really changed anything. I don't know what happens, but it seems most likely."

"Don't make me miss out on you." He spoke so softly he

sounded like a different man. "Don't change our future before we get a chance at finding out what it is, Walker. We've come this far. I want to find out where this road goes."

The part of me that didn't know when to shut up almost pointed out he wouldn't know any better, if everything did change. The part of me that occasionally said the right thing got there first, and said, "So do I."

Morrison's shoulders dropped about six inches, and I had the dizzying realization he'd actually been afraid. I got up and wrapped my arms around his waist. "I'm sorry. I don't know what to do, Morrison. It's my grandmother. I don't even re-member her, but I can't blame Dad for wanting to try."

"He must know better." Morrison sounded shaken, which made me hug him harder.

"He does. He's just not thinking. Or he knows more than we do. We'll go ask. We'll find out. Come on." I moved half a step and bumped into something.

I looked down to find Joanie gazing up at Morrison with starry-eyed adoration. She tugged my pant leg and pronounced, "He vewy handsome," in a stage whisper that would've been audible in the rafters.

I laughed out loud and said, "Yeah, he is," as Morrison crouched and grinned at mini-me. "And you're very pretty," he informed her, which made me laugh again. Joanie skipped off, pink and happy as could be. I offered a half-hearted kick at Morrison's shin as he stood. "Imprinting yourself on me young, are you?"

He looked horrified, then slightly uncomfortable. "She's a cute kid, Walker. She— You— Ah, hell. I wasn't think-ing about her being you. I was imagining her being—" He stopped abruptly and his ears flushed red.

My eyebrows went up. "As being what?"

He said, "Nothing," so hastily that I followed his train of thought and turned as pink as Joanie had.

"Oh. Um. Okay. Um. Let's, um. Let's go find Dad and tell him he can't do this."

Still hastily, Morrison said, "Good idea," and we skittered off my grandmother's lawn like a couple of guilty kids.

Dad hadn't gotten all that far, really. He was about half a mile down the road, at what I suspected was the crash site. The road and sky were both clear, no standing water to make the old boat of a Pontiac slip or to create glare that might have blinded my grandmother as she drove. There were no fallen trees, no lurking deer, nothing to drive her off the road. I went up to him, hands in my pockets, and said, "Maybe she was just driving too fast."

He shook his head once. "That's all you, Joanne. Your grandmother never broke the speed limit in her life. I don't know where you got the daredevil streak."

"You're telling me you never sped on all those trips across the country?"

He slid a perplexed glance at me. "With my daughter in the car? No. There was never any hurry great enough to risk you."

And the hits just kept on coming. I tipped my chin up and stared at the sky, absorbing that. Then I reversed my gaze, sighing at the view again. "You know you can't save her, Dad."

"I know I shouldn't. It could change everything. But don't tell me you're happy with the way things turned out, Joanne. You've hated me since you were a teenager."

Air whuffed out of me. "Hated you. No. I just couldn't figure out what the fuck I had to do to make you love me. Your daughter, so disappointing you decided to call her by a boy's name."

"Is *that* what you think?"

"Come on, Dad. I mean, it was pretty clear you didn't want to be saddled with me in the first place, but the point kind of got driven home when Aidan said you were teaching *him*. Sorry I wasn't born with a penis, Dad. So glad you got a grandkid who was."

"Joanne, I was trying to *protect* you—"

"Yeah. By keeping us moving all the time. By not telling me about my heritage. By letting me get so fucked in the head that I did the stupidest things possible to try to get attention. From you, from anybody, whatever the hell. Good job, Dad. Banner job."

Dad, through his teeth, said, "I started teaching Aidan because I'd realized how badly I'd done by you. I thought I was protecting you, Joanne, and for the love of God, I didn't call you Jo because I wanted a boy. I thought it made it you and me against the world, Big Joe and Little Jo—"

"That's what I thought until you started looking at me like I was a stranger!"

"You were growin' up and no matter what I did you kept recognizin' more and more about the shamanism I was practicin'! If I was lookin' at you like you were a stranger it was 'cause I was tryin' ta figure out how to keep you out of it!"

Having grown up with it, I almost never actually heard my father's North Carolina accent, but when his temper got up, it got thicker, until he was almost indecipherable. The same thing happened to me if I got pissed enough, and I was fast approaching that level of anger now. "Like I said, banner goddamned job, Dad! You—"

"And then you said we were comin' back here, hell or high water, back to where your grandmother died, and I knew I'd lost you—"

"I was thirteen years old, Dad, you don't lose somebody

when they're thirteen years old unless you goddamned well *give up on them!*"

The rest of the argument was shattered by the Pontiac screaming around the corner, a fallen angel in pursuit.

All the what-ifs fell away. I didn't think, I just reacted. I threw a wall of magic up between the Pontiac and the angel— it *could not* be an angel, fallen or otherwise, but it sure as hell looked like one, with black-soot wings spread wider than the road and a beautiful face scored by misery and despair— I threw magic, and the angel smacked against it at full speed.

Smacked against and burst through, almost all at once. The strength I was so proud of was utterly meaningless by comparison to its. Dad gasped, *"Kolona Ayeliski,"* and the Cherokee language Renee had revived translated it—*Raven Mocker.*

Even I knew about Raven Mocker. He was one of those legends I'd sarcastically dismissed as a teen determined to turn her back on all things Cherokee. He was a demon, a monster, a fallen angel, sure. Something from the Lower World that disguised himself as a creature from the Upper, pretending to provide spiritual guidance and safety while sucking the soul out of his victims. Raven Mocker was the specific thing that vigil-keepers were keeping vigil against, when they watched over the bodies of the dead.

He was not a daylight monster, and there was no way in hell he should be chasing my grandmother down the road at deadly speeds. I gathered strength again to throw another wall up, or to catch him with a net, anything to at least slow him down so the Pontiac could slow down, too. I waited for a straight stretch, a place where Grandmother would have time to apply the brakes without going flying off the mountainside, and I dug deep, getting ready to throw everything I had between her and the Raven Mocker.

Shields as strong as my own wrapped me, muffling my

power, and rebounding it back into me when I let it go. An echo banged around my head, magic left with nowhere else to go, and I staggered a few inches. Dad caught my shoulders, steadying me, and I recognized the steady, implacable touch of his magic as what was shielding me. "What the hell!"

"Who do you think *Kolona Ayeliski* is, Joanne? Who do you think your mother was trying to protect you from when she brought you to me? He must have been waiting here for some sign we'd returned. We just gave it to him. We stepped through time and landed where we weren't supposed to be. If I had agreed to go into town with your grandmother...."

Any hold I had on my magic dissipated. "She obviously knew he was chasing her," I said dully. "And he must not have known we weren't—I wasn't—in the car. She..."

She leaned on the gas pedal, the Pontiac picking up incredible speed on the straight stretch. There was another curve up ahead, a hairpin bend.

Grandmother never hit the brakes as she approached the bend. Dad closed his eyes, unable to watch as the car soared went off the narrow road, briefly and beautifully unbowing to gravity's call. It sailed farther than I imagined possible. I stood in Dad's grip, unable to take my own gaze away until it fell from my line of sight and the first scream of metal sounded. Then my own eyes closed, and Morrison was there to hold both of us up.

We skipped forward through time.

CHAPTER TWENTY-ONE

I knew where we were before I even opened my eyes. It was the smell, the faint scent of antiseptic, that sharp astringency in dry air that hospitals never quite manage to erase. I hated that smell, and I said, "No. No. Get me out of here. Get me out of here, I can't do this again," without ever opening my eyes. My heart was sick in my chest, pounding so hard I thought I would throw up. "Get me out of here, Daddy. Get us out of here now. Please. Please. I don't want to see. Not again. Please get me out of here, Daddy. Please." Tears squeezed through my lashes and left hot streaks on my face, but I would not open my eyes.

I heard the men catch their breath as they figured out where we were. I was sobbing by then. We were in a hospital ward and there were two very small babies nearby, and there was only enough life in the both of them for one. Morrison caught me, holding on hard as I thrashed against him, the words tearing at my throat. "Get me out of here, get me out of here, I can't stand it, I can't stand it I hate it I hate it I hate it get me out of here please please please *get me out of here I can't I can't I can't* not now *why weren't you here!"*

I tore myself out of Morrison's arms and hit Dad as hard as I could. "You're a healer, you're a goddamned *healer,* why weren't you here to save her, why weren't you *here?"*

And my father, terribly, whispered, "I was."

My eyes flew open. Beyond Dad-now I saw Dad-then, standing outside the ward windows, his hands clenching and opening with impotence. It wasn't the distance, I knew it wasn't the distance, they would let him in, he was their grandfather, and besides, I didn't believe for a minute he couldn't affect a healing from a mere few yards away. Not when the babies were so fresh and new, with no expectations placed on the world. Dad could do it. He could do it.

But he didn't. His walking-stick spirit animal sat on his shoulder, its face hidden behind long thin arms, as if the anguish twisting my father's features hurt it just as badly. "You have to See, Joanne," my now-father said in a thick voice. "You have to understand."

"I don't want to see!"

"Don't." Morrison sounded dangerous. "Don't do this to her, Joseph."

Somehow that gave me the strength to look, even though my father said nothing. I reached for Morrison's hand, crushing his fingers with mine, and steeled myself to look, just once, at the babies.

My whole life I'd had the idea they'd only had enough strength for one. That Ayita had given up her strength for Aidan so that at least one of them would live. I Saw now, for the first time, how incredibly right I had been. The babies, born just minutes apart, already lying so close together, shared more than the strength of their bodies. They shared the strength of their souls, as well, Ayita's dancing, laughter-filled soul merging and melding with Aidan's more serious, contemplative personality. Her yellows and pinks wound around his blues and greens, the colors brightening and burgeoning until the single surviving child's aura burned almost white, all the time.

Two-spirited. No wonder Aidan had so much raw power. Two-spirited souls, people who carried both the masculine and the feminine within them, were sacred to most Native Americans, the Cherokee included. They were respected and believed to have a closer connection to the spirit world than most, making them natural shamans and guides.

And Aidan was literally two-spirited. Like my friend Billy, he actually shared his body with his sister's spirit, but there was one huge difference. Billy's sister, Caroline, had died when she was eight, a developed personality of her own already. She'd remained with Billy for decades because of their close bond, and that had affected him, but it wasn't the same as being born from the same womb, together for every moment of their brief existences, and given unto one another in death as in life. Aidan and Ayita's spirits were melded from birth, incomplete without one another. Aidan's power was boundless, with Ayita's spirit a part of his.

And it was his only chance against the Executioner.

I knew it in my gut, inside the sickness that still boiled within me. I turned away, wishing I could throw up. I wasn't one for Seeing the future, but Renee, on my shoulder like the walking stick on Dad's shoulder, showed me something that was, to her, so close in time to right now that it was all the same. Now and then were so close together, from an unchanging insect's viewpoint, that there was no particular difference in Seeing what lay in the children's future. Maybe Dad could have saved Ayita, but it would have been at the cost of both their lives, when the Master came for them. And the Master, Raven Mocker, *Kolona Ayeliski, was* coming for them.

There'd been some question about it, with me. Maybe Mom had hidden me well enough. Maybe keeping me out of the traditional training had been enough to slip me under the radar. But the walking stick had shown Dad what lay in Aidan's future. What lay in Ayita's future, if they both lived.

Death had lain in their future, if they both lived. They only stood a chance together, as one, two-spirited.

Ayita Walkingstick had only lived a few minutes, but she was the bravest person I had ever met.

Empty, drained and exhausted, I said, "Take us home," to Renee, and she did.

Thursday, March 30, 12:12 p.m.

The sky was unbearably bright when we stepped back into our own time. Petite was where she'd been, sitting quietly under a thin film of dust. The Impala was gone, with no recent tread marks to say when. I was glad I'd taken out full insurance on the thing, and kind of wondered why Petite was still there—and undamaged—if the Impala was missing. I unlocked her doors and sat down in the driver's seat to turn the radio on and find out what day it was.

Thursday, according to the DJ. That made no sense. Morrison and I had gone into the mountains on Saturday. We'd lost most of a week.

They were not lost, Renee said. *The days passed as you ran the ancient forests.*

Of course they had. We'd overnighted in the valley with the isolated tribe, then it had taken us three days to get to the Ohio. I slumped in Petite's front seat, wrung out and with no idea at all of where I should start. Morrison leaned in the open door, concerned. "You okay, Walker?"

"I'm really not. I'm really, really not." I closed my eyes, and after a moment Morrison closed the door gently and went to talk to my dad. I heard the explanation without letting myself listen to the words, and all but felt Morrison's sorrow roll toward me. I still had afterimages burned into the backs of my eyes, things I hadn't let myself look at, in the hospital. Doctors. My fifteen-year-old self, stone-faced to keep anybody from suspecting I was screaming inside. I had never let my grief and rage and helplessness go the way I'd just done while in Morrison's arms. Eventually it would probably be cathartic, perhaps finally allowing wounds that were scabbed over to properly heal. Right now I was just exhausted and fragile, prepared to shatter again if anything hit me wrong.

I leaned forward and touched the bottom edge of Petite's windshield. It was whole, unmarked—I never risked dings turning into cracks—and the world beyond it was slightly hazy from the thin film of dust. Other than that, though, perfect. I reached for the image that had risen from within me the day my shamanic powers had awakened: the idea that Petite's windshield reflected the state of my soul. In my mental image, there was a massive hole punched through the windshield, spiderwebs and long cracks radiating out from it. Over the past year the cracks had begun sealing up, the spiderweb receding, glass fusing back together. Recently it had become more whole than broken, but the puncture wound was still there.

Its edges, though, were maybe a little softer than they'd been before. The spiderweb had closed up around it until the entire fracture was only about the size of my spread hand, instead of spreading from one side of the windshield to the other. I didn't think the damage would ever be completely fixed. Eventually it might just be a warped spot, though, just a wobble in the windshield where resin had been poured in and sealed to the unbroken whole. I tried fixing the idea of a glass-sealer to the windshield, seeing how much I could smooth out if I put actual effort into it.

To my surprise, a delicate layer of new glass appeared, splootching across the bullet-size hole itself and filling in more of the spiderweb around it. I flattened a piece of film over it to make sure it stayed in place, and sat back to study it. I couldn't say the whole of the scar had shrunk any, but it was bandaged, which was more than it had been for over a decade. I patted Petite's dashboard and whispered, "Looking good, girl."

My father and Morrison were still talking. I thought the topic of conversation was probably what to do next, and knew I should be taking part in it. I didn't want to. I wanted to curl up in Petite's passenger seat and sleep for about sixty hours. It wasn't even that I hadn't had enough sleep, because for once I was getting reasonable amounts. I couldn't, as usual, remember when I'd eaten last, except for a vague awareness that I had been a coyote when I had. My stomach rumbled, reminding me that Morrison had been right, I was too skinny. I'd cannibalized my body's extra resources and been burning up muscle with all the shapeshifting I'd done in Ireland, and hadn't come anywhere near returning to fighting weight. Food suddenly sounded more important than sleep, even if I was an emotional basket case. I got out of the car.

Both men stopped talking like they'd been caught doing something naughty, and looked at me guiltily. I deduced they had not been discussing a game plan, but had instead been talking about me. "I don't even want to know."

Relief replaced guilt, which made me want to know after all, but it was too late. "Do you guys have a plan? Because I don't have a plan, and we've missed a week and I don't know where the hell Aidan is and I don't know what to do and some-body's got to go tell Sara her husband is dead and I'm hungry enough to gnaw my arm off and, and, and..." I put my arms on the top of Petite's door and put my forehead against them, completely out of steam. Muffled, I asked, "Is that diner we used to go to still open, Dad? Because I could really go for about three pounds of applesauce biscuits and grits."

My father, cautiously, said, "There's going to be a lot of magic coming our way, Joanne. Eating—"

I lifted my head to give him a flat stare. "I. Don't. Care. Having food in my stomach has never weighed me down when I needed to work magic—" which may have been because I never remembered to eat while running around on adventures, but he didn't need to know that, because "—and even if it did, I've been running on empty for most of two weeks, how can it *possibly* have been only two weeks since that dance concert? Two and a half weeks? Since I shot Raleigh?" That was addressed to Morrison, who half smiled.

"Because despite your best efforts, Walker, the calendar only passes one day at a time."

"I guess." I kept looking in his direction, but I wasn't focusing on him anymore. "Oh, hell, Morrison. It's Thursday. Never mind Dad and Lucas. *We've* been missing for most of a week. And Aidan..."

Aidan had been pulling down power strong and focused enough that he wasn't as wedded to arriving at the same times or places we were. For all I knew, he could have come back within minutes of us leaving. He could have returned to an entirely different location. For all I knew, he'd stepped into some already volatile location and dropped a massacre's worth of death magic into it. If we'd been missing most of a week, we could be screwed.

"We need to get into town."

★ ★ ★

Cherokee was deserted. It wasn't like high tourist season anyway, when people came by the thousands to go to the casinos and visit the mountains, but at noon on a Thursday there should be traffic, people coming and going to lunch, little kids out of school, buses carting older students on field trips—the usual signs of life in a small town. But it was all missing. Petite crept down the main drag, no traffic to make me drive at a normal speed, and we all peered down side streets and into blank, black business windows. Vehicles were idle, dust-sprinkled like Petite, *CLOSED* signs hung on normally open doors, and no one was to be seen on the streets. It felt like a ghost town.

None of us said anything, because we all knew none of us could answer the questions we all wanted to ask. Dad was wedged into Petite's tiny backseat, nose all but pressed against her window. Seeing the town like this had to be worse for him than me, and I found it disconcerting as hell. We passed a guns-and-ammo store and Morrison said, "Stop."

I did. He got out of the car and, to my eye-popping astonishment, broke the store's front window to let himself in. Three minutes later he came out with new ammo for our duty weapons and the shotgun, and a guilty expression. "I left a couple hundred dollars on the till," he muttered defensively.

Grinning, I leaned over to kiss him, whispered, "Good thinking," against his mouth, and got back to the business of creeping down Cherokee's main street.

We all three saw it at the same time, glimpsed out of the corner of our eyes as we passed another side street. I hit the brakes, not that we'd been moving fast, and hovered my hand above the gearshift, not quite willing to put her in reverse yet. "Was that…?"

Dad and Morrison said, "Did you—" and, "Was that—" at

the same time, making me pretty sure we'd all seen the same thing. I said, "What the..." and cautiously put Petite into Reverse. We backed up a few feet, all of us looking to the left.

A CDC truck sat at the other end of the street. I killed Petite's engine and we all sat there staring at it. I'd never seen one except in movies. It wasn't particularly menacing in and of itself, but the words blazoned on the side were by their nature scary: *Centers for Disease Control*.

There were no circumstances ever in the whole wide world that a person wanted to see a vehicle with those words in her hometown. In fact, a person never wanted to see a vehicle with those words anywhere, because the CDC was not an agency that fucked around. They were the people called in for anthrax scares. They were the people who maintained—for reasons I would never, ever understand—live smallpox samples. They were the people who went into Ebola breakouts, who fought the plague, who, for sweet pity's sake, *kept the live smallpox virus* under lock and key within their facilities. CDC workers were goddamned superheroes, and any circumstances that required superheroes were not good circumstances for the local population.

"Walker," Morrison said in a thunderous voice, "please tell me we haven't triggered the zombie apocalypse."

I said, "We have not triggered the zombie apocalypse," obligingly enough, and Morrison relaxed a hair. I said, "Aidan might have," and Morrison tensed up again, glowering at me in a fashion reminiscent of the tried-and-true Almighty Morrison.

My father, unable to believe we were making light of the situation and possibly a little afraid we weren't, said, "The zombie apocalypse?"

Right about then the CDC guys came pouring out of everywhere and surrounded my car.

CHAPTER TWENTY-TWO

A fully bio-suited man in orange threatened Petite's window with a fist. I unrolled it slowly, trying to keep my hands visible as I did so. Morrison put his hands on the dashboard, and my father put his on the back of Morrison's seat. The bio-suit man did not look reassured by any of that, and my brain, scared silly of what a bio-suit suggested, disengaged from smart and went straight to smart-ass.

"Hello, officer," I said in the most chipper voice I could come up with. "Was I speeding?"

Morrison groaned and the bio-suit man didn't look like he thought I was funny at all. "Who are you? How did you get in here? This whole county is quarantined."

"Holy crap, really? How are you controlling the bor—" That was not a helpful question. Neither was "You can't possibly have managed to roust everybody out of the hills, have you?" which I also got halfway through before Morrison growled, "Walker," as a suggestion that I shut up.

I said, "I'm sorry," after a few seconds of trying to get my mouth and my nerves under control. "We were camping. We had no idea anything was going on."

"We've been doing low flyovers for the past three days, broadcasting messages to come to a center for inspection. How could you have missed those?"

I glanced at Morrison, who had no helpful answers written on his forehead. I swallowed and looked back at the CDC guy. "…we were spelunking?"

"Where's your gear?"

The only answer to that was "In the trunk," and I really did not want paranoid government officials opening a trunk full of shotguns and other monster-hunting gear. I did have carry permits for all of it, but they were carry permits for Washington State. I wasn't sure how well that would go over, two thousand miles from home. I tried for distraction instead. "Officer, what's going on here?"

"Lady, you wouldn't believe me if I told you. I need you to drive down toward the van, very slowly. When you get there you're going remove yourself from the vehicle. You will be isolated, tested for disease and disinfected. The car will undergo forensic scrutiny—"

A tingle of outrage danced up my spine. "Excuse me? Undergo *what?*"

"Forensic scrutiny, ma'am. It means the vehicle will be stripped—"

"Like hell it will be."

"It's necessary, ma'am. We need to inspect it for any foreign material that may be able to carry disease. You've been inside the epicenter of a plague. The vehicle has to be thoroughly examined, even if that means destroying it."

Morrison put his chin in his hand and his elbow in the passenger side window, looking the other way. I didn't know if he was fighting laughter or despair, but he was ostentatiously not getting involved in this particular argument. I smiled at the CDC guy, who took it as a good sign and therefore didn't quite understand when I said, "Over my dead body."

When he caught up to what I'd actually said, he got grim. "If necessary, yes, ma'am. I have military reserves on hand and at my command—"

"Really." My voice squeaked with interest. "You've got the U.S. military on the Qualla? On land that belongs to a foreign and sovereign nation state? How's that playing on the news, Officer? How's that going over with the Eastern Band of Cherokee, or the Navajo Nation? You making it nice and clear they're next, after an already embittered history of governmental dismissal of Native rights? Are you—"

Somewhere in the middle of my little rant, I started to recognize what I was describing as being *exactly* what the Master, his Executioner, and the wights were probably after. I broke off with a whispered, "Holy shit. It's that easy, isn't it. It's really that easy."

"Walker?"

"I'm sure the government has got a media blackout on this anyway, but holy shit, Morrison, it's perfect. Whether there's a real disease or whether Sara didn't listen and burn the bodies—"

My father said, "Burn *whose* bodies?" but I wasn't going to stop and explain just then.

"—and if they rose and have created more wights, either way it's a perfect excuse to bring the government into the reservations. And there's still bad blood there, there's always going to be, so once word gets out that the government is trampling Native rights and invading reservation territory again, it's all

over. Either the First Nation peoples are going to revolt and
be killed, or they're going to be taken away, spread out, and
assimilated into nonexistence. It's putting a shiny red bow on
the genocides. And I bet anything Aidan's out there stirring
up the will to fight instead of to sit back and take is all pas-
sively. Where *is* everybody?" I demanded of the CDC guy,
and behind his glass plate mask I saw a hint of uncertainty
flicker across his face.

"You don't have them, do you." A smile started to stretch
my mouth. "You people came in here like a load of bricks,
threatening and angry and scared, and the People told you to
fuck off, didn't they. I mean, I'm sure some of them stayed.
Lots, even, I mean, not everybody in this area has Native
blood, never mind cares enough to stand up to the Feds, and
somebody called you in, after all. But a whole lot of 'em just
went to the hills and now you can't find them, can you. You're
afraid there's a whole disease center out there somewhere, and
it's completely out of your control. Tell me, who called you?
Was it Sara Isaac from the FBI?"

The guy's whole face pinched up. "We have an FBI agent
missing?"

My grin went wild and broad for a couple seconds. "No.
She's not missing. She's just chosen her side. Look, listen to me,
buddy. If you come across bodies with an ash mark on their
forehead, like a fingerprint burned in? Just burn them. Don't
do an autopsy, don't try to figure out what killed them or if
it's infectious. It's not infectious, except through a touch like
the one on the bodies, and you will never understand what
killed them, not really. If you want to help, burn the bodies
to keep them from rising—"

CDC Man turned white. I took that to mean he'd seen
some of them rise, and I was fairly certain he'd lost some men
to the newly risen.

"—and otherwise, stay out of the way and let me do my job."

He rallied a little. "Who are you? What do you know about this? Disease control is our job, not yours. Who *are* you?"

"My name," I said, mostly under my breath, "is Siobhán Grainne MacNamarra Walkingstick, and I'm the answer to all your prayers."

It seemed appropriate to throw Petite into Drive and roar off down the road after a line like that, so that's what I did. CDC guys flung themselves out of the way, I pulled a 180, and we tore back the way we'd come, hitting ninety miles an hour in about a quarter mile. I cackled the whole way. Morrison covered his eyes with one hand, then dropped it. "I can't believe you told them your name."

"Oh, come on, Petite is unique. It would only take them about fifteen seconds to find out who I was anyway, and it was a *great* exit line. C'mon, Morrison, you gotta admit, that was an *awesome* exit."

"Walker, I'm a police captain. From the law's perspective, that was not only incredibly dangerous—you could have killed someone!—but also unbelievably stupid. They're only doing their jobs, and we should help them with that." The corner of his mouth twitched. "From a personal perspective, though, yes, I've got to hand it to you, Walker. You do know how to make an exit."

My father said, "You should have seen the exit when she left the Qualla," and right about then the military boys started giving chase.

There was no chance they'd catch us in land vehicles. Unfortunately, they had a helicopter. I gunned Petite, sending her well over a hundred miles an hour, and we shot up a mountain road that wasn't intended to be taken at fifty. I downshifted ahead of a sharp corner that my reflexes remembered more than my eyes saw. Morrison hit a high note I didn't think a man of his size could produce as we swung around a curve with nothing but hope keeping us on the road. Then he clamped his eyes and mouth shut and hunkered down while I proved to myself, my God, and anybody else within a six-mile radius that I was still the best damned driver in the Qualla. All my shakes and emotions disappeared into the adrenaline rush of dangerous speeds. It was as good as, better than, a drum circle: this was all me, skill and a love of the road tying together to make the best possible antidote for fear and exhaustion.

Raven bounced around in my head, cawing and *klok*ing and squealing with excitement that only encouraged me. Rattler swayed, hissing gleefully, and I tapped into the speed he'd been known to offer me, increasing my reflexes just that much more. The downshifts came half a heartbeat later, the upshifts that much sooner, eking extra yards out of each action. I didn't care that a helicopter had the advantage. I was going to outrun it, and disappear us into the hills right under the military's noses. I bellowed, "Renee, what can you give me?" and my newest companion animal, who didn't seem naturally inclined to outrageous activity, stepped up.

Time slowed down. That happened a lot, when things were going badly, but for once it was just for the pure outrageous joy of pushing myself, my car, and my magic to the limit. I saw—Saw—the road unfold in front of me with astounding clarity. Saw patches of gravel, fine sprays of water, the smear of some unfortunate possum who'd played chicken with a car and lost. I twitched the wheel fractions of an inch, feeling Petite respond to the most minute requests, and over the roar of her engine I shouted, "Where we going, Dad?"

He yelled, "We're not going to make it!" back, but that

wasn't what I'd asked. "It's an eight-mile drive, Jo! The chopper is going to catch up!"

"Just tell me where we're going!"

"There's a track off the road up there—" He pointed at a site about two mountains over, his fingertip bobbling with our speed.

I remembered when he said it. It wasn't much of a track, not something a car could go up. It was rocky for the first several hundred yards, rough enough terrain that it wouldn't take footprints or other signs of passage to any meaningful degree. He was right, though: through the twists and curves of the mountain roads, it was about eight miles away, even if I could see the stretch of road it branched off from where we were. There were chunks of green valley and steep hollers between us, nothing a 4x4 could traverse, never mind my lowslung 1969 Mustang. We hit a straight stretch, a familiar straight stretch, the last one my grandmother had ever driven, and all sorts of crazy ideas came together in my mind.

I remembered the Pontiac's massive blue weight, the black soot wings of Raven Mocker making mockery of its attempt at flight. I thought of the helicopter coming up the mountain the short way, blades hauling awkward dragonfly shapes through the air, and I thought, *hell.* I thought of Wile E. Coyote and the Road Runner laying down road over empty sky, and I thought, *well, hell,* whispered, "Chitty Chitty Bang Bang," and slammed Petite off the side of a mountain.

We flew.

The Rainbow Connection came together beneath us, every ounce of my shielding magic slapping blocks of bright-colored roadway together under Petite's wheels. It wasn't going to last, it couldn't possibly last, but it didn't *have* to last. It just had to get us across half a mile of clear air, an impossible shortcut to the hidden path into the hills. I drew strength from the astonished earth, pulling it up as fast as it would let me to braid it into the air bridge. I felt like Indiana Jones crossing the invisible bridge, except moving at 110 miles per hour instead of creeping on hands and knees.

Dad made apoplectic sounds in the backseat. Morrison clutched the dashboard and stared at treetops three hundred feet below us. I grinned so broadly my face hurt. I had never had so much fun in my life. I desperately wanted to turn around and see if the helicopter had caught up, if they could see what we were doing, and how they were taking it if they could. I didn't dare, afraid if I looked away the path I was building would fall apart, but I could imagine their expressions.

I did not imagine them firing missiles at us, which is what happened next. Dad gave a strangled warning shout at the same time I heard them, high whistles that sounded a lot like they did in movies. Morrison roared something incomprehensible, but I didn't dare listen. I didn't know how fast missiles traveled. I knew how fast *we* were going, Petite's speedometer clocking well over 130 now, but I was pretty sure missiles flew faster than that. I wondered if they were heat-seeking or targeted or what, then remembered everybody's favorite deep-sea maneuver and hit the brakes, spinning the second 180 of the afternoon.

I wished to God I could see it all from the outside. The shields I drew from the earth rearranged so fast I heard them clattering, blocks of magic crashing together to keep a surface under Petite's wheels. She fishtailed from turning at such high speeds, but bless her little steel soul, she leapt right forward again as I leaned on the gas. All of a sudden we were charging a helicopter, and I did get a chance to see the pilots' faces after all. There were two of them, a man and a woman, and their faces showed a range of emotion from shock and bewilderment to outright fury and determination to take us down.

The woman, however, also looked like her every prayer had been answered, that she was seeing living proof that the world was as awesome and amazing as she'd ever hoped. She looked like someone had just proven to her that magic was real, and nothing was ever going to take that away from her. I gave her a big cheesy grin and a thumbs-up.

The missiles behind us swung around and smashed into each other, creating a smoking fireball in the sky. I threw Petite into Reverse, not risking the time to turn around again, and flung my arm over the passenger seat so I could turn and drive backward through the airborne wreckage. I was starting to see stars, nothing to do with the missiles and everything to do with blatantly ignoring the laws of physics. I chanted, "I can do it, I can do it, I can do it," between my teeth and clenched my stomach muscles, like the tension there could translate to magic beneath my sweet old girl's wheels.

Twenty feet from the mountain road, I spun Petite around again and slammed us back toward solid ground. The bridge fell apart beneath her back wheels and they whirled, trying to gain purchase. Dad and Morrison both threw themselves forward, adding another few hundred pounds of forward momentum, and gravel caught beneath her wheels. She surged onto the road and I twitched a light-bending invisibility shield up around us while I slowed down enough to stop safely.

I killed the engine and it rumbled to a slow stop. We all sat there in the silence, my vision winking in and out. There was something I wanted to tell Dad. Something important. Something about keeping us hidden. I opened my mouth, said, "Ablbhlg," and passed out.

CHAPTER TWENTY-THREE

I awakened to Morrison's patient repetition of, "Wake up, Joanie. Wake up. Wake up, Walker. Wake up. Walker, I need you to—" and then a rough quiet gasp when I rolled my eyes open. "There you are. Drink this."

I was willing to drink anything, especially if it had a high alcoholic content. What he fed me didn't: it was bottled water, warm, brackish, and probably good for me. I coughed a couple of times and tried sitting up. That was when I noticed I was lying down. Mostly, anyway. Petite's front seat had been laid as flat as it went, and I was no longer buckled in. Morrison knelt beside the door, strain deepening the lines around his eyes. "Stay down awhile, Walker. It took Joe twenty minutes to stabilize you. You shouldn't have done that."

"Prolly not." My voice was weirdly hoarse. I cleared my throat and tried again. "Did it work?" Obviously it had worked. We were still with Petite instead of arrested by military mooks. That was good. I wondered where Dad was. I wondered if we'd found the missing Cherokee, except clearly we hadn't because we were still with Petite, who couldn't possibly make it up the ravine.

"It worked. That was the…" Morrison cleared his throat in turn. "I don't even know what that was, Walker. That was the most incredible thing I've ever seen."

"Better than time travel, huh?" I felt like I'd been drinking sand. I fumbled for the water and Morrison poured a little more down my throat.

"Time travel," my staid, sensible boss-former boss said, "is almost comprehensible, Walker. I pay some attention to science. I get the idea that time is how we perceive it. I can just about understand that if we can alter our perceptions enough, we might not have to be so linear."

"You're amazing," I told him solemnly. "Best ever. Best Morrison ever. I love you. Can't believe you're okay with time travel. That's amazing. You're the best." Now I sounded like I'd been on a three-day bender and was equal parts hammered and hung over.

Morrison crooked a smile. "I love you, too. But yeah, Walker, I can almost wrap my head around time travel. Flying Mustangs, not so much."

"I shoulda named her Pegasus." The thought was inordinately funny, and I giggled until I coughed. When I finished coughing I was weak as water. "What's wrong with me?"

"Your father said you drained yourself dry."

I mooshed my lips into a duck face. "Nah. Not me. I'm Supershaman."

"Not even supershamans are supposed to make three-thousand-pound cars fly through the air, Walker. Apparently you pushed the laws of physics too far that time."

"Bah. Do it all the time. Invisililliby, bility…in…vis…i…

bil…ity. Shields, time travel, healing. It all defies physics. That's why it's *magic*." I was not getting any less punchy, but the litany of powers I usually worked with did seem to have something in common. Invisibility shields were just bent light, and almost anything, including water, the most common element on the planet, could bend light. Morrison had just deconstructed why time travel might not be quite outside the laws of physics. Healing was incredible stuff, but what I did essentially sped up the normal process rather than redefining it entirely. My physical shields were, in fact, perhaps the most physics-defying thing I did, since as far as I knew nobody'd figured out how to turn air solid. So it was possible Morrison was right. It was possible I'd pushed that one juuuuust a little too far.

"Nah," I said again. "Nothing wipes me out."

"Except curing cancer." Morrison's eyebrows challenged me.

"…" Nope. I couldn't come up with an argument. Curing cancer had left me just about this rattled, and it was just about as impossible a task as building a road out of thin air. I shut my mouth, then decided changing the subject was my safest bet. "Where's Dad?"

"Making sure your invisibility shields hold. He says he never thought of doing anything like them, so he's got to pay attention. You kept them going." Morrison's voice dropped a note, respect blending with bewilderment. "Even unconscious, you kept them going until he was able to pick them up."

"Had to, or they woulda found us. Woulda defeated the point of all of…" I waved a hand toward the valley. "That. Do we have any food? Shoe leather will do."

"Sorry."

"Okay." I tried sitting up again, and was able to this time. "How long've I been out?"

"About an hour, and you should've been out a week, and in the hospital. You were in bad shape, Walker. You were gray. If your dad hadn't been here..." The strain returned to Morrison's eyes.

I leaned over to flop against him, relieved to not stand up yet. "But he was, and I'm okay now. I could eat a donkey, but I'm okay." I wondered how many times I could say that, and whether any of the repetitions would make Morrison believe me. "I think I gotta go talk to Dad. We need to go find everybody. We have to..."

My thoughts disintegrated again. With Dad, without Dad, whatever: I had pushed myself way too damned far and my brain was full of static. It took a long time just to remember the problem: that we'd disappeared out from under the military's nose, after they'd fired missiles at us. Even if I suspected a media blackout on what was happening in the Qualla, somebody was going to notice that. It would behoove the military to get to us before the news broke. They'd no doubt been searching the mountains already, but they were going to redouble their efforts now. I drifted from that into "I'm sorry, Morrison."

He tipped me back so he could frown at me. "For what?"

"I'm going to make a hash of your career, aren't I? Seattle police captain involved in high-speed military chase. Involved in the mystery of the missing Cherokee. Involved in the zombie apocalypse. That can't look good on a resume." Exhaustion and weariness made my eyes fill with apologetic tears. I was screwing up *everybody's* lives.

"Good thing you only gave them your name." His mouth curved again, rueful little smile. "And at least you quit the department two weeks ago, before you riled up the military."

"*Riled*. You've already been in the South too long, using words like *riled*. I didn't hand in a letter, Morrison." At least,

I didn't think I had. It was hard to remember. I stared at him, trying to hold my thoughts together. "I just told you I was quitting, right? Is that enough?"

My former boss looked ever so slightly shifty. "I may have taken some liberties there, Walker."

For a few seconds my haze-filled brain didn't get it. Then I blinked at him in astonishment. "You forged my resignation letter?"

His voice went soft. "I didn't think you would be coming back. Not as a cop, anyway. If you've changed your mind..."

"No." Fuzzy-minded or not, I was firm on that. It meant finding a job when I got home again, but that was the least of my problems, given that right now I was too tired to stand up. I sent a feeble request to my spirit animals for help, and they all gave me flat looks. I mumbled a silent apology to them and returned my attention to Morrison. "No, it was a good call, especially with this going on now. At least it makes me a former employee, and..." I exhaled, unable to complete the thought without effort. "And I guess, I don't know, we keep us under wraps for a little while? Until people stop talking about this?"

"Is that what you want?"

"Not really, but I want to cost you your job even less." I snorted. "Besides, if we keep it quiet awhile the department will start a betting pool on when we'll come out. Maybe we can get Billy to game it for us. Okay. Help me up. I'm...God, I'm tired, Morrison. I shouldn't be this tired. I don't tap out like that."

"You're too skinny, you haven't eaten, and you've been throwing magic around like it's fairy dust, Walker. Nobody can keep anything up forever. Not even you. C'mon."

He did help me up, an arm around my waist to keep me steady, and we went to find Dad, who was sitting just far enough away that he could pretend he wasn't eavesdropping. I didn't believe it, but I didn't care enough to call him on it. He spoke when we got close enough. "You got the invisibility shields idea from that comic you used to read, didn't you? The one with the blonde woman and the rock man. It's a good idea. Unique. I'm not sure you'd have thought of it if I'd trained you. I'm more traditional than this."

That was, in fact, where I'd gotten the idea. I'd loved Sue Storm as a kid. "You seem to have gotten the hang of it."

"Once I saw what you'd done, sure. I don't know how you kept it up until I took over, Jo…anne. You shouldn't have been able to. I've never seen anyone that deeply drained of energy and still alive."

I said the same thing I had to Morrison: "I had to, or it all would have been pointless. The real question is how we're going to keep it functioning once we head into the hills, because no way am I leaving Petite exposed up here for the military to find and tear apart."

"No, Joanne." Dad got up, hands in his pockets, a crease between his eyebrows. "The question is how you did that. You're not understanding me. When I say you shouldn't have been able to I mean I've been a shaman for more than forty years and I've never seen anyone do any of what you've done today. We use power circles and sweat lodges to alter perceptions and to heal. We don't just fling ourselves in without preparation. We shield ourselves against sorcery, but we don't wind that magic into nets and walls that affect wide spaces or many people. We don't drive cars across open air and then keep invisibility shields active when our hearts are stuttering. You barely had enough life in you to keep breathing, Joanne, and you were still pouring magic out into the world. We don't do that. It would kill us. We'd be dead before we began. We *can't* do that."

"You can't." I had no other argument, and barely enough energy for this one. In fact, *I* wasn't having an argument. Maybe Dad was, but from my perspective it was a detailing of rote information. "I don't know, Dad. Maybe it's the two heritages. Shaman and mage. Maybe it's being a brand-new sparkly fresh soul. Maybe it's not being hobbled by tradition. Maybe it's because I learned the hard way. Maybe it's that I just don't know what I can and can't do, so I do it anyway. I mean, hey, yeah, okay, it's pretty clear I shouldn't try the flying-car stunt again. Or healing cancer," I said with a sideways glance at Morrison. "But mostly the only way I find out I shouldn't do something is by doing it. I don't have any preconceptions, Dad. I have no fucking clue what I'm doing. I never have."

That wasn't true anymore. I actually had a pretty good idea what I was doing now, and it had become clear that most of my limitations were self-imposed, failures of imagination rather than failures of raw power. I couldn't figure out how to track magic, for example. I'd never been able to convince my slightly near-sighted eyes that it would be okay for me to heal them, though I had no doubt if I went in for LASIK surgery that it would work just fine. I accepted that I shouldn't try healing major illnesses without a power circle to support me, at the very least. That kind of shit was dangerous, and despite my reckless behavior I wasn't really trying to get myself killed. I just didn't know where the line was until I crossed it.

And when I got right down to it, I didn't have a problem with that. I was not going to become increasingly conservative as I grew to understand my power more fully. In fact, backed by Rattler and Renee and Raven, I saw no reason why I shouldn't become less conservative, especially in cases where I'd learned where the lines lay.

Looking at my father, at the worry pinching his face and at the barely restrained disbelief in his eyes, I thought for the first time that maybe I was more like my mother than I'd imagined. I'd never thought of Dad as conservative, but it was the first word that would've come to mind for Mom. The second one was *stubborn,* or maybe *willful.* The woman had concentrated herself to death, after all, to make sure she could be in the right spiritual place and time to save my *tuchus* more than once. It was inconceivable that she would let some piddling opinion like *"you shouldn't have been able to"* stop her from doing anything. I rolled that thought around in my mind a few seconds, then spread my hands and shrugged. "This is how it works with me, Dad. You're just going to have to get used to it. Now, what are we going to do about Petite?"

My father looked at me for a long time, with much the same expression he'd often had when I was younger. It was the one I'd interpreted as "How the hell did I get stuck with a kid?" but now I thought maybe it was really more like "How the hell do I roll with the insane punches this kid throws?" After a while he shook his head and pointed his thumb up the mountain. "There's a cave system up the road a ways. We can bring her up there and tuck her in. If you don't know where it is, it's hard to find."

The military was likely to be combing every inch of the mountain, and I doubted they'd miss it, but it was better than nothing. Maybe I could do something very rash, like bring a little rock-fall down over the cave mouth, except that would leave fresh scars for them to find, which would again defeat the point. And besides, the idea made me stumble with exhaustion, even though I wasn't moving. Morrison tightened his arm around me and my father glanced at us, worry etching his face again.

I hadn't quite put that together, that he might be worried about me, and shifted uncomfortably. "I'm okay, Dad. I'm fine."

"You're not," he said stubbornly. "I told you. Your reserves are completely depleted, beyond anything that should leave you on your feet, and it's not the first time that's happened recently. What have you been *doing,* Joanne?"

I wet my lips and frowned at the mountain above his head. It was certainly true that this wasn't the first time I'd been totally wiped out in the past few weeks, but last time I'd gotten this flat it had been followed up by the most invigorating spirit dance I would probably ever encounter. I'd have thought that had fueled me sufficiently that the drain wouldn't leave any marks, but I supposed running beyond empty left scars on any engine. "It's a long story, Dad. We'd be here for a week if I tried explaining it all. Am I okay to get up the mountain?"

"No. We could bodily carry you up there," he said grudgingly, "but if we don't do something about your reserves you're not going to be any help if things go badly."

"Things will go badly," I assured him. "Let's get Petite into that cave and we'll worry about the rest later."

"Later" came a lot sooner than I expected. We rolled Petite up the mountain and into the cave, which is to say, Morrison and Dad rolled Petite up the mountain and into the cave while I steered with a focus and ferocity previously known only to kittens intent on a piece of string. I managed not to crash her, which in my book was a huge triumph. Proud of myself, I got out of the car. Morrison put me right back in, and dragged my drum out from behind the driver's seat again. I stared at it like I'd never even seen it before. So did Dad, with more justification: he *hadn't* seen it before, at least not with its new modifications. I'd just totally forgotten about it. After a while I mumbled, "Wish I'd remembered that was there. It probably would've helped with…flying the car."

When I said the words out loud it struck me just how amaz-

ingly stupid that stunt had been. I mean, I really had been utterly, absolutely confident of my ability to do it, which meant
I'd *been* able to do it. But I would never be able to do it again,
because I was now far too aware of the cost. Maybe if the
choices were Morrison being eaten by monsters or me flying
Petite again, but short of genuine life and death it was never
gonna happen again. And really, that was okay, because although I didn't want to tell Morrison, I could barely feel my
arms and legs, never mind fingers and toes. I wasn't at all sure
I was still functional on any meaningful level.

"Yes," Morrison said dryly. "I'm sure it would have helped
with flying the car, if any of us had been calm and rational
enough to think of taking a drum out and performing some
theme music for your James Bond meets Harry Potter special
effects. But since we weren't, *now* I'm going to drum until
you stop looking like something the cat dragged in. Don't
argue with me."

I nodded mutely, and honestly didn't remember more than
the first beat or two of the stick against the drumhead. I had
odd, flitting dreams of healing power washing through me,
like I was one of my own patients, and every once in a while
I felt my breath catch like maybe I'd stopped breathing and
someone was getting it started for me again. The drumbeat
broke through every few minutes, dragging me toward the
surface of sleep before losing its grip on me again. It was pleasant, in a soft, surreal way. I could feel the earth's weight above
me, its steadiness below me, and the stillness of the air within
the small cave. I felt comforted, contained, *safe*. I wanted to
stay there for weeks, though a niggling, uncomfortable feeling suggested that wouldn't work.

After a far-too-brief forever, Dad's voice broke through my
reverie. "We're going to have to leave if we want to get into
the mountains before dark."

"She still looks like death warmed over, Joseph."

"Her aura's stronger."

Morrison's sigh matched the last beat of the drum. I opened my eyes, unable to focus on the dark cave wall beyond Petite's windshield. I wasn't sure I felt better. I didn't feel *worse*, though, and I could wiggle my toes with a reasonable confidence that they were still attached. It would have to do. I said, "I'm good," and hoped I sounded more convincing to the men than I did to myself.

I swung my legs out of the car, stood up, and swayed as hunger galloped through me. Morrison made an alarmed noise and I shook my head, hanging onto Petite's roof a minute. "No, I'm okay. I am. Just getting my feet under me. How long was I out this time?"

"Another hour. Not enough," Morrison opined. I had no argument there, but it was astounding the military hadn't found us yet as it was, so we really couldn't waste any more time. I wobbled out of the little cave and glanced back.

Petite barely fit in it, honestly. I supposed it was ever so slightly possible that when the military came around using radar, or whatever they might be using, that her big back end would make the whole stretch read as solid rock. It would be better, though, to hightail it into the mountains, find the missing tribe, and finish this thing before it turned into a new round of Indian wars. I tried concentrating on that idea instead of my stomach gnawing on itself as we headed into the hills.

Helicopters and Humvees were audible in all the hollers, their engines echoing even when the vehicles were far out of sight. Dad maintained the shields, though every once in a while I noticed them shivering as his concentration lapsed. I fell back a few steps to walk with Morrison, murmuring, "He's not all that good at this."

"Give him a break, Walker. Apparently it's impossible."

"Yeah, well, I'm a little worried. I'm still tripping over my feet, and if something nasty comes out of the hills—"

"Then you'll flatten it and pay the consequences later." Morrison didn't sound especially happy about the prospect, but he did sound like he understood it was exactly what would happen. "Are you going to kill yourself setting this straight, Walker?"

"I hope not."

"If it comes down to it?"

He meant if it came down to me or Aidan, and we both knew the answer to that, so I didn't reply. We walked for hours, very slowly, because I absolutely couldn't move faster than I was doing. We stopped for water occasionally, and Dad found some of last fall's apples. I didn't even pretend to object when he and Morrison both passed their shares to me. I wolfed them down, burped the early warning of a cramped tummy, and didn't care. The hint of food made me need more, but I felt a little better anyway, and we were all able to pick up the pace. Dad knew where he was going, and we were content to follow along.

Just before nightfall, Dad dropped the shields. "We're almost there."

I figured they'd be hunting for us with infrared at sundown anyway, so the shields didn't seem to matter "Almost where? Is this some kind of retreat plan that's been in place for decades, or something?"

"In a way. It started out as a game, with some of the young people trying out their woods skills. A few of them were interested enough to ask the elders what they knew or remembered. A while ago it started to become a rite of passage for the ones whose heritage was important enough to them." Dad deliberately didn't look at me. I wanted to kick him, but refrained for fear of losing my balance. "There's territory out here that nobody lives on, nobody camps on or explores. It's hard to imagine when you think how close we all live together, but there's a lot of land to live off still, if you're willing to do it. Kids started coming out here for summers, and some of them, when things went bad at school, came out for the winters, too. There are always a few adults who keep an eye on the place, to make sure nobody gets hurt or in trouble, but we mostly let them get by on their own. They hunt and fish traditionally so nobody wonders about gunshots in the mountains. They do a good job."

I still felt like I was being reprimanded, but kept my mouth shut. I'd explored the hills some, but never gone this deep or imagined camping out for whole summers at a time. "So it's the kind of place that people who were inclined to walk away from government interference in the Qualla would already know about."

"Yeah. I'd guess there's probably four or six hundred folks out here, if they've left town."

I thought about Cherokee town's population. "That's not very many."

"It's as many as rebuilt the tribes after the Trail of Tears."

I was definitely being rebuked. Lucky for Dad, it took enough energy just to grind my teeth that I thought I'd better save what spark I had for what was coming, rather than snarling at him. "The military's not looking very hard, if they haven't found them. That many people would show up like a wildfire on infrared."

"You think they don't know that? You think they're not taking steps to avoid being found? Kids shelter in cave systems out here, or old mines. Hunters pack themselves with mud. We've got a lot to lose, Joanne."

I pressed my lips together, reminding myself I was unwilling to be drawn into an argument, particularly one I basically agreed with. If the escapees were out here living off the land through traditional methods I had nothing but respect for them, and didn't think it was any of the government's business. Especially since I was pretty confident there was no zombie apocalypse going on. Hunting the refugees down would only emphasize the level of control the federal government still held over reservations, rather than providing any level of actual help.

For one crazy moment I wondered if this mess could help the Native cause in America. If it would provide a rallying point that would bring all the tribes together to make a stand that would give them the autonomy that had been stripped away centuries ago. Then reality kicked in. With the bleak magic Aidan was wielding, if they made a stand it would turn into a slaughter. Political protest would be swept aside in the bloodshed, and when it ended, there would be no more pesky Native population on thousands of acres of American soil. We weren't going to let that happen.

Danny Little Turtle stepped out of the forest with a silence and expression so like the Cherokee warriors Morrison and I had encountered that if it weren't for his trappings—a rifle, jeans and a T-shirt instead of leathers and spears—I would have thought we'd fallen through time again. Moreover, *those* warriors had intended to capture us. Danny looked like he'd be happy to put a bullet in each of us, and a butterfly-fluttering sense of alarm awakened in my stomach. Back then I'd been confident of stopping their arrows and spears. Right now I wasn't at all sure I could stop flying bullets.

"Give me an excuse," he said, and a goddamned military chopper buzzed us.

CHAPTER TWENTY-FOUR

I think the only thing that kept Danny from shooting us right then was the probably unbased fear the rifle's report would be heard above the chopper's blades. We all hit the ground, dampening our heat signals with leaves and mud. I folded my white coat under myself, cringing at the exhaustion that left me unable to protect it with the thin magic sheen I'd used before. The chopper skimmed past us, treetops whipping and snapping with its passage. Danny snarled, "That's an excuse," but my father snaked a hand out and wrapped it around the rifle's muzzle.

"We're not your enemies, Dan. You know that."

"Maybe you're not, but all this trouble started when Joanne came back to town."

That was entirely untrue. It had started several days before I'd come back, but I didn't think Danny would appreciate the distinction. "Is Aidan with you?"

"Of course Aidan is with us," he snapped. "Who do you think is keeping the military off our backs?"

We hadn't been being loud to begin with, but all three of us got really quiet. That was not an angle I'd expected, and it shot a spark of hope through me. Maybe Aidan had thrown off the wights' influence. Maybe he was the hero of the hour, and we were just coming late to the party to offer our congratulations. My head throbbed with relief at the idea, even if I didn't so much as half believe it. I was happy to hunt wights and fight the Executioner if Aidan was already safe. I'd happily fight them every day for the rest of my life, if he was safe.

Morrison broke our silence. "When did he join you?"

"He came and got us," Danny spat. "Sunday evening, right before the CDC showed up. He came down to the school and said they were coming and that we'd all be quarantined if we didn't get into the hills."

Sunday evening. If Aidan had been here Sunday evening, then he hadn't lost days and days to his time travel stunt. He'd been able to land back where he came from, which just wasn't fair. I wanted to rail at Renee for that, but at this juncture, it seemed useless. Instead I took a deep breath and tried to focus on something far more important: "Danny, did you burn the bodies? The ones who'd been keeping vigil, did you burn them?"

I felt his blistering glare through the darkness. "Sara said we should. She got outvoted."

"Jesus. How many more people died when they rose?"

"How do you know what happened!"

"I think," Morrison said under our increasing volume, "that we should take this discussion elsewhere. The helicopter is gone. This is probably our best chance to move."

"Who the hell are you?"

"My name is Michael Morrison, and I'm with Joanne. If

you don't like that, fine. But the longer we stay here, the better our chances of being discovered are. If I were searching these woods I'd be doing more than one pass, but they've got a lot of territory to cover and we may be able to get out of their sweep range if we move now."

"What are you, military?"

"Police."

Dan said a word his grandmother wouldn't have approved of and rolled to his feet. The rest of us followed, mouths shut and ears sharp to listen for the chopper coming back. Dan led us into an old mine shaft when we heard it, taking us deep enough that there wasn't a hint of moonlight to illuminate the way. He stepped up beside me and breathed, "I could drop you in here and nobody would ever know," in my ear.

I said, "Don't be absurd," out loud, because if nothing else, drawing attention to a threat frequently removed it. Women weren't good at that, as a rule. Societal convention told us to not raise our voices, even when we felt threatened. Police academy had done a good job of breaking that training, and I wasn't about to lend credence to Dan's theatrics by whispering back. "First off, Dad and Morrison are here, and they know you don't like me, so if I fell in the shaft they might be suspicious. Second, I'm the shaman here, Dan. I can See perfectly clearly in the pitch dark. If you try throwing me down a pit, you're probably a lot more likely than I am to end up in it."

That was obviously not how Danny had planned for the conversation to go. He made a sound of impotent rage and stomped a few feet away. Only a few feet—I bet he wasn't kidding about the dangers of the mine, and that there was indeed a shaft close enough to get thrown down.

My father said, "Dan?" incredulously, but Morrison only chuckled. Apparently he wasn't too worried about me being pitched into pits, which was heartening.

After a few minutes we ventured out again, this time avoiding any further chopper passes. Within half an hour we were in a moonlit vale that, from ground level, had the faintest signs of human habitation. I thought they must be less visible from above, and wondered how far from modern civilization we were.

The cave system Dan led us into was natural and deep. I was astonished it hadn't been exploited for minerals, but even the most assiduous explorers sometimes missed things. There could've been a rainstorm the day they went through this valley, who knew, or maybe somehow they'd just never come this way. Whatever the reason, he led us a fair distance down, stopping to turn a flashlight on once we were well past the cave's mouth.

The light caught attention down below. A number of people came to greet us, most of them expecting Dan and wary when they caught sight of the rest of us. Some relaxed at Dad's presence, but more of them tensed up at mine. I was not exactly endearing myself to my former townspeople.

Les's grandfather pushed through to the front, shaking Dad's hand, patting Danny on the shoulder and subtly ushering them both into the crowd behind him, which necessarily left Morrison and me on our own. Dad realized what had happened about half a step too late. I splayed my fingers when he made to come back, trying to stop him. If they threw us out, we, and probably they, would be better off with Dad in there. At least he had some idea of what was going on, and they might listen to him if we were ejected.

"There's a problem, Joanne." Les Senior looked pained but determined. Me, I only nodded. I was sure there was a problem. It was just a question of whether his interpretation of the problem lined up with mine. "We've been warned, you see," Grandpa Les went on. "Wasn't much of a surprise, what with all this trouble starting just before you came back, but it's coming from a source I trust, you see?"

I waited. He would nerve himself up to the confession soon enough, but I wasn't going to make it any easier for him.

"It's Aidan, you see," Grandpa Les said after a moment, and my heart dropped. Aidan hadn't thrown off the infection after all. He was still the source of the CDC's hunt, maybe imprisoned by, or worse, damaging the Cherokee who had retreated into the woods. I was about to ask to see him when Grandpa Les finished, "He says it's you who's been taken by *Kolona Ayeliski*."

Of course he does. I didn't think I said it out loud, but the thought rocked me back on my heels and shuttered my eyes for a moment. Of course he did. I should have seen that coming. I really should have, and I really hadn't. Clever damned child. Clever Master, manipulating him. I heard Dan bark a triumphant sound, and my father and Morrison start to protest.

I raised a hand, trying to silence them, and met Les Senior's eyes. "It's not true, but obviously that's what I would say. I'm afraid that Aidan's been taken by Raven Mocker, but obviously I would say that, too. And I'm completely flat, totally out of power right now, so I don't even think there's any way I could use magic to prove myself to you. I was going to ask for a drum circle," I said wearily. "I was going to ask for your help, so I could try to protect you and this valley from an evil that's coming."

"We know about that evil," somebody growled. "We hear their helicopters and know they hunt the hills for us."

"The military is not the problem." That was grossly untrue. The military was potentially a huge problem. But there were other problems on the plate first, like "The wights are part of the problem. Will someone tell me how many there are now?"

Somebody else muttered, "She oughta know, if she's *Kolona Ayeliski,*" but another person hawked in disbelief. "She wouldn't let on if she knew, would she."

"We burned them." Sara pushed her way to the front, red spots high on her cheekbones. Her gaze darted from me to my father and back again, but she focused on answering the question. "After the first ones rose, we burned the ones they killed, but the seven got away. They spread out and we don't know how far they got. When we found bodies, we burned them, too, but we only found a few." She looked between me and Dad again, then focused on me with cold fear in her eyes. "Where's Lucas, Joanne? You found your dad. Where's Lucas? Where's my husband?"

"I'm sorry, Sara."

She went white, making the hot spots on her cheeks stand out all the more. She wasn't surprised: she'd known, really, from the moment Dad and I showed up without him. "What happened? Where is he? What happened, Joanne?"

"The Nothing pulled him into another time, onto a battlefield. Dad followed, but it was too late. I'm so sorry, Sara. I'm so sorry."

Even the red faded, now, though she kept herself bolt upright. "Another *time?* There's not even a body?"

"I'm sorry." Dad spoke this time. "I did the rites. I bathed him and I buried him so no sorcerer could steal his soul. I don't know if it's what his people would have done, but it was all I could do."

Sara's attention snapped to him, but she was so rigid that the motion unbalanced her. I reached to support her and she slapped my hand away, swaying. "You're sure it was him? It could have been anyone—"

"He was wearing jeans and a Lakers T-shirt, Sara. We were

out of time. No one else was dressed that way. It was Lucas. I'm so sorry. I'm sorry I wasn't there sooner."

Sara made fists, shoulders high as she stared at the ground. "Would it have helped if I'd called Joanne sooner? Would it have made a difference?"

Dad shook his head. "I don't think so. We'd have had to have gone through the Nothing together for him to have a chance. I just wasn't soon enough. Joanne couldn't have made a difference."

"You said through time." Her voice was turning harsh with swallowed sobs now. "Can you...can you go back? Can you rescue him?"

"I can't." Dad looked at me this time, and Sara's entire body filled with tension.

There was really only one thing I could say. "I'll try. I can't right now, Sara, I really am wiped out, but I'll try as soon as I'm powered up."

To my utter surprise, she stepped past Les Senior and took up a place by my side. "Then I'll drum for you."

"Sara..." Grandpa Lester's voice carried a warning note.

Sara's head came up, color high again as her eyes flashed a warning of their own. "What, maybe I'm siding with the enemy? I don't care, Grandpa Les. If it gets me my husband back, I don't care. Besides, Joanne's a lot of things, including dumb, but she's not evil. I've seen her at work. She's the thing evil runs from. If she thinks Aidan's the problem here, then he probably is. Don't say she didn't warn you, when it's all over."

She was the last person on earth I expected to defend me. A hundred times over the past year I'd thought I didn't deserve the quality of friends I had. Right now I didn't even deserve the quality of nemeses I had. Sara outshone me on every level, and I swore to God I would do everything I could to get Lucas back for her.

One more person pushed through the crowd, her dark eyes haggard. "How sure are you? About Aidan. How sure are you?"

"Pretty sure. We saw him caught up in some bad magic. He's got it in him to fight it, but it's going to be bad. I've got to help him. Dad, me, anybody who's willing."

Ada Monroe nodded once, and stepped to my side of the line.

CHAPTER TWENTY-FIVE

That was it. Five of us: two shamans, one grieving widow, a desperate mother and a police captain with the magical aptitude of a horseradish. Sheriff Les watched us go, his gaze uncertain, but he didn't join us, and the others were more strongly swayed by Grandpa Les and Danny Little Turtle. And by Aidan, for that matter, and the bitter thing was I couldn't really blame them for trusting him more than they trusted me.

"He leaves every night at sundown," Ada reported in a low, tense voice as we abandoned the caves to look for a sanctuary of our own. "He says he's going out to make sure the valley is shielded from the searchers, but I don't like him being alone in the dark. And how did the CDC know to come to Cherokee anyway? How did he know to warn us about them? It doesn't add up, Joanne. It doesn't add up."

Worse, it did add up, but she didn't like the sum it came to.

Neither did I. "He always used to tell me everything," Ada went on. "Now he won't talk to me at all."

That sounded a lot like a typical preteen, but the timing was too convenient for me to say so. Aidan would almost certainly clam up and stop telling his mother everything, but chances of it happening naturally on the same day he'd gotten pumped full of death magic was an unlikely coincidence. "We'll get him back, Ada. He's a tough kid, with a lot of power. He's going to be fine."

"You can't know that."

I stopped in the middle of the forest and turned to her, a finger of fire awakening in me. "Yes, I can. I know it because I'll die trying to make this right, if I have to, and no way am I going to the extreme of dying and then *failing* to make it right." It wasn't very sound logic, but it was heartfelt.

Ada gave me a peculiar look. "You were always a strange girl, Joanne." She passed by, following my father and Sara.

Morrison stayed at my side, both of us looking after Ada. "She's right, you know. I don't know about always, but you do say strange things."

"Like I'm not going to die trying and fail? I don't know, I think it makes sense. It would be embarrassing to fail if you died trying."

"You didn't say that to Sara."

"Sara wouldn't appreciate the hyperbole. Not that I'm being hyperbolic. But you know what I mean."

"I'm not sure I do, but I'm not sure it matters, either. Joanne, how are you going to manage this? Even I can tell your energy is low, and you still haven't eaten anything but some apples."

"I should've asked them for some food." I glanced back, then started walking again. "Oh well. Too late now. They probably wouldn't have shared anyway, if they think I'm

Raven Mocker. You don't even know what that means, do you. Argh."

"Your dad told me."

"When? Oh." When I'd been in Petite, trying to pull myself together, no doubt. Dad had explained everything about the scene at the hospital, and probably about Raven Mocker chasing Grandmother off the road. Neither of those topics accounted for their sudden silence when I got out of the car, but now, as then, I wasn't absolutely sure I wanted to know what they'd moved on to saying about me. "Good. Raven Mocker isn't something you defeat, Morrison. He's an archetype, a demon archetype, like a trickster only malevolent instead of…flaky."

"Like the Master." It was guarded, almost a question.

I exhaled. "Yeah. I'm sure Raven Mocker is an aspect of the Master. I'm not sure if he *is* the Master. If he is I don't know… you remember the banshee, right?"

"It's hard to forget, Walker."

"Heh. Yes, it is. Those murders interrupted a banshee ritual that fed the Master. My mother interrupted one twenty-eight years ago, too. He's starving, and I'm not sure he can break through to this plane of existence when he's this hungry. It's why he needs the wights and the Executioner, to funnel food to him. So I'm not sure Raven Mocker can be the Master, because Raven Mocker came after Grandmother himself, see?"

"Did he?"

I frowned at Morrison as we climbed over a fallen tree in my father's wake. "You saw him. We all did."

"We saw an apparition. A manifestation of something you recognized as a specific Cherokee demon. But none of us touched it, Walker. None of us fought it hand to hand, not even your grandmother. It just chased her off a mountain. It may never have been something physical, just frightening.

Especially to someone who believed she had a great deal to lose. You."

That, I believed was possible. The Master had been lurking at the edges of my subconscious for months. He'd come close to breaking free of the bonds that held him more than once, and had finally, briefly, walked in the Lower World just last week. I could believe the possibility that he had at least once gathered himself strongly enough to force an apparition into this world, even if he'd been too weak to follow it bodily. "I'm going to have to ask— Dad! Hey, Dad!"

Dad ducked under a branch, looking back at me, and that was what saved his life.

The bullet's crack followed so close on my shout that it almost drowned me out. Leaves exploded above Dad's head, falling in a rain of green and branches. Ada screamed. Sara grabbed her and hit the deck. Morrison snatched his duty weapon from its holster and spun so fast I expected him to be able to sight by the rifle's still-bright muzzle flash.

Sight by the rifle. I shoved my feet under Morrison's, slapped my hand on top of his head and commanded, *"See!"*

Power rushed out fast enough to leave me woozy. I didn't fight it, dropping to the ground so I was well and truly out of Morrison's way. Two guns fired at once, and a scream followed.

It wasn't Morrison's. That was all that mattered. It came from behind us, in the direction he'd fired. It was a man's scream, though, and I ran through the list of possibilities. Les. Les Senior. Danny Little Turtle. Dozens of others, but they were the most likely candidates, the ones we'd been interacting with. I barely got my feet under me enough to scramble back toward the screams, supporting myself with my hands as much as my legs. I was going to end up with a bad case of poison ivy.

It was Danny, which kind of relieved me. Morrison had taken him in the right collarbone, a debilitating shot that probably wouldn't kill him. It was a hell of a shot, actually, since judging from where the rifle currently lay, Dan was right-handed and had no doubt had the gun against that shoulder. Sharpshooting with the Sight was apparently a distinct advantage. I thought I'd probably better not ever let Morrison, or anybody else, do that again.

Danny had gotten his screams under control and was making a terrible, high-pitched, breathless whining sound instead. I'd never been shot, but I was pretty certain I wouldn't be able to stop screaming that fast. I admired his pride even as I whispered, "You damn fool," and reached for healing power.

It started, sputtered, and failed. I yelled, not nearly as loudly as Danny was doing, but with far more frustration. "I'm sorry, okay? I'll never build a rainbow bridge for a car again! Can I please have my power back now? *Please?*"

Raven, Rattler, and Renee all pretty much said, "Pblbbl-htht,"— inside my head. As much fun as the crazy drive had been, throwing together an instantaneous air bridge had apparently taken it out of all of us.

I said, "Shut up, Danny, you're going to be fine," and Dad came out of the forest to say, "He is?"

"Of course he is. You're going to heal him."

"He just shot at me!"

"He's sick, Dad. His heart is broken. His grandmother just died and he sees us as at fault. He's a perfect vessel for Raven Mocker to guide. If you can't forgive him for being weak, then build a power circle right here and start drumming so that I can heal him." I couldn't blame Dad. Barely two weeks ago I'd walked out on the woman I'd shot, unwilling and unable to heal her after she'd nearly taken Billy Holliday's life. Nobody was perfect, but this particular burden was one I could shoulder if Dad couldn't. I just needed a power jump.

A laugh broke from somewhere deep in my chest. If only I'd thought of it in those terms when I was back with Petite. I was pretty certain I could've gotten a jump from her sweet inanimate soul, the very image of my own. It was so easy to envision, the jumper cables locked onto her battery posts, me holding the other ends with a manic grin. Her big beautiful engine roaring to life, feeding power into my worn-down magic. A few minutes of hanging on, and my own engines would restart, battery coming to life again, and everything would be okay.

A single shot of sparkling purple magic arced over the mountains and slammed into me. It knocked me flat, dropping me on top of poor Danny, who justifiably shrieked with pain.

Healing power sparked, lit, and flooded into him. Fragments of bone were like debris in the gas line, swept together and tidied back into place rather than flushed out. Torn flesh stitched back together under the image of ragged hoses replaced. Within a few seconds, Danny's shoulder was a massive black-and-blue bruise, the shattered bone repaired and the ruined flesh healed.

Mostly, anyway. I let go and shoved myself back a couple feet, stopping the flow of magic. Danny's eyes were huge in the moonlight, his breath coming in short fast pants. "It doesn't hurt as much."

"Good. It should still hurt enough that if you take another shot at us it's going to knock you on your ass and maybe re-break that bone. I'll fix it all the way once we're clear of this, but I don't have time for you to be playing hunter while we're trying to hunt something a lot more dangerous."

"You bitch," he said in breathless astonishment. "You can't do that. You're a shaman."

I seriously considered rebreaking his shoulder, and had to take several steps away to make sure I didn't. "Looks like I can. Morrison, if you wanted to handcuff him to a tree or something, I wouldn't hate that. No, don't. God forbid we couldn't find him again later and he starved to death tied to a tree."

"How did you do that?" My father's eyes were gold in the darkness, studying me with the Sight. "Where did the power come from?"

I opened my mouth and shut it again. Turned out I didn't want to confess that Petite, the big purple heart of my soul, had so much of me invested in her that she really could jump-start my magic again, even from miles away. I would tell Morrison about it later, and maybe Gary, who would think it was awesome. But Dad belonged to another tradition from mine, and while I loved him, I wasn't quite sure I trusted him with that kind of information. So I sent a mental apology winging toward Petite for belittling her role, and shrugged. "I told you. I do what I have to do, Dad. Somebody should find out if he's got anybody else with him, and we should move before—"

Before helicopter blades started cutting the air, the military alerted to a large presence of hot-bodied humans by their infrared scanners. The sound had to have been somewhere at the back of my mind for a couple of minutes before I started recognizing it and feeling the need to move, but that was a problem with being of the modern era. Helicopters, planes, cars, sirens, heavy machinery, all of that was background noise to the subconscious. It was easy not to recognize it until verging on too late, and Danny had provided plenty of distraction. By the time I finished speaking, vast white searchlights were flashing through the leaves, and a relentless loudspeaker voice was announcing that this was the U.S. military, lay down your weapons and surrender to their authority.

They had guns. They had missiles. We were never, ever going to outrun them. I gave my recharged power a little push, seeing how much of it there was to respond. Not very damned much, really. The problem with recharging a car battery was that if you had to kill the engine again, it was going to stay dead. Morrison's drumming had gotten me back on my feet, and maybe I'd built up a little bit of reserves as we'd walked, but I'd shot that wad giving Morrison the Sight. Petite's boost had basically started the battery once more, but I needed to be eyeball-deep in magic in order to keep my engines going. I didn't really dare wrap us in invisibility, much less shield us, without some kind of external power source. I still needed some quality time with a power or drum circle. Morrison had my drum, but the whole "rest in the caves, replenish the spirit" thing hadn't worked out so well, and I didn't really think the military was going to let us convene for a little midchase drum circle.

The last thing I could think of—the *only* thing I could think of—was asking for a boost from the people around me. Even this wrung out, I should be able to borrow strength from Dad and Morrison, if we could distract the guys in the helicopter long enough for me to ask. I wished I'd thought of it earlier, and allowed myself exactly three seconds of self-mockery and recrimination for thinking Dad was traditional and hide-bound when I, too, had been so focused on the traditional drum circle that I hadn't thought of doing something a little more outside of the box. Then I raised my hands in a classic surrender pose, and said, "Put your hands up, guys. We surrender."

Morrison put his hands up, but said, "We do?"

"Not really." The others put their hands up, as well, and I

shouted out an explanation of what I wanted to do while the helicopter buzzed its way closer to the earth.

The result was sort of beautiful, actually. Energy began to coalesce between everybody's upraised hands: Morrison's familiar purples and blues, my dad's less familiar greens and grays. Sara's aura was ochre and red, and ragged with grief. Ada offered up an utterly fierce protective forest-green streaked with blazes of orange determination. We had the feel of a small coven, everyone confident in what they were doing, everyone able to share without reservation.

In this case, of course, it was because we were going to get our asses handed to us if we didn't, rather than us all being so much on the same page in terms of what we wanted from and for the world, but whatever worked. I spread my hands a little, expanding the gunmetal ball between them, and a net began to form, threads dancing from me to Morrison, to Dad, to Ada and Sara. Raven gave a shout of joy and took wing, bright spirit spinning through the net, and Rattler sighed with satisfaction as my strength returned. Everything was going to be fine. I could shield us, I could pin the helicopter down, I could do what was necessary to get us out of here, and then we were going to rescue Aidan and bring this thing to a close.

Then Danny took a potshot at the U.S. military.

CHAPTER TWENTY-SIX

The bullet *spanged* off the helicopter's side, behind the large doors, just one superfast bright spark that disappeared as quickly as it came. The silence that followed was thunderous, never mind that there were chopper blades roaring through the air, never mind that the damned rifle shouldn't have even been audible above that sound. I heard it anyway, and I heard the clang of metal against metal, and I heard the incredulous shock that silenced everything else.

In that silence I thought, *Fuck*.

I had bigger fish to fry. I had a mystical enemy out there, one who was driving Danny's stupidity. If I didn't go stop that bigger bad, then Danny Little Turtle's name was going down in history as the guy who fired the first shot in the Second Indian Wars. And there I was, literally standing between one side and the other, metaphorically split down the middle myself, and it seemed utterly ludicrous that I was going to have to *stop a war* before I could go do my job. I was not cut out for peace negotiations. I liked hitting things as an action of first resort. I was supposed to fight the impossible things, not get embroiled in politics extended to other means.

I didn't know when I'd triggered the Sight. As we'd started pooling our collective energy, since I'd been Watching that. But it was certainly burning full force now, and I could See the soldiers in the helicopter. I could See their indecision even as they readied their weapons. Firing on American citizens was not lightly done, but they had every right, every expectation, to protect their own lives, and Danny goddamned Little Turtle had fired the first shot.

There was a woman at the helm. She stared at me through the windshield with exactly the same expression she'd had earlier that day: hope and disbelief, with the hope so much stronger than the disbelief it made me want to cry. I said, "Don't," into the impossible silence. Just one ordinary word, not even shouted. Just, "Don't."

I Saw her hear it, Saw her flinch back half an inch and Saw her hand hovering above a panel that I had no doubt would launch our destruction. I took every ounce of energy my people were offering, and turned the air around us to shields. Nuclear bunkers, that's what they were, and I put everything I had into making them visible.

The night lit up with white magic, shimmering and sliding around us in a half dome. It even covered Danny, which I thought was very generous of me, as I was feeling that throwing him to the wolves wouldn't be a bad move.

Every single face in the chopper went awestruck, maybe terror-struck. More than one of the weapons began spitting bullets, a rattle of silver that smacked into my shields, crumpled, and slid to the ground. Everybody, including me, flinched, but after the first hail fell harmlessly to the ground we all got our nerve back and held it together, watching the chopper's pilot to see what happened next.

I saw the shape of the words on the captain's lips, and the sudden steely resolution in her aura. *Hold your fire,* she said. *Hold your fire.*

Indecision spattered across every face, but they were military, and they did what they were told. The smash of bullets ceased, gunmen waiting on further orders. The captain, her gaze darting between the dancing white shield and me, did something ridiculous.

She took her hands off the flight controls. Lifted them very, very slowly, and cocked her head slightly, like she was saying *"your move, lady."*

I wanted to kiss her. I wanted to give her a medal. I wanted to grab her and dance her around the forest, shouting my relief at hope and magic just this once overriding training and cynicism. Instead I relaxed some of the shield and wove it back into a net that I slid under the chopper, then up around the base of its blades, being very careful not to catch the blades. That would end badly for somebody, and I didn't know if it would be them or me. I didn't want to find out, either. Once I had the chopper wrapped safely in the net, I cautiously drew it down to the ground. Without the captain steering it in the other direction, it wasn't difficult, just nerve-wracking.

After a minute it settled. The captain shut it down, then ordered her people to stay where they were as she jumped out to approach us. She stopped on the far side of the still faintly shimmering shields and stopped at ease, hands locked behind her back and feet in a wide solid stance. "Captain Sandra Montenegro. Who the hell *are* you? *What* the hell are you? And who the *hell* was shooting at my boys?"

The last was pretty obvious, since Danny was over there on the ground, moaning and clutching his rebroken shoulder, with a rifle barely out of his reach. I decided Captain Sandra Montenegro wanted the other answers more. "I'm Joanne Walker, and I'm a shaman. And," I added thoughtfully, "I think you're going to have to surrender."

Montenegro laughed. She was pretty in the way military women often seemed to be: fit, strong-shouldered, strong-jawed, like she'd walked into a lot of fists in her life and didn't figure she was done yet. I liked her. Of course, she'd decided not to shoot us all to bits, which would make me like her anyway, but she had a solid presence, a confidence in herself, that was highly appealing. "*I'm* going to have to surrender?"

"I'm sure we won't call it that when it comes time to do the paperwork, but yeah." My thoughts were skittering all over the place. "Look, Captain, may I safely say you've had an unusual day?"

She laughed again, a big open sound that bounced around the valley with no concern at all. "You could say that. How the *hell* did you do that with the car? Beautiful car, by the way. Your work?"

For a brief moment I considered throwing Morrison over and running away with Captain Montenegro. I swear to God the man knew what I was thinking, because he arched an eyebrow at me and gave me the slyest, sexiest grin I'd ever seen from him. I reconsidered my consideration, but I still beamed at Montenegro. "Yeah, my work. I've had her since I was—" This was not the point. I shook myself and tried again. "Magic. It was magic, Captain, and the mess down in Cherokee that the CDC is trying to clean up is also magic, and by tomorrow morning you're probably not going to remember this right, much less believe it, but—"

"The hell I won't."

I paused. Most people confronted with magic turned a blind eye. They found excuses to explain away what they'd seen, or let themselves start to believe they'd imagined it: anything, in essence, to deny the metaphysical in the world. I'd had a lot of sympathy for that position. Still did, in fact, mostly because magic was hard to believe in. Or at least it was for most people.

Captain Montenegro might just be a believer, though. I'd met a couple, people who weren't magical themselves but who accepted its realism. There'd been a young woman working at a morgue when the zombies had risen last Halloween, and when I met her several months later, she still knew and recognized the truth of what had happened. There'd been the false FBI agents up in Mount Rainier National Park when I'd been hunting the wendigo. There were Morrison and Gary, for that matter.

For some reason I really wanted Captain Montenegro to be like them. It wouldn't make her life easier, but it might make it happier, because she was the first person I'd ever seen who'd looked *joyful* when she saw the impossible unfolding in front of her. "All right," I said happily. "You'll remember it tomorrow, but there's a good chance they won't." I waved at her crew, who looked nervously back at me. "Anyway, the point is, I really do need you to surrender, Captain, because there are about six hundred Cherokee out here and they all think the military is coming to arrest them, put them in quarantined concentration camps, and ultimately murder them."

"If they pose no threat—"

"Captain."

Montenegro actually shut up, sucked her cheeks in, then nodded. She was right, of course. If they posed no threat nothing bad should happen to them. There wasn't a genocide in history that supported that theory, though, and the Cherokee had already been down that road. The people in this valley weren't going down it again.

"So if you don't surrender, they're likely to fight, Captain, and if a massacre breaks out, it's going to be your name that goes down in infamy. That's the first reason you should surrender."

"And the second?"

"Is that if a massacre happens it's going to be because some bad magic has peaked. I really can't afford to babysit you while I go stop it, so I need you to surrender and be on your best behavior under Cherokee watch."

"Who's going to make sure they're on *their* best behavior?"

"I am."

I just about jumped out of my skin and whipped around with pointed irritation. Sheriff Lester Lee came out of the woods with a sigh. "Sorry, Jo. I should've let you know I was here before. I followed Danny out."

Still irritated at being surprised, I snapped, "And you didn't stop him from shooting at us?"

"Some of us can't see in the dark, Joanne. I didn't know he was that close, much less shooting, until he fired. Everybody's okay?"

"Yeah, but that's not the point!"

"I think it is, Walker."

I made a face at Morrison, but he was probably right, so I let it go and turned back to Montenegro. "This is Cherokee town Sheriff Lester Lee. He'll, er, accept your surrender and make sure you remain safe."

"Just one problem, Ms. Walker. How am I going to explain to my superiors how you took down a military helicopter?"

"Oh." I looked at the undamaged chopper, then at Danny. "You stopped to provide humanitarian aid?"

"To the guy who was shooting at us?"

"He wasn't shooting at you," I said blandly. "He was deer hunting."

"At *night?*"

"It's all been a terrible mistake." I kept the look of blank neutrality until Montenegro let go another one of her big laughs.

"I guess it has been. Remind me again why the hell I surrendered?"

"Because it was clear to you that no one here wanted to be involved in a firefight, but that they were in fear of their lives. In the name of peace between nations, you relinquished your arms and offered humanitarian aid. You'll probably get a medal."

"I don't want a medal. I want a flying purple car." Montenegro lifted her voice a little. "Put down your weapons, men. We're here for humanitarian purposes, not to call down trouble. Come on out unarmed."

I thought they were actually going to do it, until Aidan and about three dozen wights burst out of the ground below us.

I hadn't felt them coming. I didn't know if I *should* have felt them coming, but I hadn't, and we all went flying as a result. Morrison, Dad, the chopper, half a dozen military guys, me, we all got flung into the air and came down in a rain harder than the bullets. The chopper crumpled when it landed, its scream of metal briefly drowning out the screams of the men it smashed.

The wind knocked out of me and I saw stars. No, not stars, after all: I saw wights, white against the dark night. They soared and pounced, driving burning fingertips against the foreheads of trapped bodies. Three of Montenegro's men were dead before the chopper stopped screaming. *First casualties of the Second Indian Wars,* I thought, and staggered to my feet.

One of Montenegro's men lifted his weapon and, with the same calm Morrison had shown a few days earlier, started methodically shooting wights. They went down easily with a bullet to the brain, but there were a lot of them and more kept popping free of the earth. I threw shields up left right and center, trying to keep the wights away from everybody on my side of the fight, and swore violently when one of the damned things laid both hands on a shield and sucked it into nothingness. Its cadaverous form filled out some, and power flooded from it toward Aidan, who soared thirty feet off the ground, spinning around in exultation.

The military guy with the gun, being no fool, looked upward when I did and trained his weapon on the boy in the sky.

I honestly didn't know which of us hit the soldier first, me or Ada. She flung herself at him bodily and I punched a wall of air at him. He slammed back and forth like he'd been caught in a two-way tackle, and crashed to the ground. Ada sat on his chest, beating the hell out of him as she shrieked about keeping her son safe. I knew I should stop for her own sake if nothing else, but a wight burst out of the ground in front of me and I discovered once again how completely helpless I was against a thing that fed on my energy shields.

Shields. God in Heaven, but I was dim sometimes. My magic sword was useless, but it wasn't the only weapon in my repertoire. The wight reached for me with a sizzling fingertip, and I lopped it off with the edge of a small, round, sharpened shield.

Copper, embedded with gold and purple. It was born of the Purple Heart medal Gary had won in the Korean War and had given to me as a protective amulet, and of the copper bracelet my father had given me when I was a teenager. It wasn't magic like the sword. It hadn't been forged by an elf king out of silver taken from his arm of living silver. It was a stronger and simpler magic than that: made of gifts from the heart and meant to protect a loved one.

I grabbed one side and swung it, Captain America style. The razored edge sliced through the wight's throat, and my second blow knocked its head off. I lifted the shield in both hands and brought it down, vivisecting the head, and turned away confident that being split in half was as effective as a bullet to the brain.

The military guy had gotten the upper hand with Ada, but had a look of intense frustration as he held her off. He obviously didn't want to hurt her, and her shrieks about Aidan being her son explained why she'd attacked him. On the other hand, Aidan was clearly a source of trouble, and military training said to take down the troublemakers. If it weren't for the fear of leaving Ada totally vulnerable to attack, I might have tried knocking her out with magic just to remove her captor's quandary. On the other hand, that would probably leave Aidan open to attack, too, which also was an undesirable scenario.

The whole forest was alight with undesirable scenarios, really. Morrison, Sara and Les were back-to-back-to-back, shooting wights from a three-point defensive position. The surviving military guys were, too, all of them concentrating on the ground game instead of looking skyward. Dad appeared to be scrambling around dead people in a panic.

Captain Montenegro was one of them.

I stared uncomprehendingly at her body for a few seconds. I'd just met her. She'd been so alive and so smart, so glad to embrace the world opening up in front of her, and it had killed her within minutes. There was a scar on her forehead, an ash mark left by one of the wights. She had to be burned before dawn, or she would rise as one of them.

Right then I hated magic. Hated it straight to the bottom of my soul, with a blind rage that went beyond comprehension. Right then I wanted to wipe all the magic out of the world, just so shit like this didn't happen. I had gotten so many people killed. Marie d'Acanto. Colin Johannsen. Caroline Holliday. My *mother.* Captain Sandra Montenegro. And nothing I did seemed to stop it, no matter how hard I tried. People kept dying, dying because magic interfered with their lives. Because *I* had interfered with their lives. And I was supposed to be the *good* guy.

Calm locked into the depths of my fury and said, *You could do it, you know. You could take the magic away.* The Sight flared up, stronger than usual, and highlighted the animistic power in everything. The purpose in existence, the continuation from then to now, the strength of magic that flowed through everything. It was a vast continuous net running through the whole world, and I was *good* with nets. My hands clawed, gathering up those threads, ready to yank them all out and twist them dry. Power roared into me, reigniting the deep magic that I'd burned out with the flying car stunt. I wanted to finish it. I wanted people to stop dying. I wanted to stop being responsible. All I had to do was give one impossibly hard yank. I was faintly aware it would probably kill me, but at least everything else would be done too.

Morrison glanced my way, his eyes still bright gold with the Sight I'd set on him earlier. He didn't hesitate, just stepped away from Les and Sara, letting them close ranks as he left the firefight and came to me.

The threads of life and light that I held ran through him, too. Tugged at him when I yanked on them, like I was pulling him toward me. His aura jounced when I did that, slipping a little free of his body. He stumbled, then straightened and kept coming. Even through rage and frustration, I didn't like to see him stumble, so I didn't pull again. Not yet, anyway.

When he reached me, he put both hands against my face and whispered, "Let it go, Joanie. Let it go. This is *Kolona Ayeliski,* not you. This is Raven Mocker, trying to turn you like he's doing to Aidan. I can See it, Walker. Listen to me, and let it go."

Then he kissed me, and my rage turned into tears.

CHAPTER TWENTY-SEVEN

They didn't last. We didn't have time for them to last, but they were hot and fierce enough to make me let go of the terrible magic I was holding, to release the dangerous temptation I'd been about to give in to. The net faded, but the supercharge remained: I'd filled up again and had enough power to wield, though I had no idea how long it might last.

The gold faded from Morrison's eyes and he kissed me again, then put an arm around my shoulder and pressed his lips against my forehead. "I know it's not all right, Walker. I know it's not okay, but it's the hand we're dealt. Stop the wights. Save Aidan. Show Montenegro's spirit that you were worth fighting for."

"The tribe is coming." I sounded wrung out. "I felt them in the magic. They've left the caves and they're on the way here. They're going to end this. They're going to start a war."

"We won't let them." Morrison, in turn, sounded confident, even though I had no clue how he could possibly stop an armed, magic-maddened mob of hundreds.

Instead of asking, I said, "Okay," because I didn't have the heart to be told he didn't know how to do it, either. I tried to pull myself together, looking beyond Morrison at the fight.

It was all going to hell. Les and Sara had run out of bullets and picked up sticks, which at least let them keep the wights more than an arm's length away. The military survivor had given up and presumably clobbered Ada, and was now standing over her limp form, shooting anything that came near them. Dad, bizarrely, was standing several yards away looking serene. I had no idea what his deal was, and didn't care enough to find out. And Aidan, who had never hit the earth again after bursting out of it, was still hovering about forty feet above the ground, body arched in an exultation of power.

The good news was there were only about a dozen wights left. The bad news was they were abandoning the fight and rising toward Aidan, spinning counterclockwise around him. I didn't need the Sight to know that couldn't be a good sign. The military guy sighted carefully and shot at one of them.

The bullet *spanged* off it just like Danny's had done off the helicopter. I Saw a hint of its trajectory as it was deflected into a tree, and watched a puff of splinters explode out as it hit. "Cease fire, soldier."

I felt very professional, or something, when he did, although his expression was highly dubious: Who was I to be giving orders, especially with his commander dead? I pointed at the drifting splinters. "That one bounced into a tree. If we're unlucky, another one might hit one of us. Cease fire unless they attack us again." I no longer sounded wrung out. I sounded preternaturally calm, which kind of worried me. It did not, however, worry the military guy, who looked somewhat reassured and stopped shooting wights. If only I had somebody being calm and telling *me* what to do.

But I didn't, so I pulled it together and barked, "Dad, report!" Apparently having military people around gave me a brand-new vocabulary. Who knew?

Dad said, "Just another minute, Joanne," like we had all the time in the world. I motioned Morrison back into formation with Sara and Les, the three of them shifting to make a protective circle around Danny, who at least had the grace to shut up during all of this. I was amazed none of the wights had gotten him, but it seemed likely he was more use alive and pouring out hate and loathing that they could scoop up and refashion into power for the Executioner.

Because it'd taken me a while, but I was finally cluing in: Aidan was by all intents and purposes missing, at this point. He had been since our little jaunt through time, and maybe since before that. The thing in the sky was shaped like Aidan, but it had very little in common with him except an ability to wield great power. Never mind the wights, the oncoming mob, the explanations to the CDC and the military: if we couldn't reach that spark I'd gotten a heartbeat-long glimpse of, we were going to lose the boy. The rest of it *mattered,* but still somehow paled in comparison. "If I could just get my hands on him…"

"Use a net."

Turned out I had a calm voice telling me what to do, after all. I shot Morrison a startled look and he lifted his eyebrows at me like *"you would have thought of it eventually,"* which was perhaps more credit than I deserved. I gathered power and flung it at the kid in the sky just as my Dad said, "Joanne, wait—!" a moment too late.

Aidan spun, caught my net in both hands, and whomped me all over the forest with it.

Trees splintered. Earth flew. I yowled. Power went *schlucking* out of me, my net exactly the right conduit to feed Aidan and his groupies even more magic. I let go of it, which had the effect of stopping the power flow, but also meant Aidan lost control of me as he swung me from one side of the gathering to the other. I was on an upward swing, too, and pinwheeled a genuinely astonishing distance across the sky before crashing violently into tree tops, branches, trunks and eventually roots.

I lay there wheezing for a little while, afraid to even check and see if anything was broken. It shouldn't be: I was still shielded on a personal, physical level, but being bashed all over a forest still hurt. Perhaps it was my magic's way of keeping me humble. It wouldn't let me get battered into bits, but it was happy to let me know, by way of pain receptors, just how much *more* damage it was sparing me from.

Somewhere south of my feet, quite a considerable distance south, actually, a power circle sprang to life. That, no doubt, was what my father had been working on. That, no doubt, was what I should have waited on before trying to drag Aidan out of the sky. That, no doubt, would have been nice to know before I went all cowboy and got my ass handed to me. I sat up gingerly, whimpering as not-quite-broken bones settled back into place. Twigs poked me in impolite places and I brushed them away once I'd staggered to my feet. A deep breath and a cautious flex of magic washed the worst of the bruising away, but it refused to all fade. Teaching me a lesson, though I wasn't sure what the lesson was. Maybe look before you leap, though I despaired of ever learning that one.

Since I wasn't going to learn it anyway, I broke into a clumsy lope and headed back for the gang. It took longer than I expected—Aidan had thrown me a long way—and when I got there, I decided the positive way to look at things was to focus on the fact that Dad's power circle was holding the wights and Aidan in place, not letting them spread beyond a relatively small circumference in the forest.

The negative viewpoint was that the entire top of the power circle had become a whirling black vortex that looked like a portal to another world.

Aidan was chanting. I couldn't hear the words clearly enough to even assign a language, but it didn't really matter. Where chanting and vortexes—vortecii? vortices?—vortexes, I decided firmly. Where chanting and vortexes occur together, bad things happen. I nudged the power circle, asking to be let in, though I wasn't certain I wouldn't be better off on the outside. Dad gave me a wild-eyed look that suggested he was in over his head, and I decided *he* was better off with me inside, even if I wasn't. I slipped through, and Aidan's shouting became clearer.

He was calling out in Cherokee, telling the story of the great things he and the wights had done, and inviting Raven Mocker to come enjoy the spoils of war. Not just inviting him, but laying down a path built on the pain and souls of the dead for him to enter on. The vortex strained at the edges of Dad's power circle, and Dad gave me another frantic look.

I tried very hard not to look frantic back at him. I'd dealt with a portal-opening coven once. In fact, to my eternal embarrassment, I'd helped them open it. None of us, however, had been flying through the air at the time, and none of us, not even me, had been fighting at Aidan's weight. A net was obviously not the way to take him down. The military guy with the gun had it trained on Aidan, but was looking at me, and clearly didn't expect to be told to shoot. Even if I'd told him to, bullets were not going to make a difference at this particular stage of the fight. The only thing—the *only* thing— I could think to do was cut off their power somehow, and so far I was batting a thousand at not managing to do that. Trying to do so with magic only fed them more. Trying to do so without magic still gave them ordinary human lives to feed on. I muttered, "C'mon, Jo. C'mon. Be clever," as I stared up at the whirling black pit of power.

Experience suggested that throwing a willing—and innocent, but I was going to overlook that requirement for the moment—soul into chasms of doom was one way to destroy them. Experience did not, however, suggest what to do if the chasm of doom in question was sixty feet overhead instead of conveniently at ground level. I could maybe just barely defy the laws of physics a second time in a day and throw myself skyward, but the thought had no conviction, and without conviction it wouldn't work. Dad shouted my name, but I waved him off, still staring upward.

Aidan remained below the vortex, his hair purely white and his voice hoarse from shouting. Hoarse like a raven's, like he was taking Raven Mocker into himself and we were running out of time. I didn't know how we could run out of time when we had our spirit animals to help, spirit animals who could stretch and slow and speed up time, but we were running out and I had no answers.

My father, exasperated, roared, "Siobhán Grainne Mac-Namarra Walkingstick, get your ass *over* here!"

To the best of my knowledge, he had never used my full legal name before. He'd never called me Siobhán. I wasn't sure he'd known how to pronounce it. Hell, *I* hadn't been sure how to pronounce it until fairly recently, even though I'd looked it up dozens of times. Shevaun Grania, that's what it sounded like, except coming from my father it also sounded sort of like the voice of God. I was hopping to it, getting my ass over there, before I even knew I was moving.

Dad put his hands out, palms up. I put mine on top of them

instinctively. He exhaled a huge sigh of relief, and without asking or explaining, transferred the weight of the power circle to me. I hadn't even known that was possible. He waggled a warning finger under my nose and stomped away, giving the distinct impression that I'd been wasting valuable time.

The circle fluctuated with the change of keepers, but didn't fade in any way. I felt the strength of everyone inside the circle helping to keep it viable: Sara, Les, even Ada, who'd woken up at some point. The poor military guy was only putting out stress and confusion, not positive energy, but with the power circulating through me I could hear Ada's murmur, her explanation to him about what he could do to help. I'd known she was a good woman before she'd wanted to adopt Aidan, but I was increasingly impressed with her resolute awesomeness. Morrison, like the others, was expending energy, but he was also carving something with a Swiss Army knife and a huge amount of concentration. Watching him reminded me of the carving he'd done in his own garden, the tiny figurine that had proven to be me, and my heart lurched.

Dad knelt in the center of the circle, taking up a number of branches that had been cut free from trees when the chopper went down. He pulled a knife from the back of his jeans, which surprised me in that I was surprised to be surprised. Of course Dad had a knife. He probably had an entire survival kit tucked into pockets and sleeves, because that was my father. He sharpened four sticks to deadly points in record time, then pulled a leather pouch out from under his shirt. I rolled my eyes at the sky because he was proving my point, but in rolling, saw Aidan again, and lost all humor.

By the time I looked back at Dad two seconds later, he'd taken a pinch of tobacco from the pouch, and Morrison was throwing him the thing he'd been carving: a small, rudimentary pipe. Dad packed the tobacco in and lit it with a match that came from the pouch, then sprang to his feet and strode from one side of the circle to the other, driving his stakes deep into the earth. By the time he was done, the pipe was smoking pretty well, leaving the rich scent of tobacco to follow him. He stopped in the middle of the circle, took a piece of black cloth from a pocket, and wrapped the pipe in it, giving it an air of permanence despite having just been carved.

The smoke created a drifting barrier inside the power circle, a secondary circle that reinforced the first one. Dad tipped his head back, blowing a deep lungful of smoke toward Aidan, the wights, and the shrieking portal. The first breaths barely touched the wights before they ripped themselves away from the circle and came, en masse, at my father.

It was all the excuse the military guy needed. The wights had taken themselves out of the shielding provided by Aidan's presence, and the guy's first shots took three of them out. For an instant they clashed together, chaotic indecision at its finest. Dad puffed another huge lungful of smoke at them and one shriveled in the air, collapsing into a dusty pile. Aidan's chanting grew increasingly determined, and I struggled not to hop in place. I wanted to *help*. I wanted to *do* something. Never mind that I had no idea what to do and that everything I'd tried thus far had backfired. I wasn't accustomed to being left holding the ball, or in this case, holding the power circle. Close enough.

As if feeling my impatience, Aidan's shouting strengthened and the vortex sped up, testing the bounds of the power circle. I curled a lip and dug in. I might've been left holding the ball, but that didn't mean I would let myself get sacked. Or something like that. Football metaphors were not my strong point.

Three of the wights had the good sense to abandon the attack on Dad and retreat to the safety Aidan offered. Less than they hoped, though: the moment they were close enough, he stretched his hands out and sucked them dry, gobbling up every last bit of magic that kept them functioning. Black light shot through the vortex, expanding it downward, since that was the only direction it could go. Aidan didn't drop, though, only became more central to the expanding darkness. My heart started hammering in overtime as I wondered what happened when he became enveloped by the vortex.

Dad, in a voice much stronger than Aidan's, began a counter-chant. He called on spirits I knew nothing about: men from the Lower World, a Red Man and a Purple Man. The Purple Man had a familiar feel to him, a Trickster feel that reminded me of Coyote. He came from the sky, dancing backward and covering his eyes with one hand as he shouted and teased at Aidan. The Red Man came from below, strong and generous of spirit, and drew arrows from his bones to fire at the vortex above.

One struck Aidan, and he fell.

It was a chance. I took it.

Aidan's garden was shockingly vulnerable. Not surprising, I guessed, since it had been invaded by the Executioner and very possibly by Raven Mocker himself. The Executioner would have very little need to guard its own personal space, though I thought Raven Mocker had a lot more self-awareness. Especially if Raven Mocker was the Master, but that thought wasn't worth pursuing. I could deal with the Executioner. Raven Mocker was a bigger fish to fry. I took a breath, trying to understand my surroundings, and put my money on Aidan's possession being mostly Executioner: I had no sense of a personal vendetta, no active will beyond drinking down the available power. The Executioner's hunger was only a funnel, passing what it took on to the Master, and what was left of Aidan's garden had that transitory feel to it.

The walls had fallen. More than fallen. They had become ragged edges of a flat earth, with once-rich soil collapsing into nothingness while rivers of water poured over the sides. Every drop that passed wore away more of the garden's area, and it ran relentlessly.

So did rain, pounding from vast black clouds against earth so water-laden it sucked at my feet, trying to hold me back. Dark shadows were illuminated by rapid explosions of lightning that struck time and again at shattered trees. Somewhere in there, I told myself: somewhere in there, a kid was huddling, holding a candle against the dark. All I had to do was find him. If the Executioner had no particular sense of self, it shouldn't be that hard. It seemed logical that something without a sense of self wouldn't think to disguise something that *had* a sense of self.

An eleven-foot-tall metal monstrosity of spikes and plate mail, bearing a sword larger than I was, erupted out of the darkness and put paid to that thought.

I nearly fell off the edge of the world, trying to escape it. Dirt crumbled under my fingers as I scrambled back to solid land. One of my knees dropped alarmingly before I lurched myself forward and crawled, then ran, for the garden's center at top speed. The Executioner lumbered after me, sending whole yards of earth falling away into the void as it ran. This was going to have to be a fast fight, or there would be nothing left of Aidan's garden to recover. I got to what appeared, in the darkness, to be about as central a location as was to be had, and turned to face the Executioner with two fists full of healing power.

If nothing else, the magic provided light, but that proved less heartening than I might have hoped, since I could now see clearly how badly damaged the land was. I didn't know how lush Aidan's garden had been to start with, though I was betting it was in much better condition than my own. Even if it was as uninspired as mine to begin with, though, the fraying landscape had taken an appalling amount of damage. I breathed, "C'mon, kid," and lobbed a ball of power into the Executioner's gut, hoping to wake in Aidan a vestigial remembrance of what it was like to be one of the good guys.

The Executioner's sword lit on fire.

"Oh, that's just not fair." The whole image was straight out of a twelve-year-old fantasy reader's nightmare, a Frank Frazetta death rider of the apocalypse. And it was happy to murder me until I was dead, whereas I couldn't afford to return the favor for fear of taking Aidan out along with it. Someday I was going to get to fight something and there would be no collateral damage, but this was not that day. Worried about Aidan or not, though, I drew my sword. I wanted to at least be able to parry if that thing came my way.

Which it did, a slow heavy swing that a sloth could have avoided. Good thing, too, because not only did it light the trees it hit on fire, but it also cut them all in half. Four of them. With one blow. I watched them slide to the earth, *fwip fwip fwip fwip,* and listened to the fire go out in a series of hisses and pops as the severed trunks slid into the sopping ground.

The Executioner was so ponderous it had to spin all the way around with the weight of the blow, which gave me time to watch the trees fall down and still get out of the way when it came back around. I ducked the next blow and ran inside its reach. It roared, dropped the sword while still wheeling from its second slash, and tried scraping me off its plate armor.

That was harder than it looked, given how many spikes decorated the armor. Ankles, knees, hips, for heaven's sake, who needed hip spikes? Or a spiky belt, for that matter, or shoulder and elbow spikes? If it tilted its head more than two degrees left or right it would pierce its own brain with the spikes. On the other hand, all the pointy bits made a pretty good ladder, and I climbed its eleven-foot self in a couple of long strides. I'd dropped my own sword, but that was okay, because it was magic and I just had to call it again for it to appear. I bet the Executioner was going to have to bend over and pick his up, and I bet if I kicked its heiny it would fall flat on its face and stick in the ground thanks to all those spikes.

That actually sounded like a better game plan than the one I was trying. I filed it away for future reference, planted my feet on the Executioner's spiny belt, grabbed hold of one shoulder spike for balance, and hauled its pointy helmet off. I expected to see Aidan in there, all big-eyed and alarmed-looking, like a tiny goblin in a great big mech suit.

Instead a black slash of nothing erupted from the armor and tried to suck my head off.

CHAPTER TWENTY-EIGHT

I yelled and let go and fell six feet to the ground, landing with a splat and a grunt. The Executioner's armor collapsed around me, pointy bits offering considerably more danger than its big flaming sword had. It reformed without the armor, looking far more like the ax-wielding thing it had been in the mountain holler, and I realized belatedly that the Frazetta suit had perhaps been Aidan's way of trying to protect me. His way of slowing the Executioner down, so I could fight it more easily. And I'd blown it.

I would have to make time for recriminations later. In the meantime, if Aidan wasn't at the heart of the Executioner's armor, that meant he was around here somewhere else, maybe holding out as a separate entity of his own, deep in the sanctuary of his own garden. That meant I could fight this thing without worrying about hurting the kid, and that made everything a lot easier. I bounced to my feet, drew my sword and called my shield. We were in a sacred place, in the heart of somebody's soul, and I figured my psychic weaponry should be stronger here than anywhere else. Nerved up by this belief, I didn't try to dodge when the Executioner swung his ax.

It slammed into my shield so hard my eyeballs wobbled. I tipped over and reconsidered my game plan on my way to hitting the ground. By the time the impact knocked the breath out of me, I'd decided that running away was the only smart choice. It wasn't a viable choice, of course. But it was the smart one. The Executioner's ax smashed down. I rolled sideways, swallowing a squeak of relief as it buried the ax so deeply in the earth that for a few seconds it couldn't get it free. While it struggled, I unwound a single strand of magic from the idea of a net, and flung the rope at the Executioner's ankles.

It wrapped around them, whiplike, and I hauled back with all my strength.

Its feet went out from under it. I leapt to mine and gave a blood-curdling shriek as I went for a killing blow, which would have worked except the Executioner dissipated and left me with my sword stuck in the ground next to its ax. That was absolutely not fair. I yanked the sword out and the Executioner reappeared on the ax's far side, where it got a better grip and hauled it free, too. We stood there a couple seconds, sizing one another up. It wasn't eleven feet tall anymore, but it thrummed with magic, still drawing in new strength from Aidan, from the wights, from the fight that was promising to shape up back in the Middle World. It was made from what seemed like a nearly endless source of power, and I'd only just barely been jump-started. If I thought about it, I was doomed.

Fortunately, it didn't give me much time to think. It swung, I parried, and for a minute or so, it was epic. My teeth rattled when it clobbered me, its skin glowed and broke apart in blue chunks where I slashed it, lightning fell from the sky in vast sheets, thunder rolled across the landscape. I couldn't for the life of me count the number of blows, or track how fast we struck at one another.

Rattler was alive in the back of my head, pouring speed into my body, and Raven soared around the Executioner's head, pulling at its barely present hair and plucking at its eyes. I wouldn't have expected Raven to be able to affect it, but it was a creature made up of death magic, and Raven was my guide between the living and the dead. Renee lent the same clarity of sight I'd had driving Petite: time slowed as I fought, until the play of the Executioner's misty muscles triggered an awareness in me of where it would strike next. I started being there before it finished the blow, getting inside its guard and smashing not just with sword but with shield, every hit driving healing power into it. I started feeling like the fantasy hero who would have fought the armored monstrosity the Executioner had first appeared as. It was fantastic, confidence and assurance building in me. The Executioner finally retreated, then ran, trying to escape me. I yelled and gave chase, crashing around the remains of Aidan's garden.

Earth crumbled under my feet with each step. Under the Executioner's, too, falling away faster and faster until I realized we were on an island in the midst of a boiling blackness. All that remained of the garden was a single broken oak tree, its roots dangling raggedly through shallow earth. There was suddenly nowhere left for either of us to go. Huge chunks of bark fell from the tree as I chased the Executioner around it, both of us slamming against the rotting wood in our haste. Then a root gave way beneath it and it fell, silent in the storm's roar.

I flung myself after him with both hands wrapped around the rapier's hilt. It felt very cinematic, the earth collapsing behind me, my body arched dramatically and the sword raised above my head for a downward blow. The Executioner was unprotected, its chest open to me, vulnerable.

It grinned.

After I'd thrown myself from the bridge was not a good time to realize I'd made a mistake. Cold coursed through me, stuttering my heart. The Executioner wasn't even trying to save itself, just leering as it fell. I twisted to look at what we'd fallen *from:* a lonesome dying tree, all that remained of Aidan's garden.

All that remained of Aidan's garden.

The Executioner was a distraction. A *distraction,* and I was a moron for allowing myself to be distracted. Yes, of course it was something that needed to be dealt with, but I had been taught time and again that fighting wasn't the only way to deal with something. Aidan hadn't needed me to come stomping in here and slay the monster with a sword. He'd needed *healing,* a lifeline to which he could cling and draw himself back out of the dark.

I screamed and pitched the sword downward. Threw it with all my strength, like it was a spear. It slammed into the Executioner's chest, blue healing magic cracking the monster apart. In that same moment I let myself forget about it, and twisted in the air, gathering magic. For the second time I threw not a net, but just a strand, trying to reach the dying oak that now seemed an impossible distance away. It fell short, terribly short, my imagination failing me: I couldn't throw that far.

Raven caught the rope in his claws and showed me what wings were for.

He flew against the storm, through lightning and falling earth, against driving rain that would pound any lesser bird out of the sky, and he swung the rope around the tree's thick trunk. Gunmetal light flared against the tree, showing me its scars as the rope sealed to itself, making a sturdy loop that would hold my weight. I drew myself up the magic fist by fist, hands stinging with the remembered feel of rope burns.

There were clods of earth still clinging to the oak's roots when I reached it. Nothing more than that: it was essentially drifting alone, dying in a vast nothingness. I wrapped my arms around it as far as they would go, until my heart was pressed against the shattered tree. I pressed my cheek against it, too, whispering, "C'mon, kid. Take what you need," and opened up the whole of my magic, no shields, no armor, no protection.

All the lights went out.

For a few long hideous seconds I thought I'd blown it. I thought I was too late, that the Executioner had won. That I'd sacrificed Aidan's life in the name of chasing a phantom bad guy all over the mindscape, and that I was going to have to live with that. I couldn't even cry. I couldn't breathe, much less sob. The air turned to ice in my lungs, blood frozen in my chest, the magic I clung to cold and dead under my hands. I forced my fingers into the tree's bark, jamming a pulse of power into it. I knew I should be reaching for a line to ham it up: *live, damn you! Live!* Anything to ease my fear, but the thought carried no laughter, no release. I couldn't draw air to cry out, *Nooooooooooo!* like a proper movie hero would. All I could do was empty my chest a little more, and slam another pulse of magic into the tree. And another, blind eyes staring into darkness like I was waiting for the *blip* on a cardiac machine's screen. And another, waiting for a doctor to say it was too late, and call the time of death.

On a cold day in Hell.

Resolve burned through the ice in my body, fire wakening not the humor I was desperate for, but a flat determination that was considerably scarier. I would quit when Hell froze over, I would stop trying when the world fell down, I would give up at the death of the universe, and even then Cernunnos would have to drag me kicking and screaming into the great beyond. I jolted power into the tree again, and again, and again, until somewhere deep in the heart of it, something responded. A flicker of a pulse, not coming back from the dead but daring, fearfully, to expose itself. A spark against the darkness, that's all it was. White magic, twin auras bound together to hold out against the night. Scalding tears slid down my cold cheeks and melted into the oak's rough bark. I whispered, "C'mon, kid. Come out here again. Let's make this right."

That was asking too much, but that was okay. I knew the glimmer of light was in there now, which meant the rest of it could heal. I had, once before, given what I could to a dying land. I reached deep to do the same again, searching for what I could in order to help rebuild Aidan's garden. It had been easier with Cernunnos: his world had only been dying, not nearly destroyed. The physicality of it had remained, but there was so little left to the garden that its substance had to be entirely remade.

I started with my own, because it was all I had. The tall stone walls slowly breaking down, the precisely cut grass only just starting to grow wild around the edges. Tidy trees, carefully laid stone walks leading to a small pool fed by a waterfall. It had all been so particular, but there had been one thing about my garden that broke my own evidently deep-set mental ideas of what my soul looked like. There had been a robin to call out and tell me of a door hidden behind a fall of ivy, because it couldn't be a secret garden without a hidden door.

I knew what that door opened onto. It opened into a vast gestalt, a place where other inner gardens could be reached from. In my experience, there were miles of empty land between one garden and another, huge amounts of territory to traverse to reach someone else's soul.

But there didn't have to be, and so this time when I dug up the key and opened the door, my garden's limited greenery spilled through into the darkness that had become Aidan's inner sanctuary, and gave it something to start with.

Trees began unfurling on his side of the door the very moment it opened. Their roots sank into the blackness, creating rich earth as they grew, and lush bluegrass sprang up. The relentless rain that had fallen provided water for the sudden growth, though all the sunlight that shone through still came from my garden. In a fit of recklessness I cast a net and caught my own garden walls in it, pulling stone down in lumps that reminded me of fallen Irish castles. More sunlight washed into Aidan's garden, the narrow doorway-size path broadening and allowing more and more life to take root. I tucked the secret door's key into my pockets and got busy knocking more walls down, alternating between pulling and kicking. Dust rose and fell again, mortar crumbling to bits, and with every stone that crashed to the earth on my side, Aidan's garden reclaimed some of its vibrancy.

My own garden began reshaping itself with enthusiasm, once the strongest barriers were down. The quiet little waterfall shifted deep into the ground and rose again as a river that sped through a half-familiar landscape. Woodhenges broke free from the earth, marked with petroglyphic storytelling. I dearly wanted to go read them, but my garden was rumbling too much, land shifting and changing beneath my feet, and the changes rolled right into Aidan's space, where they individualized themselves according to his tastes. Beyond the henges, my space grew into low Appalachian mountains and Irish fields; on Aidan's side, a fine rash of poison oak grew up, threatening to anyone who came in uninvited. It went on and on, until all that separated his garden from mine was a hand-built stone wall of about hip height.

I waited, hoping, but he didn't come to the wall. The oak tree stood in the distance, still recovering: its black bark shone with strength, and new leaves budded, but its height had been broken, and I had no idea if it could recover. I didn't know if I should stay and encourage it, or if it was better to let it re-build on its own. I was still hesitating when Aidan stepped out of the tree and came toward me.

He looked more fragile within the confines of his garden than in the world outside. No surprise, given what he'd been through, but I thought it was more than that. His image of himself reminded me of Billy Holliday, whose garden self was more delicate and lightly built than the big man who lived in the Middle World. Billy had been a child when his sister died and their bond made her choose to stay with him. Aidan and Ayita had both been infants when their souls had become one.

He wasn't feminine. It wasn't as if here at the heart of his soul he reflected only what Ayita had been. It was more evenly balanced than that, their spirits so well-melded that either's strengths could come to the forefront at any moment. But in the Middle World he seemed fairly serious, and here there was more sense of impishness, as if Ayita's presence was will-ing and able to wink at the world. And I thought maybe right now she was the stronger of the two, because he was the one whose physical form was undergoing the transformations and power surges brought on by the Executioner's presence and the opening vortex. She wasn't protected, exactly: their two spirits were too completely one for that. But she had given up her physical body a long time ago, and I thought that might be strengthening her spiritual presence now.

He sounded exactly like himself, unbroken voice as easily feminine as masculine. "Your garden looks better."

I laughed, taken aback, and humor sparkled in his eyes. "Well, it does."

"It does. So does yours."

"Eh." He wrinkled his nose, looking around. "Not better than it was before. I didn't mean for this to happen. I'm not one of the bad guys." A tremulous note shook his voice, like he was hoping I would confirm that, and wasn't absolutely certain I would.

I shook my head. "No, kiddo, you're not. This kind of crap… happens. It happened to me, too."

"Why does it happen? I mean, if we're the good guys…"

"Because good guys put on white hats and let themselves be shot at," I said softly. "Because sometimes it's hard to tell if people are good or bad, and it's our job to assume they're good until they've gone so far overboard there's no hope of bringing them back. I believe that doesn't happen very often, but it happens."

"This magic was never good. The Nothing, the hole in time, the monster inside me, it wasn't ever good."

"The monster infected you, Aidan. It wasn't inside you. Big difference. And you're right, this magic was never good, and it got to you because of me. Because you're powerful, and because it would be a big win for the bad guys if they brought you over. But I don't think that's even possible. I've never seen anybody human who burns as bright as you do."

He perked right up. "You've seen people who aren't human?"

I grinned. "Quite a few of them. I'll introduce you sometime."

Solemnity rolled back into place. "You mean, you'll introduce me if we get out of this alive."

"We'll just have to, won't we?"

"How?"

"We took out the Executioner. We can manage Raven Mocker. Trust me, Aidan. You're gonna be fine. Nothing's going to happen to you as long as I'm still alive." I rolled a bit more power into my shields, knowing they would help guard the still-recovering garden that lay close to mine.

Aidan's eyebrows drew down. "You mean that, don't you? How come? You don't even know me. Is it 'cause you're my birth mom?"

"Partly. Mostly, maybe, but really, what kind of asshole would I be if I let monsters tromp around in kids' heads if I could stop it?"

His eyes popped and he laughed. "You're not supposed to say things like that. Mom would yell at you."

"This," I said dryly, "is one of many reasons why she's a good mom and I'd probably be a terrible one. Look, Aidan, you know your strength comes from being two-spirited, right? Some of it, anyway."

He rolled his eyes. "Yeah. Some of the kids at school wanna know if that means I'm gonna start dressing in girls' clothes." The eye-rolling turned to a sudden wicked sparkle. "I oughta do it, huh? That'd freak 'em out."

I grinned. "You probably should. Don't take me wrong, but you'd make a pretty good girl, at least until your voice changes. You've got great cheekbones. Anyway, listen, not the point. The point is you've got reserves to draw on. I know the Executioner's got his claws in you deep, out there. But we've loosened his grip in here, and sweetheart, you burn bright. You and Ayita together, honey, I don't think much of anything can stop you. Just hold on to that, okay? Hold on to Ayita and you're going to be fine. All I need to work with out there is that spark, and I can get you free of the rest of this."

"You don't sound scared."

"I was scared when your garden was falling apart. Now I know it's going to be okay." Even I believed me, more or less. "You ready to go back out there?"

Aidan took a deep breath. "No."

I laughed. "Yeah, I can't blame you. Look, just hang on a few minutes, kiddo, and this will all be over. I promise. Okay?"

He took another deep breath, then put his hand in mine and nodded. "Yeah. Okay."

I said, "Okay," one more time, and we walked out of the gardens back into a battle zone.

CHAPTER TWENTY-NINE

The last couple minutes in the garden had been so calm that returning to the Middle World was a violent shock. Aidan, despite having just had a reassuring conversation with me, was in fact still twenty feet in the air: the black magic had caught him, kept him from falling when the Red Man had shot a bone arrow into him. The Red Man, the Purple Man, and my father had all taken up points around the circle, each of them at one of the stakes Dad had driven into the ground. Sara and Les appeared to be arguing over which of them should go to the fourth, and while they argued, Morrison ran for it.

With four of them in place, they began hauling the vortex closer to the ground. It was no longer spinning: it was simply a hole ripped in the sky and pierced by the Red Man's arrows. There were no stars beyond it, and the arrows seemed to be just stuck in the black, which bothered me on a profound level. But there were ropes, or threads, or roots, falling from the arrows, and that was what the men hauled on, dragging the vortex down. Dragging Aidan down, too.

I barked, "Sara!" and she stood straight upright, startled out of her argument. I didn't think the distraction was her fault: the encroaching magic made me want to fight, too. "Come here, both of you. You need to hold the power circle in place."

"What? I can't—"

"You certainly can." Ada Monroe sounded just like a mother as she stomped over to join us. The poor military guy followed her with the expression of someone who had no idea what shit he's stepped in but was willing to follow any solid leadership available. Ada said, "Just focus your energy as positively as you can and I'll do the rest," to him, then sent him to stand at a quarter-point in the circle. He went meekly. I felt sorry for him.

Les and Sara both radiated disbelief as Ada pointed them toward other quarter-points, too. Apparently so did I, because her chin came up a little as she met my eyes. "I told you, my family had medicine men once."

"Ada, you are positively amazing. Go!" That was at Sara and Les, who scampered away like kids. I did the same kind of transference that Dad had done with me: palms up, warm magic dancing on them. Ada pressed her hands against mine, taking the weight of the circle, and went a little ashy. For an instant I saw fear in her eyes, the certainty she couldn't handle it, but I was startlingly confident as I said, "You've got it. You're fine."

She nodded once, then backed away, taking up the final eight-point around the circle. Energy flared from the four of them, making a softer white shell inside the vast magic Dad was working. That accounted for everybody but Danny, who was still sniveling about his rebroken shoulder. I left him where he was and turned to wait on Aidan's descent.

He had wings. My heart clenched. Sooty, fiery raven wings, spread wide and beating the air with outrageous determination. Raven Mocker wings, struggling to bring the boy and his power back under their control. I flexed my hands uselessly, afraid to draw magic and refuel the thing trying to eat Aidan's soul.

Except there was power flying like crazy around here and the wights were all dead. They were the conduits, the things that fed power to the Executioner and ultimately the Master or Raven Mocker or whatever the hell I wanted to call him. The Executioner had been defeated. Which might mean this was the one shot we had at a full-frontal attack, and it would be a terrible mistake for me to miss it.

I whispered, "Screw it," and reached for the sky.

Power poured out of me, silver and blue winding together in a rush. I didn't think I could defeat the oncoming Raven Mocker. I just wanted to shore up Aidan's reserves, give the kid's bright spirit a chance to fight back on its own. The rip in the sky came closer, Dad and Morrison and the magic men pulling it down. It had stopped expanding and was beginning to tear, like their efforts were pulling it beyond its ability to stretch.

My magic washed over Aidan, and for an instant his wings turned white.

Black rushed in again, swallowing the gain, but the vortex didn't widen any: we *had* cut its power sources. If it couldn't keep Aidan, it would lose all its strength. It might take a while, because it was still feeding on centuries of pain, but if we could wrest Aidan back, the darkness would burn itself out. Hope caught me in the teeth and made me grin, fierce and resolved. I extended another rolling wave of magic.

It left me woozy. My vision went black and starry, then faded back in, but I felt my power failing within me. There were two circles surrounding me that I could draw on, Dad's internal smoke circle and the larger one Ada was holding. Dad and Morrison had the vortex within ten feet of the ground now, and it was shredding. I didn't want to risk setting it loose again. Ada's exterior circle was fragile. Borrowing power on the level I'd been using it at would knock all four of them off their feet. That would do us exactly no good. And there was nobody to bang my drum, to help my stuttering power refill again, because everybody was busy trying not to let any of us get killed.

I swore. One more. I could probably manage one more healing wave into Aidan before my eyes rolled back. It would have to be enough.

He was closer now, at least. I ran toward him, dodging the massive sooty wings as they swept the air, and wrapped my arms around him, breathing, "Now would be good, kid."

To my astonishment, Renee came to bright dramatic life and leapt from me to Aidan as I unleashed one last splash of healing magic. Aidan snapped a hand up, catching her. A second walking stick appeared in his other hand. Then Dad's joined them, balancing on Aidan's chest. They blended into one another and faded, not into Aidan, not into the vortex, just…disappeared. It seemed like a bad sign.

My knees cut out, whatever magical strength I'd had utterly depleted. I was never ever *ever* flying a car again. Aidan fell with me, landing on my chest hard enough to crunch my back. I wheezed, trying to focus beyond Aidan's still-white hair in my face. His head lolled to the side, and panic spurted through me. Me collapsing was one thing. Aidan going unconscious was something else. I rolled him off me and got to my knees, hands shaking with fear.

The Raven Mocker wings remained in the air, the empty space where Aidan had been now filling with the last ragged pieces of the vortex. I cast a frantic look at my father, but he didn't look distressed by the congealing vortex. The Red Man drew another arrow and fired, a smooth perfect shot that should have pierced the very heart of the spirit monster. Raven Mocker tore in two, the arrow passing harmlessly through empty air as the winged vortex shot forward and into Danny's chest.

I realized, quite clearly and suddenly, that we'd lost.

Aidan would have been a wonderful prize, with all the power rife in his youthful spirit. But it seemed blindingly obvious, after the fact, that he was just one more conduit. The last of them, a source of life essence to allow Raven Mocker entrance to this plane of existence. Aidan was, at heart, a good kid.

Raven Mocker didn't want a good kid. He wanted someone he could use and control. Someone who was already angry at the world. He wanted someone emotionally damaged, easy to manipulate and willing to strike out. He wanted Danny Little Turtle, or someone like him.

It struck me that I had very narrowly avoided being the *perfect* host for Raven Mocker, and my gratitude ran so deep it raised shivers on my arms. Without Mom, without Morrison, without Gary and Billy and all the lessons I'd learned over the past year, it could've been bitter angry me, chock full of potential power, who offered a host body to the Master. I owed my friends more than I could ever repay them. I'd known that all along, but watching Danny get to his feet, awkward with pain and then resplendent with that pain fading, I knew it all the more deeply, and promised to thank them yet again.

Daniel Raven Mocker smiled, folded his wings around himself, and leapt straight up, smashing through the power circles and disappearing into the night.

The circles shattered, magic ringing like gongs. Fragments

of power exploded everywhere like a grenade going off. The bits that hit me settled into my skin, absorbing, renewing my strength, but when they hit the nonadepts in the group, they knocked them silly. The entire inner circle, and Morrison, were flattened. The Red and Purple men disappeared, no longer bound by the circle and magic to this place. Dad clutched a tree to stay upright, his gaze betrayed and astonished as he looked skyward.

I looked too, blank with confusion. Danny couldn't be gone. I hung up on that thought, even though it was blatantly wrong. He had to be up there somewhere, soaring on raven wings. I croaked, "Raven?" and my spirit animal appeared, looking like he'd gone three rounds with Mike Tyson. I shut my mouth on asking him to go after Danny. Wiping myself out always seemed bad enough, but wiping my spirit animals out was guilt-inducing. Raven croaked in return, then went back inside my head where it was nominally safe. I couldn't blame him.

Dad, faintly, said, "He shouldn't have been able to do that," which made me laugh. Not a happy laugh, but a laugh. Dad tried glaring at me, but didn't have enough oomph left for it to carry any weight. "That ritual is meant to kill a Raven Mocker, Joanne, and there were two power circles. He shouldn't have been able to break through."

"Most Raven Mockers aren't packing a few genocides worth of life force, Dad. Or death power. Whatever. We..." I didn't want to say it aloud, certainly not while meeting his eyes, so I looked up again, trying to find the shape of wings against the stars. "We lost."

"Nah." Aidan spoke from beside me, sounding exhausted but certain. I squeaked and turned toward him, hands pressed over my mouth. His skin had returned to normal, except tired bruises beneath his eyes, but his hair was still bone white. I didn't need the Sight to catch a glimpse of his aura, a kernel of power burning bright within him. He put a hand on my shoulder and shoved himself to his feet, wobbling a little before dropping his chin to his chest and whispering, "Nah. Not yet."

Eyes closed, he extended his hands, arms crossing at the wrists, like he was holding himself in the loosest hug possible. Like he was gathering someone else close: gathering Ayita, maybe, and when I thought it, I could nearly See it, his other half, the shared spirit that gave him so much strength. A slim girl, taller than Aidan but looking very like him, with the same cheekbones and jaw, but with a nose that was a little more like mine. I Saw her resolve, the same strength of character that she shared with her grandmother, the resolve that had let her face death in a time and way of her choosing. That, I thought, was the spark that the Executioner hadn't been able to defeat: that was the chance Aidan had been given, that would allow him to survive. He hugged Ayita more tightly, and she stepped within him, their auras igniting into brilliance.

Renee and Dad's walking stick appeared on Aidan's arms, coming up from the bones. The third, Aidan's own, rose up from his hands, balancing itself delicately on his extended fingers. Power dropped through them, magic so heavy it seemed to lower the floor of the valley. I was glad to be kneeling, for fear otherwise I would have been flattened. Dad did drop, kneeling, as well, and nobody else had gotten further than sitting anyway. Aidan was the only one left standing.

The earth beneath us frosted, white magic creeping over leaves, over branches, over the wrecked helicopter and beyond. My breath turned to fog, though my skin didn't feel cold. Magic carried silence with it, washing away the memory of battle sounds and making the valley serene. Aidan gathered his arms a little closer to his chest, embracing the walking sticks, then lifted his arms.

Soft white magic heaved upward, the ice-like frost rushing to treetops and to the distant sky beyond. I saw Raven Mocker then, a far-off shadow against the spreading brilliance. His wings cut the air, loud enough to be heard now that silence held sway everywhere else. He didn't want to fight. He wanted to escape, so he could wreak havoc in the world beyond. He wanted to escape so I would have to hunt him, and so my attention would be split in a dozen directions. I gathered the idea of a net, knowing I didn't have enough strength to pull him back even if I managed to catch him, but hating not to try.

Before I even tried to cast it, Aidan's auras became blinding, lighting the whole of the valley, and an echo ran through the mountains. Power reverberated, awakening a touch I knew. Barely knew, but I recognized it. After a moment I placed it, too, and, stunned, looked to the hills.

My whole life I had wanted to be rescued by the cavalry. That scene always got me in the movies, even when I knew it was coming. Especially when I knew it was coming. The moment where the hero is desperately outnumbered, about to die, but he smiles and looks up, and that makes the bad guys look, too. The sheer cliffs are always empty in the first moment, but then they begin to appear. The ferocious chief on a painted horse. The resentful, respectful warrior whose life the hero saved at the beginning of the film. They're the first to appear, and maybe it's just that they're there to stand witness to a hero's death.

But no: then the others come. Dozens, hundreds, sometimes thousands, all lining the cliffs, all surrounding the gulley where the hero isn't about to die after all, because if he does, the bad guys will die with him. I'd stayed up until all hours of the night watching old Westerns I'd seen time and time again, just to watch that scene again. I loved it beyond reason, and I had always wanted to be part of it.

They were ghosts, this cavalry. They didn't ride, but stood. Stepped out of the trees as light and silver, as faces and names from the past. Aidan, focused by the three walking-stick spirits, called them, guided them, and welcomed them into the present. They were so many, and so old, that the valley chilled with their presence. A power circle came to life beneath their insubstantial feet, burning more brightly and gaining speed as it passed beneath each ghost. The entire horizon came alight, every dip of the valley peopled by the serene dead, and when it reached the place it had begun, an old woman stepped forward.

I knew her. I'd had no idea we were in that same valley, my sense of the hills far too limited to notice that. But of course we were: *of course*, because it was a place where Cherokee had lived once, and it was sympathetic to the youth coming to find a way back toward tradition. There were no coincidences, and just this once I was glad for it. A laugh broke in my chest, bringing tears to my eyes. I whispered, "Greetings, old one," and the ancient shaman smiled at me from the distance.

"This pain is ours," she said. "This pain is old, and it is ours. We have waited, Walkingstick. You gave us what knowledge you could, and we have waited to repay that gift. We have stayed long past our time to rest, to take this pain back to the time it was born of. We will not let it poison our children after they have rebuilt from so little. This pain is ours, and we will die from it, but you will live. Live well, and do not forget us."

My father didn't know where I drew my power from, but I had *nothing* on the magic the old shaman threw down. She rebuilt the power circle, sending magic widdershins, redoubling its strength as the Cherokee ghosts began to sing their death songs.

Far above the valley's hills, Raven Mocker's wings began

to shed their sooty feathers, his strength being drawn into the ghosts. Soot and ashes fell faster, breaking away. Danny careened toward the earth, trying to control his fall. He was too far to hear if he cried, or maybe he was brave enough not to, while pieces of his wings fell to the earth like melting wax, as the ghosts called home their pain.

CHAPTER THIRTY

I looked away when Danny fell, not, in the end, as brave as he was. I still saw the impact from the corner of my eye, a flare of white where he hit. We would have to find the body later, but for now the despair and anger riding us all began to fade. There were hundreds of people in the forest now, the modern Cherokee who had come up ready to fight the military and now who stood silent and stunned in the wash of magic and in the presence of their ancestors.

The old shaman stomped one foot, unraveling the power circle she had built. The ghosts faded as the magic came undone, each retreat lightening the valley's weight a little. She remained a few moments longer, looking over a valley full of people who were in spirit her children. I got to my feet awkwardly, feeling stiff and uncomfortable. She looked at me and I spread my hands. "I need to come back with you, if you'll let me."

Her iron-gray eyebrows rose. I gestured at Sara. "The magic took her husband to your end of time. I need to try to save him. I don't know if I can, but I promised I'd try."

Aidan spoke for the first time in what seemed like hours. "Lucas? What happened to Lucas?"

Our hesitation in answering was answer enough. His breath rushed out of him and his hands turned to knots at his sides. "I can hold it open until you get back."

"What happens if he does that?" Sara's voice cracked, and she didn't look at us when she asked the question, but at the old shaman instead. "What happens if we hold this time rift open? Can we save him?"

"Does he live, in my day?"

I shook my head, lips compressed. The shaman frowned. "Then perhaps. Maybe if his soul is still his own, or if you reach him before death takes him, perhaps he could return. But it would be dangerous. We do not die out of time, Walkingstick. We die when we are meant to. I think his soul is already lost, if he is dead in my time. I think he would return to life a sorcerer, and this battle today would be for nothing."

"I have to try. I've dealt with sorcerers before. Maybe I could…" I trailed off, because really, dealing with body-snatching sorcerers in the past hadn't gone all that well for the host bodies.

"No." Sara slumped, hands useless in her lap. "No, you don't, Joanne. If the risk is having to do this all over again… he wouldn't want that. I do." Her voice broke, harsh and miserable. "I want you to go save him, I want to make all of this unhappen, I want to go home and be happy again, but if a sorcerer stole his soul and came back in his place…Lucas wouldn't want you to try. He wouldn't want to risk it. He would say it was a good life and to let it go. So I have to, too, don't I. Because what're you going to do if you go back and save him but it's not really him? Kill him again?"

That was possibly the worst prospect I'd ever been presented with, and I'd been given a lot of unpleasant choices over the past year. Sara glanced at me and actually laughed at my expression. Not a healthy laugh, but a laugh. "Yeah. That's what I thought. No," she said to the ancient shaman. "No, go home. Sing for him, too, even if he wasn't of your People. And don't ever cross my path again."

The last was to me, and I couldn't blame her for it at all. I nodded, though she wasn't looking my way. Sara got up, brushed her knees free of debris, and left the ruin of her life along with all the rest of us.

Most of the rest of us. Les cast Morrison and me a look, then followed Sara. Ada lurched to her feet and ran for Aidan, catching him in a hug that made him grunt and squeak with protest. Not much protest, though: he hugged her back, face buried in her shoulder, while my Dad sat down hard and rubbed his hands over his eyes. Gosh. I wondered where I'd gotten *that* habit from. After a minute, he said, "So this is your life, Joanne?" into his palms, but I was busy crawling toward Morrison and didn't want to answer. Dad didn't seem to expect an answer, either, and for a few minutes we all simply sat there, wrung out, with no thoughts for the future.

The poor military guy finally broke the silence. Not by asking what the hell had just happened, which would have been legitimate, but by saying, "I'm going to have to radio this in. They'll already be wondering why we haven't reported. You probably won't have long to get your people out of the valley."

I couldn't help asking, "What are you going to tell them? And, look, I'm sorry, but what's your name?"

"Lieutenant Dennis Gilmore." Lieutenant Gilmore rightfully looked as though he'd seen ghosts, and like he didn't want to give the only answer he could. "I'm going to tell them that we had an encounter with the epidemic's source and were able to eliminate it, but at great personal cost. We'll send out a search team for the body, and I will identify it as our target."

That reminded me. I closed my eyes, breathed, "Jesus," and opened them again. "Lieutenant, I'm really, really sorry, but you're going to have to burn Captain Montenegro and everybody else who died out here tonight. By sunrise."

He turned his wrist over, looking at a watch, then looked through broken trees at the starry night. "Four hours. We can do that, ma'am, but it'll complicate things if the tribe is still in the woods."

"Won't it complicate things if they all come back to town, too? The CDC—"

"Ma'am, the CDC is not going to let this go. But if we can obtain the source and return it to the CDC, I believe that once they've satisfied themselves that the epidemic has run its course, they'll leave Cherokee town and the Qualla Boundary without unduly disturbing its residents. The sooner you get them home so blood tests can be run, the sooner we'll be out of your hair." He sounded so professional I wanted to cry for him. His entire team was dead, and he was holding it together admirably. I wondered what he would let himself remember.

Dad stood up. "We'll get them home and we'll get the blood tests underway. Thanks for your understanding here, Lieutenant."

"I can give you half an hour." Lieutenant Gilmore went to the bodies of his fallen comrades, standing over them in silence. Dad gestured to the rest of us, and we got up to abandon the valley together.

Choppers flew overhead when the collected tribal members were barely out of the valley. Not all of the fight had gone out of them, nor would it ever, I thought; there was just too much bad blood between Natives and the government. But they'd been there when the ghosts had come to lay the pain to rest, and that went a long way toward sobering even the most hotheaded of them. Sara and Les were among them, but I stayed well out of their way, trailing near the back with Morrison. Dad, who'd taken up a position of leadership, eventually fell back to join us, and repeated the question he'd asked earlier: "Is this what your life is like, Joanne?"

"By and large, yeah. You get used to it. Kind of." I drew breath to lay down the accusations and the arguments we'd already started once, then sighed and let it go. He should have told me about my heritage a long time ago, no doubt about it. But he hadn't, and that was the hand I had to play. There were no do-overs, no matter how badly I might want them. Eventually I said, "You were pretty awesome back there, actually. Those Lower World guys, that was kinda great. You should, um. You should teach me how to do that, huh?"

"I'd like that." Dad hesitated as much as I had, then repeated himself. "I'd like that. Does that mean you're going to stay awhile?"

My hand crept into Morrison's. "Probably not. Morrison's got to get back to work soon, and I have to go find a job."

"I thought you worked for the police department."

"I quit a couple weeks ago. This—" I lifted my hand in Morrison's, gesturing a circle with both of them. I meant the motion to encompass the entire magical mess we'd just gone through, but realized that our entwined fingers were just as much a part of *this* as the magic was "—this was starting to get in the way of the job."

"What are you going to do?"

"I don't know. Slay demons and fix cars, probably. Isn't that what most people want to do when they grow up? Oh, God, my car. I have to go get Petite. I am not leaving her on the mountain for another night."

Dad pursed his lips and glanced at the throng of people heading down the hills. "They won't miss us. Come on, I'll take you across the mountains."

"Are you sure? Because I'm not exactly Ms. Fitness. It might be faster to—"

"Change shape and run?" Morrison asked blandly.

"…I'd been going to say, 'Go down to the highway and hike back up.' Are you volunteering to go for a run on the wild side with me, Morrison?"

"I thought you and your dad could go. Family bonding time."

The amazing thing was he said it with an utterly straight face, as if perfectly serious. My father, however, wrinkled his eyebrows at us both. "Shapechanging is a spiritual transformation, Mr. Morri—"

I twitched. "Captain."

"Mike."

Dad waited a moment to see if we were going to argue about that, then said, "Mike," cautiously. "Spiritual, not literal. People can't shapeshift."

Morrison said, "Oh, I see," while I tried so hard not to laugh that tears spilled down my cheeks. Dad looked increasingly offended, until I finally gasped and wiped my face, then patted his shoulder. "You sound just like me, Dad. Just like me. Okay. Tell you what, let's go for a hike. Morrison, you coming?"

He shook his head. "I'll catch up with you in town." Apparently he thought we really did need some bonding time, which was probably true. I kissed him, took the empty shotgun back just in case we met any wights that needed clobbering, and Dad and I slipped off to the west while everyone else headed downhill.

For bonding time, it was remarkably silent, punctuated

mostly by my swearing as I clambered over things that Dad just seemed to melt over. I really didn't know what to say to him, nor he to me, at least not until the sun broke behind us. Once we were in the full gold and pink light of morning he stopped to study me until I became uncomfortable from it. "What?"

"I haven't seen you in years, Jo…anne. I just wanted to get a look at you in daylight, without a war going on around us. You grew up nice."

"I'm working on it, anyway." I put my hands in my jeans pockets, shoving the long coat out of the way to do so. It made me feel like a superhero again, which once more made the coat easily the best money I'd ever spent. "You're not going to turn out to be a horrible monster now, are you? Because this is usually about when that would happen."

"Not planning to, no. Will you tell me what happened?"

I let out a short breath. "Starting with what?"

"Whatever you want. It's a long walk."

"And I still don't have any food." I honestly didn't remember the last time I'd eaten, besides the shriveled apples. Four hundred years ago, in the valley we'd left behind, maybe. I really needed to start taking better care of myself. With my life, that evidently meant always having a three-course meal in my pocket, which I didn't see happening, but it was a nice idea. I fell into step beside Dad again, getting into the rhythm of motion before I started at the beginning.

It was a long walk. Talking helped distract me from climbing over hill and dale, though with Dad's lead it seemed like we covered a lot more territory than Morrison and I had alone. Still, it was well past noon and I'd gotten most of the way through hunting the wendigo when Dad drew up again, nodding down a narrow holler. "This is your place."

I blinked down it, then hiccupped as a particularly gnarly

old tree resolved into familiarity. We weren't that far from our back door now, this little gulley one I'd retreated to often as a teen. I blinked again, then scowled accusingly at Dad. "This isn't anywhere near Petite."

"I know. I'll drive you back up to her, but I thought you might want to visit this place without…Mike." He said the name cautiously, like maybe I wouldn't know who he meant, since I clearly habitually called Morrison, well, Morrison.

I pushed my hand through my hair, which stood up in sweaty spikes. "You know, Dad, he's a grown man. If I said I wanted to come up here without him, he'd say, 'See you later, Walker.'"

Dad pounced like he'd been waiting for the chance. "Is there a reason you two call each other by your last names?"

Clearly I hadn't started early enough with the History Of My Life, As Related By Joanne Walker, since the last names thing was really sort of a way to get in an eternal dig. I mean, most people at the precinct called each other by their last names anyway, but somehow Morrison and I had managed to turn it into a way to avoid referring to each other by our respective, and therefore respectable, ranks. I decided not to try explaining right now and just went with "It's a work thing."

"You don't work together anymore."

"Dad, I just quit, give us some time. The point is he wouldn't have flipped out if I'd headed into the hills alo…" Okay, under the current circumstances, he might have. "I'm going down there now."

Dad crouched, flat-footed on the slanted earth, and wrapped his arms around his knees. I'd seen him sit like that for hours when I was a kid, and didn't expect him to move again until I came back up from the holler. I slipped and slid my way down grass and dirt, catching branches to keep myself from tumbling, and in a minute or two was at my teen hideaway.

The old tree hadn't changed much. There were a few new knots where branches were bursting out like miniature trees of their own, but mostly it was the same crooked old beast it had been. I half closed my eyes, letting memory guide me as I wandered around it, fingers trailing against the bark. There was a particular twist of roots I remembered, almost a braid, that had always been the best place to climb the sloping trunk from. Still only half looking, I found the roots and scrambled upward, guided by my hands and muscle memory. About halfway up there was a dish of a branch, wide enough for my teenage butt to fit into nicely. To my ego's satisfaction, I still fit. I settled down, back against the trunk, and slid my left hand around the rough bark. My fingers stopped when they found the edge of the hollow there. I'd discovered it this way, sheerly by accident, and had done the same thing then as I did now: scootched around on the branch until I was on my belly, dangling, so I could peer around the tree into the opening.

God. There were things in there I'd forgotten I'd left. Bleached by weather, but still remarkably intact, given that they'd been stored here for over a decade. I struggled out of my coat and made a sack with it, then gingerly took everything from the hollow. Almost everything: I'd banged a little wooden shelf into place above the hollow's mouth so my stuff would be more protected, and it had swollen too much to remove. I took everything else, though, and clambered back down to sit among the roots and go through my teenage bounty.

There was a journal I barely remembered keeping, though as soon as I saw its embossed red leather cover I remembered it vividly. I'd had the presence of mind to put that in a sealed plastic bag, and the seal had held all these years. I picked it up carefully and opened it, then rifled through the journal, astonished that the pages weren't a pulpy mash. My teenage self's handwriting looked fatter and loopier than I remembered.

The last entry was about Lucas. About bringing him up to the holler and my dumb bid to make him like me by having sex with him. There weren't any graphic details, but when I written it I'd pretty clearly been thrilled, amazed and proud of myself for taking such a big step toward adulthood. But a couple weeks later I'd realized I was pregnant, and I'd never come up here again. I'd stopped keeping a journal, in fact, the date written on the last page my last-ever entry. I closed the book and tucked it into my coat.

There were other things that made me laugh: a coat pin of Raphael from the original TMNT movie, now so weather-bleached it was recognizable only because I knew what it was. A pair of plastic badger earrings, likewise bleached. Sara had given me those after we'd done her spirit-animal quest, so I'd kept them even though I hadn't pierced my ears until about three months ago. A handful of photographs that fell from the journal, faces of people I hardly remembered. Nostalgia and memorabilia, that's what was in the tree.

That, and a small wooden box, maybe five inches by three, which I had never seen before. It wasn't weather-worn or swollen from humidity. I let it sit beside me a long time while I went through the other bits and bobs, aware of its presence but not yet ready to open it. Eventually I put everything else aside and looked at the box a long time, wondering if I really even wanted to open it. It could be Pandora's Box, filled with things I didn't want to let loose in the world, or more rele-vantly, in my mind.

Of course, the thing I'd never understood about Pandora's Box was that she'd opened it, releasing all evil into the world, but slammed it shut again before hope escaped. That never made any sense to me. I thought she should open the damned box again and let hope escape into the world, too, because it certainly didn't seem to me like it did any good locked in a box. At least if it was released like evil was, then like evil, it would have the ability to chase through the world on the wind, offering...well, *hope*.

With that in mind, it was inevitable that I opened the box.

There was a photograph in it, nothing else. Me, fifteen and prettier than I'd imagined myself, my short hair spiked with gel and stronger freckles than usual standing out across my nose, leavings from the summer sun. Sara, her own thick blond hair bleached lighter than usual, too, also from the sun, and her skin richly gold from the tan she'd picked up. I'd thought she was beautiful, back then. Looking at her picture, I still did.

And between us, where he'd always been and always would be, was Lucas. Dark eyes and black hair, a bright grin stretched across his face, and who could blame him? He had his arms around two pretty girls, like he was king of the world and knew it.

I remembered the day it had been taken, just a few days after school started. Lucas had been in Cherokee for a couple of weeks already. Sara and I had met him at the diner and we were all great friends by the time school started. It would be another few weeks before it all fell apart, but right then, man, we were happy. We were the Three Musketeers, *los tres amigos,* the good, the bad and the ugly. Right in that moment, we were perfect. We were all vibrant, full of life and laughter. Full of love.

Full of hope.

I turned the photograph over and found one word written in pencil on the back: *Sorry.*

"Yeah." I turned it again, brushing my thumb over our faces. "Yeah, me too, Lucas. For everything. Rest in peace."

I opened my hand, releasing hope.

CHAPTER THIRTY-ONE

Friday, March 31, 7:37 p.m.

Dad didn't ask, when I came out of the holler, and I went back to telling him about the adventures of the past fifteen months as we worked our way home again. He occasionally interjected with stories about his own past several years, and by the time we got out of the mountains I thought maybe a hatchet had been buried. It felt good, if a little weird, and I ended up saying so just as the sun started slipping over the horizon.

Dad, watching it, crooked a smile. "And all it took was a day alone. I'm sorry, Jo…anne. For the mistakes I made. I thought I could protect you by keeping you away from your heritage, and for years I watched you heading right down that path anyway. I should have known better."

"Probably, but—and I can't believe I'm saying this—I'm not exactly one to throw stones about knowing better." I hesitated, then offered my hand. "Friends?"

He looked at my hand, then took it and pulled me into an awkward hug. I grunted and knocked him on the back a couple of times, more overwhelmed than I wanted to admit. Then, very guy-like, we broke apart clearing our throats and pretended none of it had happened. I giggled about that all the way back to town.

When we got there, it turned out we'd been missed, after all. Half the CDC and all of the military was looking for me, apparently. A red-eyed Sara and patient Morrison were handling the crush when we arrived. The truth was I had no better answers than they did about what had happened, but I had been appointed ringleader in my absence. Sara got out of my sight as soon as she could, and Morrison stood by me as long as he could. After I gave the authorities a series of unsatisfactory answers, they hauled me off for blood testing and a military grilling which eventually led to me flopped in a chair-and-desk unit in a high school classroom with its windows boarded over, repeating, "The car doesn't fly, General. It's a car. I'm sure your people are completely reliable, but don't you think a flying car would have come up on somebody's radar before now?"

The general in question, a slender man in his late fifties who looked like he still ran a ten-mile PT course every morning, glowered at me so ferociously I reviewed what I'd said and winced. "I didn't mean radar like...radar. I wasn't trying to be clever."

"I'm certain of that. Start again from the beginning."

I sighed and started again. High-speed chase, yes. Impressive air under the wheels, sure. That happens in a car with a souped-up V-8 engine. But really, *flying?* I was okay with that party line until they brought Lieutenant Gilmore in. He was the only survivor of the chopper crew who'd seen Petite roar across empty air, and knew perfectly well that she had. Guilt stabbed me, but Gilmore kept a very calm steady voice as he denied their afternoon reports. It had been a mirage, a combination of dust and heat and the strain of awareness that they were working within American borders and were yet also on unfriendly territory. Yes, he knew what the in-flight recorders had them saying, but, permission to speak freely, General, thank you, frankly, sir, didn't it sound like they were all a little hysterical? Himself included, sir, and no disrespect meant to the dead, but it had been an unusual and stressful situation—

Gilmore talked the entire military off the cliff, saved Petite from being eviscerated by men trying to figure out how she'd flown, and did it all with only the occasional glance at me that let me know he was absolutely aware he was feeding them a line of bullshit and had no other choice in the matter. When they finally, finally let us go, unsatisfied but unable to come up with any plausible answers to fit the described scenario, I was left alone with Gilmore for a minute or two.

I stood up, then grabbed the back of my chair as a head-rush slammed me around. He put his hand under my elbow, concerned, and I wobbled a minute, waiting for the dizziness to pass. "Sorry. I haven't eaten in days. I just wanted to say thank you, and that I'm sorry. And…did they burn the bodies?"

"Yes, ma'am. All of them." Concern flickered over his face. "We've been unable to locate the source's body, though."

For a few seconds that made no sense. Then clarity came like a knife's point in my gut. "You mean Danny? You can't find his body?"

"Not yet. We will, though." Gilmore looked determined but not especially convinced.

I did not want Danny Little Turtle's Raven-Mocker-infested body out tromping around the world, and had an unpleasant flashback to my little Pandora's Box scenario earlier. "Let me know either way, will you?"

"Yes, ma'am. How will I contact you?"

I gave him my phone number and checked my phone at the same time, idly surprised to discover it still had a battery charge. There was a voice mail notification on it. I figured it was Morrison, calling sometime earlier in the day to wonder where the hell I was, and slipped it back into my pocket with a mental note to check it later. Gilmore escorted me out of the high school, where we both blinked in tired surprise at the rising sun.

Wonderful. Now I had neither eaten nor slept for days. My stomach roared and I got dizzy again. "If somebody doesn't get me some food in the next ten minutes I'm going to start chewing my arm off."

Gilmore smiled faintly. "Wish I could help, ma'am, but I have some duties to attend to."

"No, it's fine. I really am sorry, Lieutenant. Call me if you just want to talk, too, okay? It's been a hell of a couple days."

"Thank you, ma'am." He left me, and Morrison, who had apparently chosen to wait all night outside the school, came down the walkway looking far more refreshed than I felt.

I staggered over and flopped against him, much like I'd flopped in the chair earlier. "Oh, God, I'm glad to see you. I'm starving. Do you have a car?"

"I thought you were getting Petite."

"Dad took me on a...thing. Side trip. And I don't know what happened to the Impala I rented. Forget it, the diner can't be more than a ten-minute walk."

"Nothing's ever as close on foot as you think it is when you usually drive, Walker. I'll get us a car." Morrison left me wondering how he would arrange that. I sat in front of the school and tested my arm for edibility until he came back ten or twelve minutes later with a set of keys. "Your Impala," he reported. "Les took it off the mountain."

"Okay." I got up, fighting off another dizzy spell. "You drive."

Morrison's jaw fell open. "Walker?"

I chortled woozily, aware that I would have startled him less by taking my clothes off and marching down the highway starkers. That was fair enough. I wasn't sure the words *you drive* had ever passed my lips before in that combination. Just this once, though, I not only said them, but also meant them wholeheartedly. "Seriously, you drive, Morrison. I'm in no shape. I can't even stand up without nearly passing out. I'm so hungry I'm dangerous."

"That diner better be open."

"If it's not I'm breaking down the back door and firing up the grill myself."

Fortunately, it was open. Even in a crisis, people need food. Especially in a crisis, maybe. The place was packed, with nobody in any visible hurry to leave. Well, not until some of them saw me, and, angry at my part in the deaths of their elders, got up and left in protest. I would worry about that later. For the moment I took a seat in one of the booths, said, "One of everything," when the waitress came by, and put my head on the table to wait for food to arrive.

Morrison said, "I think she means it," to the waitress, which made me lift my head again. "I do. I want one of everything except coffee, I can't drink coffee right now, my stomach is too empty. But one of everything else, starting with the breakfast menu. Include the desserts. No, hold off on them, I don't want the ice cream to melt. Otherwise, one of everything. No, wait, start with a piece of pie, you can bring that right away, right? Apple pie. With ice cream. I don't care if it's warm. The pie. The ice cream probably shouldn't be. And then cherry pie if there's nothing else ready yet. Pie until food. Yes. Please."

The waitress stared at me, then looked at Morrison as if expecting rescue. He smiled. "She's hungry. I'll have some of hers, and some coffee." After a few more seconds, the woman shrugged and went to put an order in for one of everything. The apple pie arrived within forty seconds and I ate it in five bites. The cherry pie appeared less than thirty seconds later, and I ate it in five bites, too. Cherry pie was followed by blueberry, and I had an ice-cream headache building by the time a couple fried eggs with bacon showed up.

I ate that, and pancakes, and scrambled eggs and French toast and an omelet and some waffles and grits and oatmeal and more bacon and lost count of how many glasses of orange juice I drank. Then I burped loudly enough to silence the conversations around me, and started in on more fried eggs and corned beef hash and hash browns and toast and a piece of lemon meringue pie, and by then enough of the edge had left that I started to get picky about my food. I retracted the one-of-everything request and ordered a cheeseburger with bacon and cheese fries.

Morrison, by that time, was starting to look ill. There were occasional respectful murmurs at the sheer number of empty plates piled at my elbow, which I thought the waitress was leaving there just to see how many I went through before I was done. Somewhere after a chili dog with onions and cheese piled so high there was no actual evidence of a hot dog in the bun, my hands stopped shaking. I ordered a Rueben with potato chips and a milk shake, and by the time I got done with that, people were taking bets on how much I could eat, and I was feeling nearly human again.

Humanity demanded greenery, apparently. I ordered three salads with three different kinds of dressing, some proper Southern sweet iced tea, and worked my way through those, finally sighing in contentment. Only then did Morrison dare to speak. "I have never seen anyone eat that much. Ever. Are you all right, Walker?"

"You said I was too skinny." I laughed at Morrison's expression, then laughed again and put my hand over his. "Joking, I'm joking, Morrison. No, shapeshifting from this and last week took it out of me, and then that stunt with Petite, I just wiped myself out. I need fuel. Speaking of which, can I get one of those brownie sundae things, Tilly?" The waitress and I were good buddies by now. She got me a sundae, and when I finished it and indicated that I was perhaps done eating now, the whole diner broke into spontaneous applause. I stood up and took a bow, then sank back into the booth. "Oh my God, that was good."

"That was disgusting." Morrison looked torn between admiration and horror, but another voice said, "Nah, it was cool."

I turned around to see Aidan a couple booths back. He looked older than he had been, and weirdly pale with the still-white hair. I wondered if it would grow back black, or if he'd been through so much it had left scars.

Ada, beside him, saw me noticing the changes and tried not to let herself look too worried. I wanted to hug her. Instead I smiled and waved them over. They came, and we scooted around our booth until we could all see each other over the mile-high stack of plates from my feast. "That," Aidan said again, "was cool. I think you ate more than a whole football team."

"I've never eaten a football team before, so I can't compare the amount of food they would be to what I just ate."

Aidan kicked me under the table, which made me yelp and laugh all at once. His mother gave him a scolding look that no one took very seriously. "How're you doing?" I asked both of them, and they exchanged glances, then nodded.

"Okay," Aidan said. "That all kind of sucked."

I was in full agreement with that assessment. "You did a good job, though, Aidan. You were…" I spread my hands helplessly. "A hero. I mean, holy crap, kid. The ghosts. Holy crap."

He got a little smile that looked like it was trying hard not to burst out all over the place. "That was good, huh? It was mostly the walking sticks. It's a good thing you found yours, Joanne. Two wouldn't have been enough."

I actually smacked myself on the forehead. I hadn't thought about it, but of course Renee had been drawing on my magic as well as her own. No wonder I'd been so utterly wiped out. I noticed the others peering at me and put my hand back down, trying to act like a grown-up. I didn't feel much like one, really. I was feeling a little floaty and relieved, like everything was going to work out, but I thought I should try. "Glad to have been of help. But what even made you *think* of it? I mean, how could you possibly know there was any old magic in that valley to bring forward? Were you just working on a wing and a prayer?"

Aidan lifted one eyebrow. "Seriously?"

"Yeah, seriously! I recognized the valley after the fact, when the ghosts showed up, but you, you weren't even there, Aidan. You got sucked off to the Ohio River Valley when we went back in time, so how could you even have any sense of what was there?"

The kid gave his mother an incredulous glance, as if she might be able to explain my astonishing stupidity, then looked back at me. "I've been going out there since I was eight, with the elders and the others who want to learn the old ways. We've been all over that valley. Don't you know what's on the north end?"

"Of course I don't know what's on the north end. How could I know what's on the north end?" Maybe I hadn't eaten enough, after all. My brain was still fuzzy.

Aidan kept giving me the bemused look for a while, then took a napkin and some crayons off the end of the table where the "keep kids entertained" material was mostly buried under my empty plates. A minute later he pushed a drawing across the table at me. I stared at it a moment, then turned red from my elbows to the top of my head.

It was a rough sketch of a pair of stick figures. A man and a woman, their bodies inverted triangles, their heads unattached to the shoulders. They were leaning back-to-back, their arms folded across their chests, and they were both looking out at the world.

One was wearing a short black jacket, and the other, a long white coat. I'd been proud of that touch, when I'd made the petroglyphs four hundred years ago: the rock had shaped itself under my will, bringing all the dark bits to Morrison's jacket and all the sparkling white to my coat. I'd completely forgotten about the petroglyphs, and I was still blushing when I met Aidan's eyes again.

"Everybody's been wondering about those for like ever," he announced. "Everybody goes up to check them out. They're obviously old, 'cause they're all soft and worn and stuff, but I didn't figure out it was *you* until I saw you and him—" he nodded at Morrison "—there in the power circle, wearing those coats. And then I knew you had to have been in that valley a really long time ago, and if you were there that meant there was some kind of power I could reach back for. So I did, and the ghosts came."

"Holy crap, Aidan. Wow. That's amazing. I don't think I could have done it myself."

"Are you just saying that?"

"No. In the condition I was in yesterday, I definitely couldn't have, and normally, well, maybe, but I don't think I would've *thought* of it. No, you definitely kicked ass and took names. You gotta keep studying with Dad, Aidan. You're going to be amazing."

His grin cracked, after all, spreading wide across his face. "Know what?"

"What?"

"I think you might turn out okay, too."

I laughed, but my heart filled up with relief so big it felt like it might pop out of my chest. "Thanks. Thank you, Aidan. That means a lot."

"Y'welcome." He slid a glance between me and Morrison. "You guys gonna hang around a while?"

"I dunno. Maybe a few days?" I looked at Morrison, who tipped his head sideways in a noncommittal maybe-trending-toward-yes manner.

"That'd be cool." Aidan hunched his shoulders. "Maybe you can tell me what happened to Lucas."

I sighed and cast Ada an apologetic look, not knowing how to tell Aidan anything except the truth. "Dad would be able to tell you better. Lucas got caught in the Nothing, Aidan, and thrown into a battlefield. Dad went after him, but it was too late. He'd already been killed. Did you know him very well?"

Aidan shook his head, eyes fixed on the table. "I met him when he and Sara would come back, but it wasn't like he was my mom or dad. I didn't want him to get killed, though."

"Neither did I."

"D'you think the ghost shaman was right? If you'd tried to rescue him do you think he woulda come back a sorcerer?"

"I don't know, kiddo. I do know changing things, messing with the timeline, makes it possible for really bad things to get a foot in the door and kick it open."

"But you woulda tried anyway, if Sara hadn't said you shouldn't."

"Yeah."

"Because that's what good guys do."

I smiled. "Yeah. Because that's what good guys do. The right thing, even if it's the dumb thing."

Morrison snorted, reminding me he and Ada were there. "It'd be all right, Walker, if you did a little less dumb."

"I'm working on it, Boss."

He gave me a look and I smiled as sweetly as I could. Aidan wrinkled his nose and nudged his mother. "They're bein' gross, Mom."

"Yes, they are." Ada smiled at us, then nudged Aidan in return. "We should go finish breakfast, sweetheart."

"Okay. Can I order one of everything like Joanne did?" They got up and Aidan ran back to their table. Ada touched my shoulder as she passed me, and my heart lightened a little more, like I'd received a benediction. I exhaled noisily and rubbed my hands over my face, then peeked through my fingers at Morrison.

"Good to be home?" he asked quietly.

I wobbled a shoulder up and down. "Good to get some things hammered out, anyway. Good to… It'll be good to be leaving, and not running away. There's still a lot of clean-up to do here, and a lot of people are going to hate me."

"You saved them."

"Maybe. Maybe I just brought trouble down on their heads. So many people are dead."

"A lot of them were tourists." Morrison's lip curled. "You know what I mean."

"You mean the locals won't hold those deaths against me. I'll hold them against myself, though, and it doesn't negate the fact that at least thirty residents did die. It might be better if I never came back."

"Aidan and your father wouldn't like that."

"Aidan and my father could visit us in Seattle, if they wanted to." But he was right, so I nodded. "It's not something to worry about right now. I'd like to hang out a few days, if you can take the time off work. Drive back across the country leisurely."

"Do you even know how to drive leisurely?"

I grinned. "You know what I mean."

"You mean drive like a bat out of hell when you're actually on the road, but pull over to see the sights and spend relaxed evenings in decent hotels on the way?"

"Yeah. Something like that." My phone buzzed in my pocket, startling me, and I tugged it out, asking, "Did you call to ask where I was, yesterday?"

"No. Why?"

"Voice mail. I forgot to check it, but I thought it was probably you." I answered with a cheerful "Hello?"

"Joanie?"

I straightened up, shock spilling down my spine. "Gary? Are you okay?" My septuagenarian best friend never called me Joanie unless something was wrong. Usually something with me, but he couldn't possibly know what had gone on the past few days. He was in Ireland, for heaven's sake.

"I called yesterday. You didn't call back. I'm in Seattle."

His voice was older and shakier than I'd ever heard it. I got up, hands cold and stomach in knots. "I only saw the message a little while ago and hadn't had a chance—Gary, what's wrong? What's going on? Why are you in Seattle?"

"It's Annie, Jo. It's my wife. She's alive."

* * * * *

to be concluded in
SHAMAN RISES
the final book of the Walker Papers

Acknowledgments

Mountain Echoes was written in a blitz, and I am particularly grateful to Kate Laity, who provided me with a spare bedroom and no distractions for a four-day writing retreat during which I wrote a full third of the novel.

I'm also especially grateful to Mikaela Lind, who is the Word Warrior most likely to show up and make me write in the mornings. I'm not sure I would've gotten it done in time without her regular appearances.

I'm *quite* certain I wouldn't have gotten it done in time if my mom, Rosie Murphy, hadn't babysat quite a lot, and equally certain that my husband Ted's taking time off work and sending me on the writing retreat was invaluable. So thank you all most particularly. I couldn't have done it without you.

(I swear, at some point I'm going to stop running so close to the line, but I don't know when...)

I'd like to add shout-outs to Paul-Gabriel Wiener for giving me one word where five would do to describe a vehicular analogy, and to Zelerie Rogers for her help with local geography. A general apology is probably also due to Zel for the liberties I've taken with Cherokee Town and the Qualla. All changes and inconsistencies are born of my mind, and should not be laid at her feet!

Props are also, always, due to my editor, Mary-Theresa Hussey (who has gone above and beyond the call of duty for the Walker Papers this past year—check out the Gary-focused short story collection *No Dominion* to see what help she's been!), to Harlequin's art department for another stunning cover, and to my agent, Jennifer Jackson. Thank you all for being awesome.

LJKAAKV349TR

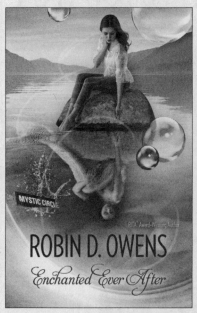

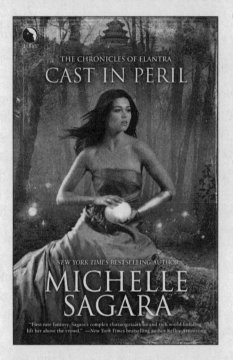